Praise for *Quieter Than Killing*:

'Hilary belts out a corker of a story, all wrapped up in her vivid, effortless prose. If you're not reading this series of London-set police procedurals then you need to start right away' *Observer* **(Thriller of the Month)**

'Sarah Hilary's debut, *Someone Else's Skin*, was widely acclaimed and won lots of awards. *Quieter Than Killing*, her fourth, is even more impressive, and DI Marnie Rome is up there in the top division of fictional female detectives' ***The Times***

'Sarah Hilary writes beautifully and unflinchingly; a dark, disturbing and thought-provoking chiller of a thriller' **Peter James**

'The most poignant entry in the series so far' ***Sunday Express, S Magazine***

'Hilary is my drop-everything writer; always original, always bang-on psychologically, always gripping. I am a huge fan' **Alex Marwood**

'Hilary writes with a menacing intensity . . . [a] dark, atmospheric novel layered with complexities, keeping the reader guessing throughout and its twist will undoubtedly take your breath away' ***Daily Express***

'It's dark, it's brilliant, and it tightens like a noose. Sarah Hilary is downright dangerous' **Mick Herron**

'DI Marnie Rome is a three-dimensional character of an emotional depth rarely encountered in the world of fictional cops'   *The Times*

Praise for *Someone Else's Skin*:

'An exceptional new talent. Hilary writes with a beguiling immediacy that pulls you straight into her world on the first page and leaves you bereft when you finish'
Alex Marwood

'An intelligent, assured and very promising debut'
Guardian

'So brilliantly put together, unflinching without ever being gratuitous . . . it's the best crime debut I've ever read'
Erin Kelly

'A slick, stylish debut'   **Sharon Bolton**

'Hilary maintains all her characters with depth and feeling'
Independent

'Hell-for-leather compelling'   *Observer*

'It's written with the verve and assurance of a future star'
Steven Dunne

'It's a simply superb read – dark and thrilling'   *Sun*

COME
AND
FIND ME
SARAH HILARY

HEADLINE

First published in 2018 by
HEADLINE PUBLISHING GROUP

1

Cataloguing in Publication Data is available from the British Library

Hardback ISBN 978 1 4722 4896 1

Typeset in Meridien by Palimpsest Book Production Ltd, Falkirk, Stirlingshire

Printed and bound in Great Britain by
CPI Group (UK) Ltd, Croydon, CR0 4YY

HEADLINE PUBLISHING GROUP
An Hachette UK Company
Carmelite House
50 Victoria Embankment
London EC4Y 0DZ

www.headline.co.uk
www.hachette.co.uk

To Victor, my victor

Seven days ago

It started stupidly, the way these things do. No conspiracy, just a cock-up, chaos theory in action. You want me to be specific? It started with a tray. Moulded plastic with a hollow for meat and a hollow for mash and all of it stained ketchup-red. This was before it all kicked off, before the rest of it – the rest of *us* – got stained.

These trays are meant to be safe, no sharp edges, no weight. If you throw one, you'll start a food fight but nothing worse. You can't kill with a tray like this, that's their calculation. Softening devices, you see. It's why prisons have vinyl floors and walls. Not here, as it happens. Here, there's a lovely hard corner in the showers on B spur where you can crack a skull wide open. But the trays are the trays are the trays, unless you count the ones melted down by men like Bayer, and you can't count that because Bayer's melted half of what's in here, it's why he's not *Bayer* to most of us but *Shanks*. Still, you get my point. The trays are for eating off, not kicking off. Not for starting fights that end with

1

people getting stabbed and definitely not with anyone getting killed.

The food stinks. Even if you've never set foot in prison, you know how bad the food stinks, takes you straight back to school and not in a good way. Tastes bad too. Tastes of the tray, mostly. Cut to the chase? All right. It's just that it's not easy for me. Not easy for any of us, but especially me. Because of what happened, because of where I am now.

All right. Okay. Listen, I'll tell you how it went. Like this—

We're eating in our cells and it's not what you see on TV, there's no cafeteria with queuing or jostling or sitting in huddles with your homeboys. That'd be too friendly, and too easy. You'd see the likes of Aidan Duffy and Stephen Keele, or Bayer and his buddies, and you'd know right away who was in charge. As it is, plenty of us haven't the foggiest until the trays start flying, faces bursting open.

It starts with—

'Hey, Mickey!'

'You're so fine . . .'

'You blow my mind—'

'Hey, Mickey!'

Rattle. Shake, rattle and roll. Tray drumroll. Tommy Walton's found an edge to slam into like the corner in B spur's showers and he's going at it like he's Keith Moon, like he's John Bonham, banging it balls-to-the-wall and it takes around six seconds for someone else to join in, then a couple more catch the rhythm and *yes* – like that. Just another day in HMP Cloverton.

Until *he* starts up.

I figured I knew him, since we shared a cell and because word gets around. Oh yes, I knew about Mickey Vokey. We all did. Wrong. We didn't, not remotely. Until it's tipping over from an improvised drumming session into a thing blacker than a cow's insides and Tommy Walton's getting smeared so hard they'll have to hose down the corridor to get rid of the bits.

Most of us stay in our cells. The smart ones, sane ones. Aidan Duffy, of course. Stephen Keele? Your guess's as good as mine, except you never saw what I saw that time in B spur's showers.

The drumming starts and there's a beat to it, tribal. You get caught up even if you're one of the sane ones and Mickey Vokey isn't anywhere near that. He had his own cell until recently, which in case you didn't know is like hanging a warning sign over his head: Mickey Vokey, madman. You don't mess with Mickey, except Tommy-meathead-Walton does. He's lost the plot, so deep with the beat he can't hear anything else, not even the siren flashing from Mickey's eyes. I'd seen that siren once before. It didn't end well then, and this time's worse because it's not contained. The mess's spilling into the corridor before anyone can catch his breath.

'You blow my mind, hey Mickey—'

Tommy goes in with the tray, hitting at the hard surfaces, anything that'll give back a note. He doesn't mean to do it, that's my guess, swinging for the wall behind Mickey's head and missing.

Have you seen a Cane Corso off its leash? Italian mastiff, direct descendant of the dogs the Romans took to war. All head and jaws, all the power packed up there. Mickey's watching the tray swing our way, and he's standing with his weight thrown forward exactly like a Cane Corso.

I don't say anything, even so. Listen, I gave up trying to reason with Mickey months ago, never mind he's my cellmate. You might think it means we're pals, that we look out for each other, but no one's looking out for Mickey because no one's stupid enough to get that close. Two sounds—

The first's from the tray when it meets Mickey's skull. The second's from Tommy Walton as Mickey punches the bridge of his nose into the back of his eyes.

Music to my ears, if I'm honest. Ask anyone, he'll say the same. Things get like that, someone's going to get hurt and hard. Every one of us was happy it wasn't our own nose, our own eyes. So, yes. Right in that minute I'm glad. Funny, when you look at me now, the state I'm in.

The police want to know how it happened. Detectives, two of them. She's so serious it makes my teeth ache. Redhead, I'd have liked that once. The pair of them at the side of my hospital bed on and off ever since. The whole week, if it's been a week. Longer, maybe. They're after a witness statement, wanting to know about Mickey Vokey, and Aidan Duffy, and Stephen Keele. Needing to know how bad it was right then and there. They've seen the walls and floors, the state of the place. Body bags zipped shut, and whatever bits of Tommy got trapped in the grids after the hoses were turned off. They've tried CCTV, but it's worthless thanks to the smoke and fire. You don't know what went down unless you were there and no one's talking, like mass hysteria with the sound switched off. Mass muteness. I don't know why they think I'll be any different except my face is okay, all my teeth intact. To look at me, I'm all right. But I'm not. I'm not. None of us are.

Prison riots. We've seen them in films, or on TV, nothing but on the news this last couple of years. This was different though, might as well compare a Peke to a Cane Corso.

What happened that morning changed everything. No one knows why, or no one's saying. Would *you* – with mad Mickey out there where your loved ones live?

4

COME AND FIND ME

Too many broken faces, blind eyes. Too much blood getting in the way of what really happened, reaching up the walls and right across the floor, one end of the corridor to the other like a heaving black lake you can't swim in, only choke and drown.

One man knows what went down that day and he's long gone, slipped the leash and ran while the rest of us were hunting for our teeth or crying for our mums.

Mickey Vokey.

Long gone.

1

Noah Jake checked his phone for messages, trying to keep warm. When he looked up, they were coming down the prison steps. She was holding hard to his arm, her best hat pinned in place, coat buttoned to the neck. He wore a mac over a blue suit he'd last worn to a wedding, his face deeply lined by this new worry. They moved slowly, as if their bones hurt or they were afraid of falling. At the foot of the steps they stopped with their heads together, regrouping after whatever they'd witnessed in the prison. Pentonville wasn't rioting like Cloverton, but it wasn't somewhere you'd want your son to spend a night, let alone nine months on remand.

Noah straightened, slipping his phone into his pocket. He crossed to where they were standing, the woman clinging to the man's arm. 'How is he? Mum?'

She turned away, showing the back of her head, red hat held in place by a white enamel pin. She smelt of talcum powder and furniture polish, the smell of his child- hood. After a minute, she pulled away, walking towards

7

the bus stop. Her bag swung at her shoulder until she held it down, her fist clenched, knuckles scrubbed and shiny.

'She needs time.' Noah's father followed her with his eyes. 'Give her time.'

'How was he? Sol.'

Dad rubbed a hand over his jaw. 'Not good.'

'I've asked to see him,' Noah said. 'More than once. I'll keep asking.'

'You should leave it for a little while.' Dad shook his head. 'Let things settle down. It's not been six weeks since— Let it all calm down.'

Since you arrested him. It hadn't been six weeks since Noah had arrested his brother, Sol.

'How's Mum?' He shivered, looking towards the bus shelter.

She'd stopped with her head held high, creases in the back of her coat from the day's sitting and waiting. Pain nagged at Noah's ribs where he wore stubborn bruises from the baseball bat which had put him into hospital just days before Sol's arrest. He kept waiting for the bruises to fade but every morning their black ache was right here below his heart, nagging when he breathed.

'You need to give her time.' Dad moved until he was facing Noah. 'And you need to take some yourself. You're thin, boy. Are you eating properly?'

Before all this, he'd have insisted on Noah coming home to eat a decent meal, a huge plate of Mum's sweet fried plantains, her cure for all ills. But not now, with her so furious. Noah wasn't to set foot inside their house. His own brother in a cell, living like that.

'I had to do it.' He'd lost count of the number of times he'd said this. 'Sol was in serious trouble. For his sake as much as anything, I had to end it.'

'Your brother's been trouble since before he was born,' Dad sighed. He touched a hand to Noah's elbow. 'Take care, boy.' He walked to where his wife was waiting.

Noah's phone rang in his pocket.

'DS Jake.' He pinched the bridge of his nose.

'Michael Vokey.' DS Ron Carling wasn't calling from the station, his voice had an underwater echo.

'We've found him?'

'Better than that,' Ron said.

What was better than finding the country's most wanted man? Michael Vokey was a sadist who'd tortured a young mother and left bloody mayhem in his wake when he'd escaped a week ago from HMP Cloverton. 'He's dead?'

'You'll want to get here for this.' Ron gave Noah the directions, adding, 'I hope you didn't eat a big breakfast.'

'I skipped breakfast. Why?' Not that Noah needed to ask. It was there in Ron's voice: a crime scene, and not a neat one.

He watched his parents climb onto the bus, Dad's arm around Mum. She kept her head high. She'd rest it on his shoulder once they were seated and it was safe to let go of the stiffness she was wearing like an extra coat against the cold. Dad would take care of her.

'How bad is it?' Noah asked.

'On a scale of one to Dennis Nilsen?' Ron sniffed. 'I'm giving this a high five.'

2

The wall was made of faces. From a distance, they resembled thumbprints, but they were faces. Old and young, male and female. Looking out of Polaroids and from newspaper clippings trimmed to the same size. Hundreds and hundreds of faces.

'See what I mean?'

No blood and no bodies, but Ron was right. The room was a punch in the gut.

A few of the faces dated back to the last century, stiff collars worn like nooses around the necks of men with rusty whiskers, women with their hair braided, one with her hand to her head as if in pain. Below her, a beautiful young man stared out with sad eyes, a cupid's bow mouth. Both images were black and white but for the red roaring from their eyes, so hot Noah could taste it on his tongue. He smelt earth on some of the square brows flinching from flashbulbs which must have fired as the old cameras captured them. By contrast the Polaroids were ferociously modern, glinting with the knife-edge of light trapped in the room. Women mostly, many young, all in pain of one kind or another. That was just the first wall.

The whole room was the same, even the window, every surface scarred with faces. Polaroids fixed like feathers, curling like scales from the ceiling, overlapping and going grey. The room smelt of gum and ink and the bitter vanilla twinge of burnt bulbs.

'Where's DI Rome?' Noah's skin crept at his neck. 'She needs to see this.'

'She's at the prison,' Ron said. 'And yeah. She really does.'

This house in West Ealing had stood empty for months. There was no longer any furniture in its rooms, no curtains or carpets, only bare boards and scuffed vinyl like the floor in here, a sitting room where the window should have looked out onto the back garden but instead looked inwards, solid with stares. The house was cold, but this room was clammy with its Polaroid-cladding, like standing inside a polythene tent. Noah found himself holding his breath hard in his chest.

'If this is Michael Vokey's house, why didn't we know about it until now?'

'Not in his name,' Ron said. 'His mum's house, we reckon. Colin's going at the paperwork. But this'll get us extra bodies on the case, right? Has to.' It was why he'd said this was better than finding Vokey. The house, even just this one room, made the investigation so much bigger.

The Polaroids amplified the silence, although whether this was due to the emulsive quality of the film or the urgent muteness of the faces, Noah couldn't be sure. He'd attended many appalling crime scenes, but few had felt as ominous as this. He moved closer to the wall on the right. Not all the photos were faces, some were paintings. The longer he looked, the more he saw. Shoulders and shins, hands and feet. But it was the faces which wouldn't leave him alone, staring from all sides.

Ron sucked at his teeth unhappily. Above their heads,

the brittle Polaroid scales expanded and contracted, as if the ceiling was breathing. Under their feet—

The floor wasn't flat, undulating in grey waves towards the window.

Noah studied the stained vinyl. 'We should take this up.'

'Shit,' Ron said. 'You think there's more, under there?'

'One way to find out.'

Of the assorted weaponry used in the Cloverton riot, smoke had done the most damage, worse even than the fire. Two men died in their beds after smoke found its way under their cell doors and into their lungs. Unlikely, Marnie imagined, that they were sleeping at the time. Stoned, or spiced; it was easier to get hold of drugs in here than it was to lay your hands on a clean towel. Michael Vokey hadn't needed a weapon, using his bare hands to maim and cripple his fellow inmates. Only the smoke had done worse damage. Five men remained in hospital including Vokey's cellmate, the one man with a decent idea of where Vokey might have gone to ground. Unless Marnie was about to catch a break, courtesy of Aidan Duffy.

'You'll want to catch him fast.' Even after a week, Aidan's eyes were wet from the smoke. 'Vokey. Before he does his worst.'

'That's the plan,' Marnie told him.

'You're thinking I can help?' The smoke had ruined his voice, stealing all the softness from its southern Irish lilt, reducing it to a rasp. 'I would, except he cut me out.'

It was the story Marnie was hearing from everyone in the prison. 'Even you?'

'Even me.' Aidan wiped at his eyes, attempting a smile. 'I'm small fry.'

'You survived, better than most.'

12

He was the same handsome devil she'd first met eight weeks ago, with his black curls and stormy grey eyes, killer cheekbones. But the riot had stolen a layer of his gloss, leaving him pale and shaken. He looked down at his hands for a moment, remembering what? The slipperiness of the corridor after Vokey had finished smearing the inside of a man's skull on the floor and walls. Aidan was a con-artist, an embezzler. He'd hurt people, it was true, but nothing on this scale.

'Tommy Walton's no friend of mine,' he whispered. 'But he didn't deserve that. No one did.'

'Who might be able to give us a lead on Michael? Nothing we have is getting us anywhere.'

'CCTV on the fritz, is it?' No sarcasm in his voice, just acceptance. He knew this prison intimately, its cracks and flaws, all the places it was failing to do its job.

'Fire damage,' Marnie said. The few working cameras had given them three long hours of thick smoke hiding everything. 'No one who was in that corridor seems to want to help us.'

'I guessed you weren't here for your health.' He bent his head over the table, rubbing with both hands until a light dusting of soot fell from his curls. 'That's after a couple of showers. This place isn't fit for habitation, not even by scum like us.'

Marnie said steadily, 'I haven't any influence over transfers. You know that.'

'I do know.' He looked up, pain sharpening his eyes. 'But you can get word to my boy, yes? To my Finn. Let him know I'm okay in case he's seen the news and thinks I'm one of those with his eyes—' He edited the sentence, as if saying the words would conjure the horror of what Vokey had done, not to Aidan but to Tommy Walton and Neil Bayer.

13

'Finn knows you're safe.' As safe as anyone here. She felt a familiar ache for Aidan's son. Finn Duffy, ten years old and ready to take on the world, was currently consigned to a foster home.

'I'd ask to see him but I wouldn't want him within a thousand feet of this place, now less than ever.' Aidan propped his head on his hand. 'Is he seeing much of his mother?'

'I doubt it. Children's Services don't seem to think that's a good idea.'

'They're right. I can't pass judgement on anyone, I know that, but she's no mother. She doesn't have a bone in her body fit for that. Not for my boy. She does harm, you know?'

Marnie wanted to ask why, in that case, Aidan hadn't taken better care to stay out of prison. If he knew Finn had only one functioning parent. 'Tell me about Michael's cellmate, Ted Elms.'

'He's a stranger.' Aidan pushed the ball of his thumb at the soot on the table. 'I've not met one quieter in here. It's like he shut himself away to save anyone else the job. Doesn't talk about what he did to deserve it. Once upon a time you knew how bad it was based on where they put you, but that's all over now.' He moved his fingers, scattering the soot. 'You've only to look at Mickey Vokey to know that's true. Transferred here because of over-crowding or underfunding, or no-fucks-given. They wanted him in with me.' He blinked at Marnie, grey eyes liquid-bright. 'Took me for a cosy chat and a cup of tea, stroked my ego 'til it could've stood up all on its little own. "Aidan, we know you're respected in here," "Aidan, you've got it all locked down." Like I'm the psycho-whisperer. Like I can take a man like Mickey and just – make him behave.'

14

He sat back, leaving his hands on the table. A shadow scarred his face from the overhead light, but he hadn't lost teeth, or eyes. He was one of the lucky ones.

'You know this place hasn't been run by the *screws*,' lavishing the word with irony, 'in a long while. Not since they stopped hiring the ex-soldiers and started bringing in the schoolboys. Saved a fortune in salaries so they could stop shouting orders and start begging us to behave. Only begging gets you about where you'd expect. Them on their knees and us . . .' He shook his head in disgust.

'They wanted Michael Vokey in with you,' Marnie prompted. 'But he ended up sharing a cell with Ted Elms. Why? Because Elms wasn't the type to object? Quiet, you said.'

'Two types of quiet, Marnie Jane. I'd've said you know all about that.'

'At least two,' she agreed.

Aidan Duffy had form with Marnie. She didn't react to his proprietary use of her name – she needed him right now, just as he'd once needed her. Noise reached them in solid waves, the unedited soundtrack of forty inmates being rehoused, the slap of feet on floors, a thumping of doors. Underneath it all, a low rumble of discontent like the shallow bubbling in the pit of a volcano. How long before it all boiled over again?

'You're not going to ask what they had planned for Stephen?' Aidan pushed his thumb at the table. 'If I'd said yes to the offer of a new cellmate.'

'Was it even an option?' Marnie asked. 'Three to a cell is the norm now, isn't it?'

'And they wonder why we riot.' He watched her, moving his mouth tenderly. 'Have you been to see him?' He used his softest voice, as if he might break her by

15

bringing the ghost of her parents' killer into this room where seven weeks ago she'd faced Stephen Keele across a table like this one, freckled now by Aidan's soot. 'Have you seen him?'

She held his gaze. 'He's not allowed visitors.'

The hospital had custody of Stephen now, shackled to a bed by the tubing needed to keep him alive. He wouldn't be looking at her across any tables any time soon, withholding his answers to her questions about why six years ago her parents had to die such brutal deaths.

'I'm sorry for you. Truthfully. Of all the ways it could've ended.'

Nothing had ended, Aidan knew that. But she didn't doubt his sympathy was genuine. Back when they were strangers he'd baited her about her foster brother Stephen, the sort of boy he was before her parents took him in, the ways in which Stella Keele had shaped her son's childhood with her abuse and neglect, and her torture. Stories which gave Marnie nightmares, stoking her guilt. Eight weeks ago, Aidan Duffy hadn't wanted her conscience clear of anything. But since then she'd tackled his son Finn away from a sociopath. Things had changed between them even before the riot.

'Is Ted Elms likely to know where Vokey's gone? Contacts, people who might hide him?'

'We're all hiding,' Aidan said in his raw whisper. 'Isn't that what they say?'

'Skipping the psychology. We've found a house that's not registered in his name but Michael Vokey was living there, we're in no doubt about that.' She paused. 'Did you see his cell here?'

'Before the mess, you mean?' Dislike danced in Aidan's eyes. 'I saw it.'

'And?' She needed his sharp eyes that didn't miss a

16

trick. Her witness, on the inside. Aidan owed her, and he knew it.

'Mickey's got a thing for photos.' He rolled his neck. 'Lots of them, all over the walls. Not family photos like the rest of us poor bastards, not unless he's sixty sisters who look nothing like him.' He scratched at his eyebrow. 'Still, I didn't get the bad vibe from him, and I've a good radar for the psychos, don't ask me how he slipped under it. Ted now, he tweaked my antennae with the cacti and the rest of it. That cell was a jungle before Vokey got to work, pinning up his pictures.'

Pictures sounded innocent but they could be deadly, like the photos Stephen Keele had gifted to Marnie the last time they met. Photos which had been burning a hole in her bag ever since.

'Ted keeps cacti.' She nodded. 'Tell me about Vokey's photos. Of women?'

'And girls, yes. Not what you're thinking, not smutty. Mugshots, you'd call them. Selfies.'

'Who were they, do you know?'

'Hybristophilia – only you said to skip the psychology.'

'What do you know about hybristophilia?'

'Too much.' He moved his legs under the table, stretching his spine in the chair. 'My therapist likes to talk about it, her pet subject. Sexual attraction to bad boys. Liars, thieves and much worse than that. There's those who think they can cure us, and those who prefer not to.' Carving a smile with his mouth. 'The ones who like us just the way we are.'

'So the photos in Vokey's cell were fan mail. From women who were writing to him here?'

'That's how it looked.' Aidan ran his fingers through his curls, dipping his head to the side.

'How many women?'

'No idea. I try to tune out the gossip.'

She looked at him. He gazed limpidly back at her.

'But this was more than gossip,' Marnie said. 'You saw the photos, in his cell.'

'He was drawing pictures from the photos.' His cheek hollowed. 'I got him charcoals. He wanted paints, but they wouldn't let him. Too messy, they said.' He stopped, looking nauseated.

Remembering the much worse mess Michael Vokey had made?

'No paints,' she prompted.

'I suppose that's why he improvised.'

Blood and ashes in place of paint, and for brushes—

From the room above them a blast of sound cut off so suddenly it left a space. Aidan didn't flinch, but he rubbed the heels of his hands at his eyes. He was bone-tired. It showed in his face and the restless movements of his fingers, the unnatural polish to his eyes. And it showed in the set of his neck and shoulders, the way he sat with his head tilted, light drawing lines along every angle of his face. When did he last get a decent night's sleep? Perhaps that wasn't possible in a place like this, even for a man like Aidan Duffy who had a knack for getting his own way, and staying wide of trouble. He'd retreated to his cell at the first sign of rioting, but the smoke had found him all the same. Marnie held hard to the questions she wanted to ask him about Stephen. How the pair of them could have been in the same cell breathing the same smoke, yet only one was in hospital, seriously ill. When she tried to picture it she saw a frantic fight for air, Aidan's teeth bared, Stephen's fists landing, the shove of their feet on the floor, a slam of bodies hitting the ground. Battling for what little air was left, a fight to the death. Did that account for Aidan's sleeplessness?

18

'Tell me about the riot.'

'I didn't see anything, stayed in my cell, we both did, 'til the smoke started coming through the vents. Then you know what they did, Marnie Jane?' Aidan shut his eyes, pain thinning his face. 'They locked us in. We were trapped, just us and the smoke. You've no idea how scary it is being locked in a box with smoke coming in and no way out. We wet everything we could, sheets and blankets and clothes. Soaked it all and stuffed it against the vent and under the door, but it was like fighting the *air* and we lost— We lost.' He pressed the heels of his hands to the sockets of his eyes. 'Stephen came off worst, but we were a *team* in there. It wasn't each man for himself. I didn't have to fight him for it, not like Arran and Jabal next door. Jesus, that was a bloodbath.' He uncovered his eyes, blinking up at her. 'I missed him. *Mickey*. He went under my radar. A psycho like that and I didn't spot him. I wasn't scared, not like I should've been, not until it was too late.'

How often did he admit to getting things wrong, missing tricks, being scared? Not often, Marnie guessed. 'Thank you. You've been helpful. One last thing.' She reached for her phone, scrolling to the images of the man they were hunting. 'Does this look to you like Michael Vokey?'

An odd question. Had DCS Ferguson been here, Marnie might have hesitated to ask it. 'It *is* him.' She held out the phone. 'But does it *look* like him?'

Aidan leaned forward, his eyes narrowed. She was showing him the image they'd released to the press and shared with police forces across the UK, with border control and passport officials, airports and train stations, anyone who might be able to help the police find the man responsible for the havoc here a week ago. Aidan studied the image for a long moment. Then he said what everyone was saying: 'It looks nothing like him.'

19

Marnie scrolled to the next photo, and then the next. Pictures published in the press, and those taken from every passport, bus pass and driving licence held by Michael Vokey. Family snaps, and ones posted on Facebook by workmates or associates. Not friends, Vokey didn't have friends, but his image turned up enough times to run the collection into double figures. She scrolled through the whole lot, pausing to allow Aidan time to consider each image in turn.

To each one he repeated the same words: 'It looks nothing like him.'

Marnie's head began to ache, the skin at her temples stiffening to a bruise.

'It looks nothing like him.'

How were they going to find Michael Vokey?

How were they going to find a man who looked nothing like himself?

'You've been staring at that foot for the last five minutes,' Ron complained. 'I'm starting to think you've got a fetish.'

'I recognise it,' Noah said.

'The foot?'

'The style.' He shifted on the stepping plate to get a better view. 'I've seen it before.'

The floor in the sitting room, like the walls and ceiling, was scaly with images. Under the vinyl, tacked into place methodically, repetitively – Polaroids again, but of artwork. Oil paintings mostly, one of a human foot, cartoonish at first glance but the longer you looked the truer it became.

'Did we know he fancied himself as Andy Warhol?' Ron was crouched on a second stepping plate, to preserve whatever DNA evidence the floor might hold.

'Dan's curating a collection of prisoner art. This style, the brushstrokes?' Noah pointed at the Polaroid of the foot. 'It's in the collection, I'm sure of it.'

'Know what it looks like to me?' Ron bent his head at the picture. 'A car crash. Like being in a smash and surviving but with the wreckage right here,' pressing his thumb to the bridge of his nose, 'up in your face.'

'*Break Out*. That's the piece it reminds me of.'

Noah took out his phone and searched, scrolling until he could show Ron the scanned thumbnail from the catalogue his partner Dan was curating. The solid block of colour at the painting's core might easily have been a burning car. Seeing it, you heard tyres ripping at the road, smelt the reek of rubber. The painting pulled you inside the burning vehicle as it bounced back into the collision to be hit again and again. You *felt* it – the shriek of metal-on-metal as the collision's perimeter spread in a savagery of shrapnel, its heart hidden under a cloud of fiery smoke. Technically, it was a tremendous painting. Horrible and horrific, the kind to give you nightmares. Not unlike the scene Michael Vokey had left behind at Cloverton.

'Jesus.' Ron peered at the picture. 'This's up your alley. Loony tunes written right through it. All else fails you can hire your boyfriend as a consultant. He's an art critic, isn't he?'

'Curator, but yes. Dan would be interested in this.' Noah tried again for a perspective on the room, but only ended up with a crick in his neck. 'We need to photograph all this, from every angle, before we take it apart. There might be a message here.'

'Other than "Dangerous Lunatic on the Loose" you mean?'

'The art of the empty soul. Didn't someone say all great paintings contain a little poison?'

'Yeah, I'd call this a tsunami. You ever seen anything like it?'

The room, Ron meant. Vokey's obsessive pinning of the

Polaroids, every surface covered, the window blacked out. 'Not like this,' Noah said. What would Dan make of Vokey's art? Profoundly disturbing, acutely wrong. These faces – who were they?

'They're right,' Ron was saying. 'The eyes do follow you.' He was studying the walls with his head cocked. 'I don't know shit about art, but I know what I don't like. Isn't that what they say?'

'Something like it,' Noah conceded. It was impossible to look away from the urgency of the faces, as if each was calling out to be found, saved.

'Who d'you reckon they are?' Ron pulled the cuff of his suit over his hand, wiping at his forehead. 'People he knew? Are we looking at more victims?'

Like the young mother Vokey had tortured, the men mutilated during the prison riot.

'Are they all his victims?' Ron wondered.

'Not all of them.' Noah pointed to the clutch of black and white photos, the woman with her hand to her head, the beautiful young man. 'I've seen these before.'

'New to me. And you're older than you look if you're remembering pre-colour mugshots.'

'These faces are famous. Medical, not police mugshots. It's the Szondi Test.'

'The what now?'

'Léopold Szondi, a Hungarian psychologist. Back in the 1930s he developed a non-verbal test to reveal a person's worst fears and impulses. Test subjects were shown a series of faces – *these* faces – and measured on their levels of sympathy or revulsion. The theory is we fear in others what we've repressed in ourselves. They used the Szondi Test on soldiers returning from Vietnam. It's been debunked for decades, but it was doing the rounds online not so long ago. It's seen as a bit of fun now but they'd have

22

locked you up once, for giving the wrong answers to his questions.'

'What questions?'

'The faces are the questions.'

'What – like snog, marry, avoid?' Ron stepped closer to the nearest wall. 'I'm just getting a whole load of avoid.'

'Szondi would say you're in denial.'

'Okay then.' Ron reconsidered the faces. 'The smiley bloke with the beard, say I chose him.'

'Snogging or marrying?'

'No, he's giving me the creeps. What's that mean?'

'Repressed maniac with a beard fetish.'

'Him?'

'You.'

Ron snorted his appreciation. 'Oh Dr Freud, with these rare old Polaroids you're really spoiling us.' He retreated one stepping plate at a time to the door.

A breeze caught the corners of the photocopied faces and fluttered them madly so that just for a second all the men and women in the room were blinking.

'I wonder what his cell's like.' Noah shivered. 'This looks compulsive. I can't imagine he stopped when they locked him up.'

'I guess the boss is finding out.'

'DS Carling, DS Jake.' One of the forensic investigators was in the doorway, his face edited by the white hood of his suit. 'You're needed downstairs.'

'This *is* downstairs,' Ron grumbled, 'isn't it?'

Noah was watching the man's face. 'There's a cellar?'

The investigator gave a grim nod. 'You'll want to see what's down there.'

3

After Aidan Duffy had been taken to his new cell, Marnie returned to the corridor where the riot had started. Michael Vokey and two other inmates, Tommy Walton and Neil Bayer, had started a fight over food. Or so the story went. Walton and Bayer were in hospital with serious head and facial injuries; both men had been brutally blinded in the attack. Vokey had gone on to start a fire with a T-shirt saturated in cooking fat. Smoke had killed two inmates and hospitalised a further two. While the alarm was being raised, Vokey had assaulted Ted Elms in the cell they shared, before making his escape through a series of doors which had been opened for the fire services. The ghost of the riot haunted the corridor in fresh white-wash specked with soot. Marnie's escort was in his twenties, peachy-cheeked and nervous, eyes jumping from the floor to the walls. He'd given his name as Darren Quayle, one of Aidan's schoolboy officers who, knowing themselves outnumbered, kept the peace by striking bargains with inmates for their good behaviour.

'Were you on duty?' Marnie asked him. 'When the riot happened?'

Darren shook his head. 'They called us in though, called everyone in.' He came to a standstill, hands twitching at his sides. 'Didn't tell us what sort of emergency, just gave out the riot gear and we kitted up and came in here.'

The corridor held onto the sour smell of bodies ripened by damage. Biohazard signs warned of the places you might slip and fall. A scroll of police tape sat in the spot where the worst of it had washed up. Not just blood. Teeth. Eyes.

'Tommy Walton's no friend of mine,' Aidan had said. *'But he didn't deserve that.'*

'We're taking the trays away.' Darren blinked at the corridor. 'Bringing the food in paper bags from now on. Meals in cells. They'll be eating breakfast sat on the toilet. And we're meant not to treat them like animals.' He wasn't looking at Marnie, staring down to where the biohazard signs stood sentry. 'How's that even going to work?'

No more bargains, or not for a long while. No promises of good behaviour, and little prospect of it. Fear would keep the peace for a while, but that couldn't last. Before long the inmates would be pushing back, needing to know the new shape of this place, where its boundaries lay. It was possible the worst was yet to come.

Marnie said, 'I'd like to see Michael Vokey's cell.'

'We showed it last time, before the clean-up.' Darren's hands moved, his fingers folding as if counting the number of empty cells going to waste in this corridor while the inmates were crowded three or four to a cell elsewhere in Cloverton. 'Nothing's changed.'

'You've cleaned up. But you kept everything in situ. We asked that nothing was moved out.'

'Except body parts.' He turned his face, light catching the fuzz of down on his jaw. He was very young. 'Eyes

25

and teeth, and bits of brain. We cleared all that out, so you lot could do your job. No one's helping us with ours, but yeah. This's important because it's *dead bodies*. They matter more than the live ones, I guess.'

Marnie couldn't offer reassurances, and chose not to offer a platitude. She walked to where Ted Elms was assaulted shortly before Michael Vokey escaped. The cell had a bunk bed and a pair of cabinets bolted next to a metal sink and toilet. Two plants sat on one of the cabinets, green cacti coated in sticky brown soot. More soot stained the ceiling and shrouded the light fitting, the dark smell of fire damage crowding the narrow space. Her team had searched this cell seven days ago, taking everything likely to yield a clue to Vokey's whereabouts. Letters and paperwork. Drugs of course, spice and pills. And Vokey's sketchpads, the charcoals procured by Aidan Duffy through the channels which ran in and out of Cloverton like overworked shipping lanes.

'Had you been in here,' she asked Darren Quayle, 'before the riot?'

He shook his head. 'Ted was a neat freak, so we didn't need to worry so much. On paper it looked like Vokey was the same. We thought it might work.'

As if this had been a flat share: *Single white male living alone seeks similar.* How close had the two men been? Vokey hadn't spared Ted Elms his share of the riot's damage; of the five in hospital, he had the worst prognosis. From the sense they'd been able to make of the night's violence, Vokey had doubled back after his spree in the corridor, to attack Elms in this cell. That spoke of personal vengeance, or a special brand of sadism.

'You know Mr Elms well?' Marnie asked Darren. 'You called him Ted.'

'We try to be friendly.' He looked at the bunk bed. 'It's

how they train us. Easier said than done with some of them, but Ted was okay. Just that one time when he swallowed batteries but everyone was doing it that week, like it was a group activity.'

'Swallowing batteries.'

'Triple A, the little ones. We have to take them to hospital so, you know, it's disruptive. That's why they do it. Low-level protesting. Nothing like what kicked off last week.' He thumbed a fleck of soot from his cheek. 'We cleaned up, but we'll need the whole wing vetted before we can start using it again. In the meantime it's four to a cell so who knows?' He glanced in the direction of Aidan's new cellblock. 'This time next week they could be rioting over there.'

'There wasn't any trouble between Michael Vokey and Ted Elms before the riot?'

'Nothing we had to deal with.' He brushed his teeth with the pad of his thumb. 'The smart ones figure out how to get along. We keep the peace as best we can, but it's up to guys like Vokey how much trouble they want to get into.'

'Ted's smart,' Marnie deduced. 'He knew how to stay on Vokey's right side.'

Darren wiped his thumb on his trouser leg, not speaking. Possibly since the evidence was stacked so steeply against the hypothesis that Ted Elms had known how to stay on the right side of the man who'd put him into hospital.

'The battery swallowing. How long ago was that?'

'A month ago?' He shrugged. 'Thereabouts.'

'So Vokey was sharing a cell with Ted when it happened.'

'Like I said, lots of them were swallowing around that time. We were about to take in new transfers, it was right after the riots in Leeds. No one was happy about that.'

'Low-level protesting. Did Vokey swallow batteries?'

'Doubt it.' He scuffed a foot at the floor, grimacing. 'It'd be on his record.'

'Do you think Ted was protesting about Vokey? Was he unhappy about *that* transfer?'

'He didn't kick off,' Darren said, as if this was the only benchmark that mattered.

Marnie considered the bed frame before crouching to examine the wall adjacent to the lower bunk. Dotted amongst the smoke stains were pale spots where glue or toothpaste had been used to stick something to the wall. Photos, Aidan had said. She touched a hand to her bag as she studied the marks, Stephen Keele slipping into her head as easily as a knife into a sheath. The slope of his shoulders, the dark of his face. Leaning across the table in the visitors' room, fixing her with his unblinking stare, daring her to swallow his lies when their deaths were already two stones in her throat. *Six years*, she'd thought that last time they sat together, *I've been asking you why you killed them for six years.* Listening to his newly broken silence, his stare burning her face like a frost until she half-expected to find its bruise on her skin the next day. His words had been bad enough, but now she had evidence. Here, in her bag. Photographs, like the ones gone from this wall.

'Who slept in the bottom bunk? Ted, or Vokey?'

Darren Quayle picked at the skin on his thumb. 'Vokey. As far as I know.'

'He had pictures here.' She indicated the marks.

'Guess so.' He looked, without interest. 'So?'

'There were no pictures in the belongings we recovered before you began cleaning up in here.'

'Guess the fire got them.'

It was a lazy lie. The fire hadn't spread into the cells. Smoke didn't burn pictures from walls.

28

'You didn't see them?' Marnie straightened. 'Photos of women, and girls.'

Darren wet his teeth with his tongue, glancing away. 'They've all got something like that.'

'Has Ted?'

He kept his eyes on the opposite wall. 'Ted's not into girls, from what I heard.'

'What's he into?'

A shrug. 'You'll have to ask him.'

Marnie thought of the hospital bed where she and Noah had been waiting to question Ted Elms. The tubes, and fluids. The dressings, the smell. She looked at the plants on the cabinet. Cacti, just as Aidan had said. They'd survived the smoke better than most inmates.

She stepped back from the bunk. 'Michael Vokey's letters. His mail.'

'Yeah?' Darren was losing what little interest he'd had.

'Where would I find that?'

'We gave you everything,' stressing the syllables, 'from in here.'

'That was a week ago. Where would I find the mail that's come for him since then?'

He paused, long enough for Marnie to suspect he knew all about the fan mail, women sending pictures, wanting to reform Michael Vokey, or worse. He'd been jailed for torturing a young mother. It was hard to believe any woman would write fan mail to a man like that, but it happened.

'The post room,' Darren said reluctantly. 'If there's anything.'

'You weren't aware of anyone writing to him on a regular basis?'

'No, but that's not my job, is it?' He squared his shoulders. An angry boil below his left ear stressed his youth.

29

How had he ended up in a prison where violence and self-harm were a normal state of affairs? Which careers officer had advised him to try this line of work?

'Did Michael Vokey write many letters of his own?'

'No idea. Some do, some don't.' His jaw bunched. 'I need to get to C spur. We done?'

'Did Ted Elms write many letters?'

'Same answer. No idea.'

Something had spooked him. The photos, which he was denying having seen? If drugs could make their way in here then so could photographs, even intimate ones. Or was it the fan mail that disturbed him? Had he seen the letters from the women who thought they could reform Vokey, or who liked him just the way he was? Had Vokey written back, encouraging confidences? Did he have a favourite fan, someone who'd shared her address in the hope of hearing from him, happy to have his attention? Craving it, even.

'*He was drawing pictures,*' Aidan had said. '*From the photographs.*'

In which case, where were those pictures and photographs? Had he taken them with him when he ran? Or had he destroyed everything before the worst of the riot took hold, knowing the letters held clues to his whereabouts? Ted Elms had seen the photos and charcoal drawings; you couldn't live this close to another human being without picking up the scent of a secret or two.

'Where's the post room?' she asked Darren Quayle. 'I need to see the mail that's come for Michael Vokey, and for Ted Elms, since the riot.'

She looked again at the pale marks on the wall by the bottom bunk. Whatever had been stuck here, however strange or innocuous or terrible it was—

Ted Elms had seen it.

30

4

I've a room to myself at last, never mind the dog lead chaining me to the bed. The hospital's like the shitting Ritz after Cloverton. I could've stood it even so, hunkered down and done my time. Until they gave me Mickey Vokey.

'You're one of the good guys, Ted. We trust you.'

To do what? I wanted to ask. Give him the bottom bunk even though it's mine and I hate sleeping so near the ceiling? It gave me a migraine being that close to the lights, but I didn't put up a fight because I could see how it was. They'd tried to cut a deal with Aidan, who wasn't getting his fingers burnt. Well, you've seen him. Aidan Duffy. Not a mark on him, and he's been inside long enough. Some people thrive in prison, that's a fact. You're not supposed to speak it, but it's a fact. For some, prison's the best thing that's ever happened. The free meals and bed, the chance to be themselves. Men like Aidan don't get rehabilitated, they don't even get reduced. The worst of them flourish, thanks to unlimited opportunities to refine their skill set. The thieves get better at thieving, the liars get better at lying, and men like Aidan get better at being smart. Keeping quiet, staying strong. I've seen him practise his smile when he thinks no one's watching, running his fingers through his hair, making his eyes dance. He's got Cloverton covered inside and out. I wonder whether the fire even touched him. When I try to imagine it, I see the flames swerve the other way.

Mickey isn't anything like Aidan, but the same rules apply.

He wasn't *in prison*. It was in him.

Prison's the one place where your identity's a hundred per cent protected. Chances are Aidan's charm only works half the time out in the real world. As for Mickey, he couldn't function out there. I know because I'm the same, needing the walls and noise. Needing the routine. Inside, if I line my stuff up and count it every day twice a day, I'm called a neat freak like it's a good thing. I get, 'You're one of the good guys, Ted. We trust you.' Out there I was called all sorts. Psycho, weirdo, paedo. Just because I had standards. They're crying out for standards inside, the same as they're crying out for anyone who can cut deals the way Aidan can. At least that's how it was back before the drugs started coming in. Speaking of—

My lucky nurse is adjusting the meds, tapping in new numbers. Increased dosage, I hope. What they're giving me's only skimming the surface of the pain, like a pebble. Three, maybe four skips before it's swallowed up. She's my lucky nurse because of the gap in her front teeth. That and the dosage, not waiting for the pebble to drop before she punches in an extra kick. They say you get addicted to morphine but I'd reckon it's the anticipation that's addictive. Counting down to when it kicks in, four, three, two— Here it comes. Icy cold *bliss*. With me, it's the anticipation.

Funny how quickly it all becomes normal. Spare a thought for the poor buggers who make a living out of smuggling shit into prisons, the girlfriends with their big smiles and bright clothes, flashing their teeth and tits around the visitors' room, pushing Mars bars across the tables, chocolate under their fake fingernails from a morning spent stuffing a mobile phone in there or whatever else will fit, the things you never knew you couldn't live without. Aidan takes care of all that now. Not the drugs, just the fancy stuff. The drugs get walked in by girls, even kids. The staff figure it's easier to keep the peace with us lot off our faces, so they nod through all the sweets and cigarettes, porn and spice. You go to Aidan if you want silk boxer shorts or earplugs, or charcoals like Mickey for his drawings. Shit, those drawings. I'd never seen anything like it.

My lovely, lucky nurse. She's punched in the numbers like it's rollover week and I'm floating on a fresh flood of morphine that's drip-dripping into my arm from the tangle of tubes. Like this, I can bear to think about Mickey's drawings, his women. He told me their names, told me everything. I didn't want to hear it, but I hadn't the nerve to tell him to shut up, so I lay there too close to the ceiling with the whole of my head caving in to a migraine as he talked about them, Ruth and Lara. Reading me their letters, showing me their photos.

He's pinned their pictures to the wall. All the time he's talking, he's running his thumb over their faces and the photos are making this sound like whispering, like squealing. I shut my eyes with the migraine setting fire to my face and *pray* for the pain to get worse, for the hammering in my head to drown out what he's saying about Lara's legs and Ruth's eyes, how they're going to look after he's emptied them out, when there's nothing left but raw red sockets and scraped white bone.

'It's what they want,' he says. 'It's why they write to me.'

33

At first I think he's making it up, that the letters are from his mum and he's only pretending to read from the pages. But he makes me recite a couple out loud, 'Like you're Lara,' and they're real. Jesus, they're so real. I can't believe letters like that make it through the post room checks.

'Do to me what you did to her.' That's the gist of the worst ones. I know who they mean by 'her' and I know about 'what you did', because Mickey talks about that too. Julie, the young mum he tortured. He won't shut up about her. How she looked after he'd finished with her. How she looked while he was doing it. He even talks about how she looked before. 'Like this.' Showing me a blank sheet from his sketchpad. Like she was nothing before he got to work on her.

'Do to me what you did to her.'

Sad, mad cows. How awful did your life have to be? Or was it just a safe suburban housewife's fantasy? That's what Daz Quayle reckons – neither of them really meant it, Lara and Ruth, they were just getting a cheap thrill out of being in touch with a violent con. I'm not so sure, Dazza. I'm not so sure anyone's got that much faith in the prison system they'd mess with a man like Vokey just because he's behind bars. Supposing he gets out, what then? What then, Dazza? An appeal, I meant. I wasn't thinking about a riot where I'd end up in here and he'd be out there, wherever he's gone. To Lara, maybe. I hope not to Julie. She's suffered enough.

'Like this.' Showing me the blank page from his sketchpad. 'Before I found her.'

Aidan got him the sketchpad. Not like the cheap ones they hand out in art classes. Mickey's pad is made of thick sheets the colour of clotted cream. He tears a page from the pad and screws it in his fist. It sounds like someone

34

stepping into new snow, the squeaky clean noise of it, like old shoes in new snow. A pulpy, sweet smell. Later, after the charcoals, it smells of ash. His sweat's the same, you find out things like that when you share a cell. I've shared with plenty. Those who never wash, and those who wash so often they stink of metal from the sink.

'Read it like you're Lara,' Mickey says, and I do.

I read, 'I want you to see me the way you saw her. I won't feel real until you do.'

He holds the letters to his lips, and sniffs. As if they're perfume samples, or porn. He smells of ash and sugar. Aidan gets him sweets. Skittles, the sour ones. Mickey soaks off the colours to use as paints. Then he wads up what's left in his mouth, slapping his teeth together as he chews. I'll be lying four feet above him, trying to hold the migraine at bay, hearing him sucking and slapping, reading the words out loud. Worst thing I've ever had to listen to, worse even than the doctors who gather to pass judgement around my bed.

'The smell of new paint turns me on.' Mickey puts on this little girl's voice when he reads from the letters. 'I set fire to a spider's web and watched it burn and I thought of you.'

I see the sweat on his head like wax, his left eye watering madly. I pray for an alarm to sound, for a fire or lockdown. I want its rattle in my skull, like metal beads in a bottle to get it clean.

'The sky smashes my head in. I need to be less, I need you to make me less.' His little girl's voice, whining, wanting. 'The skin behind my knees bruises when I pinch it.'

Did it turn him on? Of course it did, but not in the obvious way. He likes to play the parts, to *be* the women buttering him up with their letters, begging him to do his worst.

35

'I need to be less. Make me less.'

He thinks he's them.

Maybe he invented some of it. I can't understand how it got through the post room: 'I bruise too easily behind the knees and at the tops of my arms. I don't feel real.'

Behind my eye, the migraine hammers, keeping time.

In here, there's no real pain thanks to my lucky nurse. But I have an idea my hands are closing, making claws. My feet too. Like I'm marching, or trying to. Stiff legs, stiff arms, claws for hands. I want her to wash my hands, get me clean. I'm scared I won't ever get clean again. Rats scrabbling around inside my head, emptying it out. Whole parts of me I can't feel, not properly. I'm mute, unable to answer the questions the detectives keep asking. I was never mute in there. Mickey got angry if I refused to read the letters out loud.

'Come and find me.' Lara, the whine of her voice like the reeling of a fishing line.

Once, my silence made him bark. Dog noises, no words. Remembering that, I try to smile but it feels wrong, hanging off my face as if my mouth's gone, and my eyes. As if the fire caught up with me in the end.

Where is he? That's what everyone wants to know. Me too, if I'm honest. Where's Mickey Vokey?

It's weird being without him, this far away from the ceiling. I'm so used to him being in the bunk below mine, reading whatever the post's brought, being Lara talking about bruises and spider's webs, and the smell of new paint. I miss him and the missing him makes me want to shout for my nurse to come and punch in more numbers to take me away from here, change my life. Set me free.

5

'It's less than six weeks since we scraped that young woman off the Embankment.' DCS Lorna Ferguson scrutinised her team. 'And here we are again with another bloody mess on our hands.'

'Welcome to London,' Ron muttered, straightening when she caught his eye. 'Ma'am.'

'No, go on.' She cocked her head, like a gun. 'Let's hear how property development works down here. Only up North when we want a bit of extra space we shove on a conservatory. We don't dig graves in our cellars. That's what you found in this house in Ealing, am I right? An open grave.'

Ron nodded. 'That's what it looks like.'

'Hard to see what else it could be, that size and shape. Unless he's putting in posh plumbing and I don't see how he'd find the time with all his other extra-curricular activities. Assault, aggravated arson, prison mutiny.' She ticked each item off on her fingers. Verbal bullet-pointing, they called it. Noah had the impression she'd like to be using real bullets. 'Michael Vokey. Who's got the profile on this charmer? DS Jake. Let's start with how dangerous he is,

37

and work our way from there. Before you roll your eyes, DS Carling, I know we've covered this ground already, but as we're making less progress than a striking snail, I'm thinking we could use the recap.'

'Vokey went into Cloverton as a Category B prisoner,' Noah said. 'But they were in the process of upgrading him. By all accounts he should have been Cat-A from the outset. Highly manipulative and aggressive. Clever enough to hide it a lot of the time.'

'Until he buried a plastic tray in the back of someone's head.' Ferguson stood five foot five in her heels. Solidly built and expensively blonde, she made a point of taking no prisoners, Cat-A or otherwise. 'That's the kind of clue they couldn't ignore. Go on. What else?'

'He's serving eight years for aggravated burglary. They've moved him around under prisoner protection rules, citing reasons of safety and disruption.' Noah referred to his notes. 'Exerting a negative influence over other offenders.'

'So they thought they'd bung him in an overcrowded prison where tensions were already running higher than the walls.' Ferguson nodded. 'That makes perfect sense.'

'Is there any other kind of prison, right now?' Ron wanted to know.

A ripple of weary assent moved around the room. Noah waited until it had died down. 'On record, Vokey's behaviour was exemplary. But the behaviour of those around him became increasingly difficult to manage. Three attempted suicides at his previous prison, one of which resulted in a death. All three had formed friendships with Vokey shortly before the incidents, except *friendship* is too strong a word. The prison governor described these men as being in Vokey's thrall. They became agitated or excited in his presence, depressive the rest of the time. Stopped sleeping, smashed up their cells . . . The governor likened it to an outbreak of rabies.'

'I'd say the governor got it right,' Ron muttered.

'This is up in Leeds?' Ferguson asked. 'Why was he shunted our way?'

'There was a riot at Leeds two months ago,' DC Debbie Tanner said. 'Wasn't there?'

Noah nodded. 'It's why he was transferred to Cloverton so quickly.'

'Thereby making last week's riot a sure-fire certainty.' Ferguson thumbed a speck of mascara from her left eye. 'Any reason to think he may've run back to Leeds?'

'No contacts in the immediate area,' Ron said, 'although his sister's not far off. West Yorkshire Police are on the lookout, like the rest of us.'

'Oh good, because last time I counted they had seven detectives covering the whole of Leeds.' Ferguson wasn't exaggerating, the cuts had been savage. 'That's a sixth of what they had four years ago and no prizes for guessing the state of the response units. So now he's on the loose, most likely on our patch, and of course he's gone to ground, lower than a slug's belly in the sand. No sightings in seven days. Forensics sifted through the slop in that corridor in record time, and came up with precisely nothing we didn't already know. CCTV may as well be bunting for all the good it's doing us.' She flicked the speck of mascara away. 'Tell me about this house with the hole in the cellar. Why wasn't it uncovered at the time of his arrest?'

'The house isn't in his name,' Debbie said. 'His mum Marion paid off the mortgage years ago. When she died there was no paperwork linking the house to Vokey. It's in probate.'

'So she died without a will.' Ferguson chewed this over.

'But we're not imagining it was *her* dug the grave in the cellar. In which case, what's it for? Who's it for?'

'Julie Seton?' Ron suggested. 'Or his next victim. Classic escalation – if we hadn't caught him when we did he'd have killed by now.'

'DS Carling's here all week,' Ferguson said sourly. 'If you're looking for a laugh.'

'I was just saying— We *did* catch him, after Julie.'

'And then we let him go again. Or Cloverton did. Which means we don't get to keep the medals or the warm feeling of having done our duty. Let's say you're right about the escalation. It means we've a killer out there looking for someone to bury in his cellar. Who's got a bright idea in that direction?' Her stare ran the room. 'DS Jake, tell us about the photos.'

'We took over five hundred from the house. The vast majority aren't attributable to Vokey. He cut them out of magazines, newspapers, textbooks. All forty-eight faces from the Szondi Test, and he'd photocopied each one multiple times. The Polaroids we found under the flooring were of artwork, life studies mostly. We think we can attribute the art to Vokey.'

'We'll come back to the art, and the Szondi Test.' Ferguson eyed the evidence board unkindly, holding her Met lanyard away from the scarlet silk of her blouse. 'Discounting the photocopies and his dodgy ideas about home décor, what're we left with that we should be worrying about?'

'Eleven faces.'

Ferguson swivelled towards Noah. 'Eleven out of five hundred?'

'We've identified these two,' he touched a hand to the images of a young mother and her daughter, 'as his victims from the Edmonton estate. Julie and Natalie Seton. Vokey

40

stole these family photos from their house on the night of the assault. Julie is the reason he was convicted, and sentenced. Aggravated burglary, eight years. But that leaves nine faces we've yet to identify.'

Everyone looked at the photocopies on the board, each face enlarged from its Polaroid original. The images of Julie and Natalie had been set to one side, a black band of shadow obscuring Julie's eyes. She looked like a warning of what might befall any one of the others.

'Seven of the nine are women,' Debbie added. 'Two might be men, it's hard to tell. But we reckon all these photos were taken in the last four or five years.'

'Don't be fooled by the Polaroids,' Ron put in. 'They look retro, but they're recent.'

'Nine potential victims,' Ferguson repeated. 'Out of over five hundred photos. Not that it isn't plenty to be getting on with, but are we absolutely certain this isn't optimism on our part?' Her gaze moved around the team until it landed on Colin. 'DC Pitcher?'

'We scanned every face,' Colin said. 'Put it all through our systems, plus a reverse image search to see which ones pre-existed online. Some needed extra digging, facial recognition software and so on. We got hits on every image except these. These nine don't exist online, or in any police or misper database we can access from here.' He blinked behind his spectacles. 'That's a lot of databases. Obviously we've checked passports, driving licences and the rest.'

'I look forward to your overtime claim. But good, well done.' Ferguson straightened up. 'So, do we need to flag these nine people as being at risk? Is one or more of them destined for his cellar? Or are we chasing shadows when we've a dangerous prisoner to catch?'

No one answered right away. It was hard to look at the

faces and declare them unimportant in the light of what was done to the inmates at Cloverton, most especially in the light of the empty grave. Noah saw it in his mind's eye, a pit in the floor surrounded by a loose margin of earth and sand. A man-sized pit, or woman-sized. Deep enough for two bodies, if both were small. It was impossible to look at the nameless faces on the board and not think of that pit. Noah had copied the nine photos to his phone, committing the faces to memory, wanting to keep faith in some small way with each one, to give them hope.

'We don't know that they're victims,' Debbie was saying. 'I mean they could be accomplices or one-night stands, or complete strangers.'

'He didn't dig that pit for fun,' Ron said. 'He took up a brick floor. It's a professional job, must've taken him weeks.'

'He didn't just collect photos of their faces.' Noah nodded at the board where they'd pinned the pictures of shoulders and shins, hands and feet. 'I don't think they're strangers in any usual sense.'

'But the vast majority of his collection are press cuttings and photocopies,' Ferguson said briskly. 'Unless I've missed something.'

Noah shook his head. 'You know as much as we do, Ma'am.'

'We've got someone on Julie Seton, yes? Since she's the one put him away.'

Debbie nodded. 'Round the clock surveillance.'

'More dents in the budget. But we can't be seen taking chances, not if DS Carling's right and he's been dreaming of his burial project all the short while he was inside. Not to mention the bedlam he left behind when he ran from prison. If we're talking escalation, we should be focusing on that. I've seen rabid dogs do less damage.' She clicked her tongue. 'I don't think Ms Seton knows what a narrow escape she had. She was lucky to hang onto her teeth, for starters.'

The photos from the corridor at Cloverton occupied the bottom half of the evidence board, a low tide of blood and soot. Vokey had improvised a black and red rainbow, working blind since the corridor was solid with smoke, smearing the carnage he'd left on the floor, picking up whole handfuls of it in lieu of a paint brush, wiping his hands and fingers onto the wall. As if the floor wasn't enough for him – the mess he'd made of the men he'd mutilated – as if he needed the walls to bear witness to what he'd done. Carnage, from the Latin *carnaticum*, meaning flesh, meaning slaughter. He wasn't an artist, not in the real sense; interested in destruction, not creation. And driven, compulsively violent. There was no coming back from what he'd done at Cloverton. Noah was reminded of a conversation with a good friend from university, Sam Amsler. Sam worked as a forensic psychologist, trying to rehabilitate offenders. Except when you tried to rehabilitate a psychopath, Sam said, you just made a better psychopath. Taught him or her new tricks, more sophisticated ways to pass below the radar of most people's threat instinct. If art was the expression of a person's soul then Michael Vokey's was black and red and ruined beyond rescue.

'D'you think his mum knew?' Debbie asked. 'About the sort of son she raised? Is that why she didn't make a will, because she didn't want to leave him the house, or anything else?'

'He has a sister, hasn't he?' Ferguson said. 'No, I've no idea how she died, but his mum probably thought she'd plenty of time to get her affairs in order before she dropped down dead. Well, don't we all think that?' She checked the gold watch at her wrist. 'I can't see how we'll justify a full-scale search for these nine people, no matter how much it might eat at our collective conscience. We need all the bodies we have looking for Vokey. When's DI Rome back with us?'

'She's on her way from Cloverton now,' Noah said.

'Good. I'll see the pair of you in my office as soon as she gets here. Anything else?' Glancing around the incident room. 'No? Let's crack on in that case.'

Marnie texted when she was within striking distance of the station. Noah went down to the car park, wanting to intercept her before Ferguson could launch an attack. Not that their new DCS had been doing much attacking of late, but Noah trusted Lorna Ferguson about as far as she could sprint in her daggered heels. Louboutins with red soles, as if she'd walked to work through an abattoir. He'd made his peace with her appointment, having little choice since Commander Tim Welland was on extended sick leave, but it was an uneasy peace, partly because Ferguson didn't want anyone to get comfortable on her watch. She gave the clear impression she didn't trust Marnie, Noah or anyone else to get the job done without her. The team had regrouped under her command, but no one was quite used to its new configuration and Ferguson's impatient pugnacity did little to help.

'Anything?' Marnie pushed her red curls from her eyes, keeping one hand on the open car door. She'd parked in the only available space, between two pool vehicles.

'Ferguson thinks the faces are a blind alley,' Noah said. 'We need to focus on finding Vokey. She agrees with Ron that the grave means he's working his way up to killing. But still no leads, and no trail. No sightings, just the press heavy-breathing down the phones. How about at Cloverton? Did Aidan have anything for you?'

'He knew Vokey had photos in his cell.' Marnie reached into the car and pulled on her jacket, hiding the seat-belt creases in her white shirt. 'Fan mail, he thought. Vokey bought charcoals from Aidan to draw pictures of the women who were writing to him. I quizzed one of the officers, but he was pretending he knew nothing about photos or letters.'

'We cleared out the cell.' Noah frowned. 'There was nothing like that.'

'Nothing we found.' She took her bag from the passenger seat before locking the car and pocketing the keys. 'Possibly because he took it all with him when he ran. But he couldn't take these.' She held up an evidence bag. 'These only arrived in the prison post room three days ago.'

Noah took the bag from her. Five envelopes, letter-sized, postmarked, the prison's address typed or handwritten under Vokey's name and number. 'More fan mail?' he asked.

'More mess.' Marnie slung the messenger bag across her body, leaving her hands free. She was wearing a black suit that washed out what little colour she had.

As they crossed the car park and climbed the steps to the station, Noah watched her with a vigilance that was new but had felt necessary ever since the sequence of events seven weeks ago, which had put first Noah and then DS Harry Kennedy into hospital, victims of a vigilante who hadn't known when or how to stop, until Marnie cracked the case. Like Harry, Noah had recovered from the physical assault. Marnie hadn't been a victim in the same sense but she'd been psychologically damaged by the case, the sort of damage that goes deep. Little things like the time she took before she spoke, especially to DCS Ferguson, and the careful way she held herself as if anticipating pain. It reminded Noah of the way his mother was with Sol, back when his brother was a baby.

45

She'd spend hours rocking Sol to sleep. When he finally cried himself out she'd hold him as if he were a live grenade and any small movement on her part might trigger an explosion. Marnie had been holding herself that way for weeks now, even before the vigilante case had closed. Noah had asked her, more than once, whether she was okay. The closest she'd come to an answer was, 'Give me time.' He was doing as she asked but it didn't stop him from staying close, watching out for her the way she'd done for him during those first days after Sol's arrest.

'Any word from the hospital,' Marnie was asking, 'about Ted Elms?'

They climbed the final flight of stairs to the incident room.

'Nothing new. And nothing on the other . . . victims.'

Noah nearly stumbled on the word. The men hospitalised by Vokey had been in Cloverton for good reason. Each had victims of his own, men, women and children injured by his actions. Stephen Keele was guilty of double murder.

'Have you been to see him?' He held the door open for Marnie.

'Elms? Not since we last visited.'

'Stephen, I meant. Sorry.'

She dropped her head, checking her phone for messages. 'No visitors allowed.'

'Still?'

'Still.' Her voice was steady, unemotional.

'And you're okay?'

She smiled at him, tucking the phone away. 'I'm guessing Ferguson wants us in her office?'

Noah nodded. 'Good guess.'

'Let's see what she makes of this fan mail.' Marnie

nodded at the handful of envelopes. 'If nothing else, we have two addresses worth visiting.'

'These women gave him their addresses?'

'Addresses, photographs and their undivided attention.' Marnie stopped to straighten the collar of her shirt, knotting her curls away from her face. 'Everything a man like Michael Vokey could want, especially now he's looking for a place to lie low.'

Noah could see the bones in her wrists, and at the nape of her neck. He wanted to let her know how much he was on her side. The loss of his mother's trust had made him more vulnerable to other people's pain, and Marnie was in pain, he was sure of it. Because of Stephen? Her parents' murderer was lying in a hospital bed with smoke-damaged lungs and she couldn't visit him, even assuming she wanted to.

'Ted hadn't any letters,' Marnie was saying. 'Just a seed catalogue.'

'That ties with no next-of-kin. We're his only visitors at the hospital.' Noah stopped short of saying, 'Poor sod,' but he thought of Ted wired to the machinery and felt pity for the man who'd been Vokey's cellmate, caught up in the madness which had prefaced Vokey's escape.

'One other thing,' Marnie said. 'Vokey's mugshots. The official ones, and the Facebook ones.'

'What did Aidan say?'

'The same as everyone else. Nothing we have looks anything like him. Aidan couldn't give me a clear description of what's missing, says Vokey passed under his radar. He made the man sound like smoke, always shifting, never in focus.' She reached to scratch at her ankle. 'Not terribly helpful.'

'Sol's like that,' Noah said. 'Or he used to be. Has this talent for altering his appearance at will, depending who

47

he's with. The first time the police brought him home, I didn't recognise him. Then Mum came into the room, and he was just Sol again.'

Marnie touched a hand to his elbow as she straightened. They smiled at one another, in solidarity. Pain could do this, Noah was learning. No matter how distinct or personal, how private it was, the pain brought you closer. Like prisoners tapping out messages on the wall that divides them, turning the separation into a connection.

'It's going to make him harder to find. If Vokey's a shape-shifter.'

'Infinitely harder,' Marnie agreed. 'Let's see what Ferguson thinks about the fan mail.' She glanced at Noah. 'What sort of mood's she in?'

'Oh, the usual.' He leavened it with a smile. 'Impatient for results, but not yet explosive. I'd say we have six minutes to reach minimum safe distance.'

'Too bad we're headed in the opposite direction.'

6

'Ask me where I draw the line.' Lorna Ferguson was drinking tea from an insulated cup. 'Go on.' She pointed the brushed steel beaker, lollipop pink, at Noah. 'Don't be shy.'

'Where do you draw the line, Ma'am?'

'PMQs. DI Rome knows what I'm on about.'

'Prime Minister's Questions.' Marnic drew out a chair and sat facing Ferguson. 'Has it come to that?'

'Some pimply-faced parasite from the arse end of the country needing to know what we're doing to protect his yokels from our metropolitan menace.' Ferguson set the cup down next to her in-tray. 'Why he reckons Michael Vokey would want to set foot in his constituency is anyone's guess. I've had veggie curries with more meat in them.' She thinned her lips. 'As for Cloverton, don't get me started. CCTV not doing its job, no one prepared to give evidence, eye witnesses all in hospital, a couple of them *without* any eyes, and they had him as a Cat-B prisoner?'

'We have a theory about the silence,' Noah said. 'All the men inside Cloverton, including the officers, have wives or children. People they're afraid for now that Vokey's out.'

'Well, it's the thin end of a thick wedge and it gets right on my wires. We're feeding the press too many headlines as it is.'

Marnie didn't point out that it was Ferguson's love of a press briefing that had sparked the red-top campaign to hold the Met accountable for its failure to find Vokey and return him to a prison cell. Even so, it was frightening how fast the spotlight had swung from Cloverton's short-comings to their own. 'We have new leads.' She shared the fan mail between Noah and Ferguson. 'Two women who've been in contact with Vokey, possibly for some time. Ruth Hull, and Lara Chorley. They shared intimate details, including their home addresses.'

'These letters were handed to Vokey with those sorts of details in them?' Ferguson looked up sharply. 'Cloverton allowed that to happen?'

'Not officially. The post room's insisting they'd have redacted information of that kind. They don't routinely read letters, however. And Lara's been using stationery from a solicitor's office which means her letters are allowed through unread, as official correspondence.'

'Funny sort of solicitor.' Ferguson turned Lara's letter over in her hand. 'Unless we're talking about the law of attraction, or diminishing returns.' She reached for one of the other letters, reading it with her eyebrows raised. 'Don't these two know what he did to Julie Seton?'

'They know exactly what he did,' Noah said grimly. 'This letter refers to Julie by name.'

'Right,' Ferguson decided. 'I want a team at each of these addresses. If Vokey's hiding out with one of these women, we'd better be prepared for that. If he's not, I want them brought in here and interviewed. Either one of them could be hiding him, or helping him.'

'Or they could be victims,' Marnie said.

'If the press get hold of these?' Ferguson tossed the pages down, tapping them with a finger. 'They'll say these two were asking for it. Begging for it. And they'll have a point.'

'They believed he was safely behind bars.' Marnie paused, picking her words with care. 'We have to assume that. They can't have known he'd escape and there's nothing to suggest they encouraged or assisted him in any way. These letters were posted on or after the day of the riot, which makes me think they had no prior knowledge of his plans. They wrote these letters not knowing he'd be in a position to act on any of the information they disclosed.'

'Back up.' Ferguson chose a page at random and read out loud: '"Julie doesn't know how lucky she is. If it were me, I'd let you do all that and more. I wouldn't ever want you to stop. Don't ever stop, darling. I'm here for you when you're ready." Excuse me if I say that doesn't sound like someone I'm falling over myself to protect and serve.'

'Even so,' Marnie said quietly. 'Unless we find evidence they're assisting him, perhaps even *if* we find evidence of that, we need to treat these women as potential victims. Targets.'

'Oh, they're targets all right. Each one of them's drawn a ruddy great sign on her chest. DS Jake.' Ferguson swivelled her chair in Noah's direction. 'You're unusually quiet. Don't tell me this's a pathology too far for you.'

Noah shook his head. 'I agree with DI Rome. I'd be surprised if these women wanted anything other than letters back from Vokey, and possibly not even that.'

'So it's just the dubious thrill of writing to a convicted

felon, is it? Well, let's say that's true. People get their kicks in funny ways and happen these two are bored rigid with daytime telly and want a rise out of someone safely under lock and key. Why hand over your address, why send dirty pictures? The post room didn't have any photos? Ruth's letter says she's enclosing a new batch.'

'This is everything they had,' Marnie replied. 'Or so I was told.'

'In other words someone at Cloverton's got a stash of Polaroids they're not letting us see. Did you get to the bottom of that?'

Noah had never suffered from workplace irritation before DCS Ferguson pitched up here.

Marnie, on the other hand, appeared to be made of patience. 'The post room removes and destroys explicit images, that's the official line. Otherwise, as long as Vokey isn't in any of the photographs, he's allowed to keep them.'

'No photos were found in his cell,' Noah reminded them. 'And no drawings. Aidan said he was drawing pictures of the women.'

'How is Aidan?' Ferguson put in. 'As enchanting as ever?'

She'd had a run-in with Aidan Duffy seven weeks ago. Marnie was with her when it happened and from the little she'd told Noah, he wasn't surprised Ferguson was having a hard time getting over the encounter. Aidan had a knack for finding the chink in your armour, and a passion for button pressing. If he'd played his usual games around Michael Vokey, he'd be in the hospital right now, in the bed next to Ted Elms.

Marnie replied, 'Aidan says Michael passed under his radar.'

'Oh really?' Ferguson curled her lip. 'Either his radar's

playing up, or he was making too much money slipping *Michael* whatever he wanted.'

'Charcoals,' Marnie said. 'For drawing the women from the photos they sent.'

'Where are these drawings?'

'Officer Quayle said the fire destroyed everything we didn't recover from the cell.' Marnie paused. 'But he was cagey about the whole idea of photos, and letters.'

'He's caught onto the size of the fan needed to deal with the shit they're trying to deflect our way.' Ferguson tapped a glossy fingernail on the desk. 'I spoke with the arresting officer up in Leeds. He can't believe Cloverton let Vokey pass himself off as Cat-B, said it was clear from one look in his eyes what sort of man he is. Stone-cold psycho.'

Marnie was aware of her silence in response to this. Aware too that Noah had her back, ready to lend his weight to whatever resistance she might offer to Ferguson's theory.

Was Michael Vokey a psychopath? They knew he was a sadist with a vicious temper and enough animal cunning to evade capture in the days immediately after he'd attacked Julie Seton in her home, in front of her daughter. A strange assault, bloodless, leaving little physical evidence other than a traumatised mother and child. By all accounts he didn't start the riot at Cloverton, certainly not single-handedly, but he'd been quick to escalate it. And he'd started the fire and escaped under cover of its smoke, knowing where the weak points were in the prison's perimeter security. He'd done all this as a Cat-B prisoner with no recent record of bad behaviour to warrant isolation or special measures. That suggested an instinct for self-preservation. Marnie thought of the images on her phone, Vokey's native camouflage. The arresting officer in Leeds might be right. They couldn't in any case afford wishful thinking.

'We'll start putting together the teams for the house searches.' She stood and collected the letters from Ferguson's desk, knocking them into a neat pile in her hand. 'I'll let you know how we get on.'

In the corridor outside Ferguson's office, Marnie turned to Noah. 'Show me the pictures of the house in Ealing?'

He took her to the office on the second floor which he was using as an unofficial incident room. It was an odd shape, arrow-headed by the emergency installation of a new heating system behind a partition wall. Winter had put its boots through the old system: months of freezing pipes and icy windows. Confronted by a blue-lipped work-force wearing enough jumpers to shame a Scandinavian crime drama, the budget holders had relented. The new heating system was a huge hit, until the temperature outside climbed above freezing. On those days, they swapped Scandinavia for Spain, with Ron threatening hourly to strip down to his boxers and a knotted hand-kerchief. One of the unexpected upsides of the new boiler was this extra space on the second floor. Too small to be useful as a regular office, it was invaluable as an overflow incident room. In here, Noah had recreated the room of faces from Marion Vokey's house, using photos of the walls, floor and ceiling as it had looked before they took it all apart.

'I keep thinking I'll find patterns here,' he told Marnie. 'But perhaps it's about the detail, the differences. There's no order to the way he's pinned the images. None that I've found, anyway.'

The colours created a kind of camouflage, pale splotches from faces, greens and browns and blues from eyes, mouths adding pinks and reds, yellows from the oil paints in the photos they'd unpinned from the floor. If you stared too long you started to see pixels, broken details in a map which might suddenly make sense seen from a sufficient distance.

'Let's find out whether Lara Chorley's face is here,' Marnie said. 'And Ruth Hull's. We need profiles for these women. We need to know if they were in direct contact with Vokey before Cloverton, or in the week since he ran.' She nursed her neck with the curve of her hand. 'And we need a better photograph of him. The ones we have . . . Everyone says he doesn't look like that. No matter which picture we show them, it's the same answer. He doesn't look like that.'

Noah nodded, but he didn't speak. It was important to let her look. Ron hadn't wanted to see this room – 'Being in that house was enough, thanks,' – but Noah couldn't shake the sense that *this—*

This was where they would find Michael Vokey.

They'd exhausted every other avenue, sifting through CCTV, alerting officials, contacting former workmates, neighbours, anyone who might have seen Vokey since his escape. At least they had the letters to follow up now. Otherwise it was starting to feel as if he'd vanished into thin air.

'The camera never lies.' Marnie was studying the photos. 'Isn't that what they say?'

'Not everyone. Diane Arbus said a photograph is "a secret about a secret, the more it tells you the less you know." That's what this feels like to me.'

'These women who sent him their photos – why?'

'Attention,' Noah said. 'Obsession. He's clearly obsessed with imagery, with ownership.'

As if he could steal their souls, capture them in emulsion.

Marnie stepped close to the wall, putting her hand on the face of the young woman with a band of shadow blacking her eyes. 'This is Julie Seton.'

Noah nodded. 'I'm thinking we should talk with her again. If anyone knows what Vokey looks like, it's her.'

'Let's do that,' Marnie agreed. 'And let's get looking for these other two. Ruth, and Lara.' She stayed standing by the wall, her hand on the young mother's face, fingers thinly splayed. 'Julie has a little girl. I want her to feel safe. I want them both to feel safe.'

7

I've been thinking a lot about Julie, stuck in here with just my lucky nurse for company. She's started calling me Ted. It was 'Mr Elms' at first, then Edward, but now it's Ted. She's a nice woman, old enough to be a mother. I wish I could ask her about her kids. Julie was sixteen when she had her little girl, Natalie. Teenage pregnancy, nothing unusual in that, certainly not in this day and age. But the way Mickey talked about her, you'd think it was an immaculate conception, that she was the Virgin Mary, untouched except by him – *until* by him.

'I was her first,' he said.

'What about Natalie?' I wanted to know.

That's when I first saw the warning siren flashing. My mistake, challenging his version of events. I wouldn't make it again. You wouldn't either, if he'd done to you what he did to me.

Batteries. Six of them. He fills his fist and I think it's a punch coming but he grabs me by the throat, shoves me face down in his pillow and feeds me the whole handful—

Six batteries clattering against my teeth, making my tongue fizz, my tonsils pop.

He's on me, all his weight in my kidneys and he's not a light man, Mickey. I'm thrashing, trying to get him off, trying to *breathe*. He has the heel of his hand on my head, grinding my face into the pillow, and I've taken worse but not with a mouthful of batteries, not without any way to breathe and now a punch to the side of my throat so that I'm swallowing, I'm swallowing batteries and I think, *They'll call this a protest, they'll say I did this on purpose*, and I can't breathe and my spine's snapping but even so I'm worrying about the hospital, who'll look after my plants if I'm out of here for too many days, and I *know*—

I know that doesn't sound normal. I should be worrying about whether he'll let me live or if he wants to choke me to death. At the very least I should be thinking of the pain, how much it hurts to have six hard fingers of plastic-coated metal fighting down your throat, how much it'll hurt at the other end, coming out. But part of me's absolutely certain he won't kill me. Because he needs me – who else is going to listen to his lies about Julie and the others? So much of it's lies. Like saying he was her first when she already had Natalie. Trouble is, *they* lie too. Not Julie, not that I know of. But Lara, and Ruth. They're lying in their letters, they must be. Who asks to be tortured? Who the hell wants to be a torturer's best friend?

When he takes his hand away, Mickey wipes it on the pillow next to my face. I see blood in my spit because I bit my tongue. He rolls me onto my side and hits my chest a couple of times, which helps. The last of the batteries dislodges itself from my windpipe and goes down with the others, into my stomach. I can breathe again and I start laughing, out of relief.

Mickey leans over me, watching my face. I'm crying as well as laughing, leaking spit and tears, snot and blood. I suppose he can't help what he does next. He reaches

58

for his sketchpad. Sits up, straddling me. Wets the square end of a charcoal with the tip of his tongue, spits sideways and starts to draw. I squeeze shut my eyes but he grunts, so I open them.

I can taste the batteries, my throat's on fire. I try not to think about them leaking acid, burning a hole in my stomach. Even so, I retch and moan. He sits on me like a mastiff with his lips hanging full of blood, his whole face altered by it, eyes long and slitted, watching me as he draws. He makes me think of the Thorn of the Cross, which is called one of the ugliest plants in the world because its leaves grow in cross-shaped spikes. Mickey's more like a succulent, the way the blood goes to his lips and nostrils as he bends over me, thighs tightening to hold me still as he sketches. I moan a bit more, but it makes no difference. He's lost in what he's doing.

The charcoal rubs at the paper, a rough sound like the padding of paws. Smoke rises from the sketchpad and hangs in a little cloud until he blows it away, which makes my eyes tear up all over again. His breath's sweet and putrid. I start to cry, I don't know why. It's not fear any more, or even pain. It's the way he's sitting on me, holding me with the long clench of his legs. It's how it makes me feel, in spite of everything. I feel—

Safe. Real. I'm right where I've always been, but for the first time I make sense to myself. This is what they want, I realise, the women who write to him. They just want to feel real, not empty or aimless, spiralling through space. Pinned down, named. Needed.

I can still taste those batteries today. Worse than ever now I'm wired up to these machines with only my nurse for company. She doesn't need to be named or needed. She's doing a useful thing with her life, helping men like me who can't help ourselves. Making us better, well enough to leave these beds and go home. In my case, back to prison. I want to go back to prison because Mickey won't be there this time, because he's gone. They think they're hunting a man who gets his kicks hurting people. Women for preference, but he's not picky. They know what he did to Julie, but they don't know the half of it. Not even those detectives, that redhead who looks so serious and so sad. I want to tell her, 'You're not hunting a man. You're hunting a monster.'

What he did to Julie was nothing. What Lara wishes he'd do to her, that's nothing. It's the stuff they never caught him for, that's what they need to be scared of. Stuff only I know about.

Lying in the bunk that was mine, rubbing at his photos, at himself, telling stories which might be fantasies but aren't. I know, you see. You can't live that close to someone without finding out the sort of man he is, and they're hunting a monster. Mickey is a monster.

I hope to God one of them works that out, and fast.

8

'Lara Chorley, and Ruth Hull.' Marnie pinned the new faces to the board. 'What do these two women have in common?'

'Apart from crap taste in men?' Ron flapped the collar of his shirt, sweating freely thanks to the heating system's lavish interpretation of 22°C.

'They started corresponding with Michael Vokcy shortly before his trial a year ago. From what we've read in their letters, he was writing back. DCS Ferguson wants us to interview both women as soon as possible. We're liaising with local police in case Vokey's gone after one of them, to hide or to harm. Debbie, what do we have so far?'

'We've traced Ruth to a home address in Danbury in Essex. If the address is right then she's living in a church mission.'

'That tallies with her letters,' Colin said. 'She's the one wanting to save Vokey's soul.'

'God-botherer,' Ron abridged. 'What about Lara?' He used his lanyard as a fan. 'She's the one writing the sickest letters.'

'Lara lives in Keswick, in Cumbria. She's divorced with two kids. A son who's studying law at university, and a daughter who works for the National Trust.'

'Jesus,' Ron said. 'Empty nest syndrome hitting hard, is it?'

'Let's stick to the facts.' Marnie nodded at the board. 'These women need to be questioned about their correspondence with Vokey, whether he shared details of places he may have gone, or gave any clues in that regard. We need local police onside, this has to be a team effort. Noah?'

'We're going to see Julie to reassure her about the measures in place to keep her and Natalie safe, and in case she has any ideas about where he might be hiding. We know he's not been near his mum's house since he ran. CCTV's tight around there and while he's not an easy man to identify, we've had three sets of eyes over everything without any joy. I don't think he went home.' Noah paused. 'We have one other possible lead. Michael's sister, Alyson. She's been interviewed once already, insists she's had no contact with her brother in months.'

'Put her on the board,' Marnie nodded. 'We'll call her after we've visited Julie.' She turned to the team. 'Debbie, I'd like you to concentrate on Lara. Make friends with Cumbria Police, let them know what's on our mind. Ron, see what you can find out about Ruth. And Colin, keep at the paper trail. We're missing too much of this puzzle. Lots to cover, so let's get to work. Thanks, everyone.'

In the station car park, Marnie's phone rang.

'It's the hospital.' She handed Noah the car keys. 'I'd better take this.'

He nodded, unlocking the pool car to discover sugary crumbs on the passenger seat. Doughnuts, from the fatty smell. He brushed the crumbs into the footwell and climbed in, watching Marnie through the car's windscreen. She was standing with her head bowed, the phone at her ear. What was the news from the hospital? Ted Elms, or Stephen Keele? Her expression gave nothing away.

Noah's own phone rang and he reached for it. 'DS Jake.'

'Noah, hi. It's Harry Kennedy. Do you have a minute?'

DS Harry Kennedy was with Trident, the Met's Gang Crime Command. Seven weeks ago he'd been fighting for his life, a victim of the same crime that'd landed Noah in hospital. Harry was back at work now and busy by the sound of it. Trident was after Sol's allegiance, had offered protection to Noah's little brother in exchange for information about his old gang. Noah had hoped it might work as a way out for Sol, who couldn't keep running or hiding forever.

'We're about to set off,' he told Harry, 'but yes. What's up?'

'It's Sol.' Harry kept his voice light, but serious. 'We've brought in a member of his gang and he's talking. We can't shut him up, in fact. A lot of it's smoke, but I wanted to give you a heads up. Some of it's bound to bounce back at you, at least in the short term. I'm sorry.'

A car pulled out of the station and just for a second Noah met his own eyes in the dark surface of the windscreen. He blinked, and looked away. 'How bad is it?'

'Enough for new questions to be asked.' He heard regret in Harry's voice. 'He's likely to be re-interviewed under caution.'

'Is it worse than what we had? If you charge him. Is it worse?' Noah had arrested his brother for importing Class C drugs. Had he known Sol would end up on remand for nine months, he'd've handled it differently. Prison was the last place Sol needed to be right now, the last place he'd get help. Far more likely he'd end up making dangerous new friends, or enemies.

Harry had gone quiet but now he said, 'Firearms, Class B. I'm sorry. Noah? Call me later. I'll fill you in as far as I can, but it's sticky right now. We're going after a production order.'

A production order meant a court appearance, his mother in her best hat again. Noah winced. Guilt was like a piece of shrapnel travelling around inside him, never in the same place twice so he couldn't ever get comfortable, accustomed to its pain. Firearms, Class B, meant a minimum sentence of five years. Sol was struggling to do nine months.

'I'm sorry,' Harry said again. He was breaking protocol by making this call.

'Thanks. I understand. And I appreciate the heads up.'

When Harry ended the call, Noah lowered the phone to his lap, cleaning the screen with his thumb. So that was it. He'd put his little brother behind bars, and the gang Sol had hoped to escape was taking its revenge. This new evidence could be a warning shot in case he was tempted to turn informant, or it could be a lesson to others in the same gang. Sol wasn't a gun runner, Noah was sure of that, but what chance would he have to prove it, now? And if the gang was firing warning shots, Sol could be in real danger. There was no good reason to imagine Pentonville was any safer than Cloverton. How had Noah not seen this coming?

You did this. Your own brother. This's on you.

His fist tightened around the phone. How was he going to tell his parents?

'Ted Elms took a turn for the worse.' Marnie got into the driver's seat. 'They've stabilised him, but it was touch and go last night . . . Noah?'

'Yes.' He put the phone away.

'Keys?' She had her eyes dead ahead, not seeing the effort it took him to smile.

He handed over the keys and she started the car, saying, 'They'll keep us posted, but it's not looking good. We're advised to hold off on further visits until we hear from them.'

Noah thought of the seed catalogue brought back from the post room at Cloverton, the sunny pictures of summer gardens. 'Poor Ted.'

Marnie was focused on reversing from the narrow parking space and missed the emotion in his voice. He was glad, not ready to share this latest trouble over Sol. 'So . . . Julie Seton?'

'Let's tread carefully,' Marnie said. 'I imagine she's very frightened right now.'

'I called her Victim Support Officer to see if she'd be with Julie during our meeting. There's Natalie to consider too.' Noah thought of the child's face from the collage in Vokey's house, a press clipping from his trial which he'd pinned to the wall as if it belonged to him. He should never have been bailed. 'Six years old and she saw Vokey terrorise her mum. The VSO said Julie's a tougher nut to crack, insisting she's okay, asking to be left alone to get on with her life. She didn't want to give evidence at the trial but she did it for Natalie's sake, to prove she's a strong mum after what Natalie witnessed that night.' Noah glanced across at Marnie. 'That grave in the cellar. Do you think there's a chance he'll go after Julie, or Natalie?'

Marnie kept her eyes on the traffic. 'Not unless he wants to be caught. We had officers at Julie's house as soon as the alarm was raised. We can't rule it out, since it was her evidence that put him away. Revenge is a motive for all manner of madness. But after what he did at Cloverton, he's looking at a life sentence. I doubt he'll want to play those odds.'

'He wasn't a killer, that's what his defence lawyer argued in court. He didn't kill Julie, didn't use a knife or any kind of weapon, and he never touched Natalie. He could control himself, that's what the jury heard.' Noah adjusted the seat belt, his bruised ribs nagging at him. 'He just chose not to, when it came to Julie.'

'We need to be careful what we disclose,' Marnie said. 'I don't want Julie hearing about the grave, or our theory that he's about to kill. Not until we have a proper profile, anyway.' She glanced at Noah. 'You saw that cellar. What went through your head? Give me your gut instinct.'

That whoever dug the grave intended to bury something, or someone.

'He wasn't acting on impulse when he dug it.' Noah rolled his neck. 'Far too neat a job for that. He put a lot of thought into it, kept the bricks so he could build the floor back up afterwards.'

'His defence lawyer was right, then. He's in control of himself.' Marnie watched the traffic ahead. 'He could have killed Julie that night. Alone in the house all that time. Do you think he meant to? That Natalie saved her mum's life by appearing when she did?'

'The judge didn't think so, going by the sentence he handed out. Vokey was bailed because he wasn't a serious threat to the public. Of course the jury didn't know about the grave, or the house full of photos.' Noah looked to where the streets were crowding, pavements narrowing as they approached the estate. 'Ron's right, prison was the perfect place for him to cultivate his worst instincts. He was never going to get better there, only worse.' The street's shadows chilled his face. 'Prison was the perfect place for him to escalate to full-blown murder.'

*

Julie and Natalie Seton lived in Edmonton, a part of London where knives were carried as routinely as mobile phones. Julie had grown up on the same estate, with her mum just a block away, her gran too. Julie worked in the chippy. Her hair and clothes stank of fish and fat no matter how much she washed, but it'd got so she didn't really notice any more. That night when Vokey told her she stank, she didn't understand what he was saying, not right away. He was talking about the grease in her hair. It was in her eyelashes, and the hairs up her nose. It was in her ears. 'You stink,' he said. 'You really stink.'

She was concentrating on breathing with the weight of him on her chest and how he looked when he leaned in to sniff at her hair and ears, at her eyelashes, all the blood in his face running to his lips, black and swollen— She was concentrating on not screaming and waking Natalie.

The entire flat stank of chips, but it was better than Julie's mum's place, which stank of Airwick plug-ins because she couldn't give up smoking. She'd tried but she couldn't do it. Same for Julie's nan. Julie'd been a smoker before she fell pregnant but she'd quit for Natalie's sake, and after that she could either afford cigarettes or nappies but not both. She hated that her mum and gran smoked round Nat, told them it was doing her head in worrying Nat'd grow up to be a smoker. Worse things to be, Mum said, but Gran agreed with Julie and tried not to smoke when her great-grandchild was round. Even so there were days when Julie caught Nat sucking on a crayon, pretending it was Silk Cut. Boys in the same year at her school were smoking Silk Cut, so it really could've been worse. It was what everyone kept saying about everything. About Vokey, that night – him sat like a slab on her chest – and everything that came after. They kept saying, 'It could've been worse, Julie.'

67

Most of this Noah had picked up from the PC who'd interviewed Julie after the assault. This was the first time he and Marnie had been on the Edmonton estate. A patrol car was parked close to Julie's house, two uniformed officers inside. In case Vokey made an appearance, and because the press were demanding a police presence, proof that they were taking his escape and the threat to public safety seriously. The two uniformed officers had a flask of tea propped on the dashboard. One of them was reading a newspaper, both looked bored rigid.

Julie answered the door in jeans and trainers, an over-sized brown T-shirt. Her hair was cut short and bleached blonde, dark at the roots. Her face was heart-shaped and would have been beautiful but for the scowl. 'Yeah?' she said to Noah's badge. 'And?'

'I'm DS Jake, this is DI Rome. Is your Victim Support Officer here?'

'Told her not to bother.' Her stare travelled to the patrol car and back. 'Didn't see the point. Haven't seen her in ages, in any case.'

'Can we come in?' Marnie asked.

Julie sighed through her teeth. 'I've twenty minutes, then a bus to catch.'

She was going to work, despite the fact her assailant was being hunted by the police. Michael Vokey knew this address. Thirteen months ago he'd seen Julie working in the chippy and followed her home after her shift ended. Even so, she'd refused the offer of a safe house for her and Natalie.

'Thanks,' Marnie said. 'We won't keep you long.'

They followed Julie to an open-plan room with a kitchen at one end and two black pleather sofas at the other. Khaki curtains were drawn at the window, letting in a little muddy light. Natalie was lying on the floor, drawing with crayons on a pad of paper. She wore denim dungarees over a green T-shirt, her hair bunched in pink plastic bobbles. Noah knew Marnie would have preferred not to talk in front of the child but with no VSO, they had little choice.

Julie cleared space on the sofas and sat. Her eyes went to Natalie then came back to Marnie and Noah. She wore no make-up but her skin, clear and smooth, didn't need it. Hazel eyes ringed with gold around the irises. Cat's eyes, Vokey had called them.

He'd sat on her, on the floor where Natalie was lying. Julie's hair had been long then, honey-blonde, her natural colour. She'd been in shorts and a vest top, her version of pyjamas. The attack took place after dark. Julie's mum had babysat Nat, but she went home when Julie returned from work. Julie went up to kiss Natalie then settled to watch TV. She'd worked a long shift and was knackered, but she needed to unwind before she could sleep. She'd thought the knock on the door was her mum coming back because she'd forgotten something, she was always forgetting stuff. When she opened the door, Vokey pushed his way inside, shoved her to the floor and sat on her. Julie, terrified of waking Natalie, had concentrated so hard on not screaming that she'd bitten through her tongue. Ten minutes later Natalie woke anyway. She came downstairs to find her mum lying under a man with long, dirty hair tied in a ponytail like a girl. Mum was making a funny noise. Natalie thought she was laughing, but she wasn't. There wasn't any blood, but the carpet under Mum's head was wet from spit and tears. She was making a really funny noise.

'Have you caught him yet?' Julie looked at Marnie and then at Noah. 'Have you?'

'Not yet,' Marnie said.

Julie hissed. 'Knew it.' She folded her arms.

69

Natalie looked up at her mum. Her face was round and blank, with pale eyes and a nub of nose. She'd been chewing crayons, yellow wax on her lower lip, drawing a picture of her mum at the seaside, sand under a fiery sky. She returned to her picture, rubbing the yellow crayon on the page.

'I've been yelled at in the street. I've had, "Julie, we hear your boyfriend's out!" The papers've been round wanting to know if I feel safe with him out there. Bad enough when I was in court, but that's what I had to do to put him away, to know we're safe. *Safe.* They told me that's what I had to do.' She watched her daughter rigidly. 'This's what I get for making a spectacle of myself for those cows sat on the steps every day, waiting for me to come out of court. Shouting abuse, asking why I was stupid enough to let him in here, like I'd wanted it. "Got yourself some attention, Julie? Seen you in the papers, how much d'they pay you? Barely even touched you and you're front page news. Imagine if he'd raped you." Like I could've made more money if he'd left marks instead of just—' She broke off, twisting her lips shut.

Natalie glanced up, but didn't speak. Her mum said, 'Finish your picture, there's a good girl.' She fixed her stare on Marnie. 'So why're you here if you've not got him?'

'We wanted to let you know we're doing everything we can to find him—'

'Yeah? That's why you're here? Think he might be hiding under my bed?' She showed her teeth. 'About as much use as those two out there in the car, stuffing sandwiches. How's this *finding* him? You just want to show your faces so I can't complain I'm being left alone.' She drew her knees together, keeping her arms folded, shoulders stiff with hostility. 'No chance of that. I can't walk

70

down the street without getting stared at, can't walk *her* to school.' She looked down at her daughter. 'It's a joke. "When's the compensation coming, Julie?" I've had boys not much bigger than her offering to get me more compensation. "I'll do you properly, love, get you the good money." And you're round here to make me feel better? It's a joke.'

'It's not a joke to us. We're taking it very seriously.' Marnie paused. 'One of our problems is the mugshot we have isn't a great likeness. Everyone tells us he doesn't look like his photo—'

'He doesn't look like anyone,' Julie hissed. 'Those pictures in the paper? Half of them make him look like a rock star. I told your lot that, spent hours doing the photo fit but it was *nothing* like him. "We've not captured him," that's what your expert said. Funny when you think about it. We've not *captured* him. You want to know what happened last week?' She fixed her eyes on Natalie. 'A boy in her class offered to sell her a gun. Not even a knife – a *gun*. He meant it too, little git. "Then you can take care of your mum next time," like there's not enough shit in her head already. That's what it's like round here in case you didn't know, that's what it means that we *look after our own*. Knives and guns, and throwing a party on the compensation.'

Her anger fizzed in the room. Natalie moved her feet out of the way of it, rubbing harder with her crayon on the page.

'In your statement,' Noah said, 'you spoke about how much he talked. Did he say anything that might suggest a place he could've gone, now?'

'He didn't talk about *places*. What, you think we were chatting about his holiday plans? You'd be better off asking those stupid cows where he's gone. You *know* what he said because it's all in my statement, and the court records.

71

Every word of it, what I put myself through, cross-examination and the rest, to put him behind bars. For Nat's sake as much as anything. I laid it on thick, just like they told me. Cried on cue, made a show of myself. Those questions in court, being made to feel like a bad mum, a stupid slag, and for what?' She bent to pick up one of Natalie's crayons, rolling it hard in her hand. 'My lawyer telling me to go on about how scared I was even though he hadn't got a knife or a gun and he never touched Nat. I did as I was told, but guess what? He's out there *right now* because some snot-nosed kid didn't do *his* job, couldn't figure out what sort of man he was dealing with. I went through all that and for what?'

Her voice shook with tears. Natalie abandoned her colouring and climbed to her feet, coming to her mum's side. She leaned into Julie, not speaking, her eyes empty and round.

Julie stiffened. 'Finish your drawing. Gran'll be here soon.'

Natalie tipped forward, butting her mother's arm with her head.

'No.' Julie moved out of range, hardening her tone. 'Finish your drawing.'

Natalie didn't make a sound. She returned to the same spot on the carpet, sitting cross-legged next to her sketchpad. Noah said, 'May I see?' He looked to Julie for confirmation. 'Is that okay?'

'Don't make a fuss,' Julie told him tightly. 'That's when she gets upset, when you make a fuss.'

She wasn't ignoring her daughter. She was trying to hold it together, her fragile family unit, putting all her energy into holding onto this. She couldn't go to work if Natalie was upset, and she had to go to work to pay the bills and keep a roof over their heads. Other people had options, people like Ruth Hull and Lara Chorley, but Julie just had this. She had to keep it together.

Noah stayed where he was. He smiled at Natalie, but she stared dead ahead. After a beat she reached for a red crayon and added more colour to her picture.

Keys sounded in the front door, knuckles rapping.

A woman's voice called out, 'Just me.'

'Gran's here.' Julie stood, reaching for a blue fleece on the back of the sofa. 'I can't be late, I'm the one opening up tonight.'

Her mum walked straight to the kitchen to fill the kettle, not looking at Marnie or Noah. Her face was weathered, sunken at the jaw with a smoker's deep wrinkles. She wore jeans and a blue fleece like her daughter's, smelling aggressively of the spray she'd used to disguise the scent of cigarettes.

'Two things, just quickly,' Marnie said to Julie. 'What did you mean when you said Michael Vokey was out because some snot-nosed kid didn't do his job properly? Which kid?'

'The prison guard, the one giving that interview. It's all over the internet what he said about that bastard. What he did in the prison, the eyeballs and the rest of it.' She pulled on the fleece. 'Looked about fifteen, acne on his neck, little twat.' She glanced at Natalie who was busy with her drawing, the tip of her small tongue caught between her teeth.

'You said you laid it on thick, for the court—'

Julie kept her eyes down, not looking at Marnie. 'Don't hold anything back, that's what they said.' There was a lick of wariness in her voice. 'It's what my lawyer told me to do.'

'He told you to lay it on thick?'

'I didn't mean literally.' The wariness was in her neck

73

too. 'Just not to hold back, not to be brave. I had to show the court how much he'd scared me, how bad it was. Because he didn't leave any marks. There were no photos to show the court. That's what I meant.'

Noah watched her, seeing all her hostility erased by this new caution. Had she exaggerated the attack in some way? He thought of Vokey's rampage at the prison, and DCS Ferguson's contention that Julie had a lucky escape. That might be true, but she was living with the aftermath. The jeers and stares in the street, her child's strange silence, this endless fight to keep it all together.

'And the women who might know where he's gone,' Marnie said, 'the ones we'd be better off asking?'

'Those cows.' Julie zipped the fleece. 'You can tell them to stop writing to me, for starters.'

'They've been writing to you?' Noah met Marnie's eyes. 'Do you have their letters?'

'I tore them up, didn't want *her* reading them.' She kept her eyes on Natalie. 'She can read now. She can talk too, just doesn't do a lot of that since it happened. Her therapist reckons it's normal. What's not normal is those cows telling me I was *lucky*—' She broke off, picking up her bag.

'Can you remember the names of the women who wrote to you?' Marnie asked.

'They didn't sign their names.' Julie fished out her keys, looking at her watch, distracted. 'Three letters, one after another. One of them wasn't so bad, but then they stopped.'

'Three letters. From three different women?'

'Yeah, it was getting mental. I was going to save the next one and report it to you lot, but there's been nothing new in days so they must've got bored.' She shot a look at her mum who was putting tea bags into

74

two mugs. 'He's not coming round. That tea'd better be for you.'

'It is.' Her mum shrugged. 'I'm thirsty. Haven't had a cuppa all day.'

'Right. Because I'll know if he's been round.'

The two women looked at one another.

'I'll know,' Julie repeated fiercely.

Her mum shrugged. 'You'll miss your bus.'

Natalie climbed to her feet, holding up her drawing. Julie passed it to Marnie without looking at it. 'Here's your mugshot.' Her voice was tight with tears. 'Here's what he looks like.'

It wasn't a drawing of sunshine, or the seaside. Natalie had used red and yellow crayon to draw fire. With a black crayon she'd drawn two stick figures, one big, the other small. The big one held the other down inside the fire. The small figure had cropped fair hair and wore a blue fleece.

'She draws these all the time.' Julie sounded helpless, hopeless. 'All the time. You want to know the funny thing? He was pathetic. He pawed at me like— He was *pathetic*.'

Marnie waited but when Julie stopped speaking she said, 'Do you mean he was impotent?'

He hadn't raped her. He hadn't touched her below the neck. His defence lawyer had made a great play of that in court. As if another man wouldn't have thought twice about rape.

'I don't know what he was.' Julie's face closed. 'But they should've kept him locked up. I gave all the evidence they asked for, made a show of myself in court, and for what? They let him walk out of there like he was *anybody*. You won't find him because he's a coward, a *pathetic* coward. He'll hide himself away somewhere until he

75

does it all again, because he doesn't think he's doing anything wrong. He thinks it's okay and he loves it. He *loves* it.'

'She wasn't what I expected,' Noah said when they were back in the car. 'I thought she'd be more frightened, or angrier at Vokey. She's angry but at us, not him.'

'Can you blame her after his escape? But she wasn't what I was expecting either.' Marnie checked the car's mirrors. 'We need to find this online interview with the prison officer. Can you get Colin to hunt that down? I want a name. Whoever he is, he shouldn't be giving interviews.'

Noah nodded, texting the request to Colin. 'These women who wrote to her. You don't think it's Lara and Ruth? She said three letters from three different women. "One wasn't so bad" – that could be Ruth, being the religious one. But who's the third woman?'

They exited the estate where the patrol car was parked, the uniforms still yawning. Six kids were huddled on the other side of the street, smoking, watching with razor eyes. If Vokey came back here they'd be the ones to spot him, before the patrol car or anyone else. Whether they would do anything helpful about it was another matter.

Noah's phone rang as they reached the main road. 'DS Jake.'

'Vokey's sister.' It was DC Debbie Tanner, calling from the station. 'Alyson.'

'She's been in touch?' Noah switched the call to speaker.

'She's in hospital, unconscious. Found at home with a serious head injury.'

'When?' Marnie didn't take her eyes from the road.

'Earlier today. Forensics are at her house now.'

76

'It's a crime scene?' Noah's neck clenched. 'He attacked her?'

'It's not clear. But given who she is and what's happening with her brother, they wanted to be sure. DS Joe Coen's on the ground there. I'll text you his number.'

'Thanks. What happened, do they know?'

'She fell downstairs, or she was pushed. That's what they're trying to establish.'

'She lives alone?' The traffic demanded her full attention, a fusion of swerving cyclists and entitled cabbies, but Noah could hear Marnie's brain ticking, working this new angle of the case.

'Yes, but she has friends close by. They saw her for coffee yesterday morning. She was in her nightie when the police found her, so this must've happened before bed last night or first thing this morning. DS Coen thinks it was yesterday, from what he's seen inside the house. He sounds like someone who doesn't miss much. Forensics are still at the scene.'

'Remind me where she lives?' Marnie asked.

'Kendal.'

'Cumbria,' Noah said, 'that's not far from Lara Chorley.'

A pit stop on Vokey's journey north to see his big sister? Alyson had told police she'd had no recent contact with her brother. Then their mother's death, the empty house in probate being used by Michael. His hiding place, full of his obsession. He wouldn't have wanted it seen by anyone else, not even his sister if they'd fallen out over the lack of a will.

'Less than an hour away by car,' Debbie said. 'I've been trying to get hold of Lara, but she's not answering calls. Local police are paying her a visit. They should be with her soon.'

'Keswick,' Marnie said. 'Is that where she lives?'

'Near Pooley Bridge. DCS Ferguson's saying she wants you up there with her, boss. If it's where Vokey's gone to ground, she wants us to be the ones who find him.'

Noah could imagine how that would play with DS Coen and Cumbria CID. Ferguson was on a mission to bring Vokey back to a secure cell in HMP Cloverton, wiping clean the Met's copybook in the process, but this tactic was a tricky one, London detectives turning up to show the locals how it was done. In Marnie's place, Noah would have run a mile from that scenario.

'Let's speak with DS Coen.' Marnie checked the car's mirrors. 'And let's wait for news of Lara. I don't want to duplicate effort on the ground if they've got it covered, certainly not before we know for certain Michael was involved in his sister's accident. Call as soon as you hear from the local police. Has Ron been able to get hold of Ruth Hull?'

'That's some good news at least,' Debbie said. 'He's spoken with her and she's okay. She's not scared of Vokey, "He's a changed man," so she's kidding herself, but at least she's safe. At home, and Ron doesn't think Vokey's with her. She was too calm on the phone, and the church mission's open twenty-four seven to anyone who wants to walk in. Not a good place to hide out.'

'He doesn't need a whole house,' Noah said. 'Just one room. We need to be sure it's not Ruth's, no matter how safe she's telling us she feels. Too many people have made mistakes about the sort of man we're dealing with. Let's not fall into the same trap.'

The traffic had slowed to a single lane crawl, London's arteries hardened where they weren't clogged, a tailback of fumes and frustration.

'Noah's right.' Marnie flexed her fingers at the wheel. 'We've all seen the pictures from inside Cloverton. We need to operate on the assumption he's capable of killing, and motivated to do it. Worst-case scenario, but we're taking no chances. Get a response unit to the church mission and tell Ron to bring Ruth in, for her safety and to answer our questions.' She found an opening in the traffic and turned left. 'We're on our way now. Call us if you get news of Alyson or Lara before we reach you.'

9

I was thinking about Ruth today, her letters to Mickey, and the letters he sent back. My lucky nurse wears a crucifix, you see. I didn't notice it until this morning. She's bending over me, checking my tubes, and there's this yellow worm wriggling at her throat where the light's catching on a gold chain and crucifix. I wonder if she prays for me. She's so close I can smell her skin, pear drops and peach shampoo. It's a lovely, lucky smell.

Ruth's always saying she'll pray for Mickey. He puts on a preacher's voice when he reads her letters, a God-fearing soul from the Deep South: 'I know you're searching, I know that's what this is. I've felt that way myself. Until He found me and brought me home. I want to bring you home, Michael. You're lost and feeling little, I know. You're searching for something bigger than yourself. But you need to stop searching and stand still. You need to let Him come and find you.'

You might think Mickey would make fun of letters like that. You might think, *Of course he loves Lara's letters, because they're filthy. He's stuck in here with no one but you and your plants for company, and her letters are porn. Of course he reads them and sniffs them and sleeps with them close to his cheek.* Ruth's letters about the Lord finding him, you can't imagine him feeling the same about those. He did, though. Re-read them just as often, slept with them as close, sniffed them even though they smelt of nothing, just the fingers of whoever was on duty in the post room, or else of Daz Quayle. Dazza liked to handle Mickey's post, part of the personal service he offered because he couldn't get enough of being Mickey's favourite.

My nurse prays for me, that's what I think. Not down on her knees, not like that. Ruth says you don't need to kneel to pray, you don't even need to be in church. You can be anywhere at all, up a mountain or in a cellar. You can be in prison. I reckon lots of people pray in hospitals. Harder not to here. Either you're sick, or you're visiting someone who's sick. You've lost someone, or you're losing her. I haven't had any visitors. My nurse is sad that no one comes to see me. Even a bastard like me, dog-chained to the bed, deserves a visitor at a time like this. Other patients get their loved ones holding their hands, whispering words of encouragement, waiting for them to wake up. I get two detectives and a gaggle of student doctors watching from the foot of the bed as I'm poked and prodded and pronounced upon.

Mickey always said his sister would come if he got sick. After the batteries, when they brought me back from the hospital. Dazza must've told him I'd had no visitors there, and of course Mickey knew I never had any in Cloverton because neither did he.

'You're lucky,' he says.

'How d'you figure that?' I'm being careful, but I can see he wants to talk. He's missed me, or he's missed having an audience. Did he read their letters aloud to himself on

81

those nights when I was gone? I bet he did. But it wasn't the same, how could it be?

'My sister wouldn't leave me alone. Until I made her stop coming.' He catches my puzzled silence and adds, 'Up North, in Leeds. It wasn't so far for her to come and visit me up there, but she'd be down here if I let her.'

He's never this talkative. I turn on my side to look down at him in the bunk that's mine.

'She likes seeing me in prison.' He snaps his teeth and touches one of the photos on his wall, one of his women. Lara, or Ruth. He screws the ball of his thumb to her face. 'Bitch.'

'Is that her?' I ask, even though I know it's not.

He punches the underside of my mattress, hard. 'I wouldn't have her picture on my wall, would I? Bitch like that.'

'What's her name?' I ask. 'Your sister?'

'Alyson.' He hisses the last syllable.

'Is she your only sister?'

'She's enough.'

'Is she older than you?'

'Yes.' He punches the mattress again. 'Bitch.'

I can't tell if he means me, or her.

'Did you get any more letters?' I ask, to calm him down. 'While I was away?'

It always calms him to talk about the letters. Days when he doesn't get mail, those are the worst. I dread those days. I've even thought about writing letters myself, getting Dazza to pass them off as part of Mickey's mail. I reckon I could write a convincing fan letter, the kind of thing he'd like. If he can get off on a soppy prayer from a Bible-basher, how hard can it be? I'd make a good Lara, I've got her voice down now. That's why he's missed me so much.

'Did you? Get any more letters?'

'Some shit from Ruth,' he growls. 'About my sins.'

I think about his sins, what I know of them. Julie was nothing, in the scheme of it all. I wonder about the letter Ruth would write if she knew what he'd done, the full extent of his sins. If she knew about the boy in Leeds, say. 'Dear Michael,' she'd write, 'I can't help you and neither can God. Burn in hell. Ruth.'

Unless I'm wrong. Unless anything can be forgiven if you work at it long and hard enough. If you get on your knees and pray. Up a mountain or in a cellar, by a hospital bed or at the side of the road with a hidden dip where cars can't be seen until it's too late. You can pray anywhere and maybe if you do it right, like you really mean it, anything can be forgiven. I'd like to believe that for my sake, if not for his. That nobody is beyond the grace of God. Not even Mickey Vokey.

10

'This is Michael Vokey.' Marnie pinned the mugshot to the evidence board. 'And this.' A second photo. 'And this.' A third. She didn't stop until she'd pinned eight images to the board.

Vokey looked like a different man in each one. Not just his hair – varying lengths and colours – but his bone structure. Rapid weight loss and gain explained some of it, giving him cheekbones then taking them away, but the overriding factor was the insipidity of his features, as if he wore a mask on which he drew a face each morning depending on his mood, the cocking of an eyebrow or curling of a lip transfiguring everything. As boys, Noah and Sol had shared a passion for a game called Fuzzy Face: moving metal filings with a magnet to bring a beard or bushy eyebrows to an otherwise featureless face. Vokey's photos reminded Noah of that game. Here was Michael with a full beard. Now the beard was gone. Here was Michael with sideburns, with a moustache. Here he was with a shaved head looking like a priest in a black and white film. Noah's eyes ached. He'd been looking through pictures for the best part of a week, snow-blind from searching.

'No CCTV sightings in London, or Cumbria,' Colin said. 'We've been through hundreds of hours of traffic cam footage already.' He removed his spectacles, massaging the bridge of his nose where the skin was red and indented. 'Ditto service stations, train stations, ports and airports.'

'We know he's not in Danbury.' Debbie glanced at her notes. 'Ron says the church was clean, no trace of him there. He's on his way back with Ruth. We're waiting for an update from DS Coen in Kendal. Alyson's in a stable but serious condition post-surgery for swelling on the brain. No sign of an intruder at her house in the last forty-eight hours, but they're not ready to rule out an assault. Aggravated burglary, maybe. DS Coen says he'll keep us in the loop.'

Aggravated burglary was the name they'd given to the offence committed by Michael Vokey against Julie Seton. It covered a multitude of sins, from robbery to abuse.

'What news of Lara?' Noah asked.

'She's with friends up in Scotland,' Colin said. 'A shopping weekend. It's why we couldn't reach her. That and the fact her house is out of range of most networks. Oh, and the local telephone exchange floods every time it rains, which it does a lot in Keswick. She's on her way home, but she was in Edinburgh on the day of the riot.'

'Then we need to find whoever posted her last letter to Michael. Because that was postmarked in Keswick on the day of the riot.' Marnie nodded at Colin, who made a note. 'What about the prison officer who's giving interviews online?'

'We're still searching. It looks like the one Julie saw was taken down.' Colin's frustration showed itself in a rare frown. 'I'm waiting for the chance to talk to her about exactly when and where she saw it. Her phone's switched off. According to the patrol, she's at work until late tonight.'

'We're sure she's okay?' Noah asked.

'The surveillance team like their chips.' Colin nodded. 'They're watching the house, the fish shop and Julie.'

'She wouldn't go to a safe house,' Debbie remembered. 'We offered one for her and Natalie, as soon as we knew he'd escaped. She wouldn't even think about it, just turned us down.'

'She's trying to hold it together,' Noah said. 'Her job, her family. We were offering a safe house on the other side of London. She'd have lost her job, apart from anything else.'

'Still.' Debbie raised her eyebrows. 'She didn't even want the police presence outside her house. If DCS Ferguson hadn't insisted on it, she'd be on her own with Natalie.'

'She's had enough of the attention. Can you blame her? And she doesn't trust us not to make it worse.' Between the press and patrol cars, and the kids hounding their local celebrity, it wasn't likely Vokey would get close to Julie, if that was his plan. But Debbie had a point. Julie's lack of fear made Noah uneasy. It didn't look like bravado, but he hadn't seen enough of her to judge. He wished he'd known her before the assault.

'I'll try her again,' Colin said, 'in the morning. Then we can track down this online interview with the prison officer and see whether it's any help to us.'

On the evidence board, Michael Vokey's eight faces were so dissimilar they didn't even look like members of the same family. Alyson's was the ninth face, resembling none of the eight belonging to her brother.

'Something we found out about the sister,' Debbie said. 'She was the key witness in a prosecution thirty years ago, when she was in her early twenties. The victim of malicious communications, hate mail.'

86

'Letters, again?' Noah turned from the board. 'Who was writing to her?'

Debbie pulled a face. 'It was her best friend, Jo Gower. She and Alyson had been mates for years, since nursery school. Like glue, everyone said. Then Alyson started getting these threatening letters. Silly stuff to start with, offers of a make-over, help with failing relationships, adverts for incontinence and acne, all that sort of thing. Jo gave her a shoulder to cry on. Except it was *Jo* who was doing it. Sending the flyers for accident insurance, even bereavement counselling. It went on for months. Alyson wanted to go to the police but Jo talked her out of it, persuaded her to hand over all the letters, said she'd look into it, she had a cousin who knew about harassment. It went on and on. By the end, Alyson was more or less having a breakdown.'

'How was Jo Gower caught?' Noah asked. 'Did she confess?'

Debbie shook her head. 'She denied it right up until the trial. But they found stacks of evidence in her house. It was an easy conviction. She got a prison sentence, eighteen months.'

Almost the same sentence Michael Vokey had been given for terrorising Julie Seton.

Marnie had listened in silence to Debbie's account of the harassment. Now she asked, 'Did Jo know Alyson's brother, Michael?'

'His name didn't come up in the trial.' Debbie examined her notes. 'But if Jo was that close to his sister he must've known her. Michael's only a couple of years younger than Alyson, and they all went to the same school. They're bound to have met at her house.'

'Marion's house, where we found the photos. That's where they were living at the time?'

Debbie nodded. 'That's the address on the system, Mum's house. Dad's been out of the picture since the kids were tiny. Alyson looked out for Michael back then, that's what she said.'

'Do we have a picture of Jo Gower?' Colin put his spectacles back on. 'I can check it against the ones we took from the house, see if we get a hit.'

In the photo on the board, Alyson's expression was distrustful, her mouth pressed shut, cheeks flushed. Noah felt a jolt of déjà vu, but blamed the snow-blindness; he was seeing faces in his sleep. This was a recent picture – salt and pepper highlights in her hair – Alyson didn't look like this now, not after the accident which had put her into hospital. Falling down her own stairs, or being pushed. Blunt trauma to the back of her skull, swelling on the brain.

'Do we have a good reason to think Michael would want to hurt her?' Noah wondered. 'She was on his visitor list at Leeds, at *his* request. But she never visited him there, that's been confirmed. He wanted her to, but she refused. When we contacted her last week, she didn't want to know, said they'd been out of touch since before his conviction.'

'She could be ashamed,' Debbie said. 'With the papers full of what he's done. Not just to Julie. At the prison. The fire, those poor men with their eyes . . .' She shuddered.

'Alyson didn't tell us about the house,' Colin pointed out. 'Or the photos we found. Either she didn't know her brother was living there after their mum died, or she's covering for him.'

'The house is in probate,' Marnie said, 'is that right?'

Colin nodded. 'Their mum died without a proper will. It's pretty clear Michael wanted the house, going by what he was up to in there. They couldn't find any definitive paperwork after their mum died, so the solicitors piled in. They're making a small fortune now.'

'In other words, there's definite enmity between Alyson and Michael.' Marnie rubbed at her wrists. 'Even if we discount his fondness for violence, that's a motive for him to attack her.'

'He's on a vengeance kick,' Debbie said. 'That's what it looks like to me. Those men he maimed at Cloverton, the grave he dug at the house. It's like Ron said, if he hadn't been caught after Julie, he'd have escalated to killing. I don't see prison having cured him of that.'

'The opposite's more likely,' Colin agreed.

He hadn't set foot inside HMP Cloverton, before or after the riot. Hadn't felt the narrowness of its walls, the low roof pressing down, or come away with the taste of the place like scalded metal in his mouth. Marnie had; Noah could see its shadow in her face. He'd smelt the prison on her clothes when she returned from interviewing Aidan Duffy. It made him think about how often she'd visited prisons over the last six years. Not only to interview men like Aidan. To see Stephen, her foster brother, who refused to give up the answers she needed about why her parents had died so violently at his hands. If Stephen died without giving up those answers, what would it do to her?

'We need to concentrate on finding Michael.' Marnie nodded at Debbie. 'When is Ron due back with Ruth Hull?'

'In the next hour, boss.'

'And Lara Chorley? How long until she gets home from Edinburgh?'

'Late tonight,' Colin said. 'She's driving, but she wants to avoid the rush hour. Might not be home until midnight, she said.'

Julie would be locking up the chippy and catching the last bus home as Lara, with her shopping bags, drove leisurely back to her cottage in Cumbria where it was just her now, two children grown and gone, husband divorced and out of the picture. No one to ask about the letters she was writing to the man who'd terrorised Julie in front of her little girl. Letters inviting Michael to do the same and worse to Lara, full of promises of all the things she'd do for him when he found her, all the things she'd let him do to her. What sort of man did she imagine Vokey to be? Which of these eight faces was the one she pictured in her mind's eye when she wrote those letters, inviting a savage stranger to hunt her down? Noah's skin crawled as he studied the faces. He thought of Natalie lying on the carpet with her crayons, Julie dragging the zip on her fleece, getting ready to go to work, leaving her mum in charge because she had no other choice, because life had to go on. Those khaki curtains at the windows, Noah wanted to tear them down, let the light back in to their lives.

'It's late,' Marnie said. 'Get some rest and we'll regroup first thing. Noah, I'll drop you home.'

He nodded, straightening up. 'That'd be great. Thanks.'

More photographs were waiting when Noah reached home. Dan had commandeered the kitchen table to plan the prisoner art exhibition, spreading glossy prints across its surface. Propped against the table leg was a canvas, twelve inches by ten, layered oils set in a soft glaze.

'A present,' Dan said. 'From John.'

Noah didn't know John's surname, only that he was one of the inmates whose work Dan was curating for this exhibition. They'd become friends, Dan and John.

'He says he's mucked up the depth, but I told him in the right light it'll look great. Here.' Dan moved the canvas to a spot where its surface swam with shadow, softening the brushstrokes to lure something less ambivalent from the heart of the picture. 'He's calling it *Sea*, as in Irish.'

'It's beautiful.' The sea curved, a tender palmful of umber and plum. After a day of looking at the haunted faces of strangers, Noah was glad to rest his eyes on the painting. He leaned across the table to study the artwork. 'Show me your other favourites?'

Dan separated the prints as respectfully as if they were first editions. He singled out a painting of a half-open window cross-hatched by glimpses of sky, the room a warm contrast to the bleak blue outside. '*Fear of Freedom*. And this one,' the print of a charcoal drawing, smudged ellipses interlinked at intervals like chain mail. '*Heart*.'

'Wow.' Noah took the print from Dan, holding it at the edges. Not chain mail, it was softer than that, like the layering of feathers, very simple and intimate, a thumb-print in each ellipsis. Noah couldn't remember the last time he'd seen a picture with so much soul.

'Funny, isn't it?' Dan slipped an arm around Noah's waist, resting into him easily. 'How much talent's going to waste in these places. Most of these men never took an art class in their lives before they ended up behind bars. We'd never have known they had this talent. Unless of course it was being in prison that gave them the impetus to start drawing, or painting.'

Dan wasn't talking about inmates like Michael Vokey, or prisons like Cloverton. He was talking about category D prisoners. Low risk, long sentence, places where art classes were intended to help offenders work through the emotions and actions that had put them in prison. Art as escapism. For Dan, and for Noah too, art was about engaging with reality, not running away from it. Reaching out at the risk of being rejected, inviting raw emotion.

91

Pain, elation, fear, loss. But it wasn't like that for most inmates. The recurring themes in prisoner art were vertical lines and visions of freedom, wide beaches soaring into blue skies. Unsophisticated but all the better for it, primal and urgent. Making art was a basic human need. The best of this work bore witness to that.

Noah hadn't liked the idea of Dan spending time inside, albeit with men like John, not men like Michael Vokey. But it was working out. 'You're still enjoying it?'

'Loving it.' Dan smiled.

What would Sol draw, if he were to attend one of Dan's classes? Noah couldn't imagine his brother's art. Unless— A few of the prints on the kitchen table were angry or evasive. But most were candid, and emotional. Most were wonderful.

'I think this is my favourite after *Sea*.' Noah reached for a cityscape in tepid shades of grey, pewter and dove. Lavender in the stoop of the sky, all the places it touched the rise and fall of the city. Spires and domes, scaffolding and cranes, each reflective surface filled with a different shade of the same silvered smoke.

'You have great taste.' Dan kissed the side of his neck.

'Mmm.' Noah dropped the print, concentrating on Dan's mouth. 'And not just in art.'

The flat was quiet. Marnie's first thought was that Ed had been held up in the office, or called out to an emergency. His work in Victim Support was made of emergencies, much like her own work. She dropped her keys into the bowl by the front door and stood listening to the silence until she could separate out the soft sound of the shower running. Ed was home. She smiled in quick relief.

In the flat's tiny kitchen, she ran the cold tap and filled a glass, drinking the water as she opened the morning's post. Roast chicken soup was warming in the slow cooker. Between them, Marnie and Ed had mastered a week's worth of recipes for the slow cooker, which had been their best investment since the Gaggia that belted out hot coffee all hours of the day and night. She reached for one of its cups now, in case of a late call from the station. Ed had pinned a note to the fridge, warning he might be home after her tonight. Amongst many things, she loved him for his optimism. Other couples, she was sure, had family photos on the fridge. Ed had two takeaway menus, an unfinished game of noughts and crosses, three Pokémon cards, and a magnet that said, 'This is a Fridge Magnet'.

It was nearly two years since she'd moved in. In twenty-two months of cohabiting, they'd acquired the slow cooker and the Gaggia, but resisted taking couple selfies. Marnie's horror of having her photo taken dated to a time when her father had wanted memories of their modern family, Marnie and her new brother. Then the press coverage of Stephen's trial, a daily battery of camera shutters like guns, her face in the papers, on the news. She'd come to dread cameras.

She reached out and straightened the fridge magnet. The blue paper wallet of photos was tucked in the bottom of her bag. Each night she expected to be ready to share its contents with Ed, knowing he'd offer sympathy and support, whatever she needed. Each night she left the photos in her bag. It was seven weeks since she'd taken the film from her father's camera to the chemist, paying for the blue wallet of prints before walking the short distance to her car. Seven weeks since she'd sat in silence looking at the evidence Stephen had warned her she'd find on the film: snaps taken at her parents' house in the days before it became a crime scene. Before he killed them. The last days of her parents' lives. She knew she

93

should put the wallet away, deep in a drawer or high on a shelf. Carrying it around with her was nonsensical, and it was dangerous, threatening to undermine her hard-won equanimity. On bad days, she heard the evidence crying out to her, demanding to be acknowledged.

The sound of sirens in the street brought her back to the flat, to this moment. She left the paper wallet at the bottom of her bag, going to the bedroom to undress.

Out of habit, she sniffed the cuffs of her shirt and the collar of her jacket, to judge how much of the prison was clinging to her clothes. She had dark suits and white shirts for every day of the week, but dry-cleaning wasn't cheap and the visits to the hospital weren't helping, adding a sickly odour of their own. How many more hours was she to spend in prisons or at the sides of hospital beds, with guards who patted her down, leaving their heavy thumbprints on her phone and keys, and on her clothes? She hung her suit and shirt on separate hangers; she'd steam the suit in Ed's tiny bathroom while she showered off the day. Naked, she considered herself in the mirror, reading her tattoos, the reversed words like hieroglyphs on her skin. At her right hip: *elixE fo secalP*.

Places of exile. Places like the room where Aidan shook soot from his hair, and the prison where Noah's brother Sol was held on remand. The house on the Edmonton estate where Julie was trying to keep her child safe, the hospital where Ted Elms and Stephen Keele were fighting for their lives. Her parents' house, and Noah's family home from which he'd been temporarily exiled. It made her sad to think of his parents siding with Sol against Noah. She hadn't seen enough of Sol to judge the likely extent of his innocence or guilt, but she knew Noah. Valued and admired his honesty and courage, felt how much the exile hurt him. Harry Kennedy hoped to persuade Sol to give evidence against a gang which was bringing guns and drugs into London. Knowing Harry, Marnie guessed he hated being the one to compound Noah's problems, but there was little sign so far of Sol playing ball.

Families were an impossible puzzle. Take Michael and his sister Alyson, or young Finn Duffy with his father Aidan in jail, his mother declared unfit for the task. 'She does damage,' Aidan had said, 'you know?' Marnie did know. Stephen's mother had damaged her birth son so badly he'd been taken from her and given to Greg and Lisa Rome when he was eight years old, an act of necessity and kindness which had condemned Marnie's parents to a brutal and bloody death.

The light altered and she blinked again at her reflection in the glass, *elixE fo secalP*—

'Hey.' Ed's hands were warm from the shower, his lips soft at her shoulder where water trailed from his towel-dried curls. 'How long've you been back?'

'Not long.' She smiled at him in the mirror, seeing his arms snake round to cover her tattoos. 'Missed the shower by a matter of minutes.'

'I rationed the hot water.' He rubbed his cheek catlike at hers. 'In case that happened.'

Much later, she woke to hear Ed moving away from her, away from the bed. It was dark, the middle of the night. She hadn't heard his phone ring, but it had to be a call-out. Someone needing Victim Support. Ed was at the top of his game, the head of a department who nevertheless insisted on getting his hands dirty, working one-on-one with the people who needed him most. There was never enough Ed to go round. She pushed upright on one elbow, watching the sweep of his shoulders half in shadow. The smoothness of his skin made her think of Harry's scars, and of the words inked on her own body. There wasn't a mark on Ed, anywhere. He was getting dressed, shrugging his hips into the frayed jeans she'd kicked to the floor earlier.

'You're going out?' she said.

He turned his head. 'Yes, sorry.' He finished dressing and stood.

She kept the sheet against her chest. He stayed in shadow, his face out of focus. 'Call me,' she said stupidly. 'To let me know you're okay.'

He came back to the bed, sitting beside her. 'Are *you* okay?' He straightened a strand of her hair with his fingers, but it sprang back into a curl when he released it.

'Yes, sorry. I was dreaming. Go. I'll be fine.'

He leaned down and kissed her, tasting of the wine they'd shared after the shower. Then he straightened and went, closing doors in his wake, locking the last one.

Places of exile.

Marnie curled on her side and sought sleep as a refuge from the nagging of her skin, the stiffening of the day's small bruises, and all the tender places he'd smoothed with his lips.

11

'What do you look like, darling? Send me a photo back, please! I've sent so many of myself. I've seen your face in the papers, of course, but I know it's not you. What do you look like, really?'

I'll tell you what Mickey Vokey looks like, but it will only be true for those few seconds while I'm telling you. It won't last because he changes, all the time. You're welcome to my first impression as long as you understand it has a sell-by date and that date, like him, is long gone.

'Ted, this's your new friend, Michael. Michael, this is Ted. Play nicely.'

That was Armitage (the man we called *Shanks* before Bayer hit his stride), one of the few guards over the age of twenty-two. Daz Quayle looked up to Armitage, until he fell under Mickey's spell.

'Hi, Michael,' I say, willing to give this my best shot, and because he looks like trouble.

That's my first impression: *He's trouble.*

He doesn't respond, standing with his arms folded like a chieftain, his face carved deep with disgust, as if the sight of me sitting on the bottom bunk trimming my bonsai ligustrum is too much to bear. A ponytail of brown hair drawn back from his widow's peak reaches to the flat pad of muscle between his shoulder blades. Tied with a ratted leather lace, it looks out of place on his head, as if he's wearing someone's scalp, a trophy taken in battle. He's neither tall nor fat. He has small feet which he plants apart on the floor, marking his territory. His smell fills the cell, cheap soap, scalded water, and a fleshy, fatty stink that makes me see butchers' windows. For a second I'm a kid again, pushing sawdust into a pyramid with the toe of my shoe as I wait for Mum to finish haggling over the Sunday joint. The butcher's shop was always cold, smelling rustily of raw meat, sausages slung in greying loops from a steel hook, knuckled slabs of beef squeezed into stiff collars of fat, pickled eggs peering like eyes from jars filled with brackish water. These are Mickey's colours. The colours of things once living, now dead. He isn't a large man, but he seems to grow as you look at him. Five eight and leanly built. The way he looks at you, though. He sneers, not just with his mouth and eyes, with everything he has. The sneer redraws his face, the way a nylon stocking smears a bank robber's. He likes to show his teeth. I'm not going to call it a smile.

Armitage says, 'Ted's okay. He'll show you the ropes.' He nods at me. 'Right, Ted?'

'Sure,' I say.

Mickey isn't looking at me, or Armitage. He's looking at my pruning scissors, wondering what bargain I struck to be allowed them in here. Good behaviour and an over-eager officer; he's too new to know how things work in HMP Cloverton. He's eyeing up the bottom bunk like he's deciding which way round he'll sleep on it. As soon as Armitage leaves, he says, 'I'll have those.' The pruning scissors.

I shake my head. 'No need. You can get your own, from Aidan.'

He doesn't ask, 'Who's Aidan?' but he does look at me, finally. His eyes are like those butcher's eggs, moving in their vinegary water.

I carry on pruning, pleased with the noise the scissors make, each snip separate and distinct. I've built up a nice rhythm and I don't appreciate being interrupted. Armitage understands, it's why he went on his way so quickly. Unless he didn't want to spend longer than he had to with Mickey. I can see how that might have been part of the incentive.

'I'll have that too.' He's nodding at my bunk, the shadow of his head swinging on the floor.

I can't tell him to ask Aidan for a bottom bunk. Aidan's good, but that'd stretch even his powers.

'I can't sleep near the ceiling,' I explain. 'I get migraines.'

'You can get migraines anywhere.'

It doesn't sound like a threat, the way he puts it. Just a fact.

'Anyway,' I say, 'this's my bunk. That's yours.' I nod at the one above me.

'No.' Again, just a fact. As if I got it wrong and it's his job to set me straight.

He walks over to the cabinet. Except walks is an exaggeration, because the cell's so small. He steps over to the cabinet, stands staring at my cacti. 'What's this then?'

'Fishhook barrel cactus from Arizona. Horse crippler. Devil's head.' I nod at each in turn.

He twists his head to look at me.

'You asked.' I shrug.

He bends over the horse crippler. 'What's that stink?'

'Chicken grit.'

He straightens. 'From Duffy?' So he knows about Aidan already, that was fast work on someone's part. Aidan's, probably. Did he roll out the red carpet for Vokey because he's heard good things, or bad things? Aidan's the cleverest bastard in here, or so he likes to think.

'From Duffy?' He nods at the horse crippler.

'Aidan. He prefers Aidan.'

'He can get me bolt cutters,' Mickey says. 'And petrol, and he can get me paints.'

He drops onto the bottom bunk, his weight see-sawing me, making the scissors snip at a part of the tree I hadn't wanted to trim, not today. I blink to clear the anger from my eyes. He's so close I can feel the heat lifting off him. Plants are a lot like people. I'm supposed to believe that, being interested in botany. Some flowers look beautiful but are full of poison. Cacti are ugly as sin but they're life givers, all that goodness stored inside. You can deform people, the way he's made me deform my ligustrum. You can twist them into different shapes, force them to grow the wrong way. I'm wondering about Mickey's mother, you see, right from our first meeting.

'Duffy can get me paints.' He shifts on the bunk, swinging his legs like a little kid.

'Chicken grit,' I say. 'And builder's sand. That's what I use. It's low maintenance so you don't need to change it very often.'

'Like your clothes,' he sniffs. 'Like you.'

'Like all of us. Why d'you think Aidan does such a good line in aftershaves?'

He sends the breath out between his teeth. I catch a whiff of sweet, ripe rot.

'This is mine.' He leans back on my bunk. 'You can sleep up there. It'll be okay. You get a migraine, I'll ask Duffy for aspirin.'

'Aidan.' As if this is the important part of everything he's got wrong. 'He prefers Aidan.'

100

'I'll take that cabinet too.' He nods to the horse crippler. 'You can have the other one.'

There's no natural light in here, so I can't argue that one of the cabinets is better than the other for the purposes of growing cacti. But it's the principle of the thing. You'd be the same if you had to organise eight feet by six into living and sleeping quarters. It's the principle.

'You'll want to move these.' He nods at my pages from the seed catalogue, taped to the wall by my bunk. 'I've got my own pictures to put up.'

Strictly speaking, he wasn't being awkward or bullying. He was simply playing by the rules of the place. Survival of the fittest. You lay down your laws on day one, and you stick to them.

'You can have the cabinet, but I'm keeping the bunk.'

And the scissors, I think. I see right away he's not to be trusted with scissors. You asked for my first impression, that was it. Mickey's not to be trusted with scissors, not even ones with blades no longer than the tip of your little finger.

The next morning I wake with the ceiling light spitting in my eyes. Just for a second, I think they've moved him out, given me someone new to share with. Because he looks so different in the morning. Different to how he was yesterday, and different to the shape I'd watched in the night, lying below me in my bunk, squeaking his fingers at the photos he'd taped to my wall. Faces, female. I'd guessed right away they weren't family.

That was just the start of it, the first night. I adjusted to most of it and quickly, because who would I be kidding otherwise? I got used to calling him Mickey not Michael, handing him what he wanted without putting up a fight or wasting my breath on words. But I didn't ever get used to how different he looked each time I saw him. As if there was something wrong with my eyes or a tumour was growing in my brain, pressing on a subtly different spot each day so that sometimes I saw a man and sometimes a hollow tree trunk, or a slab of meat, or a lounging silverback gorilla.

Once, before I'd opened my eyes properly, I could've sworn a giant pike was lying under the blankets. Black and glistening, its fat-bellied grin running up the wall beside me, hooked jaws trembling as it laid its cheek on my pillow, the iron stare of it reaching up through the bunk and the bed's metal frame, through the mattress and my clothes, to bite its cold teeth at the back of my neck.

12

'He was out of his depth,' Ruth Hull said. 'In prison. He shouldn't ever have been put there, of course, but that's a separate issue.' She delivered a soft, brisk smile. 'I hope you're asking a lot of awkward questions at Cloverton because nothing that happened there can be explained away. Not the fact he was denied access to the chaplain, and certainly not the fact of his escape.'

'How do you explain his escape?' Marnie asked.

Ruth nodded, as if the question pleased her. 'Michael was afraid. He didn't feel safe in Cloverton. He'd asked to be put into isolation, that's how very afraid he was.'

'And you knew this how?'

'It's in his letters.' A hint of colour in her cheeks. Pride, or pleasure? 'He wrote to me every week, sometimes twice. I sent him stamps so he could write whenever he wanted. It was important he knew I was here when he needed someone to listen, or talk to. I wrote to the prison chaplain on his behalf, and to the governors. I've written to the Home Office.' She swept her fair hair behind her ears. 'I made certain he knew his rights because it's too easy to be misled when you're an inmate. "Governors must ensure faith provision is available to all prisoners in accordance with the Service Specification, Faith and Pastoral Care for Prisoners." I sent him the paperwork, and copies of the letters I received in response to my appeals to the chaplain and governors.' She waited for Marnie to respond to this, but was quick to fill the silence: 'He saw that I took it seriously because it was so important to him, and therefore important to me. I knew his rights, and I made sure he knew them. I told him, "It's your fundamental human rights we're talking about, no matter what you did." And of course he didn't do a fraction of what they claimed in court.'

Again she waited until the silence forced her on: 'That woman was all about the compensation, you could see it in her eyes.' She sat up straight, filling the shoulders of her faded denim dress. 'I don't blame her. I expect she was told to put on a performance for the court.' A brisker version of the same smile, less soft now. 'But the prosecution couldn't provide evidence of bruises let alone the rest. He was sorry, he'd told her he was sorry. It was a mistake and of course he was willing to pay for that, but they should never have sent him to prison.'

'You say you don't blame Julie Seton for his sentence,' Noah said, 'but it sounds as if you do.'

'Oh, I'm sure she was just doing as she was told by her counsel.' Ruth dismissed the idea of Julie, setting her aside as if she were incidental, of no interest. 'It's just a shame she didn't have anyone else, someone impartial, giving her advice.'

'Did *you* offer any?' Noah asked. When Ruth looked puzzled, he said, 'In letters, perhaps.'

Three letters, from three different women. Julie had binned them, but Ruth didn't know that.

She held Noah's gaze. 'It was too late for that. She'd

104

already done the damage in court. Michael made his apologies, but she wouldn't accept them. Apologies don't come with compensation, of course. So yes, I was helping him. And I understand why he ran.'

'Were you helping with that?' Marnie asked. 'His escape.'

Ruth gave her a pitying look. 'You have to ask, I understand. But no. I was pursuing all legal avenues for appeal. He wouldn't have let me break any laws for him even if I'd wanted to.'

'Did you want to? It's clear you feel very passionately about Michael.'

'Passion isn't a dirty word, DI Rome.' Her mouth spread in a wide smile. 'No matter what anyone tells you.' She moved in the chair, settling her hands in her lap. Large hands with square fingernails, polished calluses on her thumbs from repetitive industry of some kind.

She wasn't what Noah had expected. Living in a church mission, writing 'Dear Michael' letters, advocating for a violent inmate's release. She was in her late twenties, tall and well-built with tanned skin and a forward thrust to every movement as if she couldn't get through her days fast enough, and anticipated resistance each step of the way. Under the denim dress she wore black tights and the ugliest green leather shoes Noah had ever seen, round-toed like a child's with a fat buckle fastening. The shoes were polished, the tights had an expensive sheen. The denim dress was tailored and she'd taken care of it. Everything about her, from the ugly shoes to her blunt-cut hair, had been selected to scream, 'I don't care about physical appearances,' but she did. Noah sensed that strongly. And she could afford to. She'd handpicked this uniform, paying good money for it. Was her tan from a holiday abroad? The kind of holiday Julie and

Natalie could never afford, even with the compensation.

'Yes, I care passionately about Michael.' Ruth lifted her chin. 'Does that mean I assisted in his escape? No, of course not. If you have any suspicions in that direction then I request a solicitor be present during this interview. You haven't cautioned me, so I'm assuming this is an informal discussion. If you've misled me in that regard then I have the right to a solicitor.'

Her father's solicitor, Noah guessed. The accent she'd ironed from her voice was well-heeled Home Counties. She was someone's high-achieving daughter, privately educated, independently wealthy. Noah could have guessed that much without Colin's research which had fleshed out the fine details: a degree in art history and philosophy after which she'd worked in shops and restaurants before turning to the church, volunteering at the mission in Danbury for the last two years, knocking on doors to recruit new believers, standing on court steps handing out pamphlets, protesting sentences like Michael Vokey's which she considered unfair. Often she was the only one pamphleting, a one-woman protest. How did her parents feel about the direction her life had taken? Her father was a local magistrate, her mother a retired GP. Neither was church-going.

'You care passionately about Michael.'

Marnie's tone was as cool as the collar of her shirt. She was making notes, a tactic which denied Ruth the eye contact she craved. It was the right strategy for this witness. Ruth was desperate to latch onto a barb in Marnie's voice, some evidence of a police conspiracy, or a sign she wasn't being taken seriously. It was very clear that Ruth wanted to be taken very seriously.

'The correspondence you received from Michael in reply to your letters. Where is it?'

'I'm afraid I didn't keep anything.'

She'd prepared a smile for precisely this question, serving it with a relish that set Noah's teeth on edge. He thought of Julie's courage, the staunch line she'd drawn under her pain, her determination to move on. Thinking of that made it hard not to despise Ruth.

'There's no space at the mission, you see. For papers, or letters. We recycle.' As if the destruction of potential evidence were a civic duty.

'You threw his letters away.' Marnie made a note, nodding as if Ruth had given the correct answer. Then she glanced at her watch. This interview, her glance said, was a formality to be got through, unlikely to yield anything of interest or importance.

Ruth glued the smile in place, but she hated being sidelined. She was here as the star witness for the defence, coveting her role as Vokey's disciple. This was her chance to fight openly for her champion, although why she wanted to do so was a mystery to Noah. Piety, or passion?

'You're imagining I kept the letters because I'm infatuated in some way. I'm sorry to disappoint you. I'm simply someone who happens to believe everyone deserves a second chance, not to mention his fundamental human rights.'

'That's quite all right,' Marnie said, a lick of boredom in her voice. 'We have the letters you wrote to Mr Vokey last week. We understand the nature of your relationship.' She gave the woman no chance to react to this before saying, 'You told DS Carling you hadn't been in contact with Michael Vokey during the last eight days. Is that correct?'

Ruth didn't move but the chair creaked under her, giving the lie to her stillness. 'You have my letters?' Hissing on the last syllable.

'And your photographs, yes.' Marnie turned the page

107

in her pad, moving on. 'You haven't heard from Michael Vokey? Despite the fact he has your address?'

'So you've interfered with his post.' The expensive tan turned patchy as Ruth paled, revealing a broken line of acne at her jaw. 'I'm on an approved list, so you know.'

'I'm sure you've researched legal guidance on offences by prisoners, including mutiny and escape with the use of force.' Marnie continued looking through her notes, ignoring the woman's increasingly agitated efforts at eye contact. 'He's facing a possible life sentence, so yes. We're investigating the matter thoroughly and from every angle.' She looked up at last, her ink-blue gaze pinning Ruth in place. 'Please answer the question. Have you heard from him?'

'No.' Ruth glanced across at Noah then away. 'I haven't.'

'Were you expecting to? You said he was writing twice a week. This would be the eighth day without a letter from him.'

'That's why I agreed to come here!' She raised a hand from her lap then dropped it back down. 'I'm *worried* about him. He hasn't written and of course he's had other things on his mind, but I'm worried about him, very worried in fact.' She allowed the Home Counties accent to the fore for the first time: 'I'm on his side. That doesn't mean I condone his recent behaviour.'

'Yes, it must have been uncomfortable,' Marnie said. 'To learn of his offences at HMP Cloverton and realise exactly how much he belongs behind bars.'

'You don't know him,' Ruth gave back. 'You've never even met him.'

'Have you?'

'I know him through his letters, and his art. I know his *soul*.'

'Which art, in particular?' Noah asked. 'The pictures he drew of you?'

But Ruth wasn't flinching from that. She nodded strenuously. 'Yes. Do you want to see?' She reached for her bag, pulling out a photo album the size of a paperback book. Tooled green leather with her initials, RH, blocked in silver. A gift from her parents? Ruth held the album in her hands before passing it across the table, keeping her grip on it until Marnie took custody.

In place of family photos the album contained a series of sketches, each preserved in a plastic sleeve sewn into the leather spine. Charcoal life studies, recognisable as Ruth if you knew Vokey's style and had seen enough of his subject to appreciate the fragile ferocity of her ego. It was there in her eyes and the angle of her jaw, the heft of her hands – all of her superiority, and her fear of going unnoticed. The sketches were damning, full of judgement. She couldn't see it, but Vokey despised Ruth. He'd seen through her piety to the shallow truth underpinning it. Noah battled with his instinct to admire the talent at work, reminding himself of everything Vokey had done. All that destruction, the trail of blood and body parts, jarred against the creativity displayed in the pages Marnie was turning. Eight sketches in total, five of Ruth's face, two of her hands, one of her naked legs leading in a series of wide vertical strokes to her bare feet knotted with corns and calluses, the outer edge of her big toes polished to horn. Feet as ugly as her shoes. Vokey's sketch was pitiless, triumphant in its cruelty.

'You see?' Ruth was no longer bothering to sit still, squirming contentedly in her seat, face glowing with pride and pleasure. 'This is Michael. *This*. Not the monster that woman described in court. A monster didn't draw these, how could he?'

'You've never met,' Marnie said. 'He drew these from the photographs you sent to him?'

'Yes! But these are so much *more* than that. Don't you see? So much more than copies of photographs. They tell the truth. He's captured me, all of me.'

Marnie reached the end of the sketches, resting two fingers on the empty plastic sleeve which followed the final sketch. 'Where's the missing one?'

Ruth blinked, her face convulsing evasively. 'No, these are all the sketches he did—'

'There's charcoal dust, here.' Marnie held the album where Noah could see the smudged evidence that another life study had once lived inside the empty sleeve. 'Why didn't you want to show us this last sketch, Ms Hull?'

'It's not— There aren't any other sketches. I moved the order around, that's all.'

She wasn't a good liar, which surprised Noah. With so much self-delusion to maintain, he'd have thought she'd be an expert.

'You felt uncomfortable sharing it with us.' Marnie flicked back through the album. 'Not as skilfully done as the others, perhaps. You didn't like it as much.'

The dismissal in her voice and the contemptuous flipping of her fingers made Ruth snap, 'You clearly know nothing about art. Michael has more talent in his two thumbs than most people have in their entire bodies.'

'Tell that to the men whose eyes he gouged out with his two thumbs.' Marnie closed the album and handed it back. 'Thanks for sharing.'

Ruth cradled the album in her palms as if it were a living thing. 'Shall I tell you about my experience as a prison visitor?' She wasn't about to be dismissed so easily. 'Authority in prison is an illusion. These places stand or fall by the cooperation of men like Michael. He was co-operating. They shunted him around like an unwanted pet, but he didn't complain. He was doing his best to fit

110

in. But you tell me, how do you fit in somewhere you've no business being in the first place? He wrote about the things he witnessed on a daily basis, degradations, petty cruelties. He accepted it as his lot, but he *despaired*. Often, he despaired. He saw officers assisting in the smuggling of drugs and weapons. Knives, guns even.'

'This was all in his letters.'

'Yes!'

'The letters you recycled.'

Ruth thrust a hand at the accusation. 'He was living in fear of his life, and his soul. They didn't believe in him. They thought his faith was *convenient*, that's the word they used. That he'd invented his faith in order to get special privileges.'

'You don't believe he did that.'

'I *know* he didn't.'

Marnie referred to her notes. 'When he was first sentenced in Leeds, he declared his faith as "none". How do you explain that?'

'He's a changed man.' Ruth gave a lofty smile. 'Isn't that what prison is supposed to achieve?'

'Like Ryan Gatt?'

'What—?' Her face blinked open then shut.

'Ryan Gatt,' Marnie repeated. 'The inmate you wrote to before Michael.'

The silence carved a hole in the room. Marnie rested her eyes on Ruth, as if she had all day to wait for an answer.

Ruth moved her feet, the rubber soles of her shoes raising a sound like shrieking. 'Well, there you are, then! This isn't anything peculiar. My faith requires I reach out to people, especially those in trouble.' She gestured with one large hand, wanting to move on.

But Marnie wasn't done. 'Ryan was guilty of aggravated

111

burglary, the same as Michael Vokey. You stayed in touch with Ryan after he was released. He spent a lot of time at the church mission.'

'Everyone's welcome there. We don't judge.'

'Oh, I think a few people may have judged you, when Ryan made off with the presents from a pensioner's wedding party.'

Ruth's tan faded at the edges of her mouth. 'You're wrong, in fact. No one at the mission would ever point the finger of blame at someone who believes in second chances.'

'You were mistaken about Ryan. He's back inside now. Are you writing to him?'

'No.' Through gritted teeth. 'But that was his choice.'

'And of course you're busy with Michael now.' Marnie turned a page in her pad. 'What makes you think he's any more capable of change than Ryan?'

'Michael's different. For starters, he wasn't guilty of half the things that woman claimed in court. Forgive me if I lack the necessary credulity for faith in our so-called justice system.'

For the first time, she looked pious. No more, no less. But Noah wasn't convinced that her chief motivation was her spirituality. She believed in Michael Vokey and it was physical, corporeal. The letters Marnie had brought back from Cloverton suggested Lara was the one with the unhealthy sexual attraction to Vokey. Ruth, they'd decided, was fixated on his innocence. But it went deeper than that. The sketch she'd removed from the album was intimate, Noah was sure of it. The eight sketches she'd allowed them to see were intimate enough, but she was clearly blind to how much they revealed of her infatuation and Vokey's manipulation of it. The missing sketch had to be even more exposing. Crude, perhaps, since she'd chosen

112

to remove it from the album. She was proud of these other sketches, had wanted the police to see them, showing off not only her hero's talent but their special relationship. She wasn't proud of the missing sketch. Or else she feared it shone light of a different kind on Vokey's talent.

'His art's going to be exhibited, you know. It deserves to be seen.'

'I doubt that will be possible,' Marnie said shortly. 'Given the gravity of his offences.'

'He ran because he was afraid. Because you people put him beyond the reach of help, denied him access to it in the most barbaric manner.'

'What was he afraid of?' Marnie closed her notebook and folded her hands on the table. 'You're his confidante. Help us to understand why he felt he had to run.'

'He wasn't safe there! You've been inside Cloverton. You know how bad it is, how bad it is in every prison in this country. Would *you* feel safe inside?'

Noah wanted to ask how safe she thought Julie Seton felt, or Ted Elms. If Vokey's idea of safety was freedom to indulge his vicious pastime, then the less *safe* he felt, the better for everyone.

'Was there anything or anyone in particular making him feel unsafe?'

'Everyone,' Ruth said. 'The guards, the governors, his cellmate, his *sister*—!'

Marnie looked up. 'His sister was making him feel unsafe. He told you that.'

'Alyson,' Ruth said in disgust. 'Threatening to sell the house, his family home. The place he grew up in. He loves that house, all of his childhood is there.' She smoothed her face virtuously. 'I tried to make him see that home comes in many different guises and family needn't mean the people you're born into. But he's scared of losing the house. It matters to him, that's what he said.'

Hardly surprising given the walls of faces, and the pit dug so purposefully in the cellar.

'If they'd let him attend services in the prison,' Ruth went on, 'he'd have felt less isolated. It was hard to make him understand that he wasn't alone.'

She'd stuck her fingers through his cage, stroked the ego of a dangerous sadist. Worse than that, she'd patronised him with her faith and education, her better understanding of what he wanted and needed. No wonder Vokey's sketches were so pitiless.

'You tried to make him feel less alone. By sending letters and intimate pictures of yourself.' Marnie cut the fat from Ruth's speech, serving her the raw meat of what she'd revealed of her obsession. 'You gave him your address.'

'It's a church mission.' The pious smile made a comeback. 'Everyone is welcome there.'

So many layers to her self-delusion, but Vokey had stripped each one away, laying her bare in those life studies she held so reverentially in her hands. It wasn't simply that she failed to see how savagely he'd exposed her. She saw some other version of the truth. About him, and about herself. And she valued this other version. In her letters she'd begged for more sketches, with all the self-scourging urgency of a fanatic. She couldn't wait for the day when he was drawing her from life, sharing the same room, breathing the same air. Together.

'We know Michael didn't go to you,' Marnie said. 'Otherwise you'd be with him rather than sitting here. On the other hand, there's evidence to suggest you may have encouraged or incited him to escape. Which is an offence, as I'm sure you're aware.'

'Why would I post him letters *after* his escape if I had

prior knowledge of it? You don't suspect me. There's no evidence or you'd have arrested me.' Ruth smoothed the lap of her dress. 'This is precisely the sort of intimidation I'm talking about. And I'm not locked in a cell with a threatening fetishist. Edward Elms.' She spoke the name with loathing, as if she'd committed it to memory. 'They let him have scissors, did you know that? He attacked Michael with scissors. That's why he asked to be put into isolation. *Begged* to be put into isolation.'

'Ted Elms is in hospital,' Noah said. 'On life support.'

She pushed her face forward, the light sitting in the cracked skin of her lips. 'Where's your evidence it was Michael who did that? Cloverton doesn't have *any* evidence of the part he played in the riot, if he played a part at all. The statements coming out are so vague it's obvious they have no idea what happened. Just because Michael's the one who ran, they think they can pin it all on him. Very convenient. But I don't believe it. I don't believe any of it.'

'Yet you don't condone his recent behaviour.' Noah studied her. 'That's what you said. If he played no part in the riot, what did you mean by his recent behaviour?'

'Running away!' Ruth swept her hand towards the door. 'He shouldn't have done that. We can't solve our problems by running away.' Rapping out each syllable like a machine gun. 'I thought he understood that, from my letters.'

It was a miracle Vokey hadn't gone after her to fill the grave in his mother's house. The kind of man he was, and Ruth with her tireless virtue-signalling. It was a miracle.

Marnie was saying, 'Harbouring an escaped prisoner is an offence under the Criminal Justice Act 1961. As you'll know from your research. For the record, no complaint was ever lodged at HMP Cloverton by Michael

John Vokey. Plenty of complaints lodged against him, but none by him. At any point.' She spoke slowly and precisely. 'No request to see the chaplain was ever made, or refused. No request was made by Michael to be put into isolation.' She watched Ruth stiffen in the chair. 'You wanted to know whether we'd been to Cloverton, and if we'd asked awkward questions there. We've seen everything Michael signed during his time inside, including his visitor list. His sister's name is on that list because he asked for it to be added. Your name is on that list because you requested it. There was a problem, however. Michael was made aware of your request to be an official prison visitor, and he refused it. He told prison staff he didn't want to see you.'

'He didn't want me going into that place.' But Ruth's smile curdled. She hadn't known this, and she didn't like it. 'He was protecting me.'

'He approved his sister's visits,' Marnie said. 'In fact, he asked that her name be added to the list. But not yours.'

'Chivalry.' Her eyes glinted palely, arrow slits in the tan fortress of her face. 'He didn't need to protect me, but I admire his instinct to do so. You see? He isn't a monster, he's a man who needs a friend. Desperately. But still his instinct was to keep me safe from that place.'

'That's the explanation he gave you for his refusal? That he was protecting you.'

'He didn't need to give me an explanation. He knew I'd understand.' She tidied her face back into a smile. 'Everything we have is founded on understanding.'

'Everything you have,' Marnie echoed.

'Friendship. Support. Love.' The smile settled and grew confident, even radiant. 'It's not a dirty word. I'm proud of what we have. What we are. It's a beautiful thing. We're beautiful.'

13

Love is a dirty word, the way Mickey says it. He uses it all the time to describe Lara and Ruth, and Julie. 'She loved it,' he says, and I've learnt to keep my mouth shut or else to agree, because that's what he needs. Mickey needs a lot of things, more than most. If he were here in hospital with me, one lucky nurse wouldn't be enough. He'd want a troop, starting with mine. He wouldn't notice the gap in her teeth or the smell of her hair. Just, 'I'll take Ted's,' and she'd go to him because that's what happens with Mickey and me. He covets and acquires, everything. Even the things he's no use for, like that bedpan or this catheter. If I've got it, he wants it.

Prison's all about learning to do without. Acclimatising, lowering your standards without losing them altogether. Unless you're Mickey Vokey. Then it's about growing, getting grabby.

'She loves me.' Sniffing at Lara's letters, and Ruth's. 'She loves me lots.'

I went into Cloverton as someone who likes to wash twice a day and can't sleep without a hollow-fibre pillow and real cotton sheets, who doesn't eat meat, eggs or fish, or anything with preservatives if he can help it. I like strong coffee, made from scratch. With tea, I put the milk in first and it has to be semi-skimmed, not skimmed and not full fat. I can't read a newspaper if someone's got to it before me, because it seems I'm the only person in the world capable of folding a newspaper correctly. I'll cross the street rather than walk under a ladder. I have my little ways, that's what Mum said: 'You have your little ways, Teddy, but I'm not complaining.' She kept that up even at the end, pretending I was awful, awkward, and she was the only one who could handle me.

'She loves me.' Sniffing. 'She loves me lots.'

I close my eyes at the closeness of the ceiling, and put my thoughts out there, away. Far away from Mickey and his women, and his blunt words like bullets. Lara sent him a photo of the view from her window: an empty acre of grass tortured into lawn. He hates it when she does that, a waste of good film. He wants photos of *her*, close-ups, the muckier the better. He despises landscapes.

So I send my thoughts out of the cell, miles away, to my favourite landscape. We lived in the countryside-proper, Mum and me, a place where it still floods every spring. We'd go walking in the hills when the winter thawed, high up where the waters couldn't reach us. I never told Mickey about that. He wasn't interested in my stories, only in his.

One spring when we were up there in the hills, Mum and I met a man walking two dogs, a big white and brown cross-breed, part-husky by the look of it, and a terrier with an apologetic grin. The terrier stayed close to the ground, its breath panting blackly. I've never liked dogs, but these two were enjoying the springtime so much it was hard not to smile and say hello. Not many walkers braved the back end of winter, so it was nice to see a new face. The earth was iron-clad, crimping underfoot, a low-lying mist giving the impression that the sky had caved in.

'Look at that!' Mum pointed to where the last of the flood was boiling downhill, swelling what had been a stream, churning it with twigs and branches.

I watched a dozen rafts take form in the water as the jumble of wood rushed together before sweeping apart again. Frightening what water can do. I've always thought it worse than fire.

'Come along!' Mum moved fast in those days, I had to stride to keep up. She hated any idea that she was ageing. Where we lived the thought of getting old was hair-raising, cut off the way we were and with the hard winters and spring floods. 'Keep up, Teddy!'

A sandstone village sat over the next hill, postcard-perfect like Lara's, woodsmoke shrivelling from its chimneys. At the foot of the hill, the flood separated either side of an oak tree, creating a small lake. There in its edging current we saw a lamb. Newborn, its ear clipped, drowned. The water carried it close to where we were walking, its little body like a phantom floating in the flood's tide. The current took it towards the trees, Mum oh-Teddying as if she hadn't grown up in the countryside, didn't know its savageries, so casual and constant. We watched the drowned lamb all the way downstream, its woolly head nod-nod-nodding, and Mum didn't shut up the whole time. So, yes. I know how to downsize my expectations. It's only Mickey who hasn't a clue.

'Love's a dirty word,' Michael says. As if he's the only person who's ever had to give anything up. 'Ruth's in love with me.' He folds her letter into a plane and flies it into the top bunk. 'Get a load of this shit.'

The plane lands on my leg. I unfold its wings, straighten the nose, smooth the undercarriage.

119

'Dear Michael,' Ruth has written, 'I've asked if I can come and visit you. I've been a prisoner visitor before so I'm sure they'll approve my request. Then we can talk properly. And we can pray together! I'm praying for you every day, that you're given guidance, shown the way.'

'Photos, too.' Mickey's busy in the bottom bunk. I wouldn't want that bunk now if I could have it. 'On her knees, praying for me. I'll draw her for you.' He kicks at the underside of my mattress. 'Stop you getting lonely up there. I'll do one just for you. Life study. Close-up.' He groans.

I block my ears by concentrating on the memory of the drowned lamb, the whiteness of it, the way it held the water in a pearly collar round its little throat. Mum at my side, nearly sobbing at the sight of it. Smoke rising over the hill where all the houses were owned by Londoners, strangers who hardly ever set foot there and never ventured abroad in bad weather.

'Life studies. You'd like that.'

I can't shut out the sound of him groaning, panting. It's monstrous. He's crude, and vicious, and despicable. I think of what he did to Julie, everything he's told me, and I have to shut my eyes I'm shaking so hard. I have to shut my eyes and wait until the hot red fades to pink and finally to white.

'Oh, Teddy,' all the way home, as if she'd never seen what happens when nature swoops in and sorts out the weak from the strong, before sending down a flood to wash it all away.

14

DS Joe Coen was training to be a pilot. His sister gave him a trial flying lesson as a birthday present and he fell in love with the sky when it opened up in a rainbow as he was coming to land, all red bands and purple spokes and the instructor saying, 'Wow, that's a gift in itself.' It left such an impression, Joe found himself learning about supernumeraries and twinned bows, cloud and moon bows. Rainbows are incredibly rare, he discovered. In any one place in England, you can expect to see fewer than ten a year. Halos and coronae occur more frequently, coronae when thin clouds scud across a bright moon. In very cold weather, if you're lucky, the sky will fill with perfect diamond dust crystals, interlacing like a glittering spider's web. Joe wanted to be up there when it happened, in the open sky, flying a plane. Until then he was a detective sergeant with West Cumbria CID.

Debbie Tanner had been right to say Joe didn't miss a trick. He'd contacted Marnie and the team to give them the scene examiner's report from Alyson Vokey's house the minute it was filed. Alyson was found at the foot of her stairs, unconscious and bleeding from a head injury consistent with having fallen from a height. The hall radiator had trapped traces of her blood and hair. No injuries other than those you'd expect from a fall down a steep flight of stairs. Bruises, but no broken bones. Alyson lived alone. Always better to be safe than sorry though, especially after Joe discovered her relationship to Michael Vokey, whose oddly forgettable face was flagged all over the system. Joe went back to Alyson's house and checked everything twice, finding no evidence of a break-in, or foul play. Just this ticking in his head like a beetle when he was inside, searching.

'It's a busy street,' he was explaining over the phone to DS Noah Jake, 'lots of people milling about. Makes it harder for neighbours to notice anything odd.'

The homes on the street were similar, but not identical. Variety was one of the things Joe liked about his part of the world. Alyson's house was a former brewery built over three storeys in whitewashed grey stone, its windows at wonky intervals. A narrow garden at the front was gated to the street but the gate didn't close, swinging open easily due to the slope of the path. No burglar alarm, but that was usual around here. Joe would've been suspicious if Alyson had fitted an alarm. He'd thought the Met team might grit their teeth at the lack of security, but DS Jake took it in his stride.

'How hard was it for you to get inside the house?' he asked Joe.

'The neighbour had a set of keys. Two locks on the front door, but she hadn't secured the second one, or put the chain on.'

Joe had knocked twice before he tried the key in the front door, calling out to let Alyson know he was police, because the neighbours were getting worried they'd not seen her in a while. Not a job he'd normally have been involved in but he knew the street and was over that way for another case, plus Vokey's name was lighting the system like Christmas. The smell hit him right away. She'd soiled herself, poor woman. Joe was just glad she was alive, and that she'd stayed that way.

'I checked the back door,' he told DS Jake. 'It was locked, but not bolted.'

'She felt safe, in other words.'

'I'd say so.' He'd knelt beside her until the ambulance came. The house felt lonely, the way some houses do. Her hand was chilly so he'd chafed it between his. 'It's a decent part of town, friendly street, good neighbours. They're the ones raised the alarm.'

'You still think it was an accident,' DS Jake said. 'Nothing's changed that?'

'Hang on,' Joe said, since his other phone was buzzing. It was a text from Annie, cheerful but exasperated. She still wasn't in labour. 'Sorry. My wife's about to have a baby so I'm on standby for a call. DS Jake?'

'Noah. And congratulations.' Genuine warmth in his voice. 'Your first?'

'Second. A little brother for our five-year-old, Bobby. He's the only one of us keeping calm.'

'Let's hope it lasts. You were saying you'd been back to the house to take a second look. Do you still think it was an accident?'

'No new reason to think otherwise,' Joe said.

'But—? It sounds like something's eating at you.'

He had sharp ears, Noah Jake, as if he could hear the beetle ticking in Joe's brain.

'My mum lives alone,' Joe told him. 'She's older than Alyson and she's never tripped on her stairs. You get to know your own house, and Alyson's lived there a long while. I went up and down the stairs a couple of times and they're steep, sure. But she'd have known that. She was in her slippers, sensible ones with rubber soles. It's eating at me, like you said.'

Sensible slippers and a bathrobe over her nightie, no belt to trip over. Nothing in the pockets of the bathrobe, other than a balled up tissue and a little loop of her own hair, tugged from a hairbrush and pocketed en route to the pedal bin. Toothpaste on her lower lip, her face wiped clean by baby lotion. She'd been getting ready for bed, her routine so like his mum's that Joe kept hold of her hand long after the ambulance arrived, talking to her so she'd know she wasn't alone.

'The neighbours haven't seen anyone else recently?' Noah asked. 'No strangers?'

'No one who raised any eyebrows. There's a house for sale two doors up, so they've had estate agents and people round for viewings. Then there's pizza deliveries, and Jehovahs, and couriers for online shoppers. It's a busy street. People are used to seeing new faces. I asked a lot of questions, but didn't get anything useful.'

'Did Alyson have any deliveries? Or – any religious pamphlets in the house?'

Did he think Jehovahs did this? Maybe they had aggressive types in London, but round here the Jehovahs wouldn't say boo to a goose, not even at Easter.

'Not that I saw. Her friends say she uses online shopping to avoid the town centre. She's not a recluse, just doesn't like crowds. And the parking's a joke.'

Joe's mum was the same, except she didn't have WiFi so Joe organised her online groceries, glad of the chance to help. Otherwise it was his sister who shouldered everything.

'Any odd post in the house?' Noah asked. 'Letters, maybe anonymous?'

Joe frowned into the phone. 'Hate mail? She'd had some trouble with that but it was years back, wasn't it? Before she moved up here.' He'd been surprised to find her name in the police database.

'These letters would be recent. She might not have kept them.'

Noah's way of asking whether Joe had checked the rubbish? He had, in fact. 'She's a shredder. Junk mail, bank statements, bills. Her recycling's full of it. But why don't I take a fresh look round for anything she didn't shred.' He'd not been looking for letters the first two times he'd searched the house. 'From her brother, you think?'

'Not necessarily. We're aware of a couple of women who were writing to Michael Vokey when he was inside Cloverton. We've seen some of their correspondence. The content is quite unusual.'

'What sort of thing are we talking about?' Joe thought of the young woman Vokey had attacked in London. 'Threats?'

'The opposite,' Noah said drily.

'Oh, *those* sorts of letters.' Joe's heart sank. He knew the world wasn't black and white. People behaved badly and irrationally, even unforgivably. But he'd wanted to believe that what happened to Alyson was an accident, even while he was exploring all other possibilities, searching her bins, looking for signs of foul play. An accident was bad enough. How could she face going home to that house if she'd been attacked there?

'We think these same women may have written to Julie Seton,' Noah was saying, 'possibly with Vokey's encouragement. Lara Chorley, and Ruth Hull. I'm wondering whether Alyson had any letters like that. These women are upset about the family house that's in probate. We've been told Alyson may have been pushing through the sale against Michael's wishes.'

125

Pushing through the sale, Joe thought. So they'd pushed back, sent Alyson down those stairs?

'You want me to look for paperwork about the house sale?' He rubbed his thumb at the screen where Annie's text was sitting. 'When I'm checking for letters from Lara and Ruth.'

'Could you? It'd be handy to know whether she's had any recent correspondence about the London property. I'll text you the address. Michael was living there, squatting really, before he was put away. We don't know whether Alyson was aware of that.'

'Wish we could ask her,' Joe said. 'For her sake.'

Her poor legs whittled with bruises from the stairs. And *white* – proper indoor legs. The fall had rucked up her nightie, showing her knees. He'd tugged it back down to give her her dignity.

'But she's doing okay,' Noah said. 'The surgery went well?'

Real concern in his voice. Joe liked him for it. 'Yes, they think so. I'm hoping to hear from the hospital later today. I'll keep you posted. And about the house, if I find any letters.'

'Thanks. We'll do the same down here. Good luck with everything. I hope you get that call from your wife soon. And that Bobby bonds with his new brother.'

'Thanks. Me too.' Joe ended the call and pulled on his coat, planning the route from Alyson's house to the hospital. Annie was three days overdue already. He'd be closer to the hospital than here at the station, and his DI had told him to do what he could to help the Met in London. No one wanted Michael Vokey on their patch. Not the police, not the public, not even Vokey's sister.

Joe thought of Bobby making space on his shelves for his new brother's books and toys. Alyson and Michael must've been that close, once upon a time. Now it looked like Michael might be a suspect in his sister's attempted murder. Unless Joe could find evidence to rule it out, or until Alyson was able to tell them the truth about what happened before Joe found her at the foot of her stairs with her poor white knees on show, looking like a sheep he'd once seen on the road out to Newby Bridge, struck by a car and stranded, dying, at the side of the road.

Noah knocked on the door to Marnie's office. 'D'you have a minute?'

She'd been on the phone, but she nodded him to a chair. 'How was DS Coen?'

'Very helpful. He's headed back out to Alyson's house to see if he can find anything from Ruth or Lara, or about the house sale. Since Ruth's so sure that's a bone of contention between Alyson and Michael, and because it gives him a motive to attack her. If he attacked her.'

'Any word on Lara?' Marnie pitched her empty paper cup at the bin, hitting it neatly.

'Not yet. Debbie's waiting to hear from the officers who went to her cottage first thing. I wanted to show you something, though.' He took out the Polaroid he'd unpinned from the wall in the other incident room. 'Vokey drew this. It's Alyson.' He handed the Polaroid across the desk. 'I almost didn't recognise her. The photo we have on file's so different, but this is one of the pictures we found under the floor at his mum's house. His artwork. It's Alyson.'

The sketch wasn't cruel like the ones of Ruth but it was sparing, half a dozen swift lines in charcoal, feathered by his thumbs. Alyson's eyebrows and eyes, her nose and mouth. He'd captured her wary look from the photo Joe had provided, but so much gentler and more questing. She wasn't a beautiful woman but she looked it, here.

127

Not because her brother had lied or elaborated. Because he'd told the truth in the same way he'd told it about Ruth in the life studies which exposed her flawed ego so efficiently. His drawing of Alyson was affectionate, and expansive. The white space between the charcoal lines conjured the whole of her face, illuminating it.

'He loves her. Or he did, when he drew this.' Noah looked at Marnie. 'I don't think he's the one who hurt her. I don't think he *could*— Not when he feels this way about her.'

'If he still does. But if he feels she betrayed him by selling the house?' Marnie put the Polaroid down on the desk between them. 'That would hurt even more if he loved her.'

'True. But they were close when he drew this. We didn't think he was close to anyone. She refused to visit him in prison. He wanted to see her, but she said no. That must've stung.'

'If we look at it like that,' Marnie touched the hard edge of the Polaroid, 'it makes it *more* likely he hurt her, not less.'

Noah couldn't argue with her logic.

'There's something else we need to consider.' She knotted her curls away from her face. 'If the house is a motive and he felt threatened by Alyson's claim on it then we need to think of what he might have done about that. What was it Ruth said: "He loves that house, all of his childhood is there." He chose to tell Ruth that Alyson was threatening to sell the house. What if he meant her to do something about that? What if he *instructed* her to do something about it?'

That smile of Ruth's, the speech about the beautiful thing they had.

A chill carded the back of Noah's neck. 'You think *Ruth* attacked Alyson?'

128

'What did Joe Coen say about visitors to the house?' Marnie stood, going to the filing cabinet for two bottles of mineral water. 'Had there been any visitors?'

'It's a busy street, lots of strangers.' Noah took the bottle from her outstretched hand. 'Couriers, delivery people, estate agents. No one that raised any eyebrows, Joe said.' He unscrewed the lid of the bottle, frowning. 'Not that Ruth raises eyebrows, until she chooses to. That outfit of hers is a deliberate disguise, and I bet she practises those smiles every morning.'

'We have two women ready to do anything for Michael Vokey,' Marnie reminded him. 'One of whom lives less than an hour away from the sister who's threatening to sell the house he loves. The house he can't afford to lose because of what he's done to the walls, and the cellar.'

'Lara?' Noah gave a slow nod. 'Her trip to Edinburgh's conveniently timed as an alibi.'

'It's a long way for Ruth to go and return in a day,' Marnie agreed.

Noah drank a mouthful of water, thinking it through. 'They were writing to Julie, harassing her. That might be indicative. It wasn't enough for them to have his attention, they wanted his approval, wanted to *win* his approval. Making sure he gets the house would achieve that.'

'There's another possibility we've not considered,' Marnie said. 'That Ruth and Lara know one another, or that they know *of* one another. I can see Vokey wanting them in competition for his attention, and using that to push each woman to up her game. I don't see Ruth being keen to share the role of his confidante, do you?'

'Not without a fight.' Noah set the bottle down on the desk, scratching at his cheek. 'But I can't see Ruth agreeing to hurt anyone, not physically. It's too important to her to have the moral high ground. She'll petition and protest

129

to her dying breath, but attempted murder? She'd never be able to reconcile it with her faith. Lara's another matter. Her letters are darker, more dangerous. More possessive, too. She belongs to Vokey, he belongs to her. That business about bruising easily behind her knees. And offering to send more photos, asking what he'd like from her, inviting him to challenge her to take risks. He'll have found that hard to resist.'

'Let's prioritise Lara. Check for footage of her car in the vicinity of Alyson's house, and double-check her alibi in Edinburgh.' Marnie got to her feet. 'I don't like the fact we've not been able to speak with her yet.'

'If she's hiding something, she's playing it cool.' Noah followed her from the office to the incident room. 'But that's not necessarily a good sign.'

'No, it's not. Debbie, what's the latest on Lara Chorley?'

'Sorry, boss, still waiting for the call.'

'Chase it, please.' She nodded at Debbie's phone. 'Colin, you have Lara's registration. Let's run it through ANPR to find out exactly where she's been in the last week.'

Automatic Number Plate Recognition. Marnie was harbouring serious doubts about Lara's movements if she was wanting to check that data.

'Will do,' Colin said. 'And I've spoken with Julie. We have a lead on that interview she saw online, the one with the prison officer from Cloverton.'

'Good, but let's focus on Lara. It's taking too long to track her down.' Marnie nodded at the team. 'As quickly as we can, please.'

'I'm in touch with Joe Coen up in Kendal,' Noah added. 'Leave that with me. We need to know where Lara's been, and how much she knows about what's going on between Michael and Alyson.'

130

15

'She calls herself your sister, but she's a traitor. That's *your* house, darling. I have plans for it, and for us. Black-out curtains and a big bed with an oak headboard. I saw one in a shop in Kendal, carved all over with flowers and fruit. Such a work of art! You never saw carving like it, knuckle-deep in places. This one spot, a crop of strawberries, where the detail's simply glorious. You can see every individual seed. I keep thinking of us in bed. I'll know exactly how many seeds are in each of those strawberries. If I shut my eyes, I'll be able to find them with my fingers. I'll be able to taste them. I want to taste strawberries every night we're together.'

Mickey grunts and shifts in my bunk, his breath reaching me in rotten waves.

I turn the page, read on: 'I want to taste limes too. Do you like limes, darling? Such a sharp taste, so bright it fucks through everything. You'll blindfold me, put me on my knees, and I'll be able to see its shape through the blackness.'

This is the stuff he's been waiting for, the good stuff. Lara knows how to serve it up, I'll give her that. The strawberries were foreplay. Lime's the main course.

'Thirst makes hot silk of my throat, salty. My thighs ache. I'm kneeling on a thin carpet on a hard floor. My hands behind me, wrists pressed together, fingers interlaced. I'm being very, very obedient.' I stumble, blinking at the page.

Lara's taken to typing her letters, like Ruth. I can't pretend it's her handwriting making me stumble. But I always want to stop at this point.

Mickey grunts: 'Go on.'

'"Open your mouth!"' I'm reading Lara's words. 'You don't wait for me to do it. My jaw makes a hollow sound as you lever it wide. I thrust my tongue for a quick taste of you, like sandalwood, earning a slap because that's breaking the rules and I know it.'

She's deluded. If she thinks this grunting ape tastes of sandalwood, she's deluded.

'I rock to the left. You wait while I get my balance, your breath grazing the air above me. You're taller than I expected. Your skin smells of freckles.'

It smells of rot, and rubbing. He's rubbing at himself in the bunk that's mine.

'You thrust a lime into my mouth. A whole one, "Bite down," you play with my jaw until I do as I'm told. Zest darts to the back of my throat, my tonsils quivering as it hits, tongue stung by acid. I have to work hard to hold the position you want. The shock of the taste hits me like a hand.'

I'd like this to be over quickly, but Lara's learnt to pace herself. Almost as if she knows how long he has to labour to reach a conclusion. Longer and longer, it seems.

'The fruit burns then numbs my lips. You wedge it deep, forcing an O from my mouth. Juice trickles down my chin, tickling. You take my face in your hands and lean in to lick around the taut shape of my lips. I swallow, tasting sherbet sweets, syllabub, martinis. The friction of your tongue brings my lips back to life. I can feel the dimpled details in the lime's waxy rind.'

I turn the page to read, 'I shudder as your teeth nip, sending a pulse of zest buzzing about my mouth. You follow the trail down my neck and lick slowly, hotly at the base of my throat. My skin rises under your touch. Your mouth reaches lower and I'm levitating, suspended from your kiss. Love— Love is not a safe word, but my mouth is crammed with colour and my skin sings so brightly it lights the room.'

I stop, realising he reached the end two sentences ahead of me. I've been reading to an empty cell. He isn't moving, isn't moaning. The air is flat and void. He's wiped himself out. Or Lara has, with her words. He'll be quiet now, for hours. I can breathe, I can move, I can *think*. She's wiped him out. I fold the letter away and climb down to the cabinet where my ligustrum is waiting.

Slipping the scissors into my top pocket, I swing back into the top bunk, settling cross-legged there to work. I bend over my little ligustrum and whisper to her all the ways in which I'm glad, each small snip of the blades a blunt, beautiful echo in the empty cell.

16

'Lara Chorley didn't drive home directly from Edinburgh.' Colin pinned a map to the evidence board. 'ANPR gives us a circuitous route, taking in Kendal on the way back. This was yesterday.'

Debbie was the first to react. 'She was in Alyson's home town at the time of the accident?'

'If it was an accident. Bloody hell.' Ron linked his hands on top of his head. 'The letters were bad enough, but he's got them *killing* for him? Trying to kill for him?'

'I'm narrowing it down,' Colin said. 'To see how close her car came to Alyson's house.'

'There was no sign of a break-in,' Noah reminded them. 'But I've let Joe Coen know what we're thinking. He's taking a fresh look around for anything to suggest Lara was in contact with Alyson by letter, or in person. We're checking phone records, of course.'

'Debbie, what news from Lara's home?' Marnie's steady tone defused some of the excited tension in the room. 'Have the local police been to her cottage?'

'Yes, but she was out. She left a note saying she'd gone into town for food and fuel.'

'She's a fan of leaving notes,' Ron said sourly. 'Has anyone actually seen or spoken to her since Vokey ran off? Or are we taking it on faith that she's alive and kicking?'

'I spoke to her.' Colin flushed. 'When you were bringing Ruth back from Danbury. It wasn't a long call, just enough to confirm she'd been in Edinburgh and was on her way home.'

'So just a couple of barefaced lies, then.' Ron rolled his eyes at the ceiling.

Colin bit his lip, stung into silence.

'Lara wasn't a suspect two days ago,' Marnie reminded him. 'We wanted to locate her, and we did that. Local police were taking charge of questioning her. We trusted them to do it.'

'We should've brought her in.' Ron folded his arms. 'Like Ruth.'

'We should have questioned Ruth in Essex,' Marnie told him. 'That's the word from on high. We cooperate and collaborate. We don't take over.'

'Local police have been dicking about for two days,' Ron complained. 'Have they even searched Lara's house for Vokey? She's running around the countryside doing his bidding. For all we know they're Bonnie and bloody Clyde.'

Noah's phone rang and he turned away to take the call, aware of Marnie's continued efforts to pour oil on the troubled waters of the team. 'DS Jake.'

'Noah, it's Joe Coen. I'm at Alyson's. You were right about the paperwork.'

'Hang on. Let me put you on speaker.'

Marnie nodded at the team and the room fell silent, listening to Joe.

'So she's a shredder, like I said. But she's also a hoarder, at least when it comes to her brother. A drawer full of prison forms, from Leeds as well as Cloverton. Visitor requests from Michael, rules about contacting inmates. And paperwork from their mum's death, certificates, solicitors' letters, all that sort of thing. Then there's this letter. Typed, no signature.' Joe hesitated. 'D'you want me to read it? I could send a photo from my phone.'

'Both,' Noah said, 'if you could.'

'Okay. It's just that it's not— Okay.' Joe drew a short breath. '"You should be standing by him, you bitch. Just like he stood by you. That house's all he has left. You don't want it, you never wanted it. So keep your hands off it. You've hurt him enough. We won't warn you twice."'

'Wait,' Noah said. '*We* won't? It definitely says that?'

Ruth and Lara working as a team, as Marnie had suggested? Or Vokey and Lara, as Ron's Bonnie and Clyde?

'*We* won't warn you twice,' Joe said. 'I'm sending the photo now. I've bagged it, for Forensics.'

'Good work. Anything in the solicitors' paperwork about the sale of their mum's house?'

'Nothing. But Alyson's the executor, so possibly she's thinking of a probate sale.'

'Can she do that?' Debbie asked. 'Sell it, I mean. Without a will?'

Colin was making notes, listening to everything Joe said.

'She wouldn't get as much money, but yes. As executor she can move things in that direction.'

'DS Coen,' Marnie said, 'this is DI Rome. Any news on Alyson?'

'She's still unconscious, Ma'am. But they think the surgery was a success. Do I need to organise protection at the hospital? The way it's looking, and with this letter?'

'It would make sense.' Marnie wore the stitch of a frown on her forehead.

'Then we're looking at attempted murder? My boss'll want to know.'

'I'll give her a call. Detective Superintendent Jafri, yes?'

'Yes, Ma'am.'

Noah said, 'Thanks, Joe. I'll send you a photo of Lara. Driving licence, so you'll have all the details. We've got her car going through Kendal on the day of Alyson's accident. She said she was travelling back to Keswick from Edinburgh.'

'Roadworks,' Joe said reflexively. 'We're chockablock with diversions following the floods.' He paused. 'Thought I'd better mention that in case you're thinking the worst.'

'We're thinking the worst,' Ron asserted grimly.

'Could you show Lara's driving licence to the neighbours?' Noah asked Joe. 'And to anyone who might've seen her.'

'Alone? Or with Michael Vokey?'

'Either. Both.'

'You think he's on our patch.' They heard Joe scrubbing a hand at his hair unhappily. 'He tried to kill his sister and he's with this woman, Lara. But she's not a hostage. She's helping him.'

Marnie said, 'We need to cover all the bases, but we can't make any assumptions. Lara may be acting alone, or under duress. We'll let you know as soon as we have more information.'

'I'll do the same,' Joe said. 'Good luck.'

He rang off as DCS Ferguson stepped into the room, wearing her war-ready scowl.

'I've had the press on the phone,' she announced. 'Just for a change. Asking what I know about an interview that's going viral. Any chance we're ahead of the curve on this one?'

'Yes, actually. DC Pitcher found the interview.' Marnie smiled at Colin, who brightened a little from the gloom which had engulfed him after the discussion around Lara's broken promises.

'Jolly good.' Ferguson settled herself in the chair along-side Colin. 'Enlighten me.'

Colin angled his monitor for the team to watch, opening a link on his desktop. 'Julie said she saw this on YouTube two days ago. It's been taken down, but I traced it to a civil liberties website.'

'Is it just me,' Ferguson put in, 'or do civil liberties websites exist purely to flout laws and bellow about it?'

Noah was near enough to smell the coffee on her breath. The tension in the room had returned, everyone wanting movement on the case, and not only because Ferguson demanded it. The letters found in Alyson's house, Lara's car seen in the vicinity – both developments were unfolding too far away. The idea that Vokey might have skipped their patch without so much as a footnote caught on CCTV was gutting.

'It's an interview with a prison officer from Cloverton,' Colin said. 'At least that's what it claims to be. He's kept his face hidden, and distorted his voice. He didn't want anyone to ID him.'

'While he took uncivil liberties with his oath of office.' Ferguson played with her police lanyard, tapping her polished nails against its edges. 'Jammy sod.'

Marnie and Noah gathered with the rest of the team to watch the interview on Colin's monitor. Filmed against an improvised backdrop – a black sheet pinned to a wall – the footage was sixty per cent pixels, an amateur attempt to protect the identity of the uniformed whistle-blower.

'They called everyone in.' The officer's voice was deep and distorted, disguising his age as well as his accent. 'All

138

of us. Handed out the riot gear. We kitted up and waded in. It was a jungle, a fucking *jungle* of blood. Wall to wall.'

In spite of the vocal distortion, the way he sat angled towards the camera with his head cocked and his shoulders sharp, betrayed his age. He was young, like the majority of those employed at Cloverton. Julie had said he looked fifteen. She was right. He was younger than Noah, and Colin.

'One of us skidded, put his hand right down in the worst of it. "Fuck's this?" he's holding it up, like it's right there in his hand and I'm not even shitting you. An *eye*. Still with the – shit, the *nerves*, whatever, attached. A human fucking eyeball.' He shaped his hands into a pair of pistols, firing at his own head. 'Mental, right? You won't find this in the papers, but it's happening in this country's prisons *right now*.' Pointing both fingers at the camera. 'They don't pay us enough to deal with this shit. And it's meant to be our fault he's out there, doing fuck knows what. Some bastard gets his eyeballs ripped out, or his face bitten through. Because I'm not even shitting you— He's the real thing, a proper maniac.' He shifted in the chair. Sounding impressed, in awe. 'Not like you've been told. Watch my lips.' Pointing at the pixels blurring his face. 'He is. The real. Thing. Psycho, cannibal, whatever. Okay? He's *it*. These are the headlines they should be writing. He's making Jack the Ripper look like *nothing*. Like your gran's pet poodle.'

Noah felt Marnie tense at his side, her focus sharpening on the distorted face.

'Yeah.' The whistle-blower dropped his hands to his sides, swaying forward, seeking the camera. 'They're making out he's an animal, but he's more than that.' His voice dropped an octave. 'He's dead clever, cunning. You have no idea. He'll blow your mind. He's out there!'

139

Expanding his arms, chest swelling. 'Top of the league, miles ahead of anyone. They'll only find him if he wants to be found. My advice? Don't hunt what you can't catch.'

He couldn't sit still, squirming with excitement as he described Vokey. 'The police've got *nothing*. No chance of finding him. He's gone. A ghost.' He held up his hands, opening his fingers as if throwing confetti at the camera. 'They're looking for a fucking ghost.'

The film ended, freeze-framing on the officer's pixelated face and his empty, splayed hands.

Everyone waited for Ferguson to break the silence, but she was staring at the screen. Thinking about the press, Noah imagined. Calculating the damage that would be done if the journalist who'd contacted her chose to run with this story in tonight's edition.

'Well, he's pleased with himself,' Ron snarled. 'Whoever he is.'

'Not just himself. He's pleased with *Vokey*. The body language, his choice of words.' Noah straightened, meeting Marnie's eyes. 'That's hero worship.'

'Who is he?' she asked Colin. 'Do we know?'

Like Noah, Marnie was waiting for Ferguson's verdict. Because of what was at stake, and because they couldn't afford to get this wrong. Nevertheless, her instinct was screaming at her to say it. Give a name to what she was thinking, a name to the man in the film.

Colin said, 'No clues from the IP address. I've cleaned it as best I can. They used a face-off editing function, and not very well. I was able to slow it down, isolate some of the frames where the blurring missed its target. You can see a bit more of him that way.'

He opened a fresh window on his desktop, showing an image of the man's face with the blurring restricted to the centre, leaving his neck and jawline visible.

'Acne on his neck,' Julie had said, 'little twat.'

There – below his left ear, an angry red boil.

'I know who it is,' Marnie said.

She stepped back from the desk, aware of Noah's eyes on her. Ferguson swivelled in the chair, to stare at the pair of them.

'He's the one who showed me Vokey's cell,' Marnie said. 'He was edgy when I asked too many questions about the fan mail. He didn't like talking about the letters, or the photos. That's him.'

She pointed at the face frozen onscreen. 'It's Darren Quayle.'

17

I'm thinking about Dazza today. High and dry in my hospital bed, my lucky nurse off on her rounds. Dazza hates his mum, that's what he told me. 'You've no idea, Ted.' She's a bully, always telling him what's best for him, laying down the law until he feels like a little kid at home. That's why he fell so hard for Mickey, I reckon, because Mickey made him feel powerful. But here's the funny thing. Mickey was bullied by *his* mum. She made him feel less of a man, just like Dazza. Not that either one of them would ever admit to that. Families, eh?

'Nice cacti.'

'Thanks, I like them.'

'They don't need a lot of sun?'

'They'd like more. I take them outside when I can.'

'And is that a bonsai?'

'Mmm. You're new.'

'I'm Darren. Daz. Dazza. You're Ted, right?'

This was his first day at Cloverton. Officer Quayle. He strolls in smelling of Lynx Africa, which is a nice touch given the jungle he's found himself in. Either he sprayed a bit too much of it, or he's sweating the stuff back to

142

life. He looks like a rich boy who signed up for a safari only to find himself kidnapped by pirates and forced to beg for his own ransom. His face is twitching all over the shop, Adam's apple stewing in his throat. Darren. Daz. Dazza. He's been told to make friends and I can see what joy he's had with that, higher up the corridor. It makes me want to give him an easy time of it, show him we're not all animals in here.

'We've an allotment.' He's watching me work the ligustrum. 'Mum's growing lilies.'

'What kind?' I ask.

'Orange ones? And white, of course. Sorry, I don't know the names.' He shuffles his feet, worrying that he sounds like a posh tit, because who grows lilies in an allotment? 'She's doing veg too, of course. She's trying for courgettes just now.'

'I can't stand courgettes.'

His face tweaks into a grin. 'Me neither.'

After that he's in my cell most days, chatting about his mum's allotment and my cacti. I give him advice on soil types, and answer his mum's questions, make myself helpful. We're getting on a storm until Mickey moves in. By then I know everything about Dazza, where he went to school, the name of his first girlfriend, how much he hates his mum. He talks about her all the time. She's protective of Dazza despite all his faults, which she names on a regular basis but also indulges and encourages. I'm sick to death of his mum, if I'm honest. It doesn't surprise me she's growing lilies on an allotment. I'm only surprised he hasn't buried her under them.

'*Lilium bulbiferum*,' he tells me on his fourth day. 'That's the name of the orange lilies. I asked Mum and she told me. She's pleased I'm taking an interest.'

I give him more gardening tips to pass on, pest control,

all of that. He's grateful, wants to be in her good books, says he's always struggled to be in her good books.

'The lily bulbs are edible,' I tell him.

'Seriously? Wow.'

Mickey makes a move on Dazza right away. Not because he wants to show him we're not all animals in here. Because he sees Dazza the way he sees his women, empty, waiting to be filled. I'm invisible after that. Worse, since Mickey encourages him to bully me, about the cabinets and whatnot. Mickey wants to get rid of my bonsai because she stinks and she's stealing his oxygen. He can't sleep at night, he says. Dazza jumps to it, all of it. I can see why he lives with his mum despite the way she bullies him. Like Lara and Ruth, he's begging for it. I start to despise him after a bit.

'You're wrong, by the way. Those bulbs aren't edible. My mum says.'

'Well, she's mistaken.'

'Mickey knows, don't you, mate?'

'You don't eat bulbs,' Mickey goes. 'That'd be like eating batteries.'

'You're both mistaken. The bulbs of the *lilium bulbiferum* are edible. Sweet and mealy—'

'Fuck off, Elms,' Dazza sneers.

He's been told to make friends. I can forgive him for sucking up to his new mate. And in a way it's good he's taking the time to make Mickey happy, because he sees what sort of trouble an unhappy Mickey might be. I don't want that sort of trouble, as I'm the one sleeping in the same space. Dazza gets to clock off and go home to his other bully, the one who cooks his meals and washes his socks and lies to him about the edible bulbs of the *lilium bulbiferum*. At least Dazza clears off. Mickey just takes up space. He's the one stealing all the oxygen, poisoning the air.

144

There's nothing like that here in hospital with my lucky nurse. She makes sure my lungs keep working, no labouring required. She washes and feeds me, and whispers while she does it, calls me 'love' and docsn't judge what I've done to deserve the dog-chain or the bed baths. I wish there was someone like her to look after my plants, that it wasn't all burnt to the ground, sticky with smoke. Cacti can't grow without sun, not the best ones. My horse crippler was always going to die, I accept that. He used to say he'd bring me a grow light. Darren, Daz, Dazza. He promised all sorts of things, little perks and privileges, before Mickey came along. After that he started saying the spines looked dangerous, might be considered a weapon. Oh, you think?

Imagine how it feels to swallow spines. Worse than batteries, I bet. Lodging in the soft roof of your mouth and the wet red of your gullet, sticking in your gums. Imagine someone holding your head back by the ponytail – handy of you to have that, Mickey, thanks – and feeding you the whole thing, the full way down. A courgette made into a mace, studded all over with hard pins. You can't grow that on an allotment. But you can bury it, with the rest of him. You can bury it in soil enriched by leaf mould until only his head's showing, its mouth sewn shut with spines, running red into the soil, helping the lilies grow.

18

'Darren Quayle called in sick the day after you spoke with him at Cloverton,' Ferguson said. 'He's not been into work since. Either you have a funny effect on men, DI Rome, or he's an oily customer with something to hide.'

'Where'd you want to start?' Ron asked. 'Hero worship, illegal interviews online, bunking off. For all we know *he's* the one hiding Vokey. He's clearly got a hard-on for the psycho.'

'He lives with his mum,' Debbie said. 'Anita Quayle. They've a house in Harpenden. No Dad, just Darren and Mum.'

'Lots of room for the psycho then.'

'Yes, thank you, DS Carling.' Ferguson eyed the team. 'Who wants to pay a visit to Officer Quayle to see if he's as sick as he claims to be?'

'That's us.' Ron nodded at Noah. 'You bring your psychology degree. I'll pack the straitjacket.'

Ferguson was watching Marnie. 'DI Rome, you're the one who had prior dealings with Darren. I suggest you and DS Jake hop on the North Circular.'

146

'Can't we arrest him for giving that interview?' Ron persisted.

'Oh yes, let's do that. Because I've not been humiliated by the CPS lately for attempting to raise a warrant without enough evidence to wipe my own arse on.' Ferguson drilled him with her stare. 'Pipe down and let's hear from someone who knows what sort of beggar we're up against.'

Ron subsided, shooting an eye roll in Noah's general direction.

'Darren was nervous at Cloverton,' Marnie said. 'Very different to the way he appears in the interview. The riot scared him. He was bitter about the police investigation and the lack of support inside the prison, worrying about another riot because of overcrowding, happy to voice his concerns. He only clammed up when I asked about the fan mail. It was clear he knew about Ruth and Lara, that he'd seen some of their letters, possibly the photos too.' She frowned. 'We could flatter his ego, the fact he knew Vokey better than most, the relationship he forged. He made great play of his training, how he gets close to the inmates to ensure their cooperation.'

'Close enough to help them escape?' Ron suggested. 'From the evidence online I reckon he'd crawl over broken glass for Vokey.'

'We should try for an informal interview,' Noah said, 'see if it's possible to call his bluff.'

'All right, let's do that.' Ferguson nodded. 'DC Pitcher, see if you can't make DS Carling's dreams come true by finding hard evidence that's Darren Quayle in that interview. DC Tanner, use your charms on the Cumbria lot. If they don't produce Lara Chorley by lunchtime, I'm heading up their way myself.'

*

The house in Harpenden faced a strip of village green which would have been picturesque but for the barricade of wheelie bins emitting a thick stink of heated plastic and methane. Anita Quayle and her son lived at the end of a thatched terrace in a brown brick house which an estate agent would've spun as 'rarely available and enviably positioned'. A narrow leg of garden had been planted with crazy paving, slimy from the morning's rain. It led to a white front door, security light to the left, burglar alarm to the right. Six leaded windows glazed by sunlight kept the house's secrets. The doorstep was chilly and exposed, traffic running behind them as Marnie and Noah waited for Darren's mother to let them in.

'Mrs Quayle? I'm DI Rome, this is DS Jake.'

'Metropolitan Police?' She pulled yellow rubber gloves from her hands, narrowing her eyes at Marnie's badge. In her late fifties, ferociously thin and plain but with a striking and unsettling face; a late Garbo given the Edward Ruscha treatment, trashed with gunpowder and graphite.

'We're hoping to speak with Darren,' Marnie said. 'We understand he's off work.'

'Yes, he's not at all well.' Olive eyes travelled past Marnie to Noah. She held the rubber gloves in her right hand, brushing soap suds from her dress with her left. A black linen shirt dress, its sleeves rolled up, accentuating her narrowness. When she lifted the back of her hand to her cheek, the bones in her wrist showed like an expensive bracelet. 'Has something happened at the prison?'

'Nothing new,' Marnie said. 'Is Darren home?'

'He's sleeping. If nothing's happened, why are you here?' She asked it as a question but clearly didn't expect an answer, adding crisply, 'You'll want to come inside.'

They were shown to a shallow sitting room with a lemon carpet, an old gas fire mounted above a bricked hearth.

Vertical blinds had been pulled shut at the window, their papery slats leaking light. Botanical prints in pallid water-colours looked lost on the walls. The only beautiful thing in the room was a blue vase of white lilies. Not the stiff variety sold in florists, these were open-hearted, deep-throated lilies, pollen like fire inside their petals. Of the little furniture in the room, an odd assortment of chairs stood as if guests were expected but unwelcome, while a low sideboard held a dozen poorly framed photographs which might have been auctioned as a job lot from a film set. Noah recognised Darren in his prison officer's uniform, fringe slicked up, levelling a smile at the camera. Other photos showed him as a chubby ten-year-old in a new school blazer standing with his mum, and as a baby in the arms of a boy with cut-glass cheekbones and a freckled nose, too young to be his dad. Black and white photos of grandparents. A girl in a 1950s sundress, smiling across her shoulder, brown hair swinging in a ponytail. Anita, Noah realised with a shock. It was hard to imagine she'd ever been this girl. She stood by the window, its vertical blinds backlighting her face with its incisive cheekbones.

'Beautiful lilies,' Noah said.

'Thank you, I grow them myself.' Pride put a crack in her defences, flushing her face.

'You must have a lovely garden.' Not the crazy paving at the front.

'I've an allotment. The gardens here are tiny. There's practically nothing at the back, and you've seen the front.' Her accent was moneyed but not flashy and not London. Old money. Less of it now than there once was; her Max Mara dress had been taken in at the waist, darned at the hem. The sitting room told the same story, its carpet indented in all the places where the best furniture had once stood. 'Should I wake Darren? I expect this is important.'

Marnie nodded. 'Yes, please.'

'Take a seat. I'll be right back.' She moved like a gymnast or a dancer, all sinew and muscle. Her legs were bare, her narrow feet in black felt slippers. They heard her going up the stairs into a room directly overhead. The click of a door shutting, then silence.

Noah looked again at the photo of the girl with the pony-tail, her smile provocative across her shoulder. The shadow of a car went past, circling the village green. The house was well insulated, muting the traffic to a murmur. Dust had settled in the indents on the carpet, the good furniture long gone, like the happy girl in the sundress. Footsteps down the stairs—

Anita reappeared. 'He's getting dressed. I'll make coffee, shall I?'

Marnie said, 'There's no need.'

'I'll make coffee.' She gave a firm nod and moved away.

Under the scent of lilies, Noah tried to pin down the dark smell in the room, not unpleasant, like spores raised by rainfall. This room was kept for guests, it gave no clues as to the character or style of Anita's home. A waiting room. Noah wanted to see the rest of the house. Marnie was looking at the photographs. Did she feel the strange pull of the place, the emptiness of this room, the packed silence from overhead? A big house, four bedrooms, it was worth a million even with the crazy paving, but it felt emptier and uglier than Julie's council house.

Footfall creaked the stairs.

The sitting room door pushed open.

Darren Quayle was red-cheeked from sleep, scraping his hair from his forehead with his fingers, dressed in dirty blue board shorts and an orange T-shirt with a surf logo. He blinked at Noah before his stare slid to Marnie. His fringe stayed where he'd scraped it in a waxy peak above his pale

150

forehead. He didn't resemble the man in the interview with the cocked shoulders and the heated speech about Michael Vokey's power. He looked like a lanky teenager late for school, bruises on his shins, bare feet. He smelt like a teenager too, stale and mushroomy. His toenails needed cutting.

'Hello, Darren.' Marnie nodded at him.

'I was sleeping,' blurring his words, 'I'm not well. Signed off sick.'

'How are you feeling?' Marnie asked.

He rubbed the heel of a hand at his eyes and yawned widely. 'Knackered.'

On balance, Noah preferred his acting in the interview.

'Sit down.' His mother returned with a tray of mugs and a pot of coffee. She nodded Darren at one of the stiff-backed chairs and he sat, giving no sign he resented her instruction or the signal it sent to the strangers in the room. He just did as he was told. Had it been like that with Vokey?

Marnie let Anita share out the coffee before she said, 'Thank you, we won't keep Darren long.' Her smile was a dismissal, polite but unequivocal.

Twin spots of colour came up on Anita's face, as if she'd pressed her thumbs to her cheeks, but her expression didn't falter. 'This is about his work, I suppose.'

'Yes. We won't keep him long.'

'He has a chest infection. He shouldn't be out of bed.'

'We won't keep him,' Marnie repeated.

Darren arched a foot, leaning back in the chair, aiming at nonchalance, landing on apprehension.

His mother made a conscious bid to relax her shoulders. Noah saw her practising yoga, disciplining her body to unwind. 'I'll be in the kitchen.' She nodded. 'If you need me.' A last glance at her son's bare feet and board shorts, before she retreated.

Marnie said, 'This is DS Jake. I'm DI Rome.'

151

'Yeah, I remember.' He reached for a mug of coffee. 'What's this about?'

'As you know, we're looking for Michael Vokey.'

'Well, yeah.' He turned the smirk into sucking coffee from his bottom lip, rebooting his expression to bland. No likeness to his mother, either in his appearance or his tone, aping a South London street voice. On his way to becoming the man in the online interview.

'We spoke with Julie Seton, the young mother he assaulted.'

'Not much of an assault.'

Noah leaned forward. 'What?'

Darren reassessed him, holding the mug to his chest. 'You should see some of the stuff that goes down, that's all I'm saying.'

'Eyeballs in the corridor?' Noah nodded, inviting Darren to mirror his loose body language. 'He was inside her house. Her little girl was sleeping upstairs.'

'Okay.' He sucked at the coffee, keeping his eyes down, quickly submissive.

Noah stayed sitting forward. He could smell Darren's skin properly now. Lynx Africa, lighter fluid and ashes. He'd been setting fire to something.

'Julie drew our attention to an interview, online.' Marnie kept her voice light, but she was watching Darren for a reaction. 'About what happened at Cloverton.'

'Yeah?' He reached to set the coffee mug down in the hearth, keeping his eyes hidden for the time this took. When he straightened, he was flushed. It could have been the blood running to his face, or whatever illness was keeping him at home.

'The thing is,' Noah said, 'we've watched the interview. Our tech expert's worked on it. Cleaned it up so we can identify the officer.'

'Yeah?' He put his hands in his lap, took them out again, propped his elbows on the arms of the chair. 'Who says it's an officer?'

He wasn't going to scare easily, but he had a habit of doing as he was told. Possibly it accounted for his career choice. Prison officer came with a set of instructions, rules to abide by. You could only break the rules if you'd been playing by them in the first place.

'We told your mum this wouldn't take long,' Noah said. 'Shall we cut to the chase?'

Darren moved, not quite a squirm, wetting his top lip with his tongue. His eyes jumped to Marnie then fixed back on Noah. 'Go on, then.'

Daring Noah to say it, so he could come out with whatever alibi he'd prepared. He'd had nearly a fortnight to dream up a convincing pack of lies. The boil on his neck looked close to eruption, a yellow pupil in a red eye. What would it take to get him excited the way he'd been in the interview? Running his mouth in admiration for a man with so few redeeming qualities you could count them in negative numbers.

'We reckon Vokey's with a woman.' Noah kept the careless edge in his voice, addressing Darren lad-to-lad. 'Lara Chorley. She was writing to him. D'you see any of her letters?'

'Your boss mentioned them.' Nodding towards Marnie, but keeping his stare on Noah.

'Letters and photos.' Noah put the span of his hand across his mouth, nursing the ache in his cheekbones for a second. 'She gave him her address. And of course he knows where Julie lives, but we've got eyes on that. Any thoughts as to where he might've gone?'

'Sorry, mate.' Darren cocked his head, shoulders sharpening. Now he looked like the man in the interview.

'Except it's meant to be *our* fault he's out there, running around—' He stopped, blinking. Realising he'd used the same words he used in the online interview?

'Like a maniac.' Noah nodded. 'A proper maniac.'

Darren reached for his coffee. 'If you say so.'

'Oh, he's it. The real thing. You waded through that corridor, saw your mates picking up the pieces of Tommy Walton. *Those* are the headlines they should be writing.'

Darren stared at Noah, saying nothing. The skin under his eyes was feverish now, his pupils like pin heads. For the first time, Noah wondered if he was genuinely sick.

'They're making out he's an animal, but they're wrong. You know, you saw him up close.' His voice dropped an octave, as Darren's had dropped at this stage of his recital. 'The rest aren't in the same league.'

Traffic ran its shadows across Quayle's face. His feet fidgeted at the floor.

Noah said, 'I'll be honest with you, Darren. We've got *nothing*. He's gone. A ghost.' He held up his hands, fingers splayed and empty. 'We're looking for a ghost. And we need your help.'

It worked, miraculously. Speaking about Vokey, using his own words back to him. Darren was hypnotised, following every utterance with his body swaying in time to the speech. He reminded Noah of Ruth. Blind thrall, joyous obedience. What was it about Michael Vokey? Nothing Noah had read or heard hinted at charisma. But first Ruth and now Darren clearly saw him as a cult leader, albeit one whose worshippers lived apart. Had they been forced to share the same physical space as Vokey the illusion would have shattered, perhaps. Distance lent a mythic gloss to his cruder qualities, allowing them to squint at an imagined horizon where their shabby hero strode like a god. Darren had less excuse than Ruth for falling under

154

the spell, being in charge of Vokey's routine, one of those responsible for locking him in and keeping him fed, settling on an appropriate level of privileges or punishment. Under that regime, Darren was the one in control. When did he decide to cede that authority? Or had it been an unconscious decision, Vokey working on him over time, chipping away at the edges of his immaturity, massaging his need for instruction? It was clear Anita ran this household, telling her son what to do, expecting and getting his obedience. Darren liked to be led. Vokey would've known exactly how far to push that preference. The scent of lilies lit the dark corners of the room.

'What were you burning?' Noah asked.

Darren recoiled, not expecting the switch of tack.

'You stink of lighter fluid.' Noah nodded at him. 'And burnt paper.'

'My clothes.' He sniffed at the sleeve of his T-shirt. 'I wore it to a bonfire party.'

'November was six months ago.'

'This was a mate's party up on the allotment—' He braked hard enough to get whiplash. 'Just a few beers, fireworks. You know. Nothing special.'

'So what were you burning on the bonfire?'

'The usual.' He drank a mouthful of coffee, gagged, wiped his mouth. 'Branches, leaves.'

Noah shook his head. 'Nah, this's paper. I can smell it. I've got a good nose for stuff like this.'

'He's right,' Marnie said quietly. 'It's one of the things that makes him such a great detective.'

Darren's eyes scared to her then away, across the room. His forehead was patchy with sweat, the fever spreading to his cheeks. Had he taken something, stronger than Lemsip?

'You see,' Noah said, 'we should've cut to the chase. You gave that interview online, our tech expert ID'd you. We

155

know you're a fan of Vokey's. Photos and letters went missing from his cell, we know that too. And here you are stinking of burnt paper and lighter fluid, and I'm wondering what we'll find if we go up to your room.' He nodded above their heads. 'Or through your bins.' He nodded in the direction Anita had taken, towards the kitchen.

Darren shifted, the chair creaking under him, his toes fisting on the floor.

A movement in the doorway brought Marnie smoothly to her feet. 'Mrs Quayle, may I have a moment?' Heading her off at the pass.

Anita glanced at her son, but Darren kept his eyes on Noah. She nodded at Marnie. 'Of course.'

Noah waited until they'd left the room before he said, 'She doesn't know, does she? Your mum. She doesn't know about the interview, or Vokey.'

'She knows he escaped.' Darren wet his lips again.

'Right. She watches the news.'

'Listens to it. Radio Four.' He scratched the boil on his neck. 'This's bollocks, by the way.' He examined his fingers before looking up, eyes spacey. 'I'm sick, feel like I'm going to puke. Are you arresting me?'

'Not in front of your mum,' Noah said. 'We're on the same side. Aren't we?'

'Not now.' Darren blinked, slurring his words. His stare moved around the room, seeing furniture that was no longer there, the pattern of dust-filled dents on the carpet. 'Not after Mickey.'

19

Let's talk about riots. Since I'm stuck here in hospital with nothing better to do, my lucky nurse on her tea break. Not the riot in Cloverton which is fresh in our minds, so fresh it's oozing. Let's talk about Leeds, Mickey's previous residence, the reason he ended up with us, with me. This's what he does, you see. Creates chaos and moves on. Like goutweed or ivy, the way he takes root so fast, smothering everything in his way. That's how it felt to live in that box with him. Ivy doesn't just block out the light. It invades the cracks in brickwork and joints, digging with its roots to cause permanent damage. English ivy, *Hedera helix*, is aggressive enough to bring down gutters and walls, if you're not careful. Dazza wasn't careful, and nor was anyone else at Cloverton. In Leeds he wrought havoc enough to warrant high security, assuming there's any room left in those places for men like that.

'I'm an artist.' He never used those words, but it's how he saw himself.

The corridor in Cloverton wasn't his first exhibition, just his latest. An exciting new direction with splashes of colour, chunks of texture. Teeth. He started small, like every other struggling artist. Smutty pictures for his friends in school, conceptual nudes of the girls they fancied. Jo Gower, one of his sister's friends. He drew her with her top up, knickers down. She wasn't very happy when she heard. Took it out on his sister, he said. Hate mail, until Alyson nearly lost her mind. He didn't own up, the way he ought to have done, and he felt bad about it, at least that's what he said. Of course he regretted sharing that particular confidence, made me swear to keep it to myself, threatened me with violence if I failed. That's what he's like, you see. Bottling it up until he bursts then full of regret afterwards, wanting the snake back in the can.

He'd drawn Jo from his imagination, but it turns out imagination doesn't do it for Mickey. He prefers to draw from life. Doesn't care for nudes, or not smutty ones. He likes to see you naked, but he isn't interested in the erotic, not like that. He'd sooner strip your mask than your clothes. If you're proud, he wants to see what you'd look like humbled. If you're brave, he wants to see you cry. It's why he did what he did to me, in that cell. Why he did what he did in Leeds.

'They called it a quick death,' Mickey says, swinging his foot in my bunk.

I'm trying to read, making poetry from the pages in my seed catalogue: Calendula Snow Princess and Gaillardia Firewheels to Scabious Black Knight.

'Painless,' Mickey says. 'They gave me a counsellor and that's what she called it, a quick and painless death. He wouldn't have felt much. Your thoughts get scrambled, that's what she said. It's over really quickly.' He wets the end of the charcoal with his tongue. 'It didn't look quick to me. Or painless. His face was set solid. One of his eyes was open.' I hear him drawing on the pad. 'Looking at me. He had a hard-on.' He passes over this detail, bored

158

by it. 'It's about blood, the places it goes inside you. His face was the thing. Set solid, black lips.'

I'm trying to see the garden, Mum's garden. The borders will need replanting by now. I want to fill her beds with colour, or perhaps the frothy white lace of *Orlaya grandiflora* which loves the sun, and flowers until the first frost lays its bitterness over everything.

'They call it blue, but it's black. He looked nothing like he did before. I thought he'd look the same only worse, but he was a whole different person. A stranger. That was interesting.'

He'd told me about this boy before. I call him a boy, but he was pushing thirty. It's the way Mickey describes him that makes me see a kid, someone who should never have been locked up with a man like Mickey. Soft, from the sound of him. He was learning Spanish, getting set for a fresh start, keeping his head down and doing all the right things but it didn't make a blind bit of difference because they gave him to Mickey, who couldn't even be bothered to learn his name.

'It's to do with where he tied the knot, that's what kept his eye open.' He shows me the sketch he's drawn of this boy who hanged himself after six weeks in the same cell.

I'm not surprised by the hanging but the picture is surprising, full of pity, wrenching at me. That one open eye so bewildered, his mouth dragged sideways, sloppy with pain. It makes me pull at my fingers until the joints crack. Yet there's no pity in Mickey. How does he do that, stay so empty when his drawings are so *full*? Seeing everything. Feeling nothing.

He studies the sketch as if he's reading a menu of things he doesn't want to eat, then crumples it and throws it at the bin. Lies back on my bunk, full stretch. 'Read me one of Ruth's letters.'

I'm past the point of arguing with him. The letters are in a brown envelope, like porn. I set the seed catalogue aside and leaf through the latest batch from Lara, for a letter from Ruth. She's written out a Bible quote at the top, but I ignore that. Mickey hates the cant.

'"I've taken to collecting sheet music,"' I read. 'Anything and everything, it's a cheap hobby. I haunt charity shops and car boot sales. So far I've filled three boxes with scores and nursery rhymes, pop songs and violin solos. Would it surprise you to hear I'm tone deaf? I can't read music any more than I can play it. That makes me sad, I'd like to be musical. You're so artistic! I'd like us to have that in common. Not that I could ever produce anything as beautiful as your art.'

I'm sick of Ruth. She's such a liar, and so patronising, pretending to lower herself to his level. I'd like to lower her. Into the ground.

'I cannot carry a tune,' I read, 'no matter how I try. And I do try! Not operas, I wouldn't dare, not until I have you to go with anyway. Just little jingles on the radio, muzak in supermarkets when I'm queuing for a bag of oranges.'

Lime for Lara. Oranges for Ruth. She's so Biblical it makes my teeth itch.

'Music can be orange,' I read, 'or blue or green. It has a scent and a colour. You don't need your ears. Let it in through your other senses! See it. Taste it. Touch it.'

Mickey doesn't need this prompt. He's been touching it since I started reading.

'Your tune's the colour of pomegranates, dearest. A quick flavour, surrendered a single note at a time. It's in my fingertips. It fills my palms and dances under my skin. I carry you with me everywhere and it makes me lighter, and it makes me less.'

160

I stumble over the last line, because this is the first time she's been honest. All these letters and this is the first time I've believed her.

'It makes me *less*.' I see her in my mind's eye, punched full of holes like a breaker where the tide comes in, water worming, wearing away the stone. She looks solid but she's riddled with holes, narrow passages where Mickey moved in. 'So until I can sit with you, I sit with my boxes of sheet music and search for you there, for the sound and smell and taste of you. I believe that if I piece together enough sheets, the right sheets, I'll be able to make a whole. Because I *believe* in *you*, dearest. Just as He does. Because music lifts us up, takes us far beyond ourselves. Sets us free.'

You're not free, Ruth. You're in a prison of your own making, wooing your gaoler.

'Your edges,' I turn the page, 'your edges are in the clefs and empty eyes of notes. I have searched, and I have found you there.'

I fold the page with the hot press of tears in my eyes.

Oh Ruth, you mad, miserable cow. You've made me cry.

Her poetry's wasted on Mickey. She's opening her heart to a brute, a minotaur. It's all wasted. The ache in her words is the ringing of a lead tongue in a ruined bell.

He grunts, and finishes.

A balled tissue's thrown towards the bin, landing alongside the crumpled sketch of the boy from Leeds who hanged himself rather than spend another night like this—

With Mickey scooping the poetry from everything, scraping it all back to hollow bone.

161

20

Anita Quayle knew her son was weak. Marnie sensed it must have troubled her when Darren chose to join the prison service, which was no job for anyone with insecurities or hoping to prove himself. Too easy to see how Darren had fallen under Michael Vokey's spell. Marnie had witnessed the same brand of slavery many times over, in homes as well as prisons. She saw it in the servility shown to Aidan Duffy by his cohorts. When it wasn't fetishistic it was corrosive, eroding one's sense of self. Some people welcomed that erosion, of course. In the case of Darren, she didn't believe it was a conscious act of self-effacement. He'd bound himself to Michael in the belief such slavery would lead to greater things – elevated status, respect – that he would become *more*, not less.

'We're concerned Darren may have recorded an interview online,' Marnie said. 'About the inmate who escaped from Cloverton last week.'

Anita's face flinched into a frown. 'Why would he do that? What sort of interview?'

'About the riot, conditions at the prison.'

'They're appalling.' She moved one hand in an abrupt

gesture of condemnation. 'Up and down the country. Overcrowding, staff shortages, drugs. It's revolting, inhumane—' She edited herself, reaching to remove the dead petals from a plant on the windowsill.

They were standing outside the sitting room, in a hall where doors were closed in all directions. Marnie had expected to be taken to the kitchen. She hadn't wanted Darren clamming up when Noah looked to be on the verge of extracting a confession, or a confidence. Unresponsive to flattery, Darren was nevertheless responding to Noah's tougher tactic. Had Michael Vokey been as quick to recognise which buttons to press to get what he wanted from Anita's son?

It was cool in the hall, with the starchy scent of polish. Anita was listening to the murmur of voices from the other side of the door, Noah's and Darren's, her body angled in that direction.

'Is there somewhere we can sit?' Marnie asked her.

'To talk about Cloverton? What is it you imagine I know? You're accusing my son of – what, exactly? Telling the truth about the state of this country's prison service?' She twisted her head away, exhaustion softening the stiff line of her jaw. 'It's making him ill working in that place, it's driving him into the ground. Just the thought of what he sees and hears every day, I can't bear it.'

Marnie touched a hand to the woman's elbow, feeling the thrum of stress there. 'Can we sit somewhere? I want to help, if I can. I think Darren needs our help, and that you do too.'

Anita searched her face for a second, before she nodded. She turned her back, showing the creases in her linen dress and the frayed heels of her slippers, all the small signs of wear and tear. The nape of her neck was narrow, fragile bones just beneath the surface, the loose chignon of her

163

hair unravelling in pale, staticky strands. Marnie caught her scent, green and opaline, Je Reviens. A jolt of memory tightened her throat; she'd not smelt that scent in years.

Anita led her to the back of the house, opening a door into a space so different to the other it was hard to believe both rooms were in the same house. Light fell from a long, wide window onto a honeyed oak floor spread with silk rugs that shone with age and wear. A tapestry sofa stood facing an upright piano used as a shelf for vases of tightly cupped white roses. Elegant bookcases, shaded lamps, small tables cluttered with glass paperweights and enamel boxes – it was a beautiful room, so unexpected. No television, just books and well-chosen pieces of art. Sculpture and pottery, a pair of tiny luminous landscapes painted in oils.

'Darren doesn't use this room. No television, for one thing.' Anita was a different woman in here. Warmer, easier. She nodded at the sofa. 'You wanted to sit.' Seeing the surprise in Marnie's face, she added, 'I was an army wife. We were always moving. I learnt not to get too comfortable, or rather to ration my comforts. Living out of boxes has a strange effect on one.'

Rationing her comforts to this one room where her son's absence was guaranteed.

'Darren's father doesn't live here?'

'He died when Darren was nine.' She shook her head before Marnie could frame an apology or offer her con-dolences. 'While he was alive I told people I was an army widow, we saw so little of him, but of course that shorthand's open to misunderstanding now.' She smiled a full stop.

An absent father, a mother accustomed to packing up and moving on, to always being in control. Did that explain some of Darren's oddness? His attraction to danger perhaps, or his failure to consider the consequences of his actions. Marnie watched Anita lift a book from a lacquered shelf, a travel guide to Valencia. Anita opened it, extracting a slim postcard. The sunlight showed the card as a white rectangle, blank. 'Here.' She held it out.

Marnie took it from her hand, seeing an address printed in cramped letters, Chalk Farm Road, London NW1. She turned the postcard over, flinching at what she found: a grotesque monochrome print. No shape or form or perspective, just a series of serrated lines jagging and tearing across the card, scarring its surface. She had to concentrate to stop herself from dropping the postcard or passing it back to Anita, who was wiping her hands on the sleeves of her dress as if her fingers were gritty from handling it. Six inches by three shouldn't look so obscenely abusive.

'Where did you get this?' Marnie asked.

'Darren brought it back from the prison, a gift from the man who escaped.'

'From Michael Vokey?'

Anita nodded. 'It was part of an exhibition, he said, held a few years ago. They're exhibiting his work again now. Lots of people find merit in it, apparently.' Her tone was baked dry with an undercurrent of revulsion. 'Darren likes it. Admires it.'

Marnie checked the back of the postcard. 'NW1?'

'Camden.' Anita twisted her fingers into a fist. 'They didn't have any kind of permission as far as I could tell from what Darren said. No licence. That man told him they needed a place to show the real works of art, all the things turned down for legitimate exhibitions. My son was so excited about it.' She pressed her lips into a white line. 'It's not healthy. You're right, I'm worried about him. This obsession of his isn't right. It feels terribly wrong.'

Marnie studied the front of the postcard. 'Michael Vokey drew this?'

'Appalling, isn't it?' Anita reclaimed the card, slotting

it back into the pages of the travel guide. 'I thought you should see it given the manhunt that's underway. I don't understand why Darren isn't more afraid of that man being out there. He could be *anywhere*.' She straightened the shelf of books and turned to face Marnie, tidying the worry back beneath the surface.

Organising everything, putting it all back in place. One room kept for visitors, discouragingly bland, exposing nothing of what was truly inside. Had she tried and failed to perform the same trick with her son? Marnie thought of the young man she'd first met at Cloverton, shrugging off her questions, wearing a mask of indifference. No, not a mask, not quite. The indifference was Darren's native expression, adopted during a childhood of orderly disruption dictated by an absent father and a mother whose competence must on occasion have felt like coldness.

'Did Darren tell you anything else about Michael Vokey?'

'Nothing worth reporting,' Anita replied. 'Otherwise I'd have gone to the police before you came here.'

'But he told you he admires Michael. Was this before or after the events of last week?'

'Before.' She tried to smile the exhaustion from her face. 'He's been different since the riot. I suppose he saw the true extent of his hero's . . . talent.'

'He sees Michael as a hero?' Marnie was surprised to hear Anita use the word.

'He latched onto Michael in that way. It's not the first time it's happened, but it's the first time with a prisoner, especially one as dangerous – repugnant – as this.' Anita looked out of the window, her profile faltering in the light. 'At one time I blamed myself for not having a man about the place. A *good* man, I mean, someone he might learn from. He was always desperate to learn, attaching himself to friends' husbands, neighbours, even gardeners on the allotment. Always going for the least savoury ones, making bad choices. If I'd known how important it was for him to have a man around, I'd have tried harder. After his father died, I mean.' She picked a stray rose petal from the piano, pushing it into the pocket of her dress. 'This interview you're saying he gave, what was it like? Not the speech about overcrowding. The parts about *him*. Michael Vokey.' She said the name with disgust, and fear. She was afraid for her son. 'What was it like?'

'Exactly as you said,' Marnie told her. 'Unhealthy. An obsession.'

Anita dropped her eyes with a nod, accepting this. 'He used to collect little model cars, you know. Not new ones, they had to be old. We went to flea markets and boot sales. He devoted all his time to it, all our weekends at one point.' She kept her hand in the pocket of her dress, pressing the rose petal between her fingers until its apricot scent filled the room. 'He collected them the way other children collect seashells, or conkers.' Her forehead creased as if with pain. 'Except the cars weren't to be played with. He had shelves and shelves of them but not to play with, only to look at.'

Loss could compel a person to collect, but Marnie hesitated to put a dark meaning to Darren's collecting. The little cars may have felt like the only constants in a volatile childhood, an innocent pastime for a lonely little boy. Or a way to bond with his mother, sending the pair of them in search of his chosen treasure, all their weekends spent together.

'Mrs Quayle. Has your son been burning letters and photographs?'

Anita didn't hesitate: 'Yes.'

Marnie waited, hearing the low knocking of a carriage clock on the table at her side. It felt wrong to speak about

167

Vokey in here, as if she'd released a polecat into the elegant room.

'At least,' Anita said, 'he's been burning something. I didn't ask what it was. I'm too afraid to find out.' She took another rose petal from the piano, turning it between her fingers. 'I'm a coward.'

'I questioned him at the prison. About letters and photos missing from Michael's cell. Darren denied it, but if he's been burning evidence we need to know.'

'There's more.' Anita's shoulders shook. She turned her face towards the window. 'He was out all night, seven days ago. The night of the riot. He didn't come home until the morning, and he was soaking wet.' Her throat convulsed. 'He wouldn't tell me where he'd been, just walking, he said. It rained all night and he was walking in it to clear his head after the horror at the prison. But it was more than that.' She swallowed. 'He took food from the house, and money. I didn't mind about the taking, but I can't bear the thought it might have been for *him*.'

'For Michael Vokey.'

Anita nodded, holding her elbows in her hands, arms tight to her chest. 'I hope I'm wrong. I'd more or less convinced myself I was, until you came. But now you're saying he gave an interview, that letters are missing. And he was out that night, I know he was. All night.' Her voice shook with tears and anger. She wasn't simply afraid for her son, she was angry with him.

Another petal fell from the vase, a miniature tremor running the length of Anita's lovely room.

She turned her ruined face to Marnie. 'Take him away. Please. I know you need to do that, it's your job. And I can't have him here, I'm afraid of what I'll say to him.' She twisted the petal in her fingers. 'I don't know him any longer. I can't understand him. Michael Vokey is an animal,

168

the things he did—' Her face cracked with pain. 'If my son helped a man like that, I don't want him under my roof. I can't live like that, with him. *Please.* Take him away.'

A squad car came for Darren, and a forensic team for the house. Anita took the team to her son's bedroom, a big dark box of a room filled with other boxes, gaming consoles, a television and two laptops. Black sheets on the bed, like the sheet used as a backdrop for the online interview. Marnie briefed the investigators, but shook her head when Noah produced gloves for the pair of them. 'We need to get back to the station. He's had over a week to dispose of any evidence in here. Let the team do a sweep, but I'll be surprised if we find anything.'

Noah put the gloves back into his pocket. 'He wouldn't admit to much, after you left the room. Just that everything changed at Cloverton after Mickey came. He denies helping him to escape, denies burning anything that amounts to evidence. And he's running a temperature, says he's sick.'

'Let's see what he has to say under caution.'

Marnie looked for Anita, finding her in the ugly sitting room, clearing away the coffee cups.

'We'll need a statement from you, Mrs Quayle. Do you want to come with us now, to the station?'

'I'll drive.' She was hiding behind the politeness of an hour ago. 'You said it would be a good idea to bring a change of clothes for Darren.'

'Yes.' Marnie held out her hand. 'I'm sorry.'

Anita paused before putting her hand into Marnie's, her fingers stiff, the handshake as brief as she could make it. 'I understand, yes. I appreciate it.' She wasn't in shock, not yet. That would come later, when she was alone in the house.

169

'Is there someone who can be with you, later today?'

Anita shook her head but said, 'I'll call someone. Thank you.' She straightened, her eyes snagging on the chair where her son had sat in his dirty clothes. 'I'd like to stay here until the search is over. I'd rather be the one locking up the house, if that's all right.'

'Of course.' Marnie nodded. She'd asked the team upstairs to be careful with Darren's mother, to keep an eye on her and to treat her gently.

Anita lifted a hand to switch off the lights in the room. She hadn't mentioned a solicitor, for her son or herself. It was as if she'd been expecting this, even preparing for it. The empty waiting room, the black dress. As if she were already in mourning.

On the path outside the house, a white cat brought Marnie to a standstill. Half-feral, the cat's eyes were pink as a rat's, its spine arching as it hissed and spat.

'He looks friendly,' Noah said.

'She's scared.' Marnie stayed still as the cat slunk past, disappearing up the side of the house.

Noah brushed a spot of pollen from his cuff. 'The way Darren caught himself when he mentioned his mum's allotment? I think we need to take a good look there.'

'Oh yes,' Marnie agreed. 'With back-up, for preference.'

In the event that Darren had done more than burn letters and photographs. In the event he'd taken food and money from his mother's house on the night of the prison riot and brought it to the place where his hero was hiding, waiting for the right moment to make his next move.

21

My lucky nurse isn't working today. They've given me an African who moves around my bed like a bin man, hauling at the dirty sheets, hauling at me. A bitter stink rises and I gag as I realise I'm smelling myself. I want to be clean, to be washed clean. My hands are sticky, disgusting. Why isn't she here, sponging my feet and fingers? That's what she does, it's her job, and I need to be clean.

The machine echoes at my side. I'm sunk in self-pity, remembering how it was when I was with the person who loved me most in the world, tucking me into bed when I was tiny, teaching me the difference between leaf mould and compost. Mum could be difficult. Well, mums are, aren't they? You only have to think of all that fierceness – pride and pain and fear and sacrifice – from the moment they give birth until the day one of you dies. 'Nothing but worry,' she used to say about me, even when things were going right. There's joy, of course, but resentment too. And grieving, so much grieving for each small stage we pass through, 'No longer my baby, no longer my little man, all grown up now,' and that's not counting the times life shakes the order of it into pieces, turns it all inside out, the way it did with Mickey and his mum, the way it did with Mickey and me.

All those long nights I spent staring at the ceiling, afraid he'd wake and it would start over. The awful noise of him, the wreck of our unspoken war.

These nights are the worst, his scorched-earth smell, the hiss and flicker of the light under the door. The cell's dark ruined by the glare and beam from the metal cabinets and toilet, the sink.

Worse, the sudden whites of his eyes as he wakes.

I stiffen as the sound of him starts up. Groaning, sobbing, shouting. He shouts even after they told him to stop. He doesn't know how to stop, because he doesn't know he's doing it. When he's like this, he can shriek all night.

I used to think, 'This is what it's like to be a new mother.'

The noise pushes at my spine and the lids of my eyes, at my armpits and groin. I jump under the impact, each flinch involuntary, pulled like a burr from beneath my skin. My eyes start to stream, my ears scrambling distress signals to my brain – *Feed him! Feed him! Make him stop!* – he has my whole body under siege.

Just as suddenly he is quiet. Flopping down in the bunk, making wet movements with his mouth, wincing as if rawness is a wound that reaches all the way into his lungs. He's yelled himself hoarse, and it hurts.

Hush, I think. *Hush*. I'm limp with gratitude. *Hush. Hush.*

It's quiet now, we could hear a pin drop. We're holding our breath, me and Mickey. His heartbeat's so close it stumbles up into my chest and patters there. If I look down, I'll see him smiling. Asleep and smiling, like green grass pushing through the parched grey of pavement.

Silence is a golden field, a rippling sea of corn bending

in a fresh breeze, soaking up the clean sun. *I can breathe,*
I can breathe, I can breathe—

I am the pin we hear dropping, the first leaf from the
tree, turning over and over in fretful, ecstatic freefall.

22

Larchfield allotment wasn't large, but it backed onto dense woodland lying in a long knot beyond the straight lines of soil and sheds, tight with trees that shut out light and sound. Perfect cover for anyone wanting to arrive unnoticed after dark.

Marnie and Noah hung back for the armed response unit to complete its sweep. Anita's shed was one of a collection of old Anderson shelters with corrugated iron roofs, wooden doors painted in contrasting shades of blue. The allotment, like the woodland behind it and the golf course beyond that, was privately owned. Full of pretty wooden boxes for growing herbs, benches fashioned from painted pallets, shallow fire pits decorated with attractive pebble sculptures. Noah had expected vegetable plots, maybe the odd poly tunnel, but this was gardening as a delightful hobby rather than a hard necessity. A sharp breeze stabbed the small of his back as he waited with Marnie for the ARU to confirm whether Michael Vokey was inside Anita Quayle's Anderson shelter. Police dogs were in the woods with their handlers, the allotment sealed off for the search. At intervals, sound escaped from

174

the tangle of trees, a throb of birdsong, the beat of boots. A group of bystanders had taken up posts across the street, watching the ARU close in on the shelters.

Marnie said, 'If he's here then was it Lara who attacked Alyson?'

Noah studied her profile. It was unlike her to speculate at this stage of an investigation, as they were poised for a discovery. Vokey was in the shed, or he wasn't. Either way, it was significant.

'We've been asking why they needed him,' Marnie said. 'Ruth and Lara. Darren. Why they needed a man like that in their lives. But why did he need them? What was he obsessed with?'

Sunlight shone from the roofs of the houses, making the cars glitter. Noah could smell bitumen and the clean cotton of Marnie's shirt. 'Perhaps it's as simple as this.' He nodded in the direction of the shelter. 'He was using them, looking for a way out.'

'Perhaps.' She sounded unconvinced.

The woods stood silent, no barking from the dogs. A breeze bent the tops of the trees as if folding them shut, sealing the wood with silence, keeping its secrets. The dogs would pick up Vokey's scent if he was in there. The allotment reeked of creosote and compost, kelp and iron.

'She asked me to take him away.' Marnie shivered. 'Anita. She didn't want him in the house. She's scared of him, of her own son.'

'I can understand why she would be. The way he speaks about Vokey, the hero worship. That's unhealthy.' Noah turned up the collar of his coat. 'That sitting room, its emptiness. The whole house felt wrong.'

'It wasn't like that at the back,' Marnie said. 'She took me to a room with roses and books. Her room.' Her gaze travelled to the woods. 'It was beautiful.'

175

Noah was quiet, standing at her side, thinking of mothers and sons. His own mother, of course, but Marnie's too. And Stephen Keele's mother, whose neglect of her son had ultimately led to the murder of Marnie's parents. 'It's going to be hard for her. Even if we don't find—'

He broke off as the ARU leader came towards them, lifting a hand to signal the search was over.

'All clear. No one in any of the huts. But we need to widen the cordon.'

'What did you find?' Noah asked.

'Food and clothing. Someone was living here all right, and recently.' He glanced to where his team was at work then nodded at Marnie, lowering his voice. 'And a firearm – nine-millimetre Baikal.'

The handgun of choice for London's gangs. Russian, designed for gas cartridges, rebored for bullets. Trident took hundreds of these guns off the streets every year, a drop in the ocean.

'In Quayle's shed?' Marnie shielded her eyes to look at the Anderson shelter.

'Concealed, but yes.'

Converted handguns were found every week in the bedrooms of young men and women, in the glove boxes of taxis, in handbags and sports holdalls. How often were they recovered from private allotments next to golf clubs where membership cost you a small salary?

'When it's secure,' Marnie said, 'we'd like to send in Forensics.'

The officer nodded. 'You've got it.'

'How recently was he here?' Noah asked. 'Can you tell?'

'The food stinks so I'd say days rather than hours. Fire pit's been used as a toilet, but not recently. That's going to be a fun job for someone.'

'As soon as the hut's secure,' Marnie said tautly, 'we need to be in there.'

'We're sweeping for other weapons, but yep. You'll be the first to know.' He headed back to the huts, sun lifting in a yellow haze from the shoulders of his flak jacket.

The wind changed direction, pulling a red smell of rotting leaves from the allotment.

Noah said, 'If Vokey had a gun, why didn't he take it with him?'

'Perhaps it's Darren's gun.' Marnie tied her hair back, away from her face. 'His father was in the army, he died when Darren was nine. Anita implied an infatuation with danger, and father figures. Infatuation aside, if I were aiding and abetting a dangerous criminal I'd like to be armed.'

'Or there's another weapon, a worse one. And Vokey's taken that.'

'He didn't need a weapon in Cloverton. Look what he did without one.'

'He likes to get his hands dirty,' Noah conceded. 'God, what a mess.'

'It's worse than we thought.' Marnie nodded. 'But Darren will have to talk now. We can charge him, even if we don't find Vokey's DNA in here.' She reached for her phone. 'Let's update the team that's watching Julie. And we need eyes on Ruth and Lara, and Alyson.'

She looked across the allotment to where the trees were bending their branches over the corrugated iron shelters. 'DS Joe Coen needs to know that Michael Vokey might be armed and even more dangerous than we thought.'

23

My lucky nurse is back. She's giving me a shot, but it's not working. I want to scream at her to get it right. It's not human what they're putting me through. I'm like that kid in Leeds, slowly strangling, my face setting solid and black. I want it to be over. If this is my life then I want my quick, painless death. Dazza was always boasting about how he could lay his hands on a gun. If I'd been shot I wouldn't be shackled to this bed with everything turning inside out, leaking, stalling, belching blood. She barely speaks to me now, my nurse. She's sick of cleaning up after me. This morning she was interrupted halfway through washing my right hand and she left it, just left it and walked away. I'm a thing to her now, an endless inconvenience. I wish I'd been shot dead.

Guns get smuggled into prisons, that can hardly come as a shock. But only idiots go down that route. Aidan Duffy wouldn't touch it. He can get you all the fancy stuff you want, but guns aren't fancy. They're foul, and stupid. No one in his right mind would want anything to do with a weapon like that. Who wants to be found with a handgun? You can't exactly flush it away when you're finished. You're stuck with it and good luck when they come for spot checks, like trying to hide a cactus up your arse, to borrow a phrase from Tommy Walton. No one in his right mind touches a gun inside. Some of the younger lads might talk about it, making believe they're better off armed, afraid of what they call 'lacking' on the street, as if owning a gun makes you safe, as if no one ever shot himself by accident or regretted reaching for a trigger when a fist would've done the job.

The boy in Leeds who hanged himself, he was done for carrying a gun. Had it for protection, he said, because he was scared of gangs. Well, who isn't? He was afraid for his family, that's the story his defence spun, his mum and brother, and it may even have been the truth – who knows? Given how seriously he took his rehabilitation, until Mickey got to work. The batteries were nothing, I got off lightly. That kid was scared and depressed and Mickey toyed with him, seeing how far he could push it. With Mickey, everything's seeing how far he can push you, what new shapes he can make. He helped the kid knot the sheet into a rope but he was surprised all the same, when he woke to find his new puppet hanging by his neck a few feet away.

'It was a game.' That was the closest he came to a confession. 'Yeah, we made a rope together but it was a game. I dared him to do it because I knew he wouldn't. He was always talking about when he got out. I thought he was safe.' He thought he could play, that's what he meant, he thought he could play his game with the kid.

When he first told me about the hanging, he drew picture after picture. The boy's feet, his fists, the crooked angle of his head. Every picture ended up screwed into a ball, chucked at the bin. He's like a child who accidentally creates art when he's messing about, squashing paints in

179

a folded sheet of paper to make butterflies. There's no thought behind what he does. It's not art, it's mindless.

'Look at Julie.' Boasting of all the things he could have done, and would have done, if he'd had more time. 'That was a good game.'

He didn't rape her, or break her. He wanted her attention, that's all. Then when he got it he didn't know what to do. Same story with me. He pushed me around because that's what you do in places like Cloverton, mark your territory, lay out your battle lines. He likes to flex his muscle, but all he really wants to do is draw. That picture after the batteries— If he could've made me cry without touching me, he'd have loved that. Touching's too much like hard work and it doesn't come naturally to him, whatever Dazza wants to believe.

'There's no one like him. He's out of your league, Elms. Out of everyone's league.'

I couldn't persuade him otherwise. Couldn't make him see that Mickey's weak, and he's lazy. He has no patience. You'd think being an artist would have taught him patience, but he's all about instant gratification, like a little kid. 'You have to have patience,' I told Dazza.

I tried to tell him a story from when I was ten years old and waited hours for this robin I wanted as a pet. It was lonely, just me and Mum in that cottage in the middle of nowhere. I'd seen Mrs Biggs bring down a robin one morning when the sun was long in the trees and the robin couldn't stop singing, darting about, taking grubs from the beds where the soil was freshly turned. The cat put up her paw and brought him down. I shouted, 'Hey!' and she ran but the robin stayed on the ground, his little breast rising and falling in shock. I knelt at the edge of the flower bed and leaned close, 'You're okay now, it's okay.' His eye flashed black at me like a bead. Mrs Biggs was circling behind us, her tail switching at the grass. 'You're okay,' I reached for the robin, wanting to scoop him into the palm of my hand where I could keep him safe. He stabbed at me with his beak and I dropped him. I didn't mean to, but I did. In a flash, she had him. Jaw and claws. And that was that. But for a whole morning the following day I sat with a tea towel spread with breadcrumbs, its hem in my frozen fingers, keeping still as a statue waiting for another bird to land. I'd save this one, I thought, keep him safe from that old bitch, Mrs Biggs. The birds didn't land, of course, they were far too clever and cautious for that. I crouched until cramp got the better of me. But I didn't give up, not until it started to rain and the birds retreated to the trees.

Mickey could never have done that. He doesn't know the meaning of patience, can't play the long game to save his life. If Dazza hadn't pitched in when he did, Mickey would be in Cloverton right now. We both would. He'd be drawing, I'd be reading Ruth's latest letter, looking at Lara's latest selfie. This was down to Dazza and his stupid strutting, his need to be seen. Boasting about the gun he had, and the hiding places, how he knew all the ways in and out of Cloverton, back and front, making Mickey's ears prick up.

This is on you, Dazza. If you hadn't walked in with your face shining like a choirboy on a bender, none of us would have ended up where we did.

24

'We've arrested Darren Quayle. Assisting a prisoner, permitting an escape, harbouring an escapee. That'll do for starters.' DCS Ferguson folded her arms at the evidence board. 'We're looking into what further offences we can chuck at him in the light of what we found in his mum's garden shed. DI Rome will bring us up to speed.'

'Forensics bagged everything in the shed,' Marnie told the team. 'Including samples for DNA testing, so we should know fairly soon whether Vokey was hiding there. We have clothes, food and bodily waste. An inventory's on the board.' She paused, needing their full attention. 'We found pictures of Lara and Ruth. And letters written to Vokey by both women. These are letters we've not seen before, so take a good look. And we found a handgun, wrapped in plastic, stashed in a watering can. No ammunition was found in the shed, or the house. The gun's serial number is in the system. When we processed him here at the station, we found matching firearms residue on Darren Quayle.'

'He has a story to account for that,' Ron put in. 'He'd been firing at squirrels in the woods after the bonfire party. He was pissed and things got a bit daft. His words. Duty solicitor's frothing at the teeth about cross contamination, whether he was in a car used by firearms officers, if the prison has access to weapons which might accidentally have brushed up against his innocent little fingers as he was making sure all of Cloverton's doors and windows were safely locked tight.'

The usual objections, in other words. Darren had cleared it all in a single bound by admitting to firing the gun at the party. He was denying it was his gun, however. Not his party, not his bonfire, not his gun. Nothing Darren did was his idea. He joined in, but he didn't ever initiate.

'DS Jake's leading on the interview.' Marnie nodded at Noah. 'First thing tomorrow morning, since Darren's solicitor is pleading sickness on the part of his client.'

'*Is* the little toerag sick?' Ferguson demanded.

'He's running a fever,' Noah said. 'The duty doctor wants a chest X-ray because he's had lung infections in the past. And he's stuffed full of medication so we need time for him to sober up.'

'DS Tanner, DS Carling, I'd like you to go through the inventory from the shed.' Marnie nodded at the board. 'We have jumpers, T-shirts, a pair of trainers, and food which Anita should be able to identify as having been taken from her house. Let's tick those off the list quickly. We have personal items, in particular a notebook with names of inmates Darren may have been blackmailing, but also batteries, a book of artwork and drawings of the cell Vokey shared with Ted Elms. And this.'

She extracted a sheet from her file and pinned it to the board. 'Vokey's work, we think.'

It was the sketch of a man's face, so furious it looked as if his skin might split open. A black scar for his mouth, lips drawn back so hard you saw the outline of his teeth.

183

Nostrils flared, eyes spitting rage, every individual eyelash quivering with it.

'We think it's Edward Elms.' Marnie pinned a mugshot alongside the sketch.

In the mugshot, Elms was unsmiling but not unfriendly. A fair-haired, blue-eyed man in his fifties with a high forehead, his expression benign, nothing like the man in the sketch. Only the depth of his forehead and the bluntness of his chin gave it away. At some point between being convicted of benefit fraud and becoming Michael Vokey's cellmate, something had happened to change Edward Elms, and not for the better.

'That's what shacking up with Vokey does to you.' Ron shook his head. 'Poor bastard.'

'Where did Darren get his hands on the gun?' Lorna Ferguson wanted to know. 'I think I'm right in saying Aidan Duffy is everyone's spiv of choice in Cloverton. Is his name in Darren's book?'

'Yes, it is.' Marnie nodded. 'We need to re-interview Aidan, and several others at the prison. If Darren assisted in this escape then it seems unlikely he was acting alone.'

'He was home on the night of the riot, wasn't he?' Ron frowned at the board. 'Then he gets called in to the prison. That's how his story goes. He kits up and wades in, finding all the mess Vokey made. That's before they know for certain Vokey's escaped.'

'The fire kept them busy for a long time,' Debbie agreed. 'And the smoke. They couldn't rule out the possibility that Vokey was gone over an hour before anyone realised it.'

Ferguson made a sound of derision. 'And yet somehow it's *our* fault he's out there.'

'We need to work the timeline,' Noah said. 'When did the fire start? When did the CCTV stop working in relation to Darren's presence on site?'

'Before or after the eyeballs began piling up in the corridor?' Ron snorted.

Marnie glanced his way. 'It isn't easy to feel sympathy for the men assaulted at Cloverton, I understand that. But this wasn't a victimless crime. None of the men he mutilated deserved it. They had a right to safety and protection, and they didn't get it.'

'We need to focus on finding Vokey,' Ferguson said. 'Before more people get hurt.'

'Innocent people,' Ron put in.

'Did you not hear what I just said?' Marnie fixed him with her steadiest stare. 'DS Carling? Did you not hear me?'

'Sorry.' Ron wiped sweat from his neck. 'I did hear you. Sorry, boss.'

She nodded, returning to the evidence board. 'These new letters found on the allotment. From Lara and Ruth, and from Michael back to them. We'll be asking Darren why he had these, whether he took the letters from the prison or if Michael gave them to him for safekeeping. Colin, what's happening with Lara?'

'Joe Coen's on his way over there. He knows about Darren and the Anderson shelter, but he also knows we haven't located Vokey yet. Oh, and Alyson's awake. Not fit for questions, but I stressed the need to interview her and Lara as soon as possible.'

'Let's do better than that.' Ferguson dusted her hands brusquely. 'DI Rome, let's you and I head up there. Since DS Jake's got the interview covered here, and given the content of these new letters we've found.' She handed round photocopied pages from the Anderson shelter. 'DC Tanner, perhaps you'd spare anyone else's blushes by being the one to read Lara's latest offering?'

The letter had been typed and printed over two pages.

'"Come and find me, darling. You know where to look. I'm wearing the red dress you like, no knickers since you asked so nicely."' Debbie frowned, but otherwise kept her face and voice neutral. 'I'm dreaming of it, darling, of pulling you into a bruising kiss, the dry heat of your skin, sucking wet heat of our mouths. We'll fit together perfectly I know, your body and mine like water finding its place, flowing into an empty hollow.' She turned the page. 'The sting of brick's what I want, cold and unyielding at my cheek. My body heat bleeding away until the blood begins its bumping, thumping me all over, your stare on me like the only steady thing in the world.'

Ron shuffled his feet on the floor. Colin was scarlet under his spectacles.

'Shall I—?' Debbie indicated the second page of the letter. 'That's probably enough, isn't it?'

'Oh, let's hear it all.' Ferguson folded her arms, pressing a smile from her lips.

'I'm clinging to the wall, bricks kissing like teeth, your mouth on my neck keeping me upright, your hand sliding hotly, long fingers teasing like steel under my dress. Anything, darling. Anything you want. I want it too. My cheek pressed to the stubble of the wall, the whole of me moulded in place by the hard heat of your body. If you weren't here to hold me the breeze would pick me off, turn me inside out, tatter me to shreds.'

Ferguson waited until Debbie put the pages down before she said, 'I don't know about you, DI Rome, but I can't wait to meet Lara Chorley.' She looked around the room. 'Chins off the floor, lads. Take a leaf out of DS Jake's book.' She nodded at Noah. 'He's not moved by any of it.'

'Not his cup of tea,' Ron muttered.

'Tea doesn't enter into it, DS Carling. Pot Noodle's the analogy you're groping for. Porn's just nasty dried ingredients until you add the hot water. Right.' She clapped her hands. 'We've a gun fired by a lad who's getting sweaty with his solicitor and coming down from his Night Nurse high. He's a fan of our escaped prisoner and everything points to him having given said prisoner a place to hide. Clothes, food, bodily waste. Let's get the DNA fast-tracked because I want to charge that toerag by teatime tomorrow. He knows where Vokey's gone and we need to get it out of him. Make sure you all get your beauty sleep tonight because it's going to be a long shift tomorrow. DI Rome, I'll see you in the car park in ten minutes.' She left the room, her heels barking at the floor.

Debbie fed the photocopied letter into the folder on the desk, setting it aside. A phone rang and she moved to answer it. Colin picked up a notebook and started studying the inventory from the allotment. Marnie touched a hand to his elbow. 'First thing tomorrow, can you take a proper look at the letters? Dates and chronology. Something's not right. I need your help making sense of it.'

'Will do, boss.'

'Who can tell me about the gun?' Marnie asked the others, keen to refocus their energies after Ferguson's fun with Lara's letter.

'That would be me.'

She turned to find DS Harry Kennedy in the doorway. The sight of him made Noah tense at her side, a muscle playing in his cheek. Expecting news of Sol?

'DC Pitcher sent me the serial number,' Harry said, 'after it threw a flag on the system. It's a match for a firearm used in a couple of recent robberies. Gang-related, so it landed on my desk.'

'Come in,' she told him. 'Meet the team. This is DS Kennedy from Trident.'

Harry exchanged nods with the rest of the room. He looked good, in a mid-grey suit over a white shirt, no tie. He moved as easily as she remembered, like a swimmer, showing no sign of the knife wound which had nearly killed him seven weeks ago. She wondered about his scars, remembering the hot pulse of his blood through her fingers as she'd fought to save him.

'Any idea how the handgun ended up in Darren's possession?' she asked.

'I wish I could tell you.' Harry ran a hand over his dark head. 'I wanted to show my face as I've been asked to coordinate from our side. Knowing how hard you're all looking for Michael Vokey and now this gun's turned up, I thought I'd pitch in, see if I could help.'

'Thanks. Noah's leading on the interview with Darren Quayle.'

Harry nodded at Noah, an apology in his blue eyes. 'I'm not going to tread on any toes, I promise. I've questions for Quayle, but mine can wait.'

'Easier if we compare notes.' Noah scratched his cheek, his voice light and friendly. 'Two sets of awkward questions might shake some answers out of him a bit faster. I'm happy for you to join the interview tomorrow, if DI Rome's okay with that?'

'Sounds good.' Marnie smiled at Noah. 'Keep me in the loop, but I should be back before you get started.' She picked up the folder of letters and photos. 'DS Kennedy, do you have a minute?'

'Sure.'

Harry went with her down to the car park. Marnie pulled on her coat, freeing the messenger bag at her shoulder. In the stairwell, she said, 'Sorry to be against the clock. How are you?'

'I'm good.' He moved loosely at her side, his shoulders sleek with muscle. 'What's up?'

'You're in touch with Noah's brother, Sol Jake.'

He hesitated and she shook her head. 'I'm not asking for details. I just need you to know how tough this is on Noah. He's hanging in there, but it isn't easy.'

'Of course. I'll be careful how I handle it.'

'Thanks.' Marnie checked her watch. Ten minutes, Ferguson had said. She stopped and faced Harry. 'And you're really better?'

'Any more time off and I'd be on a malingering charge. They signed me back to work, clean bill of health, just battle scars.' He smiled, seriously. 'I'm a mess with my shirt off, but I'm good.'

'I'm glad. It's good to see you.'

'You too.' His blue stare searched her face. 'You came to the hospital, I think? Everything's a bit trippy from back then.'

'I came to the hospital.' Marnie nodded.

It was strange to stand so close to him with the memory of his blood heating the palms of her hands. She'd been afraid he was dying, bleeding out, no sign of the paramedics. By the time they arrived, she was thirteen floors away, too far to see the struggle to keep him alive. Just the itch of his blood between her fingers and the fear he was dead, that she'd left him to die. That urgency had stayed with her. It had happened so fast, no time to sort her feelings into order, and she hadn't wanted to let it go, hadn't wanted the moment to pass unnoticed or unremarked.

'Good luck.' Harry held out his hand.

She took it. 'And you.' His fingers were lean and cool. 'I'll see you when I get back.'

'I'd like that.'

189

Her phone was fizzing at her hip: Lorna Ferguson, calling her to heel.

An escaped prisoner to find, an obsessed woman to interview. Letters and photos and sketches telling unpalatable truths about people who couldn't defend themselves. People like Ted Elms, wired to machinery in the room next to Stephen's where the ventilator moved his chest in a relentless parody of breathing.

'Take care, Harry.'

'You too. Travel safe.'

25

Noah pushed back his chair, rolling his shoulders to work the crick from his neck. He was paying the price for the dead air in the station, his day spent searching the room of photographs. It wouldn't matter so much if he'd learnt anything worth knowing.

'Come here,' Dan said. 'You look like someone threw you down a flight of stairs.'

'Not this week.' He dropped his head forward as Dan's fingers found the first of the knots in his neck. 'Okay, that's— *Right there.*'

'You're a hot mess.' The heel of Dan's hand pressed the pain towards the point of Noah's shoulder, slowly and with care. 'We need to get you in the pool.'

'Hmm. Or you could just do this twice a day until the end of time.' Slow heat was spreading up his spine, promising to dissolve every last ounce of discomfort. 'Damn, you're good.'

'I should be, the amount of time I spend around works of art.' Dan put his weight into what he was doing, chasing the ache from Noah's neck. 'Form and beauty. I know exactly what I'm doing.'

191

'Yes, there. *God.*' Endorphins made Noah sigh. He pushed back into Dan's touch, shutting his eyes, letting go of the day's stress. It was getting harder and harder to do that since Sol's arrest, like prising his fingers free from a high ledge. 'Don't stop.'

'No chance of that while you're wound this tight.' Dan smoothed the last of the pain into submission, working it to the inner edge of Noah's shoulder blade where it vanished in a warm pulse like a magic trick.

Noah twisted sideways in the chair. 'We really,' he pulled Dan's hands to his mouth, kissing his palms, 'need to get these insured.'

'You should hold out for some better reasons to say that.'

'I'm not going anywhere.'

After supper, Noah checked in with the custody sergeant at the station who told him Darren's X-rays were clear and Quayle was sleeping, should be fit for interview in the morning. Noah texted Harry to let him know, resisting the temptation to ask for news of Sol. There was nothing, he knew. Harry had promised he'd be the first to hear if fresh charges were brought against his brother.

While Dan put in an hour's work on the prisoner art, Noah studied the inventory from the allotment. By the time Dan joined him on the sofa, he was looking through Vokey's artwork for the sixth time. He'd stapled the photocopied pages into a book the same size and shape as the original: a pocket-sized sketchbook, each image drawn at the right-hand edge so that flicking through the pages conjured a narrative of sorts, disjointed and disturbing.

'Help me kick the tyres on this?' He offered the book to Dan, who took it, passing a bottle of Becks in return.

Noah drank the beer, watching Dan flick through the

pages, his expression wavering between admiration and repulsion. 'Shit . . .'

'Right?'

Dan turned another page, dipping his head at the sketch of a man's feet suspended, kicking at empty air. 'Whoever drew these, you have him in custody, right?'

'We *had* him in custody.'

'Shit,' Dan said again. 'Wait, this is Michael Vokey?'

He was studying the sketch of a kneeling figure, as intense and fiery as the *Break Out* painting that Noah had saved to his phone.

'It's Vokey, yes.'

Dan held the book more carefully, as if he'd been told it was a living thing. Noah shut his eyes for a second, wishing he hadn't put the pages into Dan's hands, wanting to take it back, rewind to the point where they were eating, smiling at one another across the table. He'd polluted their evening with this obsession. Not just Vokey's. His own. He couldn't stop looking, searching. He wasn't even sure he'd be able to stop after they'd found the man.

Vokey's obsession had a smell and a taste. It had colour and weight and depth, but when you stripped it right down it was a small thing and sour, fretted to nothing by Vokey's attention. Did he even call it art? If he did then he must think art was what happened up against brick walls in filthy side streets. Art was what rats did, and dogs in heat. Dan was studying the drawing of the bare feet kicking at empty air. HMP Leeds, where Michael Vokey had goaded a young man into suicide. How? What did he say or do to push the other man to that point? There was a high-pitched buzzing in Noah's skull at the thought of Vokey whispering long into the night, never letting up. Had he whispered to Ted, and to Darren? It added a new, sly dimension to the man they were hunting.

Dan turned the page to a sketch of Lara, her face and her hands filled with a sticky pain which Vokey might've called lust. He'd seen so much, and cared so little. Lara's face was a pale moon, her eyes a brown stain. He'd drawn her lying on a bed with a large handprint at the inside of one splayed thigh. All that hunger and humiliation, captured in a dozen lines of charcoal. It made Noah wonder what Marnie was finding at the cottage in Cumbria. Not Vokey himself, or she'd have called it in. But Lara had sent the photos from which Vokey had drawn these images. Noah didn't see how she could be happy, or well. Was she dangerous, or simply disturbed?

'No wonder you're not sleeping.' Dan turned the pages, his fair hair falling into his eyes until he scooped it away with one hand, the other holding the facsimile sketchpad.

Vokey's art had no shape. It was the opposite of shape, a series of craters, torturous. The welted paint at the foot of a cell door, a stained shower unit, cacti shaped like weapons. The sketchpad tricked you into staring, searching for clues. Dust clotting the wheels of a hospital gurney. A close-up of Ruth's face. Lara kneeling. A thing like worms writhing in soil. The hollow spaces in a man's skull as his face peeled away, the skin reluctant to leave, tongue taken by its root. A puppetry of light lifting from scalpels, leaving a halo of hair around the tattered margin of a scalp.

Noah wanted to shout. Not words, just noise. Life, protesting. The sound Julie would have made if she hadn't been so afraid for her daughter sleeping upstairs. Vokey's art wasn't just ugly, it was brutal, entering his head like a slow shove of steel, hurting his eyes and their sockets, bruising the roof of his mouth. The whole of him ached and felt bloody.

The flicker of the pages was like insects whirring.

The bitten palm of a hand, open. Too small to be Ruth's. Julie's perhaps. Laid aside, away from the rest of her body. Coaxing meaning from the images was like trying to grab the form of a pot from a fast-moving wheel of wet clay. It was like untangling a snarl of razor wire.

Noah leaned into Dan's side and listened, hearing his heartbeat under everything else, such a small sound. *Flak-flak-flak* as his brain puzzled over his pulse, trying to make sense of what it was hearing in the context of what it was seeing.

Dan drew a deep breath when he'd finished, putting the book away from them, reaching for his beer. 'Okay, so . . . Certain people collect artefacts with dark or violent associations because they're seen as charms against darkness and violence. Sections of the hangman's noose were sold to bystanders after public hangings to guard against meeting with the same fate, you know the sort of thing. That's what this feels like to me.'

Charms against darkness and violence.

'Talismans.' Dan balanced the beer bottle in the hollow of his hand. 'It feels superstitious. He's scared, that's what I'm getting from this.' He nodded down at the sketchbook.

'These women he drew,' Noah said. 'They're writing to him, demanding his attention. They don't see how little he thinks of them. It's as if he's cast a spell, and not just over them. Over prisoners, over a prison officer. One of the inmates committed suicide.'

The young man's bare feet, kicking.

'Lost people,' Dan murmured. 'Thinking he'd immortalise them?'

'Instead he did this.' Noah held the cool of the beer bottle to the side of his face. 'Reduced them to black scratches in a sketchpad. So much *contempt* for their dignity and privacy, everything that affirmed their lives.'

195

Michael Vokey had stolen from Julie and Natalie, taken family photos and pinned them to the wall in his dead mother's house. Like the burglar who'd targeted elderly people on another housing estate, robbing their precious memories of ever having been young or valued or loved, leaving behind only puzzlement and shame, indignity.

'He isn't happy,' Dan said. 'Not that I'm advocating sympathy, but this is someone who's feeling very lost. And scared. Are you getting that?' He nodded at the sketchpad. 'Fear?'

'I hadn't thought of it in those terms,' Noah admitted. He'd been preoccupied with Julie's fear, and his own at the thought of Vokey out there, free to do whatever he liked. 'Did you have any dealings with him, for the prisoner art project?'

Dan shook his head. 'I've seen *Break Out*, of course. But that's as close as I've come. Unless you count the catacombs.'

'Which catacombs?'

'Underground exhibition in Camden. Under the market, a couple of years ago. I'm pretty sure that's where I first saw his work. It's funny none of the press reports have mentioned his art.'

'Not really.' Noah swallowed a mouthful of beer. 'He's an escaped prisoner, and he's dangerous. He attacked a young mum in her own home. Why spoil that story by mentioning he has a talent for anything less violent?'

'Not that much less.' Dan nudged his toes at the sketchpad. 'I bet he's good at hiding.'

'Oh, he's good. And he's got help, at least that's what we think.' Noah rolled the cold bottle at his cheek, thinking of Sol who was also lost and good at hiding. Or he had been, until Noah put him in a place where hiding was impossible. 'He's obsessed, isn't he? That's

what these drawings look like to me. Obsessed with –
ownership?'

'Or oblivion. Art as an escape, his way of not having
to live with himself any longer.' Dan moved his hand to
Noah's neck, subduing the new stress which was building
there. 'You need to let it go,' he said softly.

'Vokey?'

'Sol.' Dan's thumb moved in small, warm circles. 'You
have to give yourself a break.'

'How? When he's in there, and I'm out here.' Out in
the cold. Disowned by his mother, and by Sol. 'It's about
to get worse, too. They're questioning him about firearms.'

'That's bollocks.' Dan didn't hesitate, his thumb circling.
'Sol and guns? Bollocks.'

'I should have seen it coming. Harry warned me about
the gang. I knew it wasn't just pills or weed. Now he's
saying it's firearms.'

'That dishy DS?' Dan had met Harry briefly, when he'd
called round to keep Noah informed of Trident's case. 'He
doesn't believe Sol's running guns. He's too smart for that.'

'Smart *and* dishy.' Noah allowed himself to be distracted,
knowing this was Dan's objective. 'Are you developing a
detective kink, Noys? Only I have a cure for that.'

'Hmm. I was hoping you might have.'

26

Lara Chorley lived in a cottage of weathered grey stone set inside a dry wall bordered by fields. The front of the cottage was a sinuous mass of green creeper bleached by floodlights which blazed into life as DCS Ferguson's Range Rover swept onto the drive.

The sudden brightness was an assault, disorientating because dusk had fallen so thickly an hour ago, swallowing the fields and woods around the cottage, which frowned its floodlights down on them as if they were escaped prisoners. At either side of a shallow porch a blue glazed pot stood planted with wind-beaten daffodils. It was eerily quiet, the kind of quiet London never knew, so that when a wood pigeon rattled out of the trees it was like a brick thrown with force through a window.

'Escape to the country,' Ferguson said sourly. 'You'll have to find it first.'

It had been a long drive, the satnav twice steering them to a dead end. Marnie eased the ache from her shoulders, looking to where Joe Coen and the Cumbria Police had parked their cars. They should have trusted Joe to conduct this interview but Ferguson was determined to be here,

staking her claim to what might prove a breakthrough in the case. The drive had been a chore which Marnie was not looking forward to repeating, her head already throbbing at the prospect of the trip back up the motorway. Hard to believe one woman could own so many musical theatre CDs.

'Come and find me.' Ferguson was still grumbling about the location. 'She wasn't kidding. I've had an easier time finding clean needles in crack houses.'

Joe Coen answered the door with a grave look on his face. Laughter lines said it wasn't his usual expression. He was Noah's age, five foot six, dark-haired and brown-eyed, upset by whatever he'd found in the cottage. 'She won't leave,' he told Marnie. 'He's not here, we've searched the house and the outbuildings. But she won't leave.'

'She isn't hurt?' None of the unmarked vehicles in the driveway was an ambulance.

'She isn't hurt,' Joe confirmed. 'But she isn't well either.' He was wearing navy trousers and a blue shirt, its sleeves rolled free of his wrists. No jacket or tie, and he'd removed his shoes. He glanced down at his socked feet. 'No shoes in the house, her rule. I thought it best to play along.'

'He's not here.' Ferguson clicked her tongue. 'Has he *been* here?'

Joe shook his head. 'Nothing to suggest it, Ma'am. She's saying not.'

'Of course she is.' Ferguson adjusted the collar of her shirt and took a step deeper into the cottage, her heels flinting at the slate floor. 'Well, let's have a little chat.'

Joe must have caught Marnie's expression because he said, 'Actually, Ma'am? My super was asking if she could have a word, couple of things she needs to check with you.' He beckoned one of the uniforms, who escorted Ferguson to the back of the cottage.

199

When she was out of earshot, he told Marnie, 'Sorry, but Mrs Chorley's not up to an interrogation right now. She's having a hard time of it.'

It was the first time anyone had referred to Lara as Mrs Chorley, reminding Marnie that Lara was a mother of two. 'I'll be careful,' she promised Joe.

'Thanks.' He nodded. 'She's up here.'

He led the way through a sitting room where the ceilings were low and beamed, walls the colour of skimmed milk. A deep fireplace was filled with a black range, pale linen sofas to either side. Shelves and tables had been planted with pottery vases, adding muted notes of colour. Windows looked out onto the blackened fells and woods which ran in all directions from the front door. The range was cold but the cottage was well insulated; there was money here and plenty of it. Artwork on the walls, rugs and antiques, and not the kind left by grandparents – these had been picked up in French markets over a long weekend by ferry. Years ago this had been a holiday cottage, and it clung to a little of that impersonal appeal even now. Colin had unearthed a cached website whose photos predated the French makeover, back when the furniture was small and shabby, the view described as 'heart-wrenching'. The clean scent of cut lilac was everywhere, but it must have been room spray because each vase was empty.

Marnie followed Joe up a slim stairwell to a bedroom at the front of the cottage. Joe knocked at the door, saying, 'Mrs Chorley, it's me. Can we come in?'

The murmur of a woman's voice, her words inaudible, came from the other side of the door.

Joe nodded, and they went into the room, Marnie following a pace behind him.

What had she expected to find? The letters and photographs, sketches in Vokey's art book, none of it prepared

her for the woman seated at a desk whose lamp sent her shadow up the wall, so much larger than Lara herself. She was big and fair, her head bent over the pages of a book, her finger following the words the way a child's does when she's first learning to read. The room was pretty, with floral curtains and a primrose bedspread, a big mirrored armoire against one wall. Lara had covered the mirror with a modest black dress on a hanger. Her reflection peeped from the edges of the glass, a slice of her face frowning in concentration, the heels of her stockinged feet. She wore a green moleskin tunic, long-sleeved, a silver pendant at her throat, a matching cuff on her right wrist. Her hair was freshly cropped, elfin-short, showcasing her wide cheekbones and the lines on her face. She looked every one of her fifty-three years. She pressed the book firmly open with the heel of her hand, moving her lips determinedly as she read.

'Mrs Chorley,' Joe said. 'This is Detective Inspector Rome, from London.'

Lara nodded, concentrating on the page. 'In a minute.'

Calm and cultured, but not quite right. Her voice, her tone, misfired. It was like watching a hologram projected onto the sweetly floral backdrop, a hologram with a glitch which made the image jump every few seconds, as if to remind the viewer it was an illusion.

Marnie crossed to the desk, holding out her right hand. 'Mrs Chorley.' A zap of static from the carpet made the ends of her fingers jump. 'I'm DI Rome. Marnie.'

'Lara,' she said automatically, then covered her mouth with her hand as if she'd lied, or given up a secret she'd sworn to keep. Her hair grew in a spiral pattern at the crown of her head, the way a baby's does. It made her look vulnerable, despite her size. She gazed up at Marnie, keeping her finger on the page she was reading, her eyes

201

the colour of camouflage, their lids heavy, lashes short. Her nose was broad at the bridge, her mouth deeply creased, a smoker's mouth. Small pierced ears. The pink skin of her face held the morning's make-up in its wrinkles, flickering with that glitch again as she held Marnie's stare. 'Yes?' she asked after a moment. 'Can I help you?'

'I hope so. May I sit down?'

'We're in my bedroom.' She stayed like a rock, solidly behind her desk. 'Where would you sit?'

Marnie moved to the window seat. 'Here is fine.'

Lara turned in her chair to face her. 'Tea, please.' She nodded at Joe. 'You offered and I said no but I think we should have tea.' She clipped the words pleasantly, as if ordering in a restaurant.

'I'll bring it,' Joe said. He left the room, leaving the door open by a crack.

The window seat was less than two feet from the desk, close enough for Marnie to see her own reflection in the woman's green-brown eyes.

'You were expecting someone else,' Lara said. 'Someone different. Another kind of woman.'

Marnie shook her head.

'Yes, you were. Taller, slimmer. Sexier.' She put each word into the space between the desk and the window seat, as if building a barricade. 'Younger. Or older. But sexier, obviously.'

'Obviously?'

'The letters,' Lara said matter-of-factly. 'You were expecting a boudoir.' She glanced at her bed. 'Satin sheets. Or a sex dungeon, were you expecting a dungeon? Not a frilled valance, anyway.'

Marnie said, 'I don't find expectations very helpful in this job.'

'Images, though. In your head. You can't help those.'

202

She pulled the silver cuff from her wrist and set it down on the desk, lifting her arms to unfasten the silver pendant. 'Would you . . .?' She bent forward, exposing the freckled nape of her neck.

Marnie reached out and freed the clasp, watching as Lara pooled the chain in the palm of her hand. She smelt of the same leather seating as Ferguson's Range Rover. It struck Marnie that they smelt the same. Of long car journeys, creased clothes and weariness.

'I've been trying to get undressed,' Lara said. 'Ever since I got home. Isn't that odd?' She blinked at the pendant in her palm. 'I managed my shoes, but I can't work out the order of anything else. This dress.' She lifted her shoulders. 'I can't remember how it comes off. I know how that sounds, but do you never have days like that? When you can't work up the energy to get dressed or undressed. And there's so much *more* now. Spanx and bodywear.' She stopped, as if the wall she'd built with her words was in danger of toppling. 'But you have questions. That's why you're here.'

She hadn't wanted Marnie to get started until the battle lines were drawn between them. Key words and phrases – *sex, undressing, images in your head* – her way of defusing the weapons she feared Marnie was about to use against her. By getting there first, she'd claimed ownership of the least comfortable aspects of the conversation. Like Ruth, she didn't want to be considered out of control, someone Michael Vokey had exploited. A victim.

'When did you get home?' Marnie asked.

'Before dark, but not much before. I needed fuel, and food. I was in Edinburgh with friends.' Reeling off the information she'd already provided, sandbagging her alibis.

'And you travelled to Edinburgh alone?'

'Yes.'

203

'And home, alone.'

'Yes.'

Behind Marnie, night was packing the window tightly, binding the cottage with its silence, sliced through with the sounds of mating or warring animals. No breath of wind, just the dark pressing its face against the leaded window. A whole forest of darkness, leaning its full weight into the walls. 'You live here on your own?'

'You make me sound like a recluse!' She laughed. 'Or am I just lonely? Is that your point?'

'I wasn't attempting to make a point. I would like to get the facts straight.'

'Then yes. I live here alone. My husband and I separated six years ago, my children have their own homes. But I'm far from lonely and can I just mention one other thing?' She leaned forward, her stockinged feet rubbing drily together. 'It's about a fire, a few years ago. It may not seem immediately relevant, but bear with me. My husband's rather well off, he always was.' She injected a little of her ex-husband's money into her accent, as if to underline her point. 'We were in a hotel in Cape Town when a fire broke out. Adrian didn't need to lift a finger before the manager came and took us away down a private stairwell at the side of the hotel.' She blinked ferociously. 'People died. Those on the lower floors, and many higher up the building. But we were safe because Adrian knew the manager, who wanted to protect his investment. We were never in any danger. The door to that stairwell was kept locked but we had a private key because of who Adrian was. People *died*. Do you understand? I've never forgotten that. I've been thinking a lot about privilege just lately. And while it may not seem relevant, I'm here today because of privilege. It's the same for you. But Michael Vokey . . .' Her face spasmed. 'He isn't here, feel free to search, but he was never here, and he never could be. Because it's another world. That's another world.'

Joe had come back into the room during the tail end of the speech, setting down a tray of mugs on the bedside table, careful not to crowd Lara. He understood how fragile she was beneath the show of solidity. Marnie met his eyes and nodded her thanks.

'How long have you lived here?' she asked Lara as Joe handed them each a mug of tea.

'Six years, it will be soon. We separated, and this cottage was my settlement. I was in London before.' She held the mug in her hands, like Ruth's hands, big and callused. 'For a long while. It's changed, I imagine. I don't go back. They say you shouldn't, and I can see the sense in that.'

'Your children are in London?'

'Fabian, yes, at college. Hannah moves around a lot, for her job.'

'You don't work?' Marnie wanted to get the measure of the woman's isolation.

'I used to. Weekends in a reclamation yard. More of a hobby than a job, that's what most people would say.' She dipped her little finger into the tea and shook it, as if removing an invisible insect. 'It was a vast yard, full of fireplaces and mirrors and doors, hundreds of doors, mostly riddled with worm but I was taught to do the key test.' She mimed pressing the teeth of a key to the wood of a door, the gesture theatrical, as if by play-acting she could delay the moment when she must speak frankly. 'Unless it gives, it's good. I've often thought they should have a key test for people.' She moved her head towards Joe. 'Don't go, please. I'd rather you didn't.'

Joe waited for Marnie's nod before settling himself a few feet away, unobtrusively.

'I liked working in the yard,' Lara said. 'I remember

205

this porch from a church, carving so deep you could bury your fingers up to the knuckle in it, and just— Oh, fifty or sixty doors, hung on wires so you could walk between rows of them. We sold sheets of stained-glass too, but it was the doors I loved. Bedroom doors and kitchens, front doors with letter boxes, back doors with cat flaps. Once, we had a devil's door. Do you know what that is?' She sipped her tea, looking at Joe.

'A devil's door?' He shook his head. 'What is it?'

'In the Middle Ages, people believed the devil lived in the souls of unbaptised children. A baptism drove him out, but he had to be able to exit the church. So they built these little doorways which they bricked up after the devil was gone. You wouldn't want him trapped in the church, you see. The devil's door in the reclamation yard was very small, and riddled with worm. I did the key test and it went right through.' She bent her head to sip at her tea again.

Joe met Marnie's eyes. She smiled a fraction, happy for him to encourage Lara to talk, wanting the woman to relax and open up.

'What about the other doors,' Joe asked, 'which were your favourites?'

'A pair of saloon gates, would you believe it? Piebald where the cream paint had peeled. They made me think of John Wayne, "Get off your horse and drink your milk," do you remember? Oh, you're too young!' She made a sound like spurs with her tongue against her teeth. 'Most of the doors had their locks dug out. If you bought one you needed a new lock to go with it. We sold antique locks too, so it was a nice money spinner for the yard.'

Doors without locks, without rooms. Leading nowhere, waiting for new homes. Each with its story, everything from cat flaps to fleeing devils. Was Lara thinking of

Michael when she said that? Or was she simply putting off the moment when she would have to talk about him?

'When did you stop working at the reclamation yard?' Marnie asked.

'A year ago, thereabouts.' Lara put a hand to her freshly cropped hair, following its new margin with her fingers. 'There were a lot of changes in the village, people coming and going. Too many of the houses here are second homes, holiday homes. We're going through a mini depression, shops closing, building projects grinding to a halt. People think that only happens in big cities, but we're suffering too. I lost all my friends, that's how it felt. No one's interested in an ex-Londoner living alone in a holiday cottage she's done up as a hobby.' She shook herself a little. 'The hobbies I've had! Everything from jam making to flower arranging. Christmas wreaths made of cranberries, hundreds of cranberries, each one pinned in place.' She inspected the ends of her fingers as if she could see pinpricks there. 'No one can say I didn't try to fit in. I made friends who moved on, new people moved in and it all becomes so exhausting, doesn't it, after a time.' She put the mug to her mouth again. 'Everyone's a stranger suddenly. I don't feel safe.'

She was lonely. She'd denied it too quickly, afraid of hearing Marnie speak the word. There was so much stigma attached to the idea of a middle-aged woman living by herself, bored and isolated. Of course she resisted the cliché. Had that been the beginning of her correspondence with Michael? An act of outrageous rebellion, setting herself beyond the realm of cliché, demanding a different kind of judgement. Even with six or seven people inside the cottage, its silence was oppressive. Her nearest neighbour was half an hour away. The roads often flooded, trapping her here. No WiFi, no phone signal. How could she not be lonely? Was it possible Vokey's hold over her had at first felt safe? Sitting here in her grey stone prison, writing to him in his. Held captive in the photos she sent him, ageless and unchanging, a form of death. Immortalised in his sketches, so much more than a bored housewife making jam and sticking pins through cranberries at Christmas to make a wreath for her door which only the postman would see. Taking long drives that caked the underside of the car with mud, coming back as the light started to leak from the sky and the night moved in.

Lara's hands tightened around the mug. 'I thought this was a fresh start, a new adventure, that I was shucking off all of London's grime and cynicism, the way it lays the world wide open when I wanted to be small again.' She looked around the room, her stare bristling with betrayal. 'I thought I could be small here, but it wasn't like that. It isn't. There's nothing here. *I'm* nothing here.'

She'd come to hide behind her floral curtains in this remote cottage with its heart-wrenching views. What did she see when she looked out of its windows? Miles and miles of nothing, the rattle of wood pigeons coming like stones. The Edmonton estate was grim, but at least Julie had her family close by. Lara had luxury kitchen appliances and acres of rural isolation. No community, only quarantine masquerading as peace and quiet. Her loneliness was like an animal crying to be let in, a child who wakes and won't settle until it's lifted and cradled, and fed.

'Now.' Lara put down the mug, empty on the desk. 'You want to talk about him. That's why you're here, yes?' She looked at Joe, looked at Marnie. 'Michael Vokey.' She said his name without flinching this time. 'You want to hear all about the letters I wrote because you're imagining I know where he's gone. You're hoping I'm hiding him. Will you arrest me?'

Joe moved his hand in a bid at reassurance but Lara shook her head at him, looking at Marnie. 'Not him, you. He's very kind.' A smile for Joe. 'You've been very kind. But now I need that to stop. I need to know what's going to happen.'

The atmosphere in the room altered, reshaped by her new severity. This was *her* room. She'd made certain this conversation took place on her territory, her terms.

Marnie said, 'When were you last in contact with Michael?'

'Sixteen days ago.' No hesitation, her eyes unblinking. 'I wrote him a final letter and then I stopped. I received two further letters from him, but I didn't reply to either one. He's not written since and to be clear? I never visited him, I never met him, I never spoke with him.'

It was easy to imagine her preamble had been a smoke-screen to knock Marnie and Joe off-balance. She was formidable now, more than able to stand up for herself.

'You haven't written to him in sixteen days.' Marnie had letters in her bag, the ones found on the allotment, which said this was a lie. Lara had written to Michael every day of the last month, before and after his escape. 'Why did you stop writing to him?'

'I could see where it was headed. His letters were getting stranger and stranger. You'll argue I started it, encouraged him. But at least I stopped before it got out of hand.'

The letter about the red dress, her challenge to Michael – 'Come and find me' – the promises of what she'd do when he tracked her down. Did she imagine the fire had destroyed it all? Or was she hoping to brazen it out, believing he would have disposed of any evidence? Her expression wasn't triumphant, or defiant. She held

Marnie's gaze without faltering and it looked very much as if she was telling the truth. Had she somehow persuaded herself that she was?

'Why were you in Kendal yesterday?' Marnie asked.

'I wasn't.' She moved her head to the right, frowning. 'Yesterday I was driving home from Edinburgh.'

'Your car was seen in Kendal.'

'I was driving home from Edinburgh,' inflexibly, 'whoever imagines they saw me is mistaken.'

'Traffic cameras don't have an imagination. And they don't make mistakes.'

Lara's breathing quickened. 'Then the route I took back.' She looked genuinely confused, her fingers moving in her lap until she stilled them. 'I may have come that way. I know I got lost, I always do. And there were diversions. You can look at my satnav, it'll tell you the route I took.'

'Thank you, we'll do that. Do you know anyone in Kendal?'

'No. That's how I know I wasn't there unless it was by mistake, a wrong turn. All these roadworks following the floods, diversions at every turn. I don't know anyone in Kendal.'

Marnie nodded, making a note. 'How many letters did you write to Michael? In total.'

'I suppose two dozen?' She held her head high. 'That seems a lot. But he didn't reply, not for a long time.'

'Did you send him anything other than letters?'

A tiny silence took shape before Lara said, 'Photographs.'

Marnie looked up from her notepad. 'Photographs.' It was an odd confession to make if she imagined the fire had destroyed everything, or if she hoped it had.

Lara moved her body a fraction closer to Marnie. 'Can we— Must he be here?' She forced a smile for Joe, but it was ghastly. 'You've been so kind, but this is very hard for me.'

Joe stood, collecting the empty mugs. 'I'll be downstairs if you need me.'

After he'd gone, Lara said, 'You know I sent him photographs and letters, that's why you're here. But I stopped. Sixteen days ago, and I was in Edinburgh the day he— The day of the riot. Yesterday I was driving home from Edinburgh and I didn't stop in Kendal.'

ANPR cameras had caught her car going through Kendal, but there was no evidence she had stopped there. She could be telling the truth about the roadworks. Joe Coen's first thought had been roadworks when they'd told him about the ANPR evidence.

'Michael has your address,' Marnie said. 'Are you afraid he'll come here?'

Or are you hoping that's what he'll do?

'I'm not afraid of him. I'm afraid of *you*. Of what you'll make of all this.' She knitted her fingers into a fist. 'Am I being arrested?'

Marnie sidestepped the question. 'Do you have the letters he wrote to you?'

Ruth had denied it, saying she'd recycled everything, but Lara nodded. 'Yes.'

'May I see?'

Lara stood and went to the armoire, moving the black dress out of the way. Marnie caught a glimpse of the clothes hanging inside. No red dress, or none that she could see. Lara swept her hand across a high shelf and brought down a black beaded clutch bag. She closed the armoire and came back to where Marnie was seated. 'Here.' But she held onto the bag, as if afraid to give it up. 'So you know, this was never about wanting him or loving him. It was about hating myself.' She lifted her

211

chin, correcting the shake in her voice. 'He's an animal. I'm sure you can tell me a hundred ways in which he's an animal, without counting what he did on the day of the riot. But I was never afraid of him because he didn't seem capable of real harm, not on that scale.' Her fingers tightened on the bag. 'This is going to sound strange, but I wrote to him because he seemed so *safe*. It was never about him, not in the way you might think. It was about myself, punishing myself. I know how that sounds, but I've had time to think about it out here on my own.' She gestured at the darkness crowded outside the cottage window. 'I was never afraid of him, only ever of myself. Can you understand? Call it an infatuation, of course you'll call it that, but it was never as simple as him. He's not the man you think he is. At least—' She frowned, losing her thread. 'I don't believe he is. I suppose if I'm honest I never took the trouble to find out what sort of man he is.'

'Mrs Chorley. Lara. We need to find him. If you can help with that—'

'I can't. He's not here. He's *not*. He wouldn't bother coming for me and if he did, he wouldn't sneak around. He'd walk right in.' She fixed her eyes on Marnie's face. 'He'd walk in here and he would look at you like you were nothing. And everything.' Her face flickered, dimly. 'As if the whole house were filled with him and you. He wouldn't speak, just look. You'd know what he wanted and you'd be revolted but you'd do it because you couldn't see a way out until you did. And because you wanted it.' She tipped her head back to keep the tears from brimming over, her eyes filling with the blonde light of the room. 'Because you wanted it. For once in your life this place wouldn't feel like a silk-lined cell. Your life would feel like living. You'd understand

212

what your body was for and you wouldn't be afraid any more. Just in that moment. You wouldn't be afraid or ashamed or sorry for all the things you ever did, never did. Because you would be everything.' She looked at Marnie through the raw running of her tears. 'Because you would be nothing.'

27

Hospitals are never quiet. I'm meant to be getting well, but how can I do that when this place is so packed with noise? It's worse than the countryside. Mum called it God's peace and quiet, but not a day went by without sheep bleating or owls hooting, hawks coughing up bones so close to my bedroom window I could hear the rattle of spit in their throats.

My lucky nurse is off duty. I haven't seen her all day. I stink of sickness and decay, rotting from the inside out. It scares me, but there's no point being afraid in here. Fear only works when you can do something about it, when you can use it to make things happen. Otherwise it just eats you alive. I wasn't afraid of Mickey, not in any useful way. Until the batteries and the stories of what he did in Leeds and to Julie. I'm not the sort of man who can stand aside and let terrible things happen. When the chips are down, I step up. Mum used to say, 'You're my hero, Teddy, a proper little gentleman.' She could be a hard woman, but she was rarely wrong. At the end, when she didn't want to go into the home because of the chairs – the *chairs*, mind you – I had to explain to them how rarely she was wrong. They didn't like it, of course, didn't want her with her own chairs, or her own opinions. All that was over, they said, and what's more, 'You'll never cope with her, not in your own home. She needs looking after right around the clock. Bed baths, medicine, and she can be a handful, you've said so yourself.'

I had said so, it's true. But you try turfing a stout old lady from her favourite chair, never mind from her own house after sixty years. She went into a care home to give me a break. Six days it was meant to be, but they called me after three. She'd found a way to split the seam on a wipe-clean chair they'd given her in the day room and she'd fed all sorts into there: sprouts, chicken nuggets, someone's dentures. The staff were furious. Mum was crying when I got there, but she laughed as soon as we were in the car, showing two fingers to the lot of them. 'Good riddance to bad rubbish!'

I tried to think of it as my privilege. It made me cross on occasion, of course it did. Just as I made her cross, I'm sure, when I was small and made a mess or wouldn't take my medicine. Benefit fraud, that's why they put me away. I forgot to cancel her pension, too busy cleaning up the house and organising the memorial and *grieving*—

Coffins are so small. Don't you think? Hers was too small. All of her life shouldn't have fitted inside there. More people came to the service than I'd expected. Churchgoers, not anyone I knew, no one who'd ever met her or me. Funny how people can make you more lonely, not less.

Anyway, I was late with the paperwork, certificates and so on, and they decided it was on purpose. That I'd set out to defraud the Government of their generous bounty given so graciously to old age pensioners and their carers. Benefit fraud, and they put me in there with the killers and arsonists, the rapists. Blame overcrowding, I was told. They locked me up with men like Michael Vokey, who only ever hurt people and wouldn't lift a finger to help anyone, not even his own family, not if they were on fire. What was I supposed to do?

What would you have done?

I'm serious, because I need to know.

What would you have done?

28

'Noah? Sorry it's late and the signal's not great, but I knew you'd be waiting for news from Lara.'

'It's not good news,' Noah guessed. 'You sound wrung out.'

'Vokey isn't here. There's no evidence to suggest he ever was. We're heading over to see Alyson at the hospital then we're coming back via Cloverton so I can question Aidan again.'

'How's Lara?'

'Not what we expected.' Marnie turned away from her reflection in the darkened window of the cottage. 'Not scared, or angry. Not like Ruth. But she told the truth, at least I think she did. And she gave me the letters Michael wrote to her.' From the beaded clutch bag where she'd been keeping the correspondence safe. 'She didn't pretend she'd destroyed them.'

'Not like Ruth then,' Noah agreed.

Marnie walked a short distance from the cottage. The floodlights followed her, showing up the patterns in the gravel that marked out the path she walked in search of this weak phone signal.

'We have a problem,' she told Noah. 'With the evidence from the allotment. What's the news from the duty doctor? How's Darren?'

'He should be fit for interview first thing. What's the problem with the evidence?'

She stood with the lights at her back, the night's dark chill on her face. 'The letter about the red dress, the one inviting Michael to come and find her. It wasn't written by Lara.'

Noah drew a short breath. 'You're sure?'

'As sure as I can be, without tests. She admitted writing to him, two dozen letters on stationery she stole from the firm who handled her divorce. She was quite candid about it, and I believed her. She admitted writing a letter to Julie at Michael's behest. But she stopped writing, to anyone, a week before the riot.'

Marnie turned. The cottage chimney was a pillar of black smoke above her. Behind the pretty curtains in Lara's bedroom, the furniture showed as shadows, crouched and huddled.

'The letters from Michael, allegedly from Michael, Lara says he didn't write them. She has earlier letters of his. The style's very different. That's why she stopped writing back, because she could tell she wasn't writing to him. Someone was forging his letters, that's what she believes.'

'Who?' Noah asked. 'Not Darren.'

Something shifted on the tiled roof, too big to be a pigeon. An owl? The chimney shrouded its hooded head, its eyes showing as flat yellow discs.

Marnie shivered. 'Let's find out. But you'll want to delay the interview until we've looked into this. If the letters we found on the allotment are forgeries, it changes everything.'

'What about the ANPR?' Noah asked. 'She was in Kendal around the time of Alyson's fall.'

'She took a wrong turn. She was driving through, but didn't stop in Kendal. We have her satnav to confirm it.'

'You believe her,' Noah said. It wasn't a question. He trusted her instinct.

'I do, yes.'

'Damn.' Because it took them back to square one.

'Let's delay the interview and regroup in the morning. Get some sleep. I'll see you tomorrow.'

She ended the call, looking up at the night sky in search of stars, wanting to see a constellation she recognised, anything to anchor her in this sea of darkness. In London, the sky never closed as completely as this, always broken by pollution of one kind or another. The sky above the cottage was pitch dark, making it impossible to see even the edges of dense cloud cover.

Lara was upstairs, put to bed. Marnie had called Fabian and Hannah, explaining their mother needed them. She'd said nothing of Lara's mistakes or her self-loathing, only that she wasn't to be on her own. She'd fallen into a pit, that was how Marnie saw it. Lara had fallen into a pit and was too tired of trying to claw her way out so instead she'd made her peace with it. With self-disgust and remorse, with despair. The pit was her home now.

An animal moved in the bushes by Marnie's feet, a swift scampering of claws. She stepped back, skin pricking in fright. Was she any better than Lara? Obsessing over Stephen, tied to him by her need for answers, unable and unwilling to give him up. He crooked his finger and she came running, again and again. If he escaped from prison, as Vokey had, would she feel compelled to follow and find him? He was the only tie left to her parents, the idea of losing him was grotesque. But he was a killer. She recognised the games he was playing, knew when she was dancing to his tune. That wasn't true of Lara, or Ruth.

219

Neither woman had an instinct for threat. Ruth was calm to the point of complacency, utterly convinced of her hero's innocence. Lara was focused on her own short-comings, exonerating him of any blame. Both women were incapable of imagining his guilt or appreciating the danger she'd put herself in by handing out her address. But neither had Julie been afraid, and she'd come face to face with Vokey, close enough to see the pores in his skin. It was one thing for Ruth with her armour-plated self-delusion to consider Vokey no threat, but Julie?

Ferguson's voice drifted from the cottage, giving her instructions to the team inside. They needed to get going. Ferguson would see this as wasted time, might even charge Lara on that basis. She'd been so certain they would find if not Vokey then fresh clues here, especially after the inventory from the allotment, those missives from Lara convincing them that she was the one hiding or helping him. Except Lara didn't write those letters. They should have suspected as much, the allotment letters being typed rather than handwritten. Lara didn't own a printer, had given up her laptop without a fight, handing over Vokey's correspondence and pointing out the change in tone and style, insisting she'd guessed the recent letters were forgeries. Just as she insisted her letter about the red dress was a forgery. So what was Darren doing with a stash of forged letters? What purpose had the forgeries served, and what part did they play in Vokey's escape? Lara said Michael was crude in his earlier letters, too lazy to write at length or with imagination. Pictures were his thing, not words. When suddenly the words became graceful and persuasive, Lara knew someone else was signing his name as Michael. Who was the forger, and what had he hoped to gain by writing so eloquently to Lara? Had he written to Ruth in the same way, persuading her that

220

what they had was special, beautiful? What else had he persuaded her of?

Marnie's phone rang. 'Noah?'

'One thing,' he said. 'Julie mentioned *three* women. Letters from three women, not two. "One of them wasn't so bad," remember? What if the third letter was from the forger?'

'Let's ask her. I'm bringing back the letters Lara gave me. Colin's looking into the ones from the allotment. Can you get hold of Julie first thing, ask her to come to the station?'

'Will do.' He paused. 'You sound shattered.'

'I think we have this wrong, Noah.' She turned a circle on the gravel, watching the small movements in the shadows at her feet, feeling the breathy stillness of the cottage at her back. 'I think we have a lot of it very wrong.'

Ferguson was waiting in the kitchen where Joe was washing mugs, tidying away the tea things. He met Marnie's eyes with a measure of sympathy, either for their wasted journey or in respect of Marnie's return trip – five hours in the car with Ferguson whose mood had not been improved by the lack of progress made here, and might struggle to be improved even by the *Phantom of the Opera*'s extended soundtrack on replay.

'Alyson,' she told Marnie. 'Next on our list. Seeing as she's conscious now. Hopefully she'll appreciate our efforts to return her brother to custody.' She rolled her eyes at the bedroom above them. 'Unlike madam up there, with her smutty missives and her smug silence.'

It wasn't how Marnie would have summed up Lara's confession. She was inclined to admire Lara's courage in speaking so plainly about why she'd betrayed herself to a complete stranger.

221

'I'm thinking we can leave Alyson to DS Coen.' Marnie trusted Joe to handle that interview, having seen the careful way he dealt with Lara. 'I'd like to get back to London as soon as possible.'

Ferguson looked across at Joe. 'DS Coen?'

'Of course, Ma'am.' He nodded, smiling at Marnie. 'I'll get over there as soon as the hospital says she's fit.'

'Oh, I'd move a bit faster than that,' Ferguson told him. 'We need to know who attacked her, if she *was* attacked, and how recently she's been in touch with her brother. D'you have sisters?'

Joe nodded. 'Three.'

'Then you'll know all about sibling rivalries. We'll need you to figure out whether she had good reasons for cutting her ties with Michael. If she happens to know where he's run to, that would be the bonus ball.' Ferguson dusted the shoulders of her shirt, glancing around Lara's cottage kitchen one last time. 'Right, DI Rome, let's get you home to your bed. It wouldn't do to be interviewing Aidan Duffy with a motorway hangover.'

29

Back in London, Marnie persuaded Lorna Ferguson to drop her at the station so that she could collect her car for the morning. Ed was away, there was no rush to get home. She headed to the hospital, needing news of Ted, and of Stephen. She needed news of Stephen.

It was nearly 2 a.m. Of course the hospital had nothing for her, only weary night staff advising her to return during visiting hours. She stood at the door to the room where Ted Elms was sleeping, trying to imagine what had happened in the cell at Cloverton to turn him into the frenzied man in Vokey's sketch. A light shone above the bed, silvering the tubes that snaked in and out of him, a riot of tubes, like a child's puzzle. A nurse was sitting by the side of his bed, holding a crucifix between her left thumb and forefinger, looking so beaten down by exhaustion that Marnie worried for her.

In the second room, Stephen was unconscious, oblivious to her presence at the foot of his bed. No nurse was praying for him. He was all alone in the room. Marnie thought of Anita begging for Darren to be taken from her house, shutting herself away with the roses and travel guides as if she could forget she had a son who'd helped a sadist to escape.

Marnie's body blazed with tiredness. She felt the pressure of tears in her throat and chest, but she couldn't weep. She didn't know what she would be weeping for, unless it was Lara's loneliness or Anita's pain. She walked down the corridors where empty trolleys were parked, away from the people waiting for news of loved ones. Whether it was tiredness or the tears she was holding at bay she didn't know, but she wanted to comfort at least one of these waiting people. The woman with the child's lunchbox held in her lap, her eyes on the muted TV screen – Marnie wanted to put her hand on the woman's shoulder and tell her it would be all right, it was going to be all right, and for that not to be a lie or a platitude but the truth.

It was cold in the car park, the sky sulphurous, the moon like something missing, a hole punched through the night's wall. She was walking to where she'd parked the car when she saw a dark-haired man standing with his head down, thumbing at the screen of his phone.

'Harry, hello.'

He looked up. 'Hey . . .' Smiling, but he was gaunt and muddy-eyed, so different to when she'd seen him at the station twelve hours earlier.

She felt a queasy jolt of distress. 'What's happened?'

'This?' He lifted his bandaged right hand. 'It's nothing. Just— They gave me a shot, said I can't drive. I'm waiting for a taxi.'

'I can take you home.'

'Thanks.' He pushed his hand into the pocket of his coat, brightening the smile. 'But I'm okay.'

His skin was bruised by lack of sleep. He looked worse than she felt.

224

'Let me do this,' Marnie said. 'Drive you home. I'd like to be useful, and I could do with the company.'

'It'll be out of your way. I'm headed back to my mum's place.' He put his phone in his pocket, rubbing a hand through his hair, glancing at the hospital. 'They're keeping her overnight.'

'Out of my way's good, too much paperwork waiting there.'

Marnie drove to an address in Highgate. When they drew up outside the house, Harry hesitated. 'I'd ask you in, but it's a bit of a mess. Sorry.'

The way he said it made her ask, 'What happened?'

'Would you believe she attacked me with a glass clown?'

Marnie blinked at him, not knowing whether to laugh. His tone was light, but his eyes were dark blue and desperately sad. He held up his bandaged hand. 'Actually her Swarovski Crystal Pierrot but you know, rounding down. So, yes. It's a mess in there. Antiques Roadshow Massacre.'

'Harry—'

'It's okay. She's in safe hands. They think – dementia.' He tensed, as if anticipating sympathy. 'But she's in safe hands.' He didn't want her to say how sorry she was, he wasn't ready for that.

Marnie unfastened her seat belt. 'Let's clean up.'

The house was a cottage, Edwardian, set back from the road by a small garden which had once been neat and was now neglected. The cottage was built over three floors, detached from its neighbours by a margin too narrow even for a cat to squeeze through. Harry searched a keyring for the right key, unlocking the front door. A hallway led to a kitchen at the back where a strong

225

smell of burnt toast battled with scalded milk and air freshener.

'Careful where you walk.' Harry clicked on the lights.

Broken glass and china on the floor, swimming in a messy slop of food and tea. Harry separated sheets from a newspaper, dropping them over the worst of the mess. Then he crossed to the sink for a pair of yellow rubber gloves like the ones worn by Anita when she'd answered the door – was that really only hours ago? Marnie stripped off her jacket, rolling up her sleeves.

'Let me do the floor,' Harry said.

'With that hand?' She shook her head. 'Quicker anyway, with two of us.'

'Okay, but you'd better wear these.' He held out the gloves.

When he crouched, she saw the nape of his neck above his shirt collar, the bronze notes in his dark hair. She crouched next to him and they sorted the worst of the glass and china onto a clean sheet of newspaper, Harry keeping his bandaged hand on his thigh, out of the way. Once all the broken bits were collected, Marnie folded the newspaper, waiting while Harry brought an empty carrier bag. 'You'll need two,' she warned, 'too much of this is sharp.'

While he was hunting for a second bag, she cleaned the food and tea from the floor, wrapping the sodden kitchen roll in more newspaper until it stopped soaking through. Harry found a heavy-duty bin liner and they loaded it with everything before he knotted the neck.

'Thanks. The rest can wait until the morning.'

The rest was dirty dishes in the sink, crusted plates and cups, at least a week's worth. And whatever was hiding in the other rooms. From the tension in his shoulders, Harry was preparing for a night of housework to get the cottage fit for his mum's return.

'Is there hot water?' Marnie asked.

'Yes, sorry. The bathroom's upstairs. You'll want to wash your hands.'

She ran the hot tap at the sink, putting in the plug, adding washing-up liquid.

'You don't need to—' He broke off. 'Okay, you're a star. Thank you.'

'It's this or the paperwork. You're doing me a favour.'

He laughed, sounding more like himself, and started clearing the table.

Above the sink, a window looked out into the garden. Too dark to see what was planted, but Marnie made out a long line of fruit trees, their branches knotted with buds. The windowsill held an African violet in a ceramic pot next to a red Roberts radio. A yellow jug painted with windmills and stuffed with wooden spoons frayed and blackened from use stood alongside a green tin bucket holding a collection of whisks and a fish slice. To her left, the fridge was stuck with magnets, photos of babies and children – a boy in a pink dress smoking a pipe – and pottery butterflies, a snow-dome filled with dice and glitter.

Harry had finished cleaning and was resting his hand on the table, a long slab of pine scarred by knives and ringed by scorch-marks from saucepans and cups. He traced its patterns with the tips of his fingers, finding the knots in the wood, resting his thumb in the shallow groove left by a blade. He'd grown up in this house, Marnie could tell by the way he moved around the kitchen and now this tracing of the table's imperfections. What was he remembering? Breakfasts here before school. Family meals, laughter, the pine infused with the different scents of butter and brown sugar, a tang of rosemary, the airy sweetness of dough. Harry curled his fingers under the lip of the table as if holding onto whatever memories were

227

stored there. Marnie dropped her eyes to the sink, conscious of intruding on his privacy.

When the washing-up was done, she removed the gloves and washed her hands, leaving her sleeves rolled up. 'What else needs sorting?'

'It can wait.' Harry raised a smile. 'Seriously. This's your night.'

'Paperwork was my night, however late it is. I wasn't joking about that.'

'Michael Vokey?'

'We're no nearer finding him. I'm afraid we won't.' She hadn't admitted this to anyone, not to Noah, not even to herself.

Harry's eyes were bright with empathy. He nodded, not speaking.

'I have to ask,' Marnie said. 'What *is* a Swarovski Crystal Pierrot?'

He laughed, welcoming the change of mood. 'I'll show you, come on.'

The sitting room was a shrine to china and glass, from ornamental plates mounted on the walls to side tables set with thimbles and tiny china figures. Harry singled out a seven-inch crystal statue of a girl in a ruffled dress holding up a miniature golden mask. 'This's Columbine, recently widowed. Pierrot's the one we just picked off the floor in the kitchen.' He set the statue down alongside a kneeling figure with a red rose. 'Harlequin, star of Mum's killer clown collection.'

He wasn't exaggerating. The room was full of clowns – on plates, on tables, as figurines and statues, even a doll or two. Marnie looked for photos of Harry, but all the space was taken up by the clowns, mournful, gleeful and gruesome.

'I'm thinking I should make up a story about this,'

228

Harry flexed his bandaged hand, 'that doesn't involve the removal of coloured crystal gems with surgical tweezers.'

'Oh, I don't know. Makes a change from vigilante knife wounds.'

'True.' He dropped his hand to his side.

She was close enough to smell the astringency of his skin and to see the shifting patterns in his irises as he aligned the two statues more precisely. His sadness hurt her at a level she was afraid to examine. She'd been on the brink of tears for days, she should leave before she wept them here. Harry wasn't a stranger, but he was more than a colleague. Her feelings for him, reciprocated or otherwise, made him more than a colleague.

'Stay for a coffee?' he said.

She met his eyes, saw the plea there, how little he wanted to be alone in the house. 'But let me make it.'

On their way back to the kitchen, Harry stopped at the door to a cupboard built under the stairs. 'Can I show you this?' As if he were exposing the ghosts in the house in the hope of laying at least some of them to rest. Marnie nodded and he opened the door, putting up a hand as if he expected a deluge from the other side. The cupboard was crammed full of packages. Boxes mostly but Jiffy bags too and dozens of bubble-wrapped parcels. It looked like ten months' worth of unopened post.

'This's what we fought about,' Harry said. 'I didn't mean it to turn into a fight. She'd been hiding all this from me. I found a credit card statement and she's run up a huge debt, thousands more than either of us can afford. Buying all this.' He blinked at the contents of the cupboard, looking dazed. 'Gifts, she said. For friends, neighbours, the nice man in the corner shop who always puts a copy of *My Weekly* aside for her. She buys these then forgets to give them. It all ends up in here.' He rubbed at his cheek with the knuckle of his thumb. 'They sell this stuff out of the Sunday supplements. Collectibles, like the clowns. She's spent a fortune.'

'Can you return any of it?'

'I can try. When I've worked up the energy to open it all, check for terms and conditions.' He closed the cupboard door, turning towards the kitchen. 'Sorry, I seem to be offloading on you. Blame it on the painkillers.'

'Show me where the coffee is.'

They sat at the kitchen table when the coffee was made, Harry with his elbows propped on the scored wood, the white cup cradled in his lean fingers. Much of the tension had bled out of him, but he was still immeasurably sad.

Marnie said, 'Talk, if you'd like to. I'm a good listener, took a training module in it.'

Harry hesitated before saying, 'I'm trying not to give in to the guilt. There's enough of it in the day job and this week's been especially bad.' He drank a mouthful of coffee. 'Two eleven-year-olds with fatal gunshot wounds. Girls. Sometimes I think eighty per cent of London is illegal guns.'

'The other twenty being targets and spreadsheets?'

'You're forgetting shift patterns and arse-covering.'

'Damn, yes.'

They smiled at one another. A clock was ticking somewhere in the house, but Marnie filtered it out. Six years ago, when she'd needed it, she had refused help of this kind, someone who'd listen without passing judgement or coercing action. She wanted to give Harry what she'd denied herself.

'Mum's not been well in years. If I'm honest, she never recovered after Dad died.' He studied the bandage on his hand. 'I've been short-tempered with her lately, before I knew she was ill. She was accusing me of everything,

230

this shopping online, all the rubbish arriving through the post. I was to blame, using her credit cards, stealing from her. I should've realised she wasn't well.' He drew a breath, a white wrenched look at the edge of his mouth. 'A couple of weeks ago, after I was out of hospital, she hit me. Not hard, but she's never done that before. Ever. That's when it dawned on me that she must be sick. Some detective I turned out to be. I was an idiot to leave it so long.'

'You were doing your best.'

'I wasn't paying attention.'

'You were doing your best,' Marnie repeated. 'I know you well enough to know nothing's ever half measures with you. You're doing what you can.'

'Thank you, for that.' He moved his hand to hers, pressing his thumb to her palm, which was soft and hot from the washing-up, and she thought—

This isn't me. My hands aren't soft. I'm not clean floors and stacked dishes. I'm calluses and black ink at my hips. I'm broken edges you need to wrap twice or risk cutting yourself—

'Marnie . . .'

She blinked the heat from her eyes. 'Yes. I'm okay. Sorry.'

'This isn't us,' Harry said. 'I know. It isn't me, and it isn't you. Not really. Otherwise how could we do the jobs we do? I don't want you to think—'

'It's all right.' She closed her hand around his for a second before letting it go. 'It's good. Tell me something happy about your mum. A memory. Tell me – the story of the photo on the fridge.'

The boy in the pink dress, smoking a pipe.

'Oh Christ, the fridge. I always forget the bloody fridge.' His eyes brimmed with real laughter. 'I was six and it was a school thing. I was Granny Clampett from the *Beverly Hillbillies.*'

'Yes.' Marnie nodded gravely. 'Yes, you were.'

'Mum made the dress, after Dad failed to talk me out of going as Jed. There was some debate about whether or not the pipe cancelled out the effect of the dress. I'm not sure we resolved that.'

'She made you the dress?'

'It took hours. I wasn't very good at standing still while she was pinning it, I remember that. But I can honestly say I've never been happier than when I put it on.' His eyes gleamed. 'Make of that what you will.'

'You haven't any brothers or sisters?'

'Just me. Just me and Mum since Dad died, six years ago now.' He reached for a refill of coffee. 'Losing her to this madness is far harder than I imagined. Dad's cancer was cruel, but this is worse. She's here but she's not. These last few weeks I've not known what I'll find when I come round. Sometimes she's my mum, working in the garden or reading a book, sometimes she's a stranger. Or *I'm* the stranger. She's scared of me, or she hates me.' He retraced the patterns on the table. 'It's not as if we ever had the perfect mother-son relationship, we were never weirdly close, but we've always known we love one another. Seeing that just – *gone*. Or worse, seeing it replaced by fear or hate, and knowing how frightening it must be for her to have this stranger in her home, to have lost any sense of being safe here, or happy, or loved. It's horrible. Violent.' He stopped, flinching. 'I'm sorry. That was— Not what I meant to say. What you went through, I know—'

'It's all right,' Marnie said. 'You're right. Violence is horrible. We think we're equipped for it because of what we do. But the violence isn't meant to come home with us. It's not meant to be *all* our lives. Just the part we put on a uniform for, or a suit.'

'God, I miss my uniform.' He was steering back to safe

232

ground, trying to make her laugh again. 'I can say that, right? After the revelation about the dress, I'm guessing anything's a bonus.'

'It's okay.' She gave a steady smile. 'You can talk about it. I get a lot of silence. Respectful, or sensitive. It's pretty wearing after a while.'

Harry searched her face for a second. Then he said, 'I'm afraid of how it's changing me. I didn't know how much I relied on that stability. Home. How much I took it for granted. The kids I see on the streets, the ones in gangs or being wooed by gangs, I tell myself if I'm good at my job it's because I can count my blessings when they can't. It's sympathy not empathy, but it works. They get hostility but they don't get a lot of sympathy, so it goes a long way.' He gave a quick frown. 'Okay, I need to edit the self pity. I can't compare this with kids who've never known a mum, or only known abuse or neglect.'

'You can't compare it with anything. It's too personal. And it's not self-pity, it's self-awareness.' Marnie reached for her coffee, conscious she was speaking words she'd never spoken to anyone, not even Ed. 'I wish I'd had that self-awareness, six years ago. I wasted a lot of time pretending it hadn't changed me.'

'But here you are.' He crooked his mouth, admiringly. 'The best detective in London.'

'Tell that to Michael Vokey.'

'Oh, I think he'll find it out for himself, soon enough.'

'DS Kennedy, you're very good for my self-esteem.'

'Just paying it forward.' He curled his good hand at the back of his neck, watching her. 'I needed this, thank you. And I'm guessing your day was long enough.'

'I wasn't ready to go home,' she said simply. 'You know how it is sometimes. The more you need it, the less ready you are.'

Harry returned her smile then looked at his bandaged hand. 'When I see her tomorrow, she'll probably give me a lecture about getting myself into trouble again. She wasn't too impressed by the knife attack. I hope she thinks this was done by a stranger. I don't want her remembering what she did, or what she said.' His gaze wandered in the direction of the fridge. 'Too bad we can't edit our memories in any useful way. I hate that she's forgotten the happy stuff.'

Marnie understood. For a long time she'd been struggling to retrieve the good memories, the ones which proved Stephen was lying about his motive for murder. He'd blamed her parents, their bid to bring his birth mother back into his life, insisting they'd forced him into a corner. But Marnie's parents weren't bad people. They were just *people*, made of good and bad, courage and cowardice, faults and strengths. Stephen didn't own her memories, however much he might wish he did. It was in her power to make peace with her past, she was the only one who could do that. And it didn't require photographic evidence or empirical truths. It was a leap of faith. Forgiveness, if she could achieve it, wouldn't be about Stephen. Forgiveness would be an act of kindness to herself.

Harry's mother would be horrified to find him hurt again, with no memory of having inflicted the damage. Marnie thought of the fierceness of mothers, all the ways in which they battle for their children, all the ways in which it can go wrong. Did Stella Keele know her son Stephen was in hospital, fighting for his life? Was Anita able to sleep, knowing her son Darren was about to be questioned by the police and possibly charged with offences which would put him in prison for a long time? How soon until Fabian and Hannah Chorley could be with their mother, keeping her safe from the havoc of her own isolation? How long until Noah's mother forgave him for Sol's arrest?

Underneath everything else, turning like the wheels in a watch—

Where is Michael Vokey?

30

I've been thinking I should tell you what I saw that time in B spur's showers. I've been thinking a lot about Stephen Keele since his sister showed up here at the hospital again tonight. Detective Inspector Marnie Rome. I thought she was here for me, but it turns out she's his sister. That's what I heard her telling my lucky nurse. Not a very clever lie to tell if you're a detective. She looks so serious, DI Rome, it makes me want to answer her questions about what happened the day of the riot, how the corridor became an abattoir, ankle-deep.

'I'm his sister.' For a second, I think she's trying to scam her way in here without showing her badge, by pretending to be *my* sister when I don't have one. No siblings, no parents, no next-of-kin. Then I hear his name, 'Stephen Keele,' and I realise she's his sister. She doesn't seem too happy about it, any more than Alyson is about Mickey. I remember the names of the people Stephen murdered. Rome. Greg and Lisa Rome. That's why she's here. She's his sister, and he murdered her parents.

I see her eyes, the sadness and anger there, like smoke. Smoke kills more people than fire, that's how it happened at Cloverton. The fire was nothing, it was the smoke sliding under doors, rolling through the ventilation shafts, making our eyes run. A tide of smoke and when it retreated, the black spittle of soot over everything. Mickey started the fire, no doubt about that, his T-shirt smeared with fat from the meal trays, week after week until the cell started to stink. That's one thing we can all agree on: Mickey Vokey's an arsonist. He started the fire which sent the smoke into Stephen's lungs and blinded the rest of us so that no one really knows whose fists and thumbs did the worst damage. But he's out now, just like the fire, and I'm in here with Stephen Keele two doors down. That's why she keeps coming back. Not for me, although wouldn't it be nice if I could clear up at least a little of this mess for her? She's here for him, for Stephen. She's angry and sad, and she can't work out which emotion's the right one. He killed her parents, that's bad, that's anger. But he's in here breathing on a machine because smoke filleted his lungs. She'd have to be a monster to be glad about that, and she's not a monster. She catches monsters, hunts them down, does all her best work on the edge of the abyss which means she's looked into it enough times to be worried about how often it's looked back. How much of her hard work goes into making sure she doesn't turn into what she's hunting?

'I'm his sister.' The monster's sister. I'd tell her about B spur's showers, if I could.

I'd missed the main performance, the full cast was gone by the time I arrived, but Stephen had hung around, for the blood. Someone has to clean up and he was nearest, being on the floor already. Not the first time he'd been assaulted, I saw that from the way he moved, keeping his back to the wall. I couldn't see the whole of him, because the corner was in the way. I didn't want to see in any case. From certain things Aidan had said, I knew to stay wide of Stephen Keele, not to get involved. Some people you don't go near.

'Don't—' He puts a hand on the wall and spits on the tiles, red. His hand's blue at the knuckles, but it's not bleeding. There's a sound like beads falling. He's weeping.

I move away, to the sinks. I need to wash because I've been at the chicken grit, its itch lodged under my fingernails.

'Don't— Stay still.' Very low and quiet. I haven't heard him use that voice before. He spreads his hand on the wall. 'Just stay still. It won't hurt as much in a minute.'

Sobbing again, but it's not Stephen. He's not the one who's weeping. I move to get a sightline, see an elbow, and a pair of skinny legs in grey sweats, bare feet. Not anyone I recognise, just a kid, closer to Stephen's age than mine. One of the new intake, fresh pickings. He's been done properly by the sound of it, full welcoming committee, wide arms.

Stephen's hand is on the wall. 'It won't be so bad in a minute.'

His other arm's out of sight, holding the kid's hand? I don't trust what I'm seeing, already finding excuses for it, putting it into the context of what I've heard about Aidan's cellmate.

Stephen did this, and he's making sure the kid keeps quiet. That's one explanation. Or Stephen's grooming the kid, for worse. That makes even more sense.

But when I see her here in the hospital, DI Rome – being his sister, battling her demons – I have to wonder what she'd do if she'd seen what I saw that day. If she'd heard his voice, the soft way he spoke to the kid on the ground. Would it make it easier or harder to hate him? Because you have to hate your parents' killer. You can't

238

not do that, especially when you're police. Her choices, the way I see it, are limited.

My nurse shakes her head at the questions, no need for words. No news of Stephen, or none that's good. His sister thanks her, moves away. I can't see her now, but it stays in the corridor after she's gone. Her sadness, her anger. Like smoke.

31

'Michael was born bad, that's what Mum always said.' Alyson looked bigger in the bed than she'd looked on the floor of her house, covered by the hospital's white waffled blanket and with her fading blonde hair freshly brushed. 'He wasn't like me. We were both naughty children, I was far from perfect but she could reason with me, or else bribe me with sweets and stories. She said Michael was unreachable. He liked sweets, but he'd rather steal them than earn them. And he hated other people's stories, only ever liked his own. He'd plenty of stories to tell to anyone who'd listen, which wasn't enough people or not often enough.' She closed her eyes, her voice falling to a sigh. 'But he's harmless, really. Underneath it all, there's nothing to him. It isn't that he's bad, whatever Mum had to say about it. He's just missing. A piece of him's missing.'

It was how psychologists described psychopaths. Not as high-functioning human beings but as people with a piece missing. Joe sat in silence at Alyson's bedside, waiting for her to be able to tell him about the accident which had put her here, stitches in her head, bruises on her legs, her face swollen and discoloured from the surgery.

'He's always falling in with the wrong crowd,' she murmured. 'Trying to fit in, find his tribe. He isn't bad, not really. He's just lost.'

It wasn't the version of Michael Vokey that Joe had been expecting. It wasn't the version DCS Ferguson would want to hear, although Joe suspected DI Rome would have more sympathy for it.

'Mum did her best with him, but she struggled.' Alyson's words were slurred by the painkillers. 'And of course he saw how she was with Dad, that was a difficult thing to go through as kids. It taught Michael some bad habits about how you can take control of a situation. I loved Mum to bits, but she wasn't very good at compromising. It was all or nothing with Dad, so in the end it was nothing. That was hard on Michael. He was forever watching the pair of them to see how he was meant to behave, as if he couldn't figure it out for himself. After Dad left, there was only Mum to watch and she was too good at getting her own way, or else freezing you out. I could see a lot of what she did was selfish. Michael needed more help than most to figure out what was right and wrong, how to behave.' Alyson moved stiffly in the bed, giving a lopsided smile. 'It's why I've never had kids. All that responsibility and power, so many ways it can go awry.'

Joe thought of Bobby, and the new baby who must surely be arriving soon. It made no sense that he was the one here in hospital while Annie was sitting at home with her bags packed, waiting for Bobby's brother to make his move.

'I don't remember the fall,' Alyson said. 'I'm sorry, but I don't. If you're worried it was Michael, it wasn't. Not the sort of thing he'd do. He wouldn't bother hurting me, why would he?'

241

'We wondered about the house,' Joe said gently. 'In London.'

'Mum's house?' Alyson looked confused. 'I told Michael we'd sell it, split the proceeds.'

'How did he feel about that?'

'I don't know. I never know with Michael. I don't think he cares much one way or the other.'

Joe waited a beat before he said, 'The thing is, the police in London went to the house after he escaped from the prison. He had photos pinned to the walls, hundreds of them.'

'He liked taking photos,' Alyson agreed. 'And drawing, have you seen his pictures? He's very good.' She moved her hands vaguely at her sides. 'A proper artist, whatever else he is.'

Joe watched her, on the alert for signs that the interview was tiring her out. He'd been warned to take it slowly, not to outstay his welcome. 'The police wondered who else had access to the house. They'd thought it was empty, you see.'

'It *is* empty. But we've keys, Michael and I, of course. Mum kept one hidden round the back too. He used that when he was a teenager and came home late. I'm not sure we remembered to put it away, after she died. Michael would know.' The confusion crept back into her voice. 'Are the police saying he went back there after he escaped?'

'Not after, no. Before he was sent to prison, while he was out on bail.' Joe needed to ask about the grave in the cellar but if she couldn't remember the fall, how could they be sure Michael didn't attack her? How could Joe be sure the grave wasn't dug for her? 'So the fall was an accident?'

'Not quite.' She shut her eyes. 'It's been coming on for

a while, weakness in my right leg. It won't do as it's told. And my voice, the slurring. It's not drugs, in case that's what you're thinking.' Her fingers plucked at the sheet. 'I hadn't talked to anyone about it because I know what it is and – I'm scared.' Her voice broke. 'I'm scared to hear them say it. Isn't that odd? I know what it is but I can't bear the thought of anyone saying it out loud.'

Joe wanted to hold her hand, but he had to be a detective first. 'Can you tell me?'

'I talked to the doctor here. I had to.' Hot tears slid from her eyes. 'They'll test me now and then they'll tell me what I already know. A death sentence, it's a death sentence. PSP. Progressive Supranuclear Palsy.' She gave a firm nod, as if underlining the words she'd been afraid to speak. 'I don't know how I'm going to tell Michael. He went to pieces when Mum died. I'll be in a bungalow for as long as I can be living alone. I can't ever go back to the house. Michael's welcome to it.'

She opened her eyes, still weeping. 'I'm sorry, I can't stop this. It's upsetting, I know. Part of the symptoms, uncontrollable emotion.' She wiped at her eyes and pulled a smile onto her face, shaking her head at Joe. 'Don't *you* get upset. This's why I was putting off getting the diagnosis, not just for myself. Because of having to tell everyone. Friends, and Michael. I've no idea how he'll cope, but I know it won't be good.' Her words ran into one another, jumbling. 'He doesn't know how to process things like grief, he just doesn't. At Mum's funeral he had to watch me, to see how to react. I don't know who he'll watch this time, because there isn't anyone left and it's so hard for him.' She swallowed. 'It's terribly hard for him, please try and understand that. I know he's not a good person, but he's not all bad either. He's just wrong. There's something amiss with him, but it doesn't make

243

him evil. I only stopped visiting because I was afraid of his questions, and after that young mum, what happened up in London.' She stared past Joe, to the window. 'Perhaps you won't find him and he'll never need to know. About the diagnosis. Perhaps you won't ever find him.'

He could see her imagining this outcome, her gaze fixed faraway, the tears running down her face to darken the neck of her hospital gown.

Her mouth plucked at a smile. 'It would be one less thing to worry about.'

32

Cloverton was packed with noise that didn't let up until Marnie was shown to the room where Aidan Duffy was waiting with a smile for her. He dropped the smile when he saw her eyes. 'Is it Finn?'

'It's not your son.' She sat. 'It's you. It's the lies you told me the last time I was here.'

'Did I lie to you, Marnie Jane?' He moved his head away from her accusation. 'Did I do that? I wasn't well, it's true. I was only just out of the hospital, but still—'

'We've arrested Darren Quayle. He has a gun. I'm betting he's going to say he got it from you.'

Aidan's face tightened reflexively. 'Bollocks to that. You don't believe it.'

'I believe you lied to me. At the very least you left something out. I want the full story of what was happening here, before and during the riot.'

'You've arrested him.' Aidan searched her face for some chink in this morning's armour. 'Quayle. For the gun?'

'For assisting in Michael Vokey's escape,' Marnie said. 'Harbouring an escaped prisoner.'

Forensics had confirmed that Vokey had been on the

allotment, in the shed. The clothes, the food, the bodily waste. All his.

The air left Aidan in a long sigh. 'He did that, then. Dazza. He helped Vokey get away.'

'You suspected it?' A pulse of anger made her eyes burn. 'Because it might have been helpful to have heard that from you a week ago.'

'A week ago I was in hospital.' He narrowed his shoulders, making less of himself, hoping for her sympathy. 'But even in the hospital I was hearing the whispers.' He nodded at the walls. 'The threats. You think it's a coincidence not one person will tell you what went down that night he ran?'

'Who's threatening you?'

'Directly? No one. But *Dazza* has a way of reminding us our loved ones are in the firing line now Vokey's on the run. The way he put it you'd think Finn was sharing a cellar with that madman.' His eyes grew stormy. 'It's the same for all of us with kiddies, wives. This's what their expensive training did for Dazza. Taught him to make friends with the inmates, get us chatting about our home lives so he can throw a few names about, make the fear more real.'

Darren's blackmail notebook had personal details from each inmate's life. Finn Duffy's name was in that book. Only two entries had no names next to them: Ted Elms, and Stephen Keele. For everyone else, Darren had a shortcut to getting what he wanted.

'All those techniques they taught him to keep the peace, and he's using them to wage war.' Aidan pressed a knuckle to the bridge of his nose. 'Not one of us feels safe talking to the police, not with Vokey out there.'

'You didn't think the solution might lie in finding him and putting him back behind bars?'

'You make it sound so easy, Marnie Jane. But it's been over a week and here you are, having to pick my brain for its crumbs because you're no nearer finding him.'

The safety glass in the windows gave Aidan three reflections instead of one. Treachery in triplicate. She'd been a fool to trust him, a fool to think he trusted *her* just because she'd saved his son when that was her job. It was her job. Finn was out of her hands now, and Aidan had other allegiances to forge, new foes to fight. Loyalty was a commodity to a man like Duffy.

'You could have made my job easier.' She held onto her temper, but barely. 'Instead, you chose to make it harder.'

'Choice didn't enter into it.' Aidan shook his head, pleading with his eyes. 'I've Finn to think about. Even Tommy Walton has a brother. We've all got someone, that's how the world works. It finds out all your soft spots with its threats. We've all got someone who keeps us soft.'

Marnie changed tack, tired of banging her head against his brick wall. 'Darren has told us he's scared, too. For his mother, for himself. He has to go home at night and it's safer in here than it is out there.'

'He's right about that. Look what happened to my boy Finn. If I was out there— The threats wouldn't work as well.' Aidan frowned at the table, looking more serious than she'd seen him in a long time. 'You kid yourself you can do something if you're on the ground. God knows I'd put myself in the way of any harm coming to him but in here? There's nothing to do but lie awake at night imagining what *Mickey* might do just for the fun of it, because he's bored or he didn't like the way I looked at him that one time. The dads have it worst, worrying about their kids. We're guilty enough we're in here in the first place, as if that's not proof enough of our shitty parenting.'

247

Marnie thought of Anita Quayle's eyes, awful with emptiness.

'Prison's a bitch for working on your guilt,' Aidan insisted. 'And Dazza took lessons thanks to his training, all those tricks they taught him for making friends.'

'Not only tricks,' Marnie said. 'He had a notebook, did you know about that? A notebook with Finn's name in it, and the names of other dependants. He was keeping tabs on everyone.'

'Not only names.' He snapped the words, fear wearing anger's mask.

'What do you have that you're holding back?' Marnie demanded.

He pulled his left hand from the table and put it into the pocket of his sweatpants. Took out a screw of paper like a grubby roll-up, pressing it to the table with his thumb. A short moment passed with his eyes on her and his thumb on the paper, before Marnie reached out and took it, uncurling the roll-up to find a sketch of Finn looking up at her. Barely half a dozen lines in pencil but it captured all the boy's bravery, his wariness and readiness to take on the world. Black brows like his father's, eyes like a storm out at sea, the line of his jaw so delicate and assertive it could have been a butterfly's wing. Marnie's fingers fizzed with recognition, sharpening the ache she carried in her chest for Finn, her fear for him and her pride in his courage.

'From a photo I had in my cell,' Aidan whispered. 'One look, that's all he got. But tell me he hasn't trapped my boy right there,' pointing at the scrap of paper, 'not just his face, his *soul*.'

'It's an extraordinary likeness.' Marnie passed the drawing back, watching as Aidan rolled it tight and returned it to his pocket. 'You thought it was a threat?'

'What else would it be – a gift? He's a crooked, intimidating bastard.' Aidan's eyes threw sparks. 'I hope you're going to put him away for good this time.'

They considered one another. He was in a corner, and he hated being in a corner. Unless Marnie could guarantee his son's safety, he would give her nothing.

'Did you know about the gun?' she asked.

'Only so far as I knew about the rest of it. Quayle's a fantasist. I may as well've told you about the old army tank in his garden, or the Samurai swords. If I'd known the bastard was going to piss all over my feet with it, I'd have mentioned the gun weeks ago. I thought it was a fantasy.'

'And yet you're the one with the reputation for getting everyone what he wants. You got the charcoals for Michael Vokey. What else did you bring in here?'

'Sweets. He had a sweet tooth. I got him Skittles.'

'What else?'

Aidan dropped his head forward, linking his hands at the back of his neck. Guilt written right through him, like words through a stick of rock.

'What else?' Marnie demanded.

'He has small feet.' Speaking the words at the table. 'Michael. He's a size seven, small for a man. He's not big, but that's *really* small feet.'

Marnie's silence forced him to look up.

'He wanted shoes.' Knuckles white on his own neck. 'I got him shoes.'

'You got Michael Vokey a pair of size seven shoes. What sort of shoes?'

'That's the thing.' The Irish lilt softened, dimming his voice. 'That's why I wasn't rushing to tell you. Running shoes. He wanted running shoes so that's what I got him, and then – he ran.'

249

It explained his guilt, and his silence. That and the vivid sketch of his son.

'We're trying to work out when exactly he ran,' Marnie said. 'How soon into the riot?'

'I was in the cell with Stephen.' He drilled a thumb at the table. 'You *know* that. I missed all the action. Once it kicked off, they locked us in.'

'But you know what went down. You'll have spoken to the others in the last week. You make it your business to know what happens around here.'

Aidan dropped his hands to the table, scratching at a mark on the metal, rolling his neck to the right. Calculating his currency with her, how far his stock had fallen with the revelation about the running shoes, what he had to claw back. Everything was a calculation with Aidan, a slow dance to make him feel in control no matter how much ground he'd ceded. Even the sketch in his pocket, his way of tugging on the leash of her affection for Finn.

She wasn't in the mood for dancing. 'Let me make it easy for you. Aidan Duffy, you do not have to say anything. But it may harm your defence if you do not mention when questioned something you later rely on in court. Anything you do say may be given in evidence—'

He didn't smile, but his mouth crooked. 'You've beautiful eyes when you're angry. Resolution blue. When Mickey wanted paints, he gave me a list of colours and that's yours, Marnie Jane. Resolution blue.' He straightened, becoming serious. 'I didn't see what went down on the night of the riot. I did the survivalist thing, stayed in my cell until they gave us no choice and locked us in. I heard the noise and I saw the smoke – nearly died from the smoke – and I heard screaming and it wasn't like any sound I've ever heard, in here and out there. It was *primal*.' He pressed his thumbs to his eyelids. 'I went with Finn into the countryside once when he was tiny. It was the day they take the calves from their mothers to get their ears clipped and whatever else they do. I don't know anything about farming or cattle, but I know terror when I hear it. The sound those cows made when their calves were taken and they couldn't see what was happening, but they remembered, or they *knew*— They knew enough to cry about it.' He dropped his hands to the table. 'I never wanted to hear that noise again. So we did the seaside afterwards, never the country. But that night?' He shuddered. 'The night of the riot, I heard it. Terror and fury and pain and grief. It was unearthly.'

Marnie heard him out. When he'd finished she asked, 'Who started the riot?'

'Which version do you want?' He put his hands in his hair, meeting her eyes. 'The one I've heard, or the one I know? Because I don't know. None of us do. We've been told. Dazza did a great job of feeding us all the official line, but we don't know.'

He'd done a lot of thinking since she was last here. Marnie could see it in his face. He'd struggled with the same puzzle she had. Here at the crime scene, shut in with the evidence. He'd made it his business to find out what went down.

'Tommy Walton. With a tray. In the corridor. Tommy, the Musical. That's how it started.'

'Go on.'

'He hits the walls, he hits the floor, he hits Mickey.' Aidan blinked slowly, his eyes going out of focus as he conjured the scene. 'Mickey hits back, breaks his nose. Now Bayer wants a piece of it because Tommy's his boy and he likes a scrap. He punches Mickey and that's when Mickey goes for his eyes. And the next one just the same, like he's a taste for it now.'

251

'Who started the fire?'

'Oh, that's Mickey too. You might think he'd his hands full what with the GBH, but Mickey's a man of many talents. He's six sets of hands, and he can be in three places at once.'

'Meaning it's a lie.' Her pulse skipped. 'Which part don't you believe? The GBH, or the arson?'

Aidan leaned towards her, hauling his eyes back into focus, pinning her with his grey stare. '*None* of it. None of it's the truth. But he's out there, and why ask awkward questions? Why give yourself extra work to do? There's a hell of a mess and a man's gone in the middle of it. So *put* him in the middle of it.' He moved his hand expansively. 'One ball to bring down all the pins.' He sat back, his stare challenging her. 'I didn't know him well, it's true, but Michael was a lazy bastard, the kind to eat soup from a can because he can't be bothered heating it. Everything's too much trouble for a man like that. He wouldn't start a fire or a fight. If there was a way around wiping his own arse he'd have found it.'

Marnie's wrists tightened. She didn't want to believe Aidan's version of events, but she was the one who'd told Noah they had it wrong. So much of this case, right from the start.

'And yet he ran,' she said to Aidan. 'That took planning, required physical exertion.'

'Oh, I'm not saying he's incapable of being desperate. We all do things when we're desperate. Things we wouldn't usually do.'

This was Ruth's version of Michael. Cornered, afraid, forced to run. 'Why was he desperate?'

'You need to ask yourself what he actually did,' Aidan said. 'What you *know* about Michael Vokey. Not what you've been told, or what you suspect. And you can forget

252

whatever you've extrapolated. Strip it all back.' His stare was the colour of polished pewter. 'Slay the beast in your head, and look at the man.'

'He attacked Julie Seton in front of her own child. Are you saying that's not true?'

'There's Julie,' Aidan said. 'And there's Charlie.'

'Charlie?'

'His cellmate in Leeds. Charlie Lamb. The reason he was transferred here. I've friends in Leeds who say Charlie would be alive if he hadn't been put in a cell with Michael Vokey.'

Attempted suicides, and one that succeeded. The prison governor had likened Vokey's influence to an outbreak of rabies. 'Charlie Lamb was a suicide.'

'Sure he was.' Aidan moved his thumb on the table, tracing a shield knot, an ancient symbol for protection.

'You know different?' Marnie said.

'I know Michael's not the sort to lift a finger to save a boy who's on a path like that.' His voice was rigid, unforgiving. 'I know he drew pictures of Charlie, showed them around the place, offered to sell to anyone who wanted to see what he'd looked like hanging in the cell they shared.'

'He has a house full of photographs,' Marnie said. 'And artwork. Pictures like the one you're describing.'

'He likes to look.' Aidan nodded. 'In my experience, there's lookers and doers. But they're not usually the same people.' He'd studied this from every angle, shut up in here with the evidence, all the whispers and rumours, and the truths no one would share with the police.

'In that same house,' Marnie said, 'in the cellar. There's an empty grave.'

Someone was kicking a ball in the yard outside, or hitting a punchbag. Rhythmic, repetitive. The table jumped

253

with the echo of it, until Aidan stilled it with his thumb, pressing the pattern of the shield knot over and over into the metal as if he could score it in place. A symbol for protection and warding, keeping malevolent forces at bay.

'A grave,' he repeated. 'Well, you've got me there. But since it's empty . . .' He spread his hands, palms up.

'Why did he run? Why go to that effort, or take that risk?'

'You'd have to be frantic,' he agreed. 'I only ever knew one other man who did it. He was being bullied by the guards, threatened by a couple of the inmates. He was scared. Not prison-is-a-scary-place scared. Out of his mind with it. It got so he couldn't see straight, he'd duck if you spoke to him, scream at his own shadow. Or else he'd kick you, throw his fists at anything that moved. They said he was mad with rage, but it was fear. A man like that would run, whatever the risk.'

'Where's he gone?' Marnie asked. 'Where would a man like Michael run to?'

'Somewhere he's sure of a warm welcome. Or some-where he thought'd be warm. A bit of peace and quiet, I'm thinking that's what he'd be after.' He dipped his head at her. 'They told you about the night terrors? He'd tear up his cell with the shouting, nothing they could do to make him stop. I don't know how Ted stayed sane. So I'm thinking Michael would want a warm bed to run to, a chance to catch up on his sleep. Peace, and quiet.'

Lara's letters, the ones she'd written and the ones she hadn't, all promised one thing. Sex. Not much peace there. And Ruth was full of lectures, wanting to pray, to save his soul.

'His sister, Alyson. What do you know about her?'

'She gave up on him. That's what Dazza said. But Dazza's the one putting it about that Mickey did the eyeballs and the teeth and the arson all at once. I wouldn't trust a word Dazza says.'

'Don't worry,' Marnie told him. 'We're not.'

In the station's interview room, Darren Quayle shifted in his seat, eyes sliding in the direction of his solicitor then across to DS Harry Kennedy. He didn't look at the letters in the evidence bags, not even when Noah said, 'Who wrote these, Darren?'

'No comment.'

'It wasn't Michael Vokey, was it?'

'No comment.'

'Why do you have a firearm on the allotment?'

'No comment.' Bruises under his eyes from the fever, but his chest X-rays were clear. Fit for interview, with no intention of talking.

Harry tried, 'Where did you get the gun?'

Darren flicked his eyes at the bandage on Harry's right hand then looked away. 'No comment.'

'Do you know where Michael Vokey is?' Noah asked.

He shut his eyes, sitting slumped in the chair at his solicitor's side. 'No. Comment.'

'You need to talk to us, Darren. You want this to go away. That means talking to us, helping us to find Michael and put a stop to whatever the two of you started back in Cloverton.'

Darren looked glassily at Noah for a long moment.

The tape turned, furring the silence in the room.

'Start at the end,' Noah said. 'If that's easier. Tell us about the day of the riot.'

Darren dropped his chin to his chest, the breath leaving his lungs like a slow puncture. 'No comment.'

33

My little ligustrum was looking lovely that last day. I'd pruned her long shoots and trimmed the branches that conceal her trunk before sealing her wounds with paste. She had beauty, balance and realism. Until— Well, I don't need to tell you.

All that hard work gone to waste, everything I'd done to keep the peace. Dazza too, because he didn't want war at the outset. He thought he could make it work and really, who was it hurting? It's common sense you don't want a man like Mickey making his own entertainment. But then it tipped over into more for Dazza, became showing off. Strutting, they call it. That was the first straw. And sometimes, you see, the first straw is the last straw. I hadn't forgiven Mickey for Julie, there's the truth of it. Hadn't forgiven the foul way he talked about what he did to her as if it were nothing, passing over Natalie as if she didn't even exist. He sat on that little girl's mother and terrorised her, all so he could draw her picture. He needed to be stopped, even Dazza could see that.

'What's he going to do next?' Dazza asked after a terrible night of terrors, the cell smashed up around us, and so I told him what he should be scared of, and what we needed to do about it. He listened, I'll give him that. He could be a good listener, Dazza, you just had to be careful who was doing the talking. 'We have to do something,' I said. Well, it was the truth, wasn't it?

What you want to understand about Mickey is the way he steals what makes you special. He snuffs you out, and moves on to the next one. That's a kind of addiction, and he's never happy. He wasn't happy when he sat on my chest, or Julie's. He wasn't ever going to be happy, or settled, or done. If you're trying to solve the puzzle of Michael Vokey then you need to understand that he wasn't ever going to be done. Look at what he did to my little ligustrum.

The last present she ever gave me, my dear old mum. Mickey waited until I was asleep and he stole the scissors from my pocket, from right out of my pocket. And afterwards he sat with a sketchpad and a stick of charcoal, waiting to draw my face. That's all he cared about, because I wouldn't give him what he wanted when I was awake. Horror, fear, rage or remorse. All the things he found so mysterious he had to try and capture them. Often he drew me in my sleep, when I shook with the fury I kept inside the rest of the time, rocketing from the balls of my feet to the back of my throat, the dead taste of batteries under my tongue. I had my little ways, Mum always said. I'd trained myself out of them, in here. But there's a line, isn't there? No one's denying there's a line. 'You have your little ways, Teddy.'

I cared for her right up until the end, my dear old mum. Through those days when the walks grew shorter but took longer because she couldn't move at the pace she once did, any more than she could settle in the house. All those sleepless nights because she didn't trust pills of any description. I can picture her bedroom with its lemon walls a little greasy just there above the bed because I should've washed her hair more often, especially towards the end, except 'Stop fussing!', her hand tapping at the bedside cabinet, searching for her glasses, or her teeth. A right state, that cabinet. Cup rings, Vaseline, used tissues, I can see it now. I never had a minute to myself, to clean.

Funny how the light in here makes everything flatter than it actually is. Hospital lighting, like someone took a hammer to the cabinets and beds, to me. Linoleum floors buzzing with the stuff they use to polish everywhere. There's a man comes in the night with a machine. He polishes up the corridor then he polishes down. He props open the door to my room and stands watching me with his jaw rolling, chewing gum, hands slack at his sides and the machine purring behind him like a dirty great cat. Mum hated cats at the end, said they scared her, the way they looked at you, judging you, 'Little brutes.' Mrs Biggs was long gone by then.

I remember the shape of Mum's head in the pillows that last day. I put my hand there, and the pillow was still warm with her. I'd started to tidy the bedside cabinet but stopped because it was too soon. I wanted it to be her room a little longer. She hated me touching her things. Half a glass of water with her teeth inside, a library book, Andrew's Liver Salts, all her rings and fancy bits that didn't fit her swollen fingers or wrists, but she wouldn't let me put any of it away in a safe place.

'Stop fussing!'

A lonely sort of love, ours. Anyone asks, I wouldn't recommend it. Look what it did to me, hitting the ditch from the pillows where her head lay, opening the windows to air a room where I was never welcome, not towards the end, not even when I brought breakfast and the post.

'Flaming bills!' Language, I'd say. 'And you can get lost!'

'Shall I turn back the bed, Mum?'

She'd look at me then, all sunken chest and self-reproach, and I'd pat her hand and pour the tea and two cups later she'd be fine.

The ligustrum was her last present, because she knew how much I loved to fuss. She bought me the scissors too, my first pair. The little bonsai sat on the metal cabinet that last day, putting down her pretty shadow. I went to bed seeing her sitting there. Such a strange sound to wake to, the snipping of my scissors.

My fingers twitch, trying to keep time, but the rhythm's all wrong, too fast and too ferocious. *Snipsnipsnipsnip.* Mindless, with no thought to it, but I know her sound. My ligustrum. The scissors are thick with her sound, and her smell too. Silvery green, the tick-tick-tick of her leaves falling. I roll sideways to see her shadow on the wall, dwarfed by his.

He's wedged her pot between his legs, its inward rim and delicate feet pressed between the meat of his knees. My little bonsai's smooth bark and the feminine curve of her trunk is facing away from him, as if in horror. Her sparse branches, always so gracefully curled, cower under his fist which is wielding the scissors like an axe as he slices into her, slices her open.

I'm frozen on my side, staring down from the bunk, my hands and feet tangled in the sheet and blanket, sleep crusting the corner of my eye.

He tears the leaves from her branches, stripping her bare, twisting her with his fists, stabbing her with the scissors, my scissors, slicing her open everywhere. I put out my hand, a shout opening my mouth, choking in my throat. It's too late. I've woken up too late.

I fall from the bunk, finally. Fall on him, the soft scrabble

259

of flesh under my knuckles and knees, turning this way and that like a pike, hot and breathy under me. I don't stop, I can't.

I hardly noticed the stink. Only later, when my breathing's calmed down. He never flushed the toilet after using it, but this was different. He'd blocked it deliberately, it was overflowing. It wasn't hard to block the toilets given the diet they fed us, but this wasn't his breakfast and supper. My cacti were missing. All but two of them, empty spaces on the cabinet, blood red like a massacre. That was my eyes, I realised, I was seeing red just like the stories say. So angry my temples pulsed, my whole head filled with the sound of drum-drum-drumming.

I don't remember what I did, precisely, or what I said. But it scared him. He stopped twisting finally and shrank, trying to make himself smaller, less of a target. I didn't stop, not for a long time. I frightened myself, if I'm honest. You never know, do you, how much you're holding in until it comes out. Only later, when I'd worn myself out and was lying up there under the lights, I heard him doing what he'd wanted to do. Drawing me.

The hiss of the light and blood walloping in my temples, and underneath—

A noise like a snake shedding its skin.

His charcoal stick moving on the empty white page.

34

The makeshift incident room was hot and felt crowded, its trapped air tasting of paste and pens. Noah rolled up his shirt sleeves, his eyes on the women's faces. Not just Julie and Lara and Ruth. The other women, and men. All the faces from Marion Vokey's house.

'Cameras make ghosts out of people.'

Bob Dylan, of all people, had said that. Noah was standing in a room full of ghosts. In contrast to the main incident room where Vokey's mugshots were pinned, each face on these walls was distinct. Noah focused on the nine nameless faces, the ones he'd copied to his phone. Who were they? Would he ever know, or had he to accept the impossibility of that? You can't save everyone—

He looked up when the door opened. Marnie had brought two bottles of water, handing one to him. 'Are they talking to you yet?' The faces, she meant.

'Not yet.' He sighed. 'And Darren isn't talking either. Silence on all sides.'

'Tell me what you see.' Marnie unscrewed the cap of her bottle, drinking a mouthful. 'What you see of Michael, here.'

'This is someone who doesn't recognise himself in mirrors. Someone searching for control and clarity, some measure of understanding maybe. He doubts himself, doubts everything.' Noah scratched at his cheek. 'I showed his artwork to Dan. He sees a lot of fear in it, and superstition.'

'He's searching.' Marnie returned to the first of these judgements. 'That means he's lost.' She stepped closer to the wall, shoulder to shoulder with Noah. 'They say you can lose yourself in art.'

'*We've* lost him. The trail's been cold for nearly two weeks. I'm afraid the only way we'll find him is if he hurts another woman the way he hurt Julie. Either that or—'

'Say it,' Marnie prompted, keeping very still at his side.

'Is he dead?' Noah turned to look at her. 'The gun on the allotment was fired.'

'Darren killed him?' She didn't blink. 'What was the motive?'

'The hero worship soured at close quarters?' Noah tried to imagine the cocksure young man in the interview room as a killer. 'But Vokey should have been on high alert. Being good at deception makes you hard to deceive. I don't see him trusting Darren, or anyone else.'

'Ruth, and Lara.' Marnie touched her hand to the women's faces on the wall. 'Why did they write to him, really? What did they want? Lara was lonely, weary, regretting an impulse, but it must have been more than that, at the outset.'

'She had a line in one of her letters: "You see me. You're the only one who does." Perhaps it's as simple as that. They become someone else, through his eyes. All that matters is him looking. *Seeing*. In Leeds, they said he brought out the worst in everyone, altered behaviours.

262

It's the way he looks at you, but it's also the way he *sees* you. Everyone's altered, in his eyes.'

'I need to talk to you about Leeds.' Marnie twisted the cap on her water bottle. 'The young man who hanged himself. Charlie Lamb. I've asked Colin to look into it, something Aidan said.' She studied the wall of faces. 'He doesn't believe Vokey was responsible for the riot, or the worst of the violence. We've built him up into a devil, he says. We need to break it all down, get at the truth of what Vokey did rather than the legend we've allowed ourselves to believe.'

'Aidan sounds like Ruth,' Noah said irritably.

'Perhaps. But he was living at close quarters with Michael Vokey. And he has a point, hasn't he? We've built a profile based on very few facts. No CCTV or eye witnesses, most of the forensic evidence destroyed in the fire.'

Noah fell silent. He wasn't able to argue against Duffy's truth, but he wanted to. He hadn't met the man, but he knew Aidan was manipulative and untrustworthy. A player of games.

'Say you're Michael Vokey.' Marnie nodded at the room of faces. 'This is your house, your mother's house. You grew up here. After she dies, you move back in. No furniture or water, and no power. You make this room into *your* room. It's where you sat together as a family, you and Alyson and your mum, but you turn it into *this* – fill it with the faces of strangers. Why? Why not upstairs, in the bedroom that was yours?'

'Not big enough,' Noah said. 'And easier to work in here. My bedroom's at the front of the house, someone could've seen me.'

'So you're cautious. You see others, but you don't want to be seen. You were coming to this house when you

263

were out on bail, after you'd attacked Julie. You put her photo up here, and Natalie's. The photos you took from their house.'

'I wanted them with me.'

'They're just pictures.'

'They're more than that. They're people. They're puzzles.'

Marnie studied the walls in silence. 'The pit in the cellar, who was it for?'

'I don't know, it doesn't fit.' Noah shut his eyes, trying to make this work. He'd role-played sadists before, and killers. He and Marnie had solved many cases like this, but with Vokey he wasn't feeling it. He couldn't connect to the man, or his motives. 'For the woman§ who came after Julie? Who *comes* after Julie.'

'People are puzzles,' Marnie repeated softly. 'You don't understand them.'

'They make no sense to me, there's always a piece missing. But that could be from me, just as Alyson told Joe Coen. Those pictures of Ruth. I showed her no mercy, or pity.' Noah gathered a breath, holding it in his chest. 'All right. I *know* there's something missing, I can feel it. I know my art's twisted, indecent. It's why I hid those particular photos under the floor. Because I know there's something wrong with my art, with me.'

'What are you going to do about it?'

'I'm doing it. I got away. I couldn't be inside, Ruth's right about that, I was scared in there. Of being found out, or kept away from the people I need. Like Alyson.'

'Alyson's sick,' Marnie said. 'Progressive Supranuclear Palsy. Joe says she hadn't told anyone about the PSP, certainly not Michael. Joe asked her about the threatening letter she'd received – "We won't warn you again" – but she dismissed it as hate mail. Colin's seeing if it matches the forgeries found on the allotment.'

'Darren didn't write those,' Noah said. 'He doesn't have the imagination, for one thing.'

'That's what Lara said, about Michael.' Marnie pushed her curls from her face. 'It's how she knew the more recent letters were forgeries. Too creative, she said. Too articulate.'

'And her letter about the red dress. If she didn't write that then who did?'

'That's what we need to find out.'

'We'll be too late,' Noah said. 'That's what I'm afraid of. He's out there, he's had days already, or someone has. We're not even close. We'll be too late to turn this around.'

'We can't think like that. We have to believe we'll find him, or that he'll hand himself in.'

'Why would he do that? What's he got left to lose?'

'There's always something left to lose,' Marnie said.

Noah was close enough to catch the clean scent of her skin; she'd splashed water on her face and neck. 'I saw my parents,' he said. 'The day we found these faces at Marion's house. I went to Pentonville because I knew they were visiting Sol. Mum didn't speak to me, wouldn't even look at me. She blames me for the arrest, of course. I thought I could make them understand but she already understands everything that matters. I betrayed my brother, betrayed them. That's how she sees it, and she's right. When you boil it down, that's exactly what I did.'

'What choice did he leave you? If you hadn't arrested him, his gang would have gone after Dan, or you. That would have been a betrayal of Dan.'

'I'm pretty sure he's in danger right now.'

Marnie looked at him. 'Dan?'

'Sol. I was stupid not to think it through. As if prisons aren't full of factions, gangs.' Noah closed a hand across his mouth, thumb and fingers pressing his cheekbones. 'I

265

told myself I was putting an end to it, getting him *out* of trouble. But all I've done is trap him in a place where he's watching his back twenty-four seven. Making new deals, worse ways to stay safe.'

'You can't beat yourself up.' She put a cool hand on his wrist. 'That doesn't help anyone. You, or Sol, or this investigation.'

'I know.' Noah nodded. 'I do know.' He drew a short breath, enough to be able to smile at her. 'How are things with you?'

He was expecting the familiar assurance, or another plea to give her time, but Marnie said, 'Can you stand to see more photos?' Her eyes were ink-blue, unwavering.

'Of course.' He watched her reach into her bag and remove a paper wallet. Judging by the creases at its corners, it'd been in her bag for a while.

'Eight weeks ago,' her fingers found the creases, smoothing them, 'Stephen gave me an answer to the question I've been asking him for the last six years.'

Noah didn't need to ask which question. He watched her face, every flicker, every pulse. She was hesitating, reluctant to share whatever secrets were inside the paper wallet. The answers she'd been seeking, why Stephen killed her parents after they gave him a home, a sister.

'He said he did it because they broke their promises to him, and to Children's Services. They made him meet with his birth mother, the woman who abused him for the first eight years of his life. Stella Keele. She's the reason he was in care.' Marnie held the wallet as delicately as if it were an injured bird, or a letter bomb. 'He told me they brought Stella into their house and made Stephen sit next to her on the sofa, drinking tea and eating biscuits. I told him I didn't believe him.' She stroked her thumb at the smiling images on the wallet. 'He said the evidence was in here. Pictures taken on my dad's camera, the last pictures he took. Stephen hid the camera, but Harry found it after the break-in at my house.' She reached out, putting the wallet of photos into Noah's hand. 'Stephen said if I developed the film, I'd see the truth for myself. What they did to make him murder them.'

The blue paper was cool under Noah's fingers.

'He dared me to look.' Marnie moved precisely, placing her wrists at the lip of the table, summoning a symmetry which was ruined by the messy spill of pain from her eyes. 'Go on, it's okay. Not what you might be thinking. Just photos.'

Noah opened the wallet, taking the content by its edges. Glossy prints, their colours intense, details sharp. A garden with a swing, the grass an unearthly green. A gravel driveway where a newly washed car was sparkling in the sun. The yellow sofa where a boy sat, his face and body rigid, eyes scribbled black by fear. In a chair with a red cushion, a blonde woman smiled easily for the camera. Another of the two together on the sofa – the woman and the boy – their likeness seated between them like a ghost. Stephen held a glass of squash, the light falling into it as fire, his fingers white around it, a plate of biscuits balanced on his knees. In the photos he looked about ten, but he was older. Fourteen, the age at which he'd killed Marnie's parents. They didn't appear in any of the photographs, Marnie's father behind the camera, her mother out of shot. Noah turned to another print of the garden, Stella Keele with her arm around Stephen's shoulders, his expression beyond terror, towards anger now.

'That's why he killed them,' Marnie said softly. 'Because they brought her back into his life. They were meant to be keeping him safe from her, but instead they did this.'

267

She moved her hand, its fingers thin and white. 'He wants me to believe it was a form of self-defence, or revenge. Not motiveless or senseless. *This* is why he did it. Because they were arrogant enough to think they could reconcile him with his abuser and— It's as if I've lost them all over again.' Shadows fractured her face. 'Six years ago it was their deaths, the violence of their deaths, but now it feels as if I never knew them at all.'

With these photographs, Stephen had robbed her of any hope of happy memories, making her an orphan for a second time. Noah, who was trying to keep his family together, felt her pain reach under his ribs, its fingers scrabbling for purchase in his chest.

'And then there's this.' Marnie took the photos from his hand, separating three from the rest of the set. 'Here. And here.' Pointing to a detail in each one. 'And here.'

All three photos had been taken outside the house with the street visible in the background. In the first photo, of the car sparkling in the driveway, a man stood under the trees across the street from Marnie's house. In a baseball cap and dark jacket, fists in the pockets of his jeans. The same man was in the second and third photos, the cap shielding his face from the camera. His body language rang alarm bells in Noah's head. A watcher. He was watching the house. 'Who is he?'

'I've no idea.' Marnie reached for the bottle of water. 'There was never anyone else. No strangers in the vicinity, no reports from the neighbours. It was always just Stephen, we never looked for anyone else.'

'He confessed, didn't he?'

'He said nothing, in fact. When the police got there he was sitting on the stairs covered in their blood and with injuries consistent with having used the knife, repeatedly.'

'He'd have denied it. If it wasn't him. Surely? All this

268

time . . .' Baiting her, bringing her back to the prison again and again, promising to tell her the secret of why he did it, keeping her close, never letting her go. 'He wouldn't have taken the blame unless he did it.'

'Perhaps he believes he did it. Or he did it. Probably he did it.' But there was a slice of doubt in her voice, in her head. The photos had put it there and she hadn't been able to let it go.

'Did he *know* you'd see this man in these photos?' Noah asked. 'Did he say anything about anyone else at the house, someone your dad might've photographed?'

'Just his mother, Stella.'

'What about Stephen's father?'

'Theo Keele? It could be him.' Marnie's tone said she'd considered this possibility. 'Perhaps he gave his wife a lift that day, but didn't come into the house. I've no way of knowing.'

'Did your dad know, d'you think? Did he see this man when he was taking the photos?'

'If he did, he said nothing about it. No reports to the police, nothing on record.' Marnie's face was open, laid bare for his scrutiny. 'I don't know, Noah. I may be going mad. Why would I even want to believe in Stephen's innocence after all this time, all the evidence he's a psycho-path, invested in my pain?' She drew a breath, reaching for the photo of Stephen with his mother. 'When I first looked at these, my worst thought was, *Why didn't you kill her? Why did it have to be them?* That was bad enough, wishing her dead. Then I became angry with them for putting themselves in danger and for what? To have him hug it out with the woman who'd screwed him up so horribly in the first place? I couldn't stop staring at the photos, every detail. That's when I spotted the lurker and it was – *relief*. I was relieved at the idea of someone else being there. Not just the three of them getting smaller and smaller in that house, suffocating.'

Noah thought fleetingly of his parents' house after he'd left home. Mum and Dad learning to live with Sol's excesses. But he could access the happy memories easily enough, nothing had happened to destroy that. The past was always tricky to navigate. For Marnie, it was treacherous.

'I want to believe there was someone else, but why?' She shook her head. 'To make my peace with Stephen because he's so ill? Or to keep this quest alive? I don't know who I am if I'm not hunting for answers about their deaths. It's been my life for so long, I'm afraid of the person I'll be if I stop. I've made it so much a part of me, an obsession, the same as Lara and Ruth. I'll be lost without it. If he dies and I don't have answers, I'll be lost.'

She marshalled a smile before Noah could speak. 'Sorry, I'm offloading and we have work to do, but I became a detective to get away from that house. Stephen knows it, he knows how unhappy I was there, with them. I've never admitted it to anyone, but he knew.'

Stephen murdered her parents, Noah was sure of it. The pleasure he'd taken in torturing her ever since hadn't come from thin air. Stephen was a psychopath. And he kept finding new ways to hurt her, this fresh doubt being the latest. Noah reached for her hand and held it.

'I know it's madness,' she said quietly. 'I do know that. He killed them, and he didn't have a good reason, it wasn't self-defence. They never meant to hurt him, or frighten him. They thought they were doing the right thing and it was wrong, you and I can see that, but it wasn't cruel. They did their best, just as they did with me. They weren't perfect, but why should they have been?' She gripped Noah's hand, attempting a proper smile. 'I just need to find them again, that's all. I've been so obsessed with their deaths I've forgotten who they were. I could tell you the exact pattern of the entry wounds on their bodies, their handprints in the kitchen. That's what I see when I shut my eyes, bloody handprints and evidence bags. I don't see living, flawed people. This is what I need to sort out. Not what Stephen did or didn't do, or why. They haven't been human to me for a long time. I need them to be human again.'

She retrieved the wallet of photos, returning it to her bag. 'But it made me think,' nodding at the room, 'photos can be weapons. Photos can *lie*—'

She stepped up to the wall of faces, closing in on the black and white ones. 'Szondi's test. It reminds me of mirrors, the way a camera inverts every image.' She touched a hand to her left lip. 'What if we're seeing everything back to front? Michael, and those women. I can't see him; that's never happened to me before. Even when I can't solve a puzzle I can usually see its pieces. But he's invisible. Smoke, like Aidan said. I can't get a grip on him.' She glanced across at Noah, a frown shadowing her eyes. 'We're used to being a step behind at the start of an investigation. Those first few days are all about catching up, but I don't feel we're on the same road as him. Even now, after nearly two weeks. Something's wrong, more than the riot and the fire and the escape. I told myself it was because Stephen was one of his victims but that's too easy.' She set her hand on one of the unidentified faces. 'I recognise these women, their emptiness. The urge to fill it with something, someone. I understood Lara, even before she started to tell me her truth. It's Michael who makes no sense to me. Why didn't he run to one of them? Lara, or Ruth, or Alyson. They look like Alyson, have you noticed? Ruth and Lara, big and blonde like his sister. He *needs* these women. This isn't someone who can survive on his own. He needs company, and he needs routine. Look how he worked on the men in Leeds, a ready-made audience. When he ran from Cloverton, he must have had someone to run to—'

Noah's phone buzzed and he answered it with a look of apology for Marnie. 'DS Jake.'

'The nine-millimetre Baikal.' It was Harry Kennedy. 'We did some digging. It's part of a batch sold out of Luton last year. A couple of convictions came off the back of it. One of those we convicted ended up in Leeds. Sharing a cell with guess who.'

Noah met Marnie's eyes, his grip tightening on the phone. 'Michael Vokey?'

'The same. I've got the cellmate's name,' Harry said. 'But you may already know it. Charlie Lamb. He told the court he had the gun for his own protection, for his family's sake. Well, who knows? But he's deceased. He died in the prison, a suicide. Vokey was given counselling, because he was sharing a cell with Charlie at the time. Something tells me you'll want to look into that.'

272

35

I wanted to spare you the sordid details, but it's too late for that. My fingers and toes won't stop twitching because my liver's packing up, that's what I heard the doctor telling my lucky nurse. I'm blue, like bad bacon. Hot then cold, my heart beating so fast I can see it under the hospital gown, under the tubes and blankets. Everything hurts, even sleeping. I can't hold onto a thought that makes sense for longer than a nanosecond. I'm on the blink, every bit of me misfiring. Broken, inside and out. Mickey did that, in case there's any doubt. Came at me through the smoke like a steam train. I never imagined he could move so fast, or that he'd want to. I ran, but he took me down and kept me down with his fists and feet, packing a year's worth of exertion into those few frantic minutes when he was killing me.

You might not believe me, of course. I know how the truth sounds coming from the likes of me. A convict, a criminal. I spent too much time around Mickey and Aidan and the others. Too much time inhabiting the fantasy worlds of Lara and Ruth, inventing stories to fill their sad lives. If I went too far, I'm sorry. My nurse says I'm okay, but the doctors don't agree. I've problems with breathing and processing, with my liver and heart and kidneys. Now they're saying hallucinations, delusions. I never said I was the perfect witness, but I'm doing my best because I'm the only one who saw it all unfold the way it did. I have to do my best, don't I? However much I'd rather lie here counting the minutes until the next shot, until my nurse washes me with sponges in the gentle way she has, the crucifix swinging at her throat so that if I could only just unfurl my fingers and lift my hand, if I could get my arm off the bed and reach—

I'd have it, the crucifix. I'd have it in my fist and then I could pull her close, enough for her to hear the thoughts inside my skull, battering to get out, all the places I'm trying so hard to tell the truth about what happened.

'Listen,' I'd say. 'I'll tell you how it went. Like this—'

Dazza doesn't know. He thinks he does, reckons he's the world expert on Michael Vokey because he spent so long shining his shoes with his spit. He knows nothing. Mickey used to mock him late at night. He'd be reading Lara's letters, and he'd swing his voice straight into Dazza's, 'You've got mail, Michael! Nice fat ones today. Photos, I'll bet. Lucky bastard, wish I had some bored cow flashing her tits in my direction.' Then he'd swing his voice again, pretending to be Dazza's mum because Dazza had told him all about her, 'Be a big boy, Darren, you're a big boy now. No one likes a cry baby. Accidents happen and we clean them up.'

I picture her in a rocking chair with a pile of knitting in her lap, jaw working as she addresses Dazza, laying out her instructions, building him up then breaking him down. That's how you take charge of people, take control. I've known women like that, mothers like that.

Mickey swears it wasn't the same for him, growing up

in a house with a cellar in West London. Not a big house but deep, that's how I picture it. One of those that runs below street level, where once upon a time the coal was dumped. A deep black throat under the house, sticky with soot where butterflies hibernate, hanging from the anthracite, wings whispering as they sleep.

Ruth didn't believe in the cellar, until I told her.

'Dearest Ruth,' I wrote, 'I'm worrying again about the house. I try not to, because I know you're right. Home doesn't have to be the place you were born. Family doesn't need to mean a mother and father and a sister who's moved away, too far to help me now. It means so much to know you're close by, but the house means a lot too. It's a place where we can start again, together. You and me. It's not consecrated but it's spiritual to me, and I hope to you. A fresh start, that's what my house means to me now. A chance for us to be together.'

Mickey grunts his approval at my choice of words. He's the sticky black rock where my butterfly clings, waiting for the spring. I can wait a long time. The grunts turn to snoring and I know he's asleep, so I keep writing. Words are my weapons, for now.

'All of my childhood is in the house. I worry how it's going, the sale and the probate. I can't imagine never being able to set foot in there again, the only place I've ever felt truly safe. It's worse than ever in here now, I'm afraid to sleep. You can't imagine what it's like to have to lie less than three feet from a man who wants you dead. After the scissors, I know he's serious. I hear his heart beating up there, just above me. All the things he says he wants to do to me, and I know he means it because of what happened the last time he lost his temper. I know he'll kill me if he can.'

Mickey sleeps on, snoring in the bunk that was mine.

275

'Thank you for your last letter.' My pen is smooth on the page, the envelope addressed and ready for Dazza to smuggle out of here. 'I read it in secret when he was asleep. If he knew I had a friend like you he'd try to destroy us somehow, twist you against me or stop your letters reaching me. He'd break my fingers if he knew I was drawing you. He hates that we have this, so special and precious and beautiful. What we have is beautiful. You say you're collecting sheet music, but *you* are my music. I'm no good with hymns, but I've always found church music a comfort. Like you, my dearest. My angel. I want to fill my house, our house, with your music.'

I thought for a long time before I wrote the next bit. Examined it from every angle, considered all the consequences. I knew I could get the letter out, with Dazza's help. Mickey wouldn't want to see it, he never wanted to see the letters I wrote. Even so, I had to consider the consequences. But in the end it came down to this – he'd left me with no choice.

'If I could find a way for you to get inside the house,' I wrote, 'my mother's house in London, you'd help me, wouldn't you? Ruth, please. Help me.'

36

'We made this monster.' Marnie stood beside the eight images of Cloverton's escaped prisoner. 'Michael John Vokey. We heard too many legends and rumours. Somewhere along the line we forgot about hard evidence. So we start over. Everything. Take apart what we know about him, separate it out from what we've heard or suspect. Two boards. One with what we're assuming, the other with the hard facts.'

'He ran,' Ron said. 'That's a fact.'

'People run for lots of reasons.' Noah was watching Marnie, on the alert for signs of stress. Not from the case, which was complex enough. From the photos she'd shared, and the guilt and grief he knew she was fighting. 'We've made a lot of assumptions off the back of his escape.'

'Then the men he maimed,' Ron argued. 'Those two he blinded.'

'We don't know he did that,' Marnie said. 'We have no evidence, no witnesses.'

It was true. Noah felt a pang of guilt. He'd judged so much about Vokey from his sketches, forgetting to think like a detective as well as a psychologist. There wasn't much to recommend Michael Vokey to a jury, but did that mean he was a maniac? If so, where was the evidence they needed in order to bring charges?

'The inmates won't speak with us because Vokey's out there.' Marnie rolled back the cuffs of her shirt. 'Posing a threat to their loved ones, that's been our working hypothesis. We haven't considered the possibility of the threat remaining present, within Cloverton. Yet we know Darren Quayle has a notebook he's using for the purposes of blackmail.'

'You're not telling me they're scared of him,' Ron objected. 'Inmates like that, and a kid like Quayle? What about Vokey's anger? That's well documented up in Leeds, and at Cloverton. Highly manipulative and aggressive. How'd they put it? "Like an outbreak of rabies." He's on record for losing his temper, shouting at night, smashing his cell, you name it.'

'That could be night terrors,' Noah said. 'We jumped to rage, didn't look for the causes of it.'

'All right, Doctor Phil.' Ron rolled his eyes. 'Aggravated burglary, how about that? He *sat* on Julie Seton.'

'Yes.' Marnie nodded. 'Put it on the board.'

'The grave in the cellar.' Ron folded his arms, planting his feet apart on the floor. 'We don't know who dug it, but the Polaroids in that room. Those are his photos, Alyson confirmed that.'

'What's the offence?' Debbie challenged. 'We can't do him for taking photos and pinning them to his walls. The best we've got is trespass, since the house's in probate.'

'If he didn't dig that grave then who did?' Ron demanded.

'Maybe it wasn't dug *by* him,' Debbie said. 'Maybe it was dug *for* him. This whole thing might be about revenge.'

'Whose? You're not saying *Julie* dug a grave.'

'Maybe, if she felt threatened by him. We know she doesn't trust us to keep her kiddie safe.'

'When would she find the time to mess about breaking into houses and digging graves? If he came at her in the street, maybe. If he went into the chippy, I can see her chucking hot fat in his face. But that pit was a proper job, professional.'

Marnie was silent, watching Ron and Debbie thrash through the possibilities. It was good for the team to look at this from other angles, refresh their thinking. She couldn't shake the feeling that they'd fallen into the trap of believing Vokey was to blame for everything. Whose trap, she didn't know.

'I still say it's about revenge.' Debbie put her hand on Alyson's photo. 'We've been assuming he's the one after it, but what if it's one of them?' She nodded at the women's faces. 'What if they wanted to punish him, pay him back?'

'Alyson can't manage her own stairs without falling down. She's sick, remember?'

'Then Lara or Ruth, or the two of them together. What about that letter to Alyson: "*We* won't warn you again." We thought that was Ruth and Lara doing his bidding, but what if that's never what they were doing, if they wanted him out of prison so they could get revenge?'

'Revenge for what? Ruth doesn't give a stuff what he did to Julie.' Ron juggled the marker pen impatiently. 'And Lara's too busy having a midlife crisis to figure out which way's up.'

'Who had access to the house?' Marnie said. 'Alyson, and Michael. Who else? Let's trace the keys, this set that Alyson said their mum hid at the back of the house. You're right about the pit. We need to know who dug it, and why.'

Ron scowled at the pictures of Vokey. 'He started the

fire at Cloverton. The T-shirt with the cooking fat, that was his.'

'Put it on the board.'

'Whoever blinded those blokes was off his head, that was savage.'

'Yes, it was.' Marnie nodded. 'But Aidan doesn't believe it was done by Michael Vokey.'

Ron moved his head like a bull negotiating a narrow corridor. 'This's the problem, isn't it? All our witnesses are either bent, blind or dead. Without CCTV, we're sunk.'

They studied the two boards. Noah could taste the defeat in the room. Everyone was tired, under pressure to get results, but the case was slipping away from them. It had been slipping for days.

'The suicide in Leeds,' Debbie said. 'Everyone's certain that was Vokey's work. Not murder, but inciting suicide. Not enough evidence to convict, but he'd tried it more than once.'

Marnie nodded at her to add this information to the clean board. 'Colin's running checks for us on the suicide in Leeds. DS Kennedy's traced a connection between the firearm found on the allotment and the young man who hanged himself, Charlie Lamb.'

'Bent prison officers?' Ron suggested. 'Not just Quayle, up in Leeds too?' He scowled afresh. 'I don't like that we're pointing fingers at everyone except the bastard who ran. It doesn't feel right.'

'We know he's sadistic, and obsessive,' Marnie said. 'We know there's something very wrong with him, but we've been assuming too much and it's getting us nowhere.' Her stare scanned the boards. 'Lara never met him. Neither did Ruth. His sister hasn't seen him in months. Julie saw him, up close and recently.' She turned to Noah. 'What was the word she used to describe him?'

'Pathetic. She said he was pathetic. We thought she was being brave, understating her fear. We know she's angry, feeling let down by us.'

'She's not scared of him or she wouldn't leave Natalie in that house, or walk back from work alone at midnight.' Marnie shut her eyes briefly before meeting Noah's gaze. 'What if we're searching all the dark corners and missing what's in plain sight?'

'Like what?' Ron grumbled. 'I can't see anything in plain sight except these bloody pictures, his creepy obsession with taking photos. Remember how it felt in that house?' He nodded at Noah. 'Like a punch in the gut. *That* was instinct. We knew we had a nutter, we need to keep hold of that.'

'I'm not saying he isn't a monster,' Marnie said, 'I'm questioning *our* monster, the one we've built from bits and pieces of soft evidence which, if we caught him today, wouldn't be enough to secure any conviction beyond the escape, and possibly arson.'

'Well that's enough to put him away, isn't it?' Ron argued. 'For a long time.'

'And if someone else did the worst of that damage at Cloverton? Don't you think we should be looking to convict that person?'

Ron wiped the sweat from his forehead with the cuff of his shirt. 'If he even exists.'

'Vokey didn't tweak Aidan's antennae—' Marnie started to say.

'It's come to this, has it?' DCS Ferguson had entered the room, standing with her arms folded and her head cocked. 'Taking our cues from an Irishman with too much time on his hands and a nose for mischief? We need results, people.'

'Aidan has a point, one we should have noted,' Marnie

281

said. 'One man doing all that damage while he was busy trying to escape? It makes no sense. Either you're running or you're wreaking havoc. Hard to do both with such a narrow window of time before you're reported missing.'

'Forensics turned up his DNA at the shed, that's right, isn't it?' Ferguson nodded at the new evidence board. 'Not to mention a firearm. He had an escape plan, in other words. Knew exactly where he was headed, and how to get there. Plus I'd ask why Aidan's so forthcoming all of a sudden.' Her eyebrows rose in a challenge. 'You're clearly buying it at any price, DI Rome, but why wasn't he sharing these great insights a week ago?'

'He was being treated for smoke inhalation a week ago,' Marnie said. 'He didn't witness the riot but he's been asking questions, finding out what he can and piecing it together.'

'Detective Inspector Duffy?' Ferguson gave a humourless laugh. 'With his little grey cells . . . Or should I say black cells, after the fire.'

'He smuggled in a pair of shoes for Vokey.' Marnie kept her tone bland, non-combative. 'He's been feeling guilty about that.'

'He wouldn't know *guilty* if it sat down next to him.' Ferguson treated Marnie to the hard stare for another moment before she sniffed. 'What sort of shoes?'

'Running shoes.'

'Right, that goes on the board.' Ron picked up the marker pen. 'No way Vokey wasn't planning this escape. Running, and hiding.'

'We know he's good at hiding,' Ferguson agreed. 'What's to say he's not skilled in other areas, such as managing to maim a couple of inmates along the way?'

'It isn't just Vokey who's good at hiding.' Noah nodded at the first board. 'Every one of these people, everyone who got close to him, has surprised us. We expected Julie to be intimidated. We thought Lara would be another bored housewife, that Ruth was a religious zealot. Every assumption we've made has been upended.'

'Is this heading towards a revelation,' Ferguson asked, 'or are we self-flagellating for a bet?'

'What if one of these women was only pretending to be close to Vokey, in his thrall like the rest? As DC Tanner said.' Noah nodded at Debbie. 'What if she got close to him not because she craved attention, but because she wanted to punish him?'

'I'm warming to your theme, but which one? Not Lara, or Alyson. Julie?'

'Maybe. She's the one with the motive for revenge.'

'Back up a bit,' Ferguson said. 'These letters that look like being forgeries. Who're we saying wrote them? Because Darren doesn't strike me as the literary type. The easily swayed type, that's another matter. If one of these women set out to seduce him for whatever purpose, I can buy that.' She clicked her tongue at Noah. 'Still no-commenting, is he?'

'I'm afraid so.'

'Lara said Michael's last letter arrived a fortnight before the riot. This is the last letter she's certain *he* wrote.' Marnie pinned Colin's chronology to the board. 'She'd stopped writing as soon as she began to suspect the letters coming from Cloverton weren't from Michael. But we found recent letters in the post room, pretending to be from Lara. So the forgeries were running both ways. Into the prison and out of it.'

'Who'd do that?' Ron squinted at the chronology. 'I mean what's the point? If you're forging stuff it's to extort money or influence. These were what, love letters? Who forges love letters?'

'Maybe Vokey liked the letters.' Noah was thinking out

loud. 'We know he's obsessive. What if the letters were a way of keeping him in line?'

'Or someone wanted him thinking he'd a place to hide if he ever got out.' Ferguson narrowed her eyes. 'Happen the letters were a trap and our friend in the cells was in on it. He's got mates up in Leeds, hasn't he? He could be covering his tracks, arranging for Lara's letters to be posted up in Keswick, setting her up nicely should the police start poking their noses around his allotment.'

'I don't know.' Ron pulled at his bottom lip. 'Sounds a bit far-fetched to me.'

'As the person sent on the wild goose chase,' Ferguson replied acidly, 'I get to say what's far-fetched or otherwise. It was certainly *far*. Hauling us up to Cumbria just when it looks likely Vokey was in Harpenden all along, what with the evidence stacking up against our bent prison officer.'

Ron knuckled his nose. 'So we're really looking at Darren for this? He gives that interview online, like a boy scout with a crush, then he what? Ups and tops his hero?'

'He's the one with the firearm, and the matching residue,' Ferguson reminded him. 'Tell me you didn't swallow that story about shooting at squirrels in the wood.'

'I can see him showing off. Protecting Vokey, even hiding him. But killing? Nah. He's too nervy, a proper mummy's boy. And where's the motive? I'm not buying the seduction routine.'

They turned when the door opened.

It was Colin, looking pink. 'The man who hanged himself in Leeds, Charlie Lamb? You asked me to see what I could find out, boss.' His eyes were big with news. 'You'll want to hear this.'

The phone rang at the other end of the room, and Debbie moved to answer it.

Colin pinned a new mugshot to the clean evidence

board. 'Charles Eric Lamb. Father deceased. Leeds had his next-of-kin listed as Anita Elisabeth Lamb. His mum.'

The image showed a young man with dark hair and eyes, cut-glass cheekbones and a freckled nose. Noah felt a jolt of recognition, his memory serving up an earlier version of the same face in a cheap frame, one of many in the ugly room with a white smell of lilies.

'Wait,' Ferguson was saying, '*Anita* Elisabeth?'

'He's Darren's brother,' Noah said to Marnie. 'She had a photo of the pair of them, remember? Darren in his school uniform and as a baby, with an older boy. That was Charlie.'

The boy in the photo, too young to be Darren's father. Charlie Lamb.

Colin nodded. 'He's Darren's older brother. They don't share the same surname as Anita reverted to her maiden name after she was widowed. Charlie was convicted two years ago of possessing a gun. He'd fallen foul of a Luton gang, argued the gun was for protection. He was sentenced for possession, sent to Leeds. Where his cellmate was Michael Vokey.'

'Shit,' Ron said. 'This's that suicide, the one Vokey talked into topping himself?'

'If Darren blamed Michael for his brother's death—' Colin began.

'He wasn't helping him to escape,' Ron said. 'He was getting him out of prison so he could kill him. He had him in his shed. He had a gun and several miles of woodland for burying the body.'

Noah couldn't take his eyes from Charlie Lamb's face, imagining how it must have felt to be locked in a cell with a man like Michael Vokey, so far from hope you had to take your own life. 'The police dogs didn't find anything in the woods.'

285

'They weren't cadaver dogs,' Ferguson pointed out. 'We weren't looking for a dead body.'

'Oh, shit.' Ron folded his hands on his head. 'Deb called it. Revenge.' He looked for her across the room. 'You called it, Tanner!'

Debbie set the phone down, coming back towards them. 'That was Julie Seton.' Her face was full of worry. 'Little Natalie's gone missing.'

Marnie's attention switched from the evidence boards to Debbie's news. 'How long?'

'Not long, an hour maybe. Julie was at work and her mum was babysitting. She let her in.'

'Let who in?' Ferguson asked sharply.

'Ruth,' Debbie said. 'Julie says Natalie was taken by Ruth Hull.'

37

Julie's mum was ashen, her mouth shrunken, voice shaking, 'I thought it were Perry. He said he'd bring sweets for Nat. Julie don't like him coming round here, but he's good with kiddies and Nat loves him. Only it weren't Perry, it were her.'

'Ruth Hull.' Marnie held up the image. 'Is this the woman?'

'That's her, Ruth. Victim Support, she said, asking for Julie. I told her Julie's at work, so she asks to check on Nat. I didn't think anything of it with you lot traipsing in and out all this time.' She fretted the unlit cigarette between her fingers. 'Nat liked her, that's how it looked. She's a clever girl, ten times smarter than me.' She started to cry, tears trapped in the lines under her eyes. 'I should've fought her. If it were a bloke I'd have gone for him, I swear. But she looked all right, dressed nice, talked proper. I thought she were one of you.'

'Did she have a car?' Noah asked. 'How did she take Natalie?'

'On foot—!' It came out as a wail. 'They walked off up the street together. I let them go!'

'Mrs Seton. Lisa.' Marnie put a hand on the woman's arm. 'Try and stay calm. We need your help. Was Ruth with anyone else? Did you see anyone else?'

'Just her. And Nat, my little nut, skipping up the street with her.' Her face worked, fighting back the tears. 'Julie's in a state, she'll never forgive me. I let her go, held the bloody door open for her!'

'Ruth was on foot. Headed in which direction, towards the shops?'

'Up the bypass, where the buses go. There's an ice-cream van up there, she said, "Let's get you some fresh air and a lolly," and I let them because Nat were that excited and she looked like one of you, an ID card round her neck and everything. Made me feel like *I'm* the one breaking the law, doing a bad job of looking after Nat with the curtains drawn and her stuck inside on a day like this, and then there's those two in the car, isn't there? *They* missed it. It weren't just me making a muck of things. It were them too.'

The police officers in the patrol car had been searching for Natalie and Ruth since the alarm was raised seventy minutes ago. They'd missed Ruth's arrival at the house, and her departure with Natalie. They didn't have an excuse, other than to say they'd been watching a gang of kids at the other end of the estate who looked like they might be trouble.

'Where's Julie?' Lisa Seton dried her tears with her sleeve. 'I should be with her, if she'll let us. I want to be with her, not sat here doing nowt.'

'We'd rather you stayed here, in case Natalie comes home.'

'How can she when that cow's got her? What's she even *want*? Who takes a kiddie unless they're a pervert, and you said she's not a pervert so what's she *want*?'

*

288

Julie's expression was unyielding – no tears, only fury. 'She walked her out of there like a dog, right under the noses of those bastards you put in the car to protect us. Up the street – *our* street – and not one person stops to ask who she is or what she's doing with Nat. They just let her go.' She was wearing Natalie's hairband around her wrist, snapping the elastic until the plastic bobble left a mark on her skin. 'That bastard sells her an ice cream out of his van and doesn't ask who that cow is, when he's only ever seen Nat with me or my mum. The whole lot of them just let it happen. Our *friends*. Our *neighbours*.'

Noah waited until she was quiet before he said, 'We know who she is. Ruth Hull. We think we know what she wants.'

'*I* know what she bloody wants!' Julie balled her fists in her lap. 'She's *his*. That's why she gave her name to my mum, wore it round her neck on a badge, so I'd be in no doubt. One of his cows from the court steps, writing letters. I know what she wants because she told me, but she never said she'd take my kid if she didn't get it. I knew she was crazy but not like that. Not like this.'

'You've met her?' Marnie asked. 'On the court steps, or more recently?'

'She came to the chippy two days ago.' Julie snapped the elastic at her wrist. 'Said you lot brought her to London to answer questions about *Michael*. I should start telling the truth, that's what she said. Because that's what it'd take to get him the help he needs. *Him*. The help *he* needs.'

'What did she mean by that?'

'He's in danger, that's what she said. You should be treating him like a missing person.' Julie set her teeth. 'Like Natalie. But you're too busy pretending he's a nutter, and that's going to get him killed.' She bit her lip, hard. 'I said she was talking shit, she's no idea what he's like.

289

That's when she starts up about how I'd lied in court, said this's on *me* because I lied and that's what got him locked up where he went mad, so mad he had to run.'

'Why didn't you report her?' Noah asked. 'This harassment—'

'This harassment's my *life*,' Julie said furiously. 'Don't you get that? I told you back at the house. I get it from friends and neighbours, I get it from kids, even my mum. I'm sick of being told I brought this on myself, that I should've done things differently. I've been doing as I'm told for *months*.' She snapped the elastic so savagely the plastic bobble cracked against the bone in her wrist. 'I didn't want to lie in that court, I wanted to tell the truth because it should've been enough. It *was* enough. Just because he didn't rape me, didn't beat me up or kill me, somehow it was nothing? It wasn't *nothing*. It was my whole life, changed.'

'You didn't want to lie in court.'

Julie shut her eyes tight against Marnie's stare. 'They said I had to build it up, that it wasn't enough because the jury wouldn't understand. They had to see me terrified, see me *cry*. I couldn't tell them he was just a creep, a nobody who followed me home from work, begging me to let him draw me, saying he just wanted to look at me. He sat here,' rapping her knuckles on her breastbone, 'and he *looked* and talked and it was just *words*, okay? He didn't hit me, didn't use his fists. It was all just words and his eyes on my skin, soaking me up.'

Pain opened her face. She looked at Marnie, at Noah. 'He wouldn't shut up. Whispering these insults, all the ways I disgusted him, the sick things he was going to do, but he couldn't even get it up. He's nobody, a *loser*. If he'd got it up, I'd have known what to do. I'd have gone for his eye, or his balls. But it was just *words* and the way he

290

stared, making me less than— Like I was *nothing*.' Her wrist was bruised blue under the elastic band. 'No one teaches you how to fight words or looks, not like that.' She swiped at her eyes angrily. 'I've been stared at in the street, course I have. Like I'm scum or like I'm meat, but this wasn't that. This was like I was *nothing*. I could see myself in his eyes. *Tiny*. He kept saying it, "You're nothing, you're empty. Just a stink and some skin. You're *nothing*," on and on. He wouldn't shut up.' She collected her fingers into fists again. 'When I gave up smoking, a mate lent me this hypnosis tape to help me quit. That's what it's like listening to him, that's what his voice does. Goes on and on and *on*. Gets inside your head so you can hear it even after he's gone.' She drilled her fingers to her temples. 'He's *here*. He hasn't gone away, not for a second. He's right here.'

Her legal team had advised her against making this statement in court, fearing it wouldn't be sufficient to secure a conviction. It was hard to imagine any jury remaining unmoved by Julie's palpable terror, her trauma. This, more than anything, convinced Noah they'd been right to label Vokey a monster. But Ruth refused to believe it. She'd taken Natalie because she wanted the rest of them to accept her version of Michael.

'We have search teams looking for Natalie,' Marnie was telling Julie. 'We have hostage negotiators on their way.'

'To negotiate what? You can't give her what she wants, because it doesn't exist. She wants her hero back with her, safe and sound. But he doesn't exist. It's a fantasy, she's a fantasist. God knows what lies she's telling to Nat.' Julie's eyes filled with tears again. 'Why'd you have to bring her up to London? Why'd you have to feed her fantasy that he's out there, waiting to be saved?'

'He *is* out there,' Noah said gently. 'We're trying to find

291

him. Did Ruth say anything about where she thinks he might be?'

Julie tipped her head back in a bid to stem the flood of tears. Her shoulders shook. It took a moment for Noah to realise she was laughing. Not happily, but laughing. 'He's dead! She thinks he's dead, or dying. Trapped somewhere, tricked by someone, God knows. She's crazy! She's crazy and she has Nat. She thinks *he* needs help, not anyone else. Not me, not Nat. Just him. She went on and on about how scared he is, asking me to pray for him, begging me to tell the truth. "I know you lied in court and I know why," as if she's doing me a favour, giving me a chance to say sorry when it wasn't even lies. It wasn't the truth, but it wasn't lies. What he did was far worse than what I said. You think I wouldn't rather have bruises, broken bones? He's in here.' She struck her head with the heel of her hand. 'He's in here the whole time since it happened.' She took a mouthful of air, shivering violently. 'You've checked the chippy, yeah? She hasn't tried to contact me there?'

'Not yet. We have officers there, in case.'

'Don't you have her phone number? Can't you find her that way?'

'Yes,' Marnie said. 'That's what we're doing right now. We have officers out looking for her and we're searching CCTV. Everyone is working to find Natalie.'

Ruth wasn't answering her phone, at least not the number she'd given to the police during the informal interview. Should they have held her after that, or escorted her home to Danbury? Why did it feel as if they'd failed to take her seriously, as a witness or as a threat?

Marnie poured a cup of water and handed it to Julie. 'Did she say anything else when she spoke with you two days ago? Anything which might help us find Natalie?'

'Just that she knew he was in London, that's why she

couldn't go home. She was looking for him, that's what she said. "Just like the police should be, except they don't care if he's dead or alive." Do you? Care?'

'We want to find him, and return him to prison.'

Julie stared at Marnie, looking ill with fear. 'The sickest thing's I understand her. If I were that empty, if my life were that empty, I'd want him to fill it. It's the way he— He sits on you like a nightmare, like one of those nightmares where you can't move and you can't breathe and he's so *solid*. It makes you want to give up.' She set the cup of water down, pulling at Natalie's hairband again. 'He forces you to think about how hard it is to keep fighting when everything's against you. The whole world, that's how it feels sometimes. He's like all of your loneliness and fear and all the things you hate most about yourself and your life, sitting here like a slab.' She spread her hands on her chest, pressing. 'You want to give up, it's like he's giving you permission to just – give up.'

'We need to trace Ruth and Natalie as quickly as possible,' Marnie told the team. 'CCTV, Misper, the full works. We might think it unlikely Ruth will harm Natalie, but we can't operate on that assumption. Where might she have taken her? We're already checking train stations, bus stations, routes home to Danbury, and churches here in London. Where else should we be looking?'

'What does she want?' Debbie asked. 'Is she punishing Julie for her evidence against Michael?'

'That might be a part of it. From what Julie said of their encounter at the chip shop, Ruth's frantic for news of Michael. Perhaps she believes this is how she'll get it.'

'We need to get Darren talking,' Ron said. 'If she's after information about Vokey, Darren's the one in the know.'

293

'Noah's on that.' Marnie nodded. 'Colin, you have the inventory from the allotment?'

He dug it from the folder, handing it across. 'Here, boss.'

She scanned it quickly, looking for the reason why her memory had been prodding her since the discovery that Darren had a brother. 'One pair of men's trainers, size seven.' She tapped her finger to the list. 'I'm willing to bet these are the running shoes Aidan procured for Michael.'

'So?' Ron frowned.

'So why isn't Michael wearing them?' Marnie pinned the inventory to the board. 'If he's out there, running, why isn't he wearing these shoes?'

'Shit.' Ron knuckled his eyes. 'He's dead, isn't he? Quayle killed him and Ruth knows it. Somehow. That's why she's going mental.'

Marnie's phone rang and she lifted a hand for silence.

'DI Rome.'

'I expect you've been waiting for my call.' Her voice was smooth with self-importance. 'This is Ruth Hull. I want to talk about Michael.'

38

'No comment.' Darren Quayle lowered his head, tucking his chin towards his left shoulder, settling in for another hour of refusing to answer questions.

'If I were you,' Noah advised, 'I'd reconsider going on record as not giving a stuff about a missing six-year-old.'

'Do what?' Darren looked over at his solicitor. 'What's that got to do with me?'

'Julie Seton's daughter Natalie was snatched by Ruth Hull two hours ago. Ruth wants to know what's happened to Michael Vokey. Where he is, whether he's safe.'

'Fuck's sake.' He folded his arms on the table and buried his head there. 'This's such *shit*.'

'What's shit, Darren? That a six-year-old is being used as a bargaining chip between two people so infatuated with a violent offender they can't see what's in front of their faces? Michael Vokey isn't worth going to jail for, I think you know that. He's certainly not worth the safety of a child who's already traumatised after seeing her mum assaulted in her own home.'

'I don't *know* where he is, okay?' He croaked the words into the crook of his arm. 'I don't.'

'Ruth thinks you do. She needs news of Michael and she's not going to stop until she gets it.'

'I wasn't there.' Darren lifted his head to look at Noah. His eyes were watering pinkly. 'I don't know what happened. They called us in before the fire was out and he was gone. He was *gone*.'

'Who started the fire?'

'Vokey! His T-shirt, fat from the trays. It was him, okay?'

'You heard, or you know?'

'He showed me.' Traces of last night's fever showed as bruises under Darren's eyes. 'Said he had to get out of there.'

'He told you he was planning to start a fire. Did you report it?'

'If I reported everything I'm told, I'd be doing paperwork twenty-four seven. I didn't think he meant it. I was keeping an eye on him. I was doing my *job*.'

'He knew which route to take that night,' Noah said. 'Which doors would be open for the fire fighters. How did he know that?'

'Fuck knows.' He shrugged the question off. 'I don't.'

He knew. It was written all over his face, the fever allowing his lies no hiding place. He'd aided and abetted, and that was just the tip of the iceberg.

'I'll tell you what I think, shall I?' Noah leaned forward under the light, waiting until Darren's eyes were on him. 'You helped him escape. You hid him in the shed on your mum's allotment, took him clean clothes and food. Money, too. Maybe you intended him to run, except he left his trainers in the shed, the ones Aidan got for him. He has small feet. You take a size ten, so why would you have trainers in a size seven? Because Michael Vokey was there, in your shed, overnight. He slept there, used your fire pit as a toilet. We have his DNA from bodily waste, and from the clothes *you* took to him, clothes and food. Your mum told us about that, said you were out on the night of the riot. You came home from the prison and went straight back out again, stayed out all night.' Noah rapped his knuckles on the table. 'Shit, Darren, we have your *gun*. The gun you hid in the watering can. We took swabs when we checked you in here yesterday, and found fire-arms residue. *On you*. You have a gun and you fired it recently.'

'At squirrels.' His voice was dull, but there was an undercurrent of panic. He hadn't known about his mother's conversation with the police, flinching when Noah mentioned Anita's evidence. 'I told you, I was pissed, shooting at squirrels.'

'Your mum told us you were out the night Vokey ran. Not just during the riot, but afterwards. You were out all night. Is she lying?'

'She got it wrong.' Darren's lower lip lengthened like a sulky child's. 'She thinks she gets to keep tabs on me just because she has to have it all nailed down.'

'All what?'

'Everything! Just because Dad was in the army, the house has to run like clockwork, checklists for everything, always packing and unpacking, moving on. No posters on the walls, not even Blu Tack because the walls aren't ours,' mimicking his mother's voice, 'the house isn't ours. Nothing is ours.' He kicked a foot under the table. 'Less rules in the fucking prison. At least there the inmates get to settle in. They get to stick posters on the walls, what-ever they like.'

Noah thought of the ugly room in Harpenden where he and Marnie had waited for that first interview with Darren. Anita was an army wife, ready for anything except permanence, and the possibility that her son had assisted a dangerous prisoner.

'Your mum's worried about you, Darren, where you went on the night of the riot. I'm guessing she's going to be a lot more worried when she hears about the firearms residue.'

'Yeah? You don't know shit about my mum if you think that.' He bit down hard on his sulky lower lip. 'You need to shut up about my mum. She's nothing to do with this. She's no clue what's going on, that's why she's freaking out. Because she's got no clue, and no *control*.'

'You don't like us talking about your mum. Okay.' Noah sat back, looking through his notes, allowing the panic time to take root. 'Let's talk about the gun. Where did the gun come from?'

Silence. Darren moved his feet under the table. His solicitor sat without speaking, hadn't spoken since Noah informed them of Natalie Seton's kidnap.

'We traced the serial number, so you may as well come clean. Where did you get the gun?'

'I found it.'

'You found it. All right.' Noah nodded. 'Well, we know it was Charlie's gun.'

Darren stared at him, the colour leaving his face, greying his lips.

'Your brother Charlie. It was his gun. Not the one he was charged for possessing, but from the same batch, so I'm guessing he bought two. Did he give one to you? He told the court he didn't feel safe, that's why he had the gun, to protect himself and his family. That's you, Darren. Did he give you the gun?'

'No.' It was a whisper, low.

'But you found it. After he died, or before?'

Darren wet his top lip with his tongue, holding the tip of it between his teeth for a second. 'You don't know what you're talking about.'

'I'm talking about your brother Charlie who hanged himself in Leeds prison after spending six weeks sharing a cell with Michael Vokey.'

His solicitor sat up. Darren slunk lower in his seat.

'Did you speak with Michael about that? It must've been a shock to find yourself working with the man who most people believe was responsible for your brother's death.'

'Charlie hanged himself.' Kicking a foot under the table again. 'It was a suicide. End of.'

He was angry, but mostly he was scared. This thing was closing in on him. His face scrabbled after his earlier insouciance, without result.

'Was Michael cut up about it, then?' Noah asked. 'He was the last person to see Charlie alive, and the first person to find him dead. That can't have been easy. Did you talk about that?'

'We didn't talk about Charlie, okay?' Darren stuck his thumb in his mouth, using it to brush at his front teeth. 'If you've made up some fantasy shit about this being *revenge*— Forget it.'

'Oh, I think we can leave the fantasy shit to you, Darren. You have that covered. The online interview you gave, calling Michael a psycho cannibal and what else was it? "He makes Jack the Ripper look like *nothing*. Like your gran's pet poodle." I'd say you have that covered.'

Darren squirmed in his seat, sliding his eyes out of range of Noah's stare.

'"He's dead clever, dead cunning,"' Noah quoted from the transcript of the online interview. '"They'll only find him if he wants to be found. My advice? Don't hunt what you can't catch."' He set the transcript aside. 'What did you mean by that, Darren? "Don't hunt what you can't catch." What makes you so certain we can't catch Michael Vokey?'

'Because you're *shit* at it! If you weren't shit at it you wouldn't be sitting here asking me dumb questions when a little kid's missing. You can't find him, and you can't find her. You're useless, all of you.' He blew a laugh through his nose. 'You couldn't find a needle in a junkie.'

'Is that how you persuaded Michael to escape, by telling him we'd be too stupid to find him? Boasting about the firearm you had. Did you tell him you'd hide him? I'm guessing he was stupid too, since he fell for that.'

Seconds passed, slowly. The solicitor leaned in to murmur advice to his client, but Darren wasn't interested. He squared his shoulders, attempting to stare Noah down. 'Yeah, he was in the shed on the allotment. *One night.* I went back next day, was going to call the police, but he was gone.'

'Gone where? Where is he, Darren?'

'I've no fucking idea, okay? And I never told him to escape, never told him where to hide. He knew about the allotment because he'd heard me talking with Elms.'

'Ted Elms.'

'Yeah.' A note of triumph in his tone, as if he'd played his ace. '*He's* the one who knew about the allotment, because he'd asked so many questions about it. He's dead keen on gardening and I was just doing my job, making connections. We talked about the soil and the size of the plot, which way the sun faces, how close the woods are. He had a *lot* of questions.'

'Ted Elms,' Noah repeated. He sat back, interested to see how far Darren would push this. He was still lying, it was all over him. Body language, eyes, voice.

The solicitor made another bid to curtail matters, getting slapped down again.

'Do we get a lot of shade from the woods, is the soil deep on the plot? How often do we turn it?' Darren's face

300

darkened. 'How big's the shed, what do we keep in it? On and on. Questions about Mum, about Charlie, but mostly about the allotment. *Yeah*. He had a lot of questions.' He ground the words through his teeth. 'You want to know about Mickey's escape plan, that's who you should be interrogating. Not me. *Ted*.'

39

'Natalie is perfectly safe,' Ruth said. 'She has food and shelter, and she's drawing. I'm surprised it was so easy to take her. I'd imagined you'd be taking very good care of everyone. Except Michael, of course, that goes without saying. But it appears your neglect is democratic. You'll blame cuts in funding, I'm sure, but I'm inclined to look closer to home.'

Marnie let her finish this sanctimonious speech before she said, 'May I speak with Natalie? It would be helpful to be able to tell her mother that she isn't too frightened.'

'She doesn't speak very much.' Ruth's voice didn't change, round with self-congratulation. 'But you have my word she's safe and well. Now before you pass me over to a professional negotiator, I should make it clear I'll deal only with you, DI Rome. Is that understood?'

'I'll make a note of your preference,' Marnie said blandly. 'But you'll understand there's a procedure I have to follow. It was put in place as soon as we were alerted to the kidnap of a child.'

'I hardly kidnapped her. We went for a walk, with her grandmother's blessing.'

'After you'd falsely identified yourself as a Victim Support Officer. Shall we talk about what you're hoping to achieve by taking a vulnerable child hostage?'

'If she's vulnerable it's because she lives with a liar.' A lick of asperity in her voice now. 'A woman who refuses to tell the truth even when it puts people at risk.'

'Natalie will be frightened,' Marnie said. 'No matter how careful you're being with her, she will be frightened and wanting her mum.' She paused, considering her next words. 'You're not a cruel person, I know that. You're not someone who wants to hurt a child who's already struggling. Let us come and get Natalie, and give her the help she needs. And let us give *you* the help you need.'

'I need *Michael*. I need to know he's safe and well. Can you give me that?'

'Not over the phone,' Marnie said. 'Not like this.'

'Then we have nothing to talk about.'

Ruth ended the call.

Marnie nodded at the team. 'I'll get hold of Toby Graves on another number.' Toby was a hostage negotiator, the man they needed for this job. She handed her phone to Colin. 'Let's treat this as the number she's calling to. Update everyone connected with the search. Who does Ruth know in London, where might she have gone? We need to know where she's taken Natalie, and we need teams on the ground there as quickly as possible.'

40

'Ted Elms is on life support,' Noah said. 'He has been since the night of the riot.'

'Yeah, well.' Darren drew a smiley face on the table with his thumb. 'That's what you get for fucking about with a psycho.'

'Ted was fucking about with Michael. In what way?'

'Every way. He said it was the only thing keeping Mickey from freaking out. He used to scream at night, a lot. And he was hard to handle, because of his moods. No one wants an inmate who's hard work. Ted reckoned he'd found a way to make him happy.'

'Doing what?' Noah asked.

'Letters. From Lara and Ruth. Lots of letters.' Darren waited for another question, but continued when Noah was silent. 'They wrote to him anyway, but it wasn't always the right stuff. Ruth was too bossy, and then Lara stopped writing. It made Mickey mad. That's when Ted started to write the letters himself. All I had to do was deliver them, pretend they'd come from Lara or whatever.'

'And you agreed to this plan.'

304

'It wasn't doing any harm.' Darren shrugged. 'It was keeping Mickey from going up the walls.'

Noah thought of the man wired to the machinery in the hospital. He'd pitied Ted Elms. He still did. It was too easy for Darren to make a scapegoat of someone in no position to defend himself. He let Darren see how little he believed in this new alibi.

'That stuff on the allotment,' Darren insisted. 'The sketchbook, batteries. It came from Mickey's cell but he *shared* that cell, yeah? With Elms. How come you're not looking at it from that angle? How come it's all about me and Charlie?'

'Ted is in hospital,' Noah said. 'On life support. Michael attacked him on the night of the riot. Just like he attacked Tommy Walton, and Neil Bayer.'

'You don't know that,' Darren shot back. 'You think because he ran, he's guilty. You stopped looking at anyone else for the fire and the rest of the mess. Fair enough, why make life more complicated than it needs to be? Only don't start pointing fingers at me because you haven't anyone else to point them at. If I'm meant to be mad at Mickey for being the last person to see Charlie alive then why would I help him escape? I had him where I wanted him, in prison. Why would I want him back out there?' Flinging a hand towards the door.

'Perhaps because you had a gun out there.'

His solicitor gestured at Darren to keep quiet, but Darren shoved his stare at the man. 'I've got this, yeah?' He jabbed a finger at Noah. 'I didn't kill him. I didn't want to kill him. I liked him.'

His face fixed into a grin. '*Yeah*. You hate that, don't you? I'm not supposed to like inmates, I'm only meant to pretend, let him think I like him, that I'm not going to treat him like shit in case it pisses him off. But I *liked* him. He was a cool guy. Bit fucked up, but aren't we all?'

'And the men he maimed? The fire, the riot. Charlie. I'm supposed to believe none of that matters to you.'

'Charlie was a suicide,' Darren hissed. 'How many more times? Charlie was *weak.*'

He wanted Noah to discount revenge as a motive. If he hadn't loved or liked his brother, why would Darren blame Vokey for Charlie's death? And if he didn't blame Vokey for that, where was his motive for murder? It was a good act, if it was an act.

'Explain the forgeries. Ted wrote the letters, you delivered them to Mickey.'

'Sometimes.' He flicked his tongue across his teeth. 'I put them in the post or got mates to post them. I didn't want it to be obvious what we're doing. Mickey wasn't stupid, it had to look real.'

What else had to look real? Darren's admiration for Mickey? *All he did was run.* If the forgeries were Ted's idea then how could they convict Darren? Ted was in no condition to defend himself, to admit or deny these fresh accusations. That was convenient, to say the least.

'You knew Mickey was hiding on your mum's allotment. One night, you said. How did you know that if you didn't help him?'

'Ted told me.' Darren drove two fingers into the metal table, leaving sweat prints in place. 'He told me Mickey was running, that he'd been listening in when we talked about the allotment and he'd figured out the shed was a good hiding place. For all I know, Ted encouraged him to go there.'

'And the clothes, and food and money, that you took from the house. How did that happen?'

'After I found out where he was, I needed him thinking

I was on his side, yeah?' He wet his lips, his tongue grey and cracked. 'Like the training teaches us, make them think you're on their side because it lowers their threat level and that's a good thing, right? That's got to be a good thing. I took him the stuff so he'd feel safe, and so he'd stick around long enough for me to tip you lot off.'

'You wanted the police to find him. But you didn't actually report the fact of his whereabouts,' Noah said flatly. 'That's what you're asking me to believe.'

'I didn't want him on my fucking property!' Darren thumped at the table. 'I knew what you'd make of it, even before you figured out what'd happened with Charlie. I knew you'd stitch me up!'

Noah studied his agitation, which was peculiar, suspended between hostility and the need to be believed. He'd had nearly two weeks to dream up this alibi, but it was full of holes, hardly CPS-proof. On the other hand, as an alibi for murder, it was functional. Not too slick, not too clever. And Darren wasn't clever. Which made his leaky alibi more credible, not less.

'I knew you'd stitch me up.' Darren threw himself back in his chair, huffing his breath through his teeth. 'So much for being on the same side.'

His solicitor leaned in to speak to him, but Darren shook his head. 'I've got this.'

That need to feel in control, how far had it taken him? To the allotment, to the woods?

'Tell me more about Ted Elms. Why would he help Michael Vokey to escape?'

'He wanted him out of there so he'd have the cell to himself again. He was sick to death of Mickey, and that was *before* the business with the bonsai.'

'What business?'

Darren wiped his nose with his hand. 'Mickey chopped

307

up his bonsai, just to see what Ted'd do. Ted was mental about that tree, about all his plants. Mickey was just mucking about, pushing buttons, but he went too far with the bonsai. Ted had a total fit, freaked out big time. Probably that's when he decided to get shot of Mickey. I'm just surprised he didn't do him there and then.'

'Do him.' Noah looked for slyness in Darren's face, but found no trace of it. 'You mean kill him? You're surprised Ted didn't kill Mickey after the business with the bonsai?'

'I've seen some nutters in my time, but Ted's in another league.' He wiped at his nose again, examining his hand before smearing the wetness onto his sweat pants.

'Ted's on life support,' Noah said again. 'How do you explain that?'

'Someone had to stop him,' Darren said tightly. 'He was going berserk in that corridor. You saw the state of the place. He was going mental.'

'Wait a minute.' Noah held up a hand, keeping his stare on Darren. 'The riot, GBH in the corridor. You're saying *that* was Ted Elms.'

'Yeah.' Darren rubbed sweat from the palms of his hands, eyes sliding south of Noah. 'That was Ted. All of it. The eyeballs, and the teeth. Someone had to stop him. And you know what?'

Noah was silent, waiting for him to compound the lie.

'It was Mickey made him stop,' Darren said. 'Your madman, the one you're all hunting. He dug Ted's thumbs out of Tommy Walton's skull. Then he ran, because he could. He dealt with the real maniac, with Ted. And then he ran.'

41

'Michael is capable of change,' Ruth insisted. 'Why won't you believe that?'

Toby Graves nodded at Marnie to answer. The connection wasn't good, the signal dropping in places as if struggling through dense walls or bad weather; Ruth had moved to another location since her first call fifteen minutes ago.

'I can talk to you,' Marnie said. 'But not while I'm concerned for Natalie. My chief concern right now is the safety of a vulnerable child; that has to take priority. We can discuss Michael, we *should* discuss Michael, but first let's get Natalie home.'

'Home to her, that liar who put him away? She doesn't deserve a child. She used Natalie in court, her *fear* for her daughter! All part of her lies to make them punish him.'

Ruth's anger was new, as if the consequences of what she'd done were only now hitting home. She'd kidnapped a child and was holding her hostage. How could she justify that other than by accusing Julie and the courts, the police, everyone except herself?

'He terrorised her.' Marnie shut her eyes to concentrate on the words she needed to talk to this woman. 'He

309

terrorised Julie in front of Natalie. Imagine what that did to Natalie, how frightened she must be right now. Even if you're being gentle with her, because I know you're not a cruel person, even if you're being very gentle with her, she's very frightened. Help us make sure she's safe and well, and then you and I will sit down and talk about Michael.'

'You don't believe in him. You didn't even acknowledge his talent, his art. You sneered at it, at me! You tried to make me feel *ashamed.*'

'If I did that then I'm sorry. I was concerned for you, because I felt Michael was taking advantage of your kindness. I wasn't sure he deserved that kindness.'

Marnie opened her eyes to see Toby Graves nodding at her. This was the tack to take with Ruth, fair but firm, giving no quarter to the woman's bluster.

'He's a changed man. You're supposed to believe in that. Prison changes people.' The line crackled, the signal losing strength. 'You're supposed to believe in rehabilitation.'

You can't rehabilitate sociopaths or psychopaths, Marnie knew that. Michael Vokey had used his art to try and understand how fear felt to Julie, and to Charlie Lamb. People were puzzles to him, but he wasn't interested in solving or admiring the puzzles.

'Why can't you believe he's capable of change?' Ruth's optimism was beginning to look like wilful credulity. She'd convinced herself of Michael's rehabilitation because the opposite was too awful to contemplate, that she'd assisted in the escape of a violent, remorseless offender. 'Why don't you believe in a way back for him?'

Toby signalled for Marnie to stay silent. This was about finding the parameters of Ruth's panic, and her rage. With the signal on the blink, every word they could get out of her was essential.

310

'Where is he?' Her voice climbed a pitch. 'Do you know?'

Toby waited a beat then nodded.

'We're looking for him,' Marnie said. 'Where do you believe he is?'

'Pray—!' The signal dropped, chopping Ruth's words. 'He's— Pray—'

'Ruth? Tell me where you are. Let us help you, please.' The line was dead.

'Hang up,' Toby said. 'She'll try again. She wants to talk.'

'It sounds as if she's underground.' Marnie said. 'We have eyes on Marion Vokey's house, yes?'

The house Michael had asked her to safeguard. Ruth had been prepared to fight Alyson for that house, saying she knew how much it mattered to Michael. She'd been searching for him here in London since the interview two days ago. But why was she suddenly so frantic for news? She couldn't be afraid that he'd be found and rearrested, because then she could be in contact with him again. No, she was scared the opposite was true. He was gone, for good.

'We don't have eyes on Marion's house,' Colin was saying. 'It was sealed off as a possible crime scene, but the location fits with the CCTV searches. Last sighting of Ruth and Natalie was on a bus headed for Northfields. There's a connecting service to West Ealing.'

'We need a team there,' Marnie said. 'Ruth knows how important that house is to Vokey. She might even be thinking he's gone there. We know he didn't, but she doesn't know that.'

She nodded at Colin, and at Toby Graves. 'We need a team at Marion Vokey's house.'

42

'What do we know about Ted Elms?' Noah asked Ron,
back in the incident room.

'He lived with his mum in Derbyshire. She died a while
back, but Ted carried on claiming her pension. That's how
he ended up in prison. Benefit fraud, so he's hardly Charles
Manson. If the prison system wasn't so screwed by overcrowding he'd never have been in that cell with Vokey.'

They stood studying the evidence boards, the photos
of Ted before and after his incarceration. Darren's solicitor
had asked for a break in the interview to allow his client
the chance to rest and eat. Marnie was in West Ealing.
She wanted Noah and Ron concentrating on the charges
against Darren, finding out exactly how much he knew
about what had happened to Vokey.

'Darren wants us to believe Ted was responsible for his
escape, and not only that. The GBH at the prison, the
blinding of those two men.' Noah nodded at the images.
'Darren says it's all down to Ted.' He moved his hand to
Vokey's angry sketch. 'He drew this after he destroyed
Ted's bonsai. That was the last straw, according to Darren.'

'A bloke who freaked out over a bonsai? Face it, Ted's

an alibi.' Ron dismissed it. 'Handy because he's out of the picture and can't answer back.'

'Darren's alibi, or Vokey's?' Noah asked.

'Both, I reckon. Very convenient that we find this cartoon of him looking like a nutter right when we might otherwise be deciding Darren did all the dirty work. Who's to say Vokey didn't draw this from his imagination?'

'He doesn't have that kind of imagination. He doesn't understand people, that's why he draws us, and it's why he winds us up first. To observe our emotions, try and figure out what makes us tick. He made Ted angry on purpose so he could draw this. We know Ted was different, before.' Noah nodded at the arrest photo. 'Sharing that cell with Vokey did this to him, you said it yourself.'

'Ted's the one on life support,' Ron objected. 'Vokey's the one out there.'

'Just because he's in the hospital doesn't make Ted innocent. The same could be said about any of the men injured in the riot.' Like Stephen Keele. 'And we know what those men are capable of.'

Ron sighed. 'This case's doing my head in.'

Noah felt his pain. 'We need to look at Ted Elms as a suspect in this. He knew too many details about the allotment, and he was almost certainly the one forging those letters. Darren isn't smart enough to have done that.' He paused, reaching for his phone. 'There's something else, too.'

'Oh Christ.' Ron rubbed at his eyes. 'What?'

'I looked back at the hospital records.' Noah scrolled for the info on his phone, showing it to Ron. 'When they took Ted in on the night of the riot, he was covered in blood, drenched in it. It was up his nose, in his mouth, under his fingernails. Blood, and vitreous fluid.'

'Vitreous. That's *eyes*—?'

313

Noah nodded. 'We told ourselves he was trying to help the injured inmates, or maybe the mess was transferred from Vokey when he attacked Ted. But what if it's simpler than that? Like Darren says. What if it *was* Ted who blinded those men?'

They both looked at the photo collage from the corridor at Cloverton, primal arcs of blood and soot wiped onto the walls like a caveman's first bid at painting. Michael Vokey's signature, they'd thought, because it was artwork. In the manner of artwork. But was it always only misdirection?

'If this was Elms,' Ron stepped away from Noah, 'then we're fucked. Because he's not waking up, is he? Not any time soon.' He banged his hand at the board, leaving it there, his fist on Ted's face. 'So in this new scenario Vokey did the world a favour, that's what we're saying. In some act of selfless heroism he stopped Elms running amok before he nicked off.'

'Ted being guilty doesn't exonerate Vokey. Not of what he did to Julie, or Charlie Lamb.'

'Good, let's get that much straight.' Ron's voice frayed. 'All this does is make everything even more screwed up. We're chasing our tails while Darren's laughing it up in the cells. Meanwhile there's a little girl out there who's been kidnapped because some God-botherer can't get her priorities straight, thinks we should be searching for her hero instead of keeping innocent kids safe. It's insane.'

'It isn't easy.' Noah wanted to believe Ruth wouldn't hurt Natalie, but two days ago he hadn't thought her capable of kidnap. 'Let's hope the boss is right and she's in West Ealing.'

'Yeah, and that being in a creepy nutter's house with a grave in the cellar doesn't send either one of them over the edge.'

314

43

In West Ealing, Marion Vokey's house was sealed as a crime scene, but Ruth had found a way inside. CCTV and her patchy phone signal confirmed it. Toby and his team were setting up a mobile unit, traffic officers redirecting cars and cordoning off the street. Unlike Noah, Marnie hadn't been here before, but she remembered his reaction to the room of faces. And Ron's: *Like a punch in the gut.* Vokey's shrine, his obsession writ large. A confession, of sorts, an admission of how little he understood people, what makes us human. He'd set Ruth on this path, primed her so thoroughly Marnie felt it in the street outside the house – the heartbeat of Ruth's confusion, which had led to this latest havoc. When her phone pulsed, she connected the call. 'DI Rome.'

'You're here, then.' The signal was crystal clear. 'It took you longer than I expected.'

Marnie looked for a shadow at one of the windows. Toby joined her, listening to the call, ready to guide her through the negotiation. 'May I speak with Natalie?'

'She's busy drawing.' A sudden flicker of warmth in her voice. 'Michael would approve.'

'He told you about the house, how much it mattered to him.' Marnie wanted the woman to talk, fearing silence above all else. She needed to hear Natalie in the background, proof that Julie's daughter was safe. 'Did he tell you where to find the key his mum hid at the back?'

'You took his photos,' Ruth accused. 'And his drawings. I was supposed to deal with those.'

'Deal with them how?'

'Bury them, so he can start over. A fresh start, that's what you're meant to do when you get out of prison. He asked me to help. This was to be our fresh start, right here.'

'He asked you to bury his drawings and photographs. Where?'

'*Here*. In the house.'

A flash of memory from the earlier interview: polished calluses on Ruth's thumbs from manual labour. 'You dug the pit in the cellar?'

'It's not trespass if you have the home owner's permission.' Ruth was trying for her old piety, but she was struggling. For the first time it sounded as if she was struggling. 'He wanted my help. I'm all he has, the only one who isn't hunting him. The only one *helping*.'

'When did he ask you to do this?'

'In his last letter, before the riot. Before he was forced to run.'

'Michael wrote and asked you to come here, to dig a pit in his cellar and bury his artwork.'

'Yes. It was symbolic, a fresh start, freeing—!'

From the little she understood of the man, Marnie found it hard to believe Michael Vokey would have asked anyone to destroy his artwork. The care he'd taken to pin the Polaroids in place, each image trimmed to the same size, each pin driven into the wall so precisely. All so a

316

stranger could undo it, destroy it? Michael hadn't written that letter, so who had? And what else had they instructed Ruth to do?

'Do you have his letter, asking you to come here?'

'I destroyed it.' Primly. 'At his request.'

Marnie glanced at Toby, who nodded at her to continue. 'Was it handwritten, or typed?'

A short silence, the sound of Ruth moving inside the house. 'What does that matter?'

'It matters because we're aware of other letters Michael is supposed to have written, but which we believe to be forgeries.'

Ruth laughed. 'This is your strategy for negotiation, is it? Divide and conquer? You're forgetting that I *know* Michael. I know his art, and his words.'

She would never believe in the forgeries, not even if Marnie sat her down with a dozen experts who could explain in detail why the letters she'd received weren't written by the man she imagined herself to be saving. 'May I speak with Natalie?'

'I told you, she's busy. May *I* speak, with Michael?'

'The last time we spoke, before the signal died, you were asking us to pray for him—'

Her laughter slid into a sob. 'I wasn't asking you to *pray*. I was telling you that's what he *is*. You're treating him like the hunter, but he's the prey.'

A sudden darkness at the upstairs window made Marnie and Toby look in that direction.

Ruth was standing in the bedroom which had belonged to Michael Vokey, her hand on the grimy pane, her face haggard from loss. 'He's the *prey*.'

44

My lovely nurse is washing me the way she did that first day, sponging away the blood, soaking each of my fingers in turn to clean the gore from under my nails. There's a lot of gore in a human head.

Of course Mickey never showed any interest in the allotment, only I did that. I knew where it was and which way it faced, the type of soil Dazza's mum was growing her lilies in, the size of the plot, location of the shed. I knew about the fire pit and how the woods crowded in behind, miles of them. Hundreds of trees, thousands of dead leaves on top of soft black soil.

Mickey thought he was shaping me, the way he shaped that boy in Leeds. Charlie Lamb, who hanged himself rather than live through another hour of Mickey's moaning, his baiting, his night terrors. He imagined I was the same as Charlie, that he could twist me into any shape he pleased, but I was the one with the scissors. I'm the one who knows how stunted things grow.

My nurse dries my hands one after the other, leaning over me with her crucifix hanging. She never looks into my eyes now, even though I know so much. I know how

318

fragile the human head is, its points of entry and the way it feels inside, so soft and slippery, hot. Two thumbs, is all it takes. She's being very careful with me, pressing the water from my hands with a towel, staying close. I smell her peachy shampoo, round and pink. The light's in her hair, all tangled up in there, teasing out her colours. What was that line of Ruth's—?

'Your edges are in the clefs and empty eyes of notes. I have searched, and found you there.'

You thought she was capable of writing those letters? You thought Mickey was? Oh, he had a talent, that's true. He could draw, and he could punch. Empty you out, and fill you with his chaos. But he couldn't write a letter to save his life. I wrote the letters, didn't I tell you as much? He made me read their letters out loud and he made me write back to them, as him.

'Get her to send me a photo of her tits.' Lying in my bunk, dictating like a cut-price romantic novelist with braided hair and stained teeth. 'Make her want to send me more photos.'

And so I did. I wrote, 'Dear Lara, I dreamt of you last night and it woke me. I went to the window to watch the moon, but it wasn't there. Windows lie. Only pictures tell the truth. In my picture, you're paler than the moon, and so much smoother. I dreamt your scent, like hot sand.'

I wrote, 'Dear Ruth, I dreamt of you last night and it helped me sleep. I have such trouble sleeping. Sometimes I lie awake all night, afraid of what will happen. There's no peace here and I want to make my peace. There's peace in you, I feel it. Like cool sand on a winter's beach.'

You think Mickey composed those letters? He couldn't even hold a pen properly. It was what he wanted, I was doing what he wanted, at the beginning. And it kept the peace. You don't know how important that is until you've

319

tried to survive in a place like Cloverton. Later on, 'Come and find me,' that was different. That was for me. He knew their handwriting by then. I'm many things, but I am not a forger. Dazza typed the letters, asked friends to post them. He'd seen Mickey on bad days, dreaded seeing him like that as much as I did. He was all for my plan with the letters, happy to take everything home, keep it safe. He loved being part of it, got a buzz from breaking the rules. I hope he kept it all safely in a single place. I hope the police found it all – the batteries and sketchpad, forged letters and photographs – everything they needed to make a case against Mickey, and Dazza. Because they deserve that, they deserve one another.

I suppose you could say I gave him a hiding place. Me, Edward Elms, I did that, and I deserve to suffer for it. The women he wanted, the ones he hurt, I was never enough. I was Julie, Lara, Ruth, all of them. I tried to be enough, but I wasn't. Nothing was ever enough for him.

He was scared, by the end of it. Most people in prison are scared, sooner or later. He had to run, of course he did. He wasn't to know he was running in the wrong direction. He thought he'd make it back to his house, or to his sister's house. As if the police didn't know where to look, as if he had any secrets left. Mickey was all about pictures, but I brought him down with words. Letters to send the police in circles, and to burn down his hiding places. The police won't ever see Ruth's last letter, the one I destroyed while Mickey was sleeping, tore it into tiny bits and ate it. Easy, after the batteries. Ruth ought to have known better than to write a letter like that, but I expect she thought she'd disguised it all nicely. It's not as if she wrote: 'I dug a grave in your mum's cellar just as you suggested.' She thought she was burying his past, paving the way for a fresh start. She didn't know she was digging him deeper into a pit of my making. I wanted to be sure the police knew what they were dealing with. You'd think his artwork would be enough, but the last time I looked no one was being sent to prison for putting up photos in his dead mum's sitting room. I wonder if they figured it out, the detectives. DI Rome, maybe. Stephen's sister, she looks like a sharp one.

Mickey wasn't hiding. He was hidden.

He didn't escape from here. He ran from me.

You can twist people into any shape you want. All I did was trim the size of his neuroses, turn him towards the light, let him grow. He had Dazza to do his dirty work, his bidding. He thought he had me in the same way. 'That's mine. I'll take that. And that.' Like a toddler with fat fists. He was angry, that's what everyone said, but they didn't put two and two together. Anger comes from *fear*. Anyone who's ever cornered a cat knows that. They saw the anger in Mickey, but they didn't see the fear. None of them got close enough, except me. Sleeping three feet above a man, you get to learn his smell and Mickey *reeked* of fear.

So yes, I took him, the blank page of him, and I reshaped it. He was hollow inside, like a tree that looks alive but isn't, eaten away by rot. I hollowed him out and then I topped him up. It was just our little game, to start with. He filled Lara with lust, Ruth with the promise of his reform. And he filled me with batteries. He stole my bunk and my wall, forced those Triple As between my teeth, into my stomach. Do you think I should have taken it lying down? You don't know much about prisons, if that's what you think. Survival of the fittest. Ruth and Lara were empty, just like Mickey. Not Julie, though. It's why she was never afraid of him, not in the same way. Ruth and Lara were houses of sticks and hay, wanting him to

321

blow them away. But Julie was bricks, built to last. She deserved to see him punished. Dazza was empty, but he had his mum, nothing like a controlling parent to plug a gap. Vokey was Dazza's bid for freedom. He thought he could swap his mum for Mickey, but he hadn't counted on the reason Mickey can see who's empty and who isn't. He sees it in you because it lives in him, the same black ruin in his blood. It's in DI Rome too, this emptiness, but she's filled it with something hard and hot. Hate, or anger, or love. Not love like Lara and Mickey, and not love like Ruth and her church. Love like water boiling downhill, or smoothing out to sea. Vast and fast and nothing you can do about it but stand and stare. Mickey never knew love like that, never felt its ruin boiling in his blood. He couldn't escape it, all the same. You can't alter the way a person's blood flows, but you can redirect it. You can build banks, dig trenches, set traps with logs and leaves. Write letters, pretend to be other people, whatever it takes to restore order, put him back in his place. He was out of control, like ivy, like bindweed, choking everything. He needed cutting back. Anyone asks, it was self-preservation.

Kill or be killed. *Fill*, or be filled.

He woke up to it too late, groping under the smoke for a weapon and finding me with my thumbs buried deep in Tommy Walton's face because I couldn't stop. I couldn't. You can't switch it off, a thing like that, not without a struggle. Except Mickey did. He got his hands on something, maybe just his hands, and he hit me until I stopped. Until I ended up in here, wired to the machines with nothing but their restive buzz-buzz-buzzing to tell me I'm not dead.

45

The sitting room, stripped of its Polaroid cladding, echoed with the sound of pencil rubbing at paper. Natalie lay on her stomach on the floor, drawing on the back of an envelope, her small face scrunched in concentration.

'Hello, Natalie. I'm Detective Inspector Rome. I came to see your mum, do you remember?'

No response. Forensic powder had put stains all over Natalie's clothes. Marnie felt a throb of anger at Ruth for bringing the child here. The house reeked of white chemicals and black damp.

'May I see your picture?' She crouched, careful not to crowd the little girl.

Natalie scratched with the pencil at the page. 'Is my mum dead?' It came out as a whisper, flat.

'No.' Pain cramped Marnie's side at the thought of her fearing the worst, trying to make sense of why she'd been taken from her home and brought to this empty, echoing place. 'No, she's safe and she's well. She's waiting to give you a big hug.'

Natalie pressed the pencil at the page until its lead snapped. Her small body stiffened, fingers fisted around the ruined pencil. She moved her mouth, but no words came.

Marnie touched a hand very lightly to her head. 'Your mum's safe, and you're safe. I'm going to take you to see her. Is that okay?'

Natalie nodded, reaching to pull herself into Marnie's arms, burying her face in Marnie's shoulder. The weight and warmth of her was so sudden and solid, Marnie stayed crouched a moment longer before she pushed upright, holding Natalie in the curl of her arms, one hand on the back of the little girl's head, cradling it. She grew heavier as Marnie carried her out of the house, the tension dropping away to leave her limbs slack, head nodding towards sleep.

Paramedics were waiting to check her over but Natalie clung to Marnie, whimpering a little as they tried to free her grip.

'You're needed in the house, Ma'am.'

Marnie nodded. 'Give me a minute?'

Natalie's skin was damp and sticky, smelling of raspberries and clean sweat. Marnie kept her arms cradled around the girl. The heat of Natalie's cheek against hers was a mnemonic, flooding her mouth with the taste of metal links, green grass, her parents' garden. The swing her father built for Stephen. He'd weighed less than Natalie, a skinny eight-year-old, not yet used to eating well.

'Here.' She handed the sleeping child to a paramedic, watching the woman settle Natalie under a blanket. 'Be gentle with her.'

'DI Rome?' One of Toby's team, reminding her that this wasn't over.

Marnie stood and faced the house. An ordinary terrace, just a little neglected, paint peeling from its window frames and door. Hollow inside, gutted of its furniture. She didn't want to go back in there. She wanted to stay out here in the fresh air, or what passed for it. London's traffic swelled around her like a sea, its rhythm familiar, comforting. She took shallow breaths to steady the panic in her chest, recalling all the times she'd gone into dangerous places, far worse than this, rushing in to save someone. But Natalie was out, safe. There was only Ruth waiting in the cellar by the side of the grave she'd dug, believing it to be what her hero wanted. She had nothing to give Ruth that would make this better. Her head flared gently with pain.

'Ma'am?'

She went with Toby's man up the short path to the front door with its paint crazed by rain and sun. Dust lay trapped in a straight line along the uncarpeted hallway, tangled by dirt and leaves. The sound of their footsteps stayed on the surface of the hardwood floor, having nowhere to go. All the sound in the house was the same, trapped on the surface.

The door that led under the stairs, down into the cellar, was varnished by fingerprints. She thought fleetingly of the cupboard at Harry's mother's house, packed full of gifts purchased and then forgotten. The door murmured on its hinges.

The cellar's smell rose to greet her, turned earth and bricks cracked by damp. The drop in pressure made her ears pop, as if she'd ducked underwater. Shadows crawled to the walls. Two, three steps down into the darkness, broken by a single bulb swinging on a frayed flex above the pit where Ruth was sitting with her lap full of sketches, the green leather album abandoned at her side. 'Is she safe?' she asked.

'Natalie? Yes.'

'I gave her the envelope and pencil.' She bent her fair head over her lap. 'She was drawing at the house on the estate, I could see she liked drawing. The place was full of her pictures.'

Marnie didn't speak straightaway. Then she said, 'Her home, yes.'

The cellar swallowed any echo which might have attached itself to their voices. Like the rest of the house it had been emptied ahead of the sale. Where was the furniture? The beds Michael and Alyson had slept in, the table around which they'd eaten their meals, books they'd read, trinkets they'd collected – where did it all go? To a house clearance, or into storage. Marnie had been in derelict houses, and houses razed by fire. This was different, like standing inside a tunnel. Her eyes struggled to adjust to the dimness. Ruth looked small, sitting there.

'I don't know why I took her,' she said. 'I wanted to see Julie, but she was at work. She's always at work. Natalie looked bored, and lonely.'

'She was safe. She was with her grandmother. Julie has to work, to pay the bills.'

'You think this is class war?' A thread of her old hostility, muted now. 'I do understand how people live, DI Rome. I'm not stupid.'

'No,' Marnie agreed. 'That's what makes this so much worse.'

She moved to sit on the second step, her feet on the cellar floor. The door stayed open at the top of the steps behind her, where Toby and his team were standing by. They'd offered to handle the rest of this, after Marnie had taken Natalie out of the house. Toby had offered to make the arrest and secure the scene, and she'd been tempted because Ruth revolted her on so many levels. But this was her job. She remembered what she'd said to Lorna Ferguson at the outset of the case, that Ruth and Lara were victims too. Seeing her now, seated beside the hole she'd dug so tidily in his cellar floor, her lap full of his sketches, Marnie wanted to feel pity for Ruth. She really did.

'I didn't hurt her,' Ruth said. 'And I let you take her without a fight. That should go in my favour, shouldn't it?' She looked up at last, the sheen of tears in her eyes. 'That I let you take her.'

Marnie had distrusted her capitulation when Ruth, standing at the upstairs window, had said Michael was prey. It was Toby who'd decided the crisis was over and it was safe to send a team into the house to search for Natalie; Toby who had cautioned Ruth.

'I was in his bedroom,' she said. 'That's where it hit me. He's gone. The house is so empty, as if he were never here.' She folded her hands over the sketches in her lap. 'It's over, I can feel it.'

'Over in what way? What do you believe has happened to Michael?'

'He's passed.' She bowed her head. 'The house. Everything. It feels finished.'

Toby could have taken her out of here, but it would have required force. Marnie hadn't wanted Natalie to witness that. 'How did he pass? Do you know?'

'He was tricked into running.' Ruth pushed her hands into the pile of sketches, until all her fingers were hidden. 'He would have been here waiting for me if he was safe.' She swung her feet down into the open grave as if she were sitting at the side of a pool and wanted her feet in the water. 'He would have come.'

'Tricked by whom?'

'Whoever helped him to escape. He'd never have risked running unless someone provoked him, or convinced him it was worth the risk.'

Noah had passed on the accusations Darren Quayle had made back at the station, the new reasons they had to doubt that Vokey was alive.

'The first time we spoke, you said Michael was afraid of Edwards Elms, his cellmate.'

'It wasn't him.' Ruth made a gesture of dismissal. 'He had scissors in the cell. If he'd wanted to kill Michael, he'd have done it then and there. No, it was someone else. Someone who wanted him out of there, free. Except he wasn't.' She picked one of the sketches from her lap and dropped it into the pit at her feet, the paper floating for a second on the cellar's sour air. 'He drew her. *Julie*. He sent me one of the drawings. He made her look so special, strong. An earth mother. That was the picture I took out of the album, the one you suspected was obscene. It was the only time he ever lied, making her look like that, like his favourite.'

Her face was dark with jealousy. Why had Michael sent her the drawing of Julie? To torment Ruth, or to tie her more closely to him by the burr of envy?

Marnie's shirt was sticking to her skin. The cellar air was solid, charged. She reached a hand to touch the spot where Natalie's cheek had pressed against hers. 'He told you to dig this pit. What else did he tell you to do?'

'To help him start over.' Ruth bent at the waist to unbuckle her shoes. 'He wanted to start over.' She pushed the ugly shoes from her feet, dropping them down into the grave, two dull thuds one after the other. Then she drove the sketches from her lap with both hands, a mad fluttering, so that her feet were obscured for a moment by falling paper. 'Isn't that what everyone wants, to start over?' One of the sketches clung to the arch of her foot until she kicked it free, sending it down into the pit with the others. She lifted her eyes to Marnie. 'Isn't it what you want?'

46

The light had gone out of the day by the time Marnie reached the hospital, making mirrors of all its many windows. Ted Elms was breathing with the aid of a machine, his chest rising and falling to its rhythm, too precise to be natural. Was he dreaming? Or were his dreams like his lungs, beyond his help now, made possible only with the aid of a machine?

She stood at the foot of his bed, thinking of everything he'd done. Forgery: instructions to Ruth, and reasons for Vokey to feel sure of a safe hiding place when he ran. Misdirection: the grave, and Lara's letters luring them away from London, allowing them to believe in a conspiracy against Alyson. Whatever role Ted had played in Darren's enslavement, and his revenge. The carnage in that corridor. Fire and smoke and savagery. This was the price Ted had paid, the machine breathing for him as the rest of his body slowly shut down. Had it been worth it? He must have hated Michael Vokey, needing to punish him in ways the system could not. Hating the police and the prosecutors, everyone who had judged him a fraud when he was buckled under the weight of loss, struggling to come to terms with his mother's death. His hands were outside the sheets, one white finger pinched by a heart monitor. Both hands looked clean, pale and smooth, making it hard to imagine the harm he'd done, all the ways in which he'd dealt vengeance to his tormentors.

Marnie left him and walked to the far end of the corridor, hesitating before she turned right towards the private room, guarded like Ted's. In here too the patient was wired to machines, his face obscured by an oxygen mask, an improvement on six days ago when Stephen had been on a ventilator. Acute Respiratory Distress Syndrome, ARDS, triggered by the inhalation of burning smoke. He'd been unconscious since they'd brought him here on the night of the riot, eyelashes clinging wetly to his cheeks, breath clouding inside the mask. From where she stood inside the door to his room, Marnie could see the dark line of his collarbone, a fist-sized bruise on his shoulder. He looked smaller than he had the last time she'd seen him. Smaller than he had looked in years. She watched him, hypnotised by the damp pattern of his breathing, the way the mask clouded and cleared. Clouded. And cleared.

'DI Rome?' A woman was standing under the shelter of the hospital's main entrance in a pale belted raincoat, holding a yellow leather handbag under her arm. Her shoulder-length hair was shot through with expensive high-lights that trapped the hard light and gave it back as rosy bronze and gold. Six years ago she'd worn her hair short and bottle blonde, but Marnie recognised her from the pictures taken at her parents' house, seated on the sofa next to her teenage son. Stephen's mother, Stella Keele.

'It is DI Rome, isn't it?' Stella tried a smile but it didn't fit on her face, restricted by whatever fillers went with the highlights. 'I recognise you from the pictures. In the papers, I mean.' She'd squeezed the accent from her voice, the way she'd squeezed her feet into leopard-print kitten heels. 'I want to see him.' She stepped closer, clutching the glossy bag. 'May I see him?'

'You should speak to the doctors.'

'I did.' Another step closer. 'If he were conscious, he'd need to give his permission. But I'm his mum and he's seriously ill, on a ventilator. Surely I should be allowed—' She broke off, flinching from whatever expression was on Marnie's face.

'I'm sorry, I can't help you.' Marnie turned and walked away, towards the place where her car was parked. Goosebumps on her neck, the skin hot at her wrists where a pulse pricked and stabbed, every cell in her body wanting her away from this woman.

'Please, I just want to see him!' The kitten heels flinted behind her.

Don't turn. Walk away.

'He's my son!'

The son you abused, damaging him so deeply he turned into a killer. He's in that hospital because of you. My parents are in the ground because of you.

'I know you can't forgive him, but *I* can. That's what he needs. Forgiveness.'

Keep walking. Walk away.

'Your parents understood that! I was grateful to them, I *am* grateful. For bringing us back together. They tried to help, they allowed me to see him.'

'And he killed them for it.' Marnie turned to face the woman. 'Because they judged it a good idea to bring you back into his life. You haven't the right to forgive anyone, certainly not the son you abused.'

'That's unfair.' Her eyelids twinged. 'I've changed. You can see that.'

'I see an expensive handbag and a lot of brickwork.' She nodded at the woman's immobile face. 'But if you're talking about forgiving *him*, you clearly haven't changed at all.'

'You don't know me.' She straightened, an inch taller than Marnie in her heels. 'You don't know what I went through. I tried to warn your parents what he was.'

'He was a child. Eight years old.'

'He was a *monster*—!' She glanced away, her eyes wild. 'He could be a monster. Surely you can believe that, after everything he did. I had eight years of him.' She dropped her head, highlights swaying. 'I hoped I'd find him changed after their care, I really hoped they could do that. Because I took some wrong paths, I'm not saying it isn't partly on me. I'm his mother, but it's not as simple as everyone makes out.'

'You didn't torture him, make him stand in the snow barefoot? You didn't write on his body?'

'What? No! *No*.' She swept the hair from her shoulders with one manicured hand. 'No.'

Aidan Duffy had told Marnie about the snow, and the words. Obscenities, he'd said, finger-painted all over Stephen while he was still a toddler. By both parents.

Stella stood tall in her heels, eyebrows plucked, lips plumped, the whole of her fixed and faked, nothing left to nature or chance. It was impossible to read her frozen face. Was that why she'd invested in the surgery, a glacial fortress for her lies?

'Where's your husband?' Marnie asked her. 'Why isn't he here?'

Stella's eyes shifted to her left. 'Theo doesn't— We separated.'

The pair of them painting words on Stephen's body in places he couldn't see, words he couldn't read. That

332

picture, indelible, had been in Marnie's head since Aidan told her about it. Now Stella was saying it wasn't true. That Stephen had been born bad, a monster.

'I haven't seen him in a long time,' she said. 'And prison changes you. I know that.'

Meaning what? That Stephen might have been made less abominable by the years he'd spent behind bars? Didn't she know what had happened to her son in juvenile detention? Attacked by a gang of girls, brutalised, put into hospital. Then Cloverton, an adult prison with the worst possible reputation for violence and self-harm. *Prison changes you.* Ruth Hull had argued the same case for Michael Vokey and look where it had got her: charged with child kidnap, unable to see any truth or hope or future through the fog of her delusion.

'I can't help you.' Marnie stripped the emotion from her voice. 'Other than to say I doubt he'd want to see you if he were conscious. He refused your visitor requests at the prison, didn't he?'

'This is different. He's on a ventilator! He could *die.*'

The woman's perfume coloured the air between them, a bruised purplish-blue.

'Speak to the doctors.'

'I'm *sorry.*' As if Marnie had dragged the word out of her. 'Is that what you need to hear? I'm sorry. For what my son did to you, to your parents. I am.'

'Just not sorry for the part you played in it. Good, well that's clear.' Marnie took out her car keys, fitting them into her fist the way she did when she was walking up an empty street after dark.

'I hoped he'd changed,' Stella insisted. 'I thought they might have been able to do that. They understood. The way they spoke to me, to the pair of us— They were good people.'

333

'And now they're gone.'

Because they brought you back into his life, forced him to sit beside you on their sofa eating biscuits. Perhaps he had changed until that moment tipped him over the edge, discovering his new family had betrayed him. They wanted redemption for Stephen, for the pair of you, and it cost them their lives. I need to stop this, before it does the same to me.

'You think this's easy for me just because you've been able to move on?' Stella swept a hand from Marnie's feet to her face. 'You don't have a son you haven't seen in over ten years!'

'You're right. It's easy for me. Goodnight.'

She turned her back, not speaking even when Stella called after her, 'If he dies without forgiveness, that'll be on you! He'll go to Hell and it'll be on you!'

Had she found religion, or was she simply shouting platitudes? Religion would be a further layer to her armour. She was a narcissist, needing to protect her version of the truth at all costs. Under the expensive makeover, she was just another narcissist.

'Prison changes you!' she shouted as Marnie got into the car. 'Your house was like a prison, that's what he told me! Your parents' house was a prison!'

It had been Marnie's line when she was an angry teenager, slamming in and out of her family's life, hating their house with a passion when now she'd give anything for the chance to be back there, holding them, thanking them for their patience and optimism, their faith in her.

'I have a right to see him!' There was the start of a bark in Stella's voice now, pitched high enough to reach Marnie when she was inside the car, firing the engine. 'At the end of the day, I'm his mother, I have rights. If he's dying, I have rights!'

She was in the rear-view mirror, her face shining with

outrage and anger. 'You don't have a son you haven't seen in years! You don't even have a brother!'

'I have a brother,' Marnie said under her breath. 'I made that promise to them ten years ago. All you've done is make me want to keep it.'

In the car's mirrors, smoke was rising from the hospital incinerators in thin grey fingers. In a room on the third floor, Stephen was lying in a narrow bed, his lungs blackened, poisoned. He might never regain consciousness, Stella was right about that. He might die tonight, or tomorrow, this damaged boy her parents had wanted for her brother.

She met her own eyes in the darkened windscreen. 'I made a promise.'

Stella Keele dwindled to a stick figure in the mirrors as Marnie swung out of the car park, back into the long snarl of London's night traffic.

47

The next day brought clouds the colour of tin cans, a storm trapped inside the sunshine that lit the station with infrequent flashes of white. By late afternoon, the sky was shaking with thunder and oppressively dry, not even the scent of rain to soften the storm's electricity.

'African violet.' Harry put the plant pot on the edge of Marnie's desk. 'To say thanks for the other night.' He straightened, scratching at his eyebrow. 'Mum says thanks too.'

'How is she?'

'In hospital still.' Harry had swapped the bandage on his hand for a plaster. 'She's much better there, for now at least.'

'I'm glad.' Marnie turned the violet towards the light, its petals a deep velvety blue. 'This is lovely, thank you.'

'It's the one from Mum's kitchen. Not because I'm a cheapskate, but because I didn't want it die, which it will if I'm left in charge of watering it.' He frowned, not quite seriously but as if he regretted what he'd just said. 'Obviously, with all the time you have on your hands, I thought you'd jump at the chance to be in charge of that.' Crooking his mouth in apology.

Marnie smiled at him. 'Have you seen Noah?'

'I'm about to. I have good news about Sol, no new charges relating to the firearms.'

'That's great news. He'll be glad to hear it.'

A petal fell from the African violet onto Marnie's desk.

'It may need watering,' Harry said ruefully.

'Leave it with me.'

After he'd gone, she fed the violet a little water, remembering the roses in the house in Harpenden, their apricot scent as Anita crushed the dropped petals between her fingers. Marnie touched the leaves of the violet, its fine hairs prickling her skin, a small friction which she felt in her fingertips even after she took her hand away.

At the door to her office she hesitated, watching Harry shake Noah's hand.

After he was gone, she walked to where Noah was working on the records from Darren's interview. 'We need to go back to Harpenden.'

Noah looked up, still smiling with the relief Harry's news had brought. 'Vokey?'

'Anita.'

'Of course.' His eyes clouded. 'We'll have to give her the news about Darren.'

Marnie nodded, waiting a moment. Then she said, 'Darren was jealous of Charlie. That's what you thought, yes?'

'That's how it looked. But Darren's difficult. Conflicted. The way he felt about Vokey, and the way he made Ted into his alibi?' He shook his head. 'Nothing's straightforward there.'

'Aidan was afraid of Ted. Not of Vokey, he was afraid of Ted.' Marnie tidied her hair from her face. 'But coming back to Darren and Charlie. If he was jealous of Charlie, resentful of their mother's preference for his brother, why would Darren want to harm Vokey?'

337

'I asked myself that. The motive's shaky, for sure.' Noah capped his pen, setting it down on the desk. 'But the evidence is strong. The gun, the firearms residue. Anita's own testimony about the cash and clothes Darren took from the house, the fact he was out all night.'

'We don't have a body.'

'We're searching the woods again, with cadaver dogs this time.' Noah frowned up at her. 'You don't think we'll find a body?'

'I think we will. And I think the motive *is* revenge. But I don't believe it was Darren.'

He searched her face, recalibrating. She saw the moment he reached the same conclusion she'd reached, seeing the petal fall from Harry's violet. 'Oh, God.'

'I'll do it.' Marnie touched his arm. 'Stay here. Give your mum the good news about Sol. Let me take care of this.'

The house in Harpenden was empty, as she'd feared it would be. Thunder had followed her from the city, lying low over the pantiled roofs of the terrace as a long spine of lightning lit the sky towards London. A team took the door down to get inside, but the house was empty.

Marnie stood in the room with the piano, smelling the sweet rot of dropped petals. Dusk had sent shadows into every corner, blinding the artwork and blunting the sculptures, turning glass paperweights into black weapons. In the other sitting room, she looked at the pictures of Charlie and his brother, and Anita with her hair worn in a ponytail, carefree, before either boy was born.

She climbed the stairs to the spare bedroom at the back with its pop-art wallpaper of big blue flowers with freckled faces. Jungle flowers. She opened the wardrobe doors, looking inside at jeans and jumpers, a young man's clothes. This was Charlie's room. They'd searched it but missed that fact, of a dead son and brother. A slim shelf, no wider than a picture frame, ran around the room at waist height where panelling had been fitted. The shelf was packed with a child's treasure. Not cars like the ones Darren had collected, just the odds and ends that a child's magpie eye had lighted on. Pebbles and seashells, nuts and bolts, polished stones and conkers that had long ago lost their shine. No trace of dust lay over any of it. Marnie shut her eyes and saw Anita touching each small treasure in turn, holding it in her hand the way she'd once held Charlie, each smooth pebble spotting her palm, leaving its cool heat in the heart of her hand.

Downstairs, the house was chilly, its hallway littered by more dead petals from dying plants, the lilies in the blue vase hanging their heads.

'She's not here,' Marnie told the team. 'But I think I know where to find her.'

Charlie's mother was at the allotment, waiting. Seated on a painted crate by the fire pit, her skin blue with cold. She'd lit a fire that threw sparks and smoke, illuminating and obscuring her face by turns. The storm was dying out, dulled by the dusk. Marnie warned the others to stay back. The fire was shallow but this case had started with smoke and flames; she didn't want it to end the same way. She watched Anita snap a slim twig and add it to the pit, her face wavering, coming into focus as the flames climbed before shrinking again in the smoke.

'Let me do it,' Marnie told the team quietly. 'Let me go to her.'

The fire coiled in the stone pit. The smell of the allotment was stronger than she'd remembered, thick with the scent of supplements in the soil and creosote on the fences and sheds. The storm's flat coppery scent made no impression here.

'Mrs Quayle. It's DI Rome. Marnie.'

Anita roped a strand of hair about her finger. She looked paper-thin, as if she might fold in the pit's heat. Her eyes found Marnie's face, her bleak stare like battery acid. It was hard to look at her, eyes and mouth like open wounds, raw and ugly. She wore a thin black cardigan over her linen dress, holding herself very upright, rubbing at her arms in the parody of an embrace.

Marnie was near enough to catch her injured animal smell. 'May I sit down?'

Anita nodded and Marnie sat on the upturned box at her side, not speaking. She held her hands out to the fire, hoping to get warm. All the storm's strange heat had gone out of the day.

'You know, then.' Anita's voice was jagged, dying in her throat. She was flushed at the temples, her eyes damp and gritty. 'You know.'

'Can you tell me?' Marnie asked.

Charlie's mother leaned towards the fire. 'Vokey's dead.' A keening came from her, like wind pulled through a paper kite. 'He's dead.'

'Let me take you to the station,' Marnie said. 'Please. We can do this later.'

'You need a statement so I'll make one now. I killed him. It wasn't Darren, but it was for him. And Charlie. It was for Charlie.' The fire threw sparks, its yellow flecking her olive eyes. 'I could see what was happening with Darren. That man was poison. Everything he touched, everyone he got close to.' She shivered. 'I couldn't lose another child to him.'

Marnie held her breath against the storm's slow throbbing overhead.

'Darren won't believe it, won't believe I killed his hero.'

Anita stretched a hand towards the fire, her square wrist roped with veins, those bones like bracelets under the skin. 'Don't you think we talk so much about the shock of our children, the terrible or wonderful things they're capable of, the people they grow into, so far apart from us? Yet we don't talk about the strangers our parents can become, the surprising things *we're* capable of, good and bad. We think we know all about our mothers because they were grown-ups before we were born, adult and unalterable. But the truth is everyone's changing, all the time. Everyone is a stranger.'

The allotment was peopled by shadows from the fire. Marnie felt its cold creeping at her feet, seeping into her ears. Behind them, the woods crouched and whispered with night birds.

'I didn't shoot him,' Anita said. 'I hit him with a shovel. It was hard and heavy, and it was easy. He died very easily. Digging the grave was the toughest part.'

She delivered the speech in the same tone, sunken and empty. Murdering Michael Vokey might have been easy, but the weight of this would never leave her.

'He was so easy to kill. It should have been harder. If it's so wrong, it should be harder.'

Marnie watched the shadows pressing at Anita's chest. She didn't want to believe it, not of this woman. Not murder. Her skin stiffened in protest. A grieving mother taking her revenge, trying to live with the loss of her son and failing, and falling. Felled by what she'd done. Why did it matter so much that this woman should have stayed standing?

'He wasn't what I expected. When those letters came from the prison. Darren brought home letters from Mr Elms, advice for the allotment, what to plant and so on. Such strange letters.' Her brow furrowed in a quick frown. 'It took me a long time to realise it wasn't advice. It was

341

warnings. Many, many warnings. "I lost a young sapling to rot. If you suspect such a thing, you must tackle it quickly." He was warning me of Michael's influence over Darren, and he was right to warn me. Look how Darren helped that man escape, brought him here!' She gestured at the Anderson shelter. 'That interview you told me about. *Vile*. Treacherous. Admiring the man who drove his brother to his death, how could he?'

The tail of the storm struggled out across the sky, clouds tearing up the last of the light.

'Charlie knew what Darren was. He told me there was something wrong, but he couldn't put his finger on it. Or he didn't want to, because Darren was his brother. That's why he armed himself, he said. Because he was afraid of the friends Darren was making. But I've sometimes wondered whether it wasn't Darren's gun.' She shut her eyes. 'It would be like Charlie to take the blame, try and protect his little brother. He kept quiet for a long time about the friends Darren was making. He was afraid, and it was much worse when Darren went into the prison service. Hero-worshipping men like that—!' She thrust a stick into the fire, stirring flames from its low beating.

When she was calmer, she said, 'Did you imagine I was setting him up? Telling you he was out all night, asking you to take him from the house. I was trying to keep him safe. I was afraid of what I'd do if he stayed. Now I know what I'm capable of. Now I know the worst about myself.' She pressed the ends of her fingers to her forehead. 'I was afraid of what I'd do to my own child.' She dropped her hand and studied its fingers as if she expected to see not perspiration there but blood.

The fire shrank at their feet, eating the twigs she'd fed it, spitting out their sap.

'It was Darren who brought home the last letter. From

Mr Elms.' She blinked the exhaustion away. 'Such a clever letter, as if he'd crawled inside my skull. All the words I'd been whispering to myself for months and months, all written down on the page. He made it so real suddenly. And so personal. The threat, and the thing I had to do to stop it. Stop *him*. I couldn't go to the police after I'd read the letter. I should have done, but he made that impossible.' She stared into the fire. 'I don't really understand how he did it, but he made murder seem like the easier option. The only option.'

One last growl of thunder, ashy against the night sky. The storm's signature.

'He wasn't what I'd expected. Michael Vokey. I don't know what I was expecting, but he was so . . . *Nothing*. He didn't understand why I was angry, as if he'd never seen grief before, or anger. He didn't know how to react to me accusing him of killing Charlie. I wanted to hear him say he was sorry and to see him scared the way Charlie must have been scared.' A hard sob caught in her throat. 'But he wasn't. I could see he'd never reach remorse. He didn't even understand why I was upset. Charlie's death meant nothing to him and never would. That's why I did it. Because it was the only thing I *could* do. The only way I'd change the look on his face of not caring.

'He said, "But you have another son, don't you?", as if the two were interchangeable when Darren's as different as— Charlie was my dervish, my darling.' A smile broke through, shining from her eyes. 'Always racing, dancing, never still for a second. His arms wide open to the world, the whole of him wide open. I thought he'd conquer the world the way he was. He noticed everything, stars in the sky, ants in the grass. And he wanted to travel, explore everywhere, meet everyone. When he was tiny, I watched him all the time in case he climbed too high and fell, but he never did. Not until that man pushed him.'

She smoothed her hands at her face. 'I could either be Charlie's mother – broken, driven out of my mind with grief – or I could be Darren's, propping up his insecurity. I couldn't be both. I tried, and I couldn't. In the end, I chose Charlie and I know how that sounds, to have chosen my dead son over my living, but how else could I keep faith with my boy?' She picked a round pebble from the ground, holding it in her hand. 'Darren doesn't need me. He just needs to grow up and for some reason, in whatever way, I'm preventing that. He's always leant too much on me. At least this way Charlie knows I didn't forget him, that I didn't just let it pass. What was done to him, what that man stole. From Charlie, and from me. From the whole world.'

A burst of laughter from back on the street. London's nightlife, unending.

Marnie wondered at the letter which had pushed this woman over the edge. Ted's letter. All that rigid self-control, managing every aspect of life for her family with an absent father and two small boys to care for. Yet Ted had unpicked her with a page of words. For what, revenge? He could have killed Vokey himself, surely, if that was all he wanted. He could have taken the scissors just as Ruth imagined and dealt out whatever sentence he felt Vokey deserved. Instead he'd driven this woman to do it. Charlie's mother, grieving for her son. As if it were somehow a gift, delivering Vokey into her hands, for her justice. There was a strange peace to Anita now, the kind of painful peace that comes at the end of a long and stony road.

She added another twig to the fire. 'He thought he could talk anyone into anything, that people were puppets to play with. He was proud of the way he made Charlie dance, kicking at the end of that rope.' Her hand closed around the pebble. 'I paid him in his own coin, that's all. He thought we would hide him, that my son would help his brother's killer. He thought he could take another of my children and make him dance.' She hardened her voice. 'If I could have put on Darren's uniform and gone into that place, I'd have killed him myself. He ruins lives. There's no other purpose to him. He brings nothing to the world, only takes from it.'

She brought her gaze to rest on Marnie's face, unblinking, the whites of her eyes exposed in a way which made her look vulnerable, and fearless. 'I killed him because it was the right thing to do. The only human thing.'

Marnie stayed on the allotment after the arrest team took Anita away. A full forensic unit was coming with flood-lighting, tents, excavation equipment. She buried her hands in the pockets of her coat, feeling the trees shuddering at her back. Thinking of all the hidden people, here and elsewhere. All the reasons we run and hide, and search and find. A moth flew out of the woods, spiralling for a second before vanishing back into the branches.

Her phone buzzed. 'Noah, yes.'

'I heard about the arrest. Anita confessed? There's a body?'

'She did. And yes.' Michael Vokey was less than four feet from where Marnie was standing. Not in the woods. Here on the allotment, deep under the lilies and rotted manure. 'There's a body.'

Tomorrow, she and Noah would take apart the temporary incident room and it would feel good to be clearing up together. Too often she found herself alone in her office at the end of a case, signing paperwork, her seniority setting her apart, out in the cold. She wanted to be with

Noah, the pair of them in shirt sleeves unpinning the photocopies from the walls, taking it all down.

'Are you all right?' Noah asked.

'I will be.' She reached for a handful of earth, scooping it over the remains of the fire. 'You?'

'I'm going to my mum's for supper.' He sounded happier than he had in a long time. 'Just the two of us. I wanted to check you didn't need me at the station tonight, for Anita's interview.'

'I've got it,' Marnie said. 'Go and eat.'

Headlights swept at the street. The forensic team was here.

'There's more good news.' Noah was smiling, she heard it in his voice. 'Joe Coen's wife had her baby. Jack Isaac Coen, nine pounds and an ounce. Whole family delighted and doing well.'

'That's tremendous news.' His happiness was infectious. 'I'll send my best wishes. Now, go and have supper with your mum. You've earned it.'

48

Noah's mum handed him the plate, piled high with sweet fried plantains. 'Eat.'

He did as he was told. She took a seat at the table, facing him. In her green dress, her party frock. She'd set the table with the best china, as if Noah were an honoured guest rather than family. He didn't mind, it was enough to be here, forgiven. Dad was working late but that might've been deliberate, to give Noah time alone with Mum. He filled their glasses. 'This is delicious.'

She nodded, not quite a smile. After a short while, she started to talk about Sol. 'I expected you to take care of him, the way you always did. You were the strong one, the one I counted on, my brave boy. Sol's my baby. I love him, my goodness, but he's made of – *nothing*. I know that. He's scared, so much of the time he's scared. I look at him and I see a boy. I look at you? I see a man. If I was angry it's because I expected you to take care of your little brother, put him first, always. But I know that's unfair. You've a job to do.'

'Not just that,' Noah said. 'I *was* taking care of him. I honestly thought this was the best way.'

'He's hurting in there.' She sprinkled a little salt over her plate. 'I've never seen him so afraid. It made me lash out. You know what mothers are, we can be tigers when our kids are cornered.'

'I was afraid for him too.' Noah blinked heat from his eyes. 'I knew he was trying to do the right thing, getting out of the gang. But it was driving him into a corner, just as you said. He didn't know which direction to take. He wouldn't stay with me and Dan, wouldn't come back here.'

'At least now we know where he is.'

'I'm sorry.' Noah reached for her hand. 'Truly.'

She smiled at him. 'I know.' She patted his hand. 'I do know.'

Ed was stretched on the sofa reading when Marnie got home. She hung her coat on the cluttered peg by the door and stood watching him, seeing the familiar furrow at the bridge of his nose as he concentrated on his book, a novel about dystopian America with a red moon on the cover, its spine cracked with re-reading. All about him, stacked in towers, were more books, and music, and films. Ed never threw anything out. Most of his childhood was here, buried at the bottom of one tower or another, sometimes shuffled to the top. Insulation. And comfort, security. No smashed china, no strangers. All of Ed's photos were happy ones.

'Hey.' He looked up with a smile, swinging his legs clear of the sofa, making space for her. 'Have you eaten? There's pasta in the fridge, or I can make something hot.'

Marnie crossed the room to kiss him, resting a hand in his curls. 'I'm fine, thanks.'

'You look wiped out.' He put the book down, reaching for her.

She let him pull her hand to his face, holding it curled to the shape of his cheek. Then she remembered the heat of Harry's thumb in her palm and a twinge of guilt cut through her tiredness. 'I might go back to thc flat, just for a couple of days.'

Ed straightened and stood, coming round the sofa to her side. 'What's happened?'

'Nothing, really. Just this case, the shape it's taken. So many parts are still in play, I'm going to be in work mode for a while. I'd rather take my bad moods back to my place.'

Ed didn't say, '*This* is your place,' but she saw the pain in his eyes and she was sorry for it.

'Stephen's mother was at the hospital, asking to see him. I'm just – struggling through it right now, trying to process everything.'

'I don't want you on your own with that.' Ed put his hands on her waist, but didn't try to pull her close. He wouldn't do that, she knew. He understood about space, her need to put distance between things. Loss and grief, work and play, pain and comfort.

'I won't be on my own.' She smiled. 'The way things are looking I shan't have much time to myself for anything. The flat's nearer the station, that's all, for when I get the chance to crash.'

The flat would be chilly, unwelcoming, unlived in. A form of exile, self-imposed. Familiar.

'I need this.' She put her hands in Ed's hair. 'Just for a while. It doesn't mean anything, not really. It's just – what I need. For a few days.'

'Take whatever you need, you know that.' He bent to kiss her, hiding the hurt in his eyes. 'But I'm here. So you know. I'm always here.'

'I do know.' She leaned her cheek to his, feeling the

sweet tackiness from Natalie's skin sealing them together. 'I'll pack a bag, just a few things. Then I'm going back to the hospital.'

'Stephen?' Ed stepped away, giving her space.

'Not just Stephen. The man we think is responsible for the worst of the riot. Ted Elms. I had a call to say it's not looking good. And I need to see his medical records.'

Gore under his fingernails, Noah had said. And there was the evidence from the allotment, and Anita's interview. It was going to be a long night.

Ed watched her pack, in silence.

'It won't be for long,' she promised.

She wanted to give him a token of her faith, to reassure him that this was temporary, she wasn't walking away, or running. But most of all, she wanted to be alone. In the empty flat, where the bed, like the lights, was too hard and all the sharp edges were on show.

49

The next day dawned white, no trace of the storm remaining, the air ironed flat and damp. DCS Ferguson joined Marnie at the hospital, early and in a good mood.

'We've heard from Julie. Natalie's back home, in good spirits. Julie wanted to thank you.'

Marnie knotted her hair away from her face. 'I'm glad they're all right.'

'Ruth's refusing a lawyer, asked to see her pastor instead. You did well to get her out of there without making more of a scene.'

'She wanted to come, in the end.'

Climbing barefoot up the cellar steps, Marnie's hand under her elbow to support her weight, her ugly shoes left in the pit behind them.

'As for this scumbag,' Ferguson nodded at the room where Ted was lying, 'Ruth would call it divine interven-tion.' She made a note of Marnie's silence. 'You and I need to talk.'

'Ma'am?'

'Detective Chief Inspector Rome.'

Promotion. She should be thrilled, honoured, relieved.

She nodded, feeling numb. Her short night in the flat had been sleepless and uncomfortable. She'd forgotten how colourless the place was, and how happy she'd once been with that lack of colour. Tonight she would take Harry's African violet home. One bright spot, at least.

Ferguson was saying, 'Hoops to jump through, of course. And it should be done on Tim Welland's watch.' She tucked her lanyard inside her jacket. 'Which means waiting until he's well enough to return to work and I've buggered off back to Manchester.'

Marnie thanked her, shaking the hand that was offered.

'You'll want to check on your other scumbag,' Ferguson said. 'I'll see you at the station. DS Jake can drive you back.'

In the private room, the narrow bed was empty, stripped down to its mattress. The monitor had been switched off, the oxygen mask packed away. The room smelt of starch and syrup. Marnie didn't trust the smell any more than she trusted the rush of blood to her chest as she saw the empty bed and feared the worst— He was gone.

Stephen was dead. Her eyes heated in a stab of tears, her throat hollowing with loss. Stephen was dead. All of them gone now. Her mother and father, and the boy they'd chosen as her brother. Her whole family— Gone. And Ed too, because she'd thought it wrong to be with him when she was drawn to Harry, as if she was rationed to one emotion, one love. Her body felt light, groundless; so much of her was made of what Stephen had done. She put a hand to her mouth, tasting the sterile smell of the room. She couldn't be made of this, of him. Stephen. Fear and hate, anchored only to the past and her need to know why it unravelled the way it did. She had to mend, move on. She'd needed to do that for six years but now it was here, the moment she'd been dreading. And she would have to face it alone because Ed was out of reach, she'd put him out of reach. She was alone with this. No Stephen to take up her time, to fill all the hours and hours of life after their deaths. She waited for tears to fall but her body was parched, sucked dry of every emotion but this emptiness. This was how they'd felt, Lara and Ruth. Now she understood. She could see Vokey very clearly, flowing like smoke into the empty places inside her. All of it made sense. Even Stella with her warped truth which'd made Marnie question everything.

Six years over, gone. What would she do? She'd turned her demons into detective work. They'd given her an edge, not just insight or empathy, but energy – she'd been tireless in her pursuit of each truth, burning a trail which left no room for regret. She felt it building in her now, a tide of grief, coiling and crouching the way a wave does before it comes crashing in. She couldn't outrun it or hold it back with her questions, with her *Stephen-Stephen-Stephen*. She had to stand and bear its weight thundering down, washing away every defence she'd erected against it, knowing it would drown or uproot her.

'They took him a while ago, love.'

She turned. 'I'm sorry?'

A hospital orderly, bringing fresh bedding on a trolley. 'You only missed him by an hour.'

Marnie stepped out of the man's way, swallowing the grief back down into her throat.

'D'you know him?' the orderly asked.

'He was my – brother.'

'Oh, sorry. Can't be easy.' He started pulling a sheet onto the mattress, its elastic snapping into place. 'My youngest was in prison once. Not for long. Shoplifting. Never easy though, is it? Seeing them in there. Worse

353

than when they're in here, really.' He tutted his tongue against his teeth.

Marnie watched him hauling at the bed, covering the mattress with a fresh sheet that smelt of burnt cotton.

He straightened his back eventually. 'Least he was well enough to be discharged.' He nodded down at the bed.

'He was discharged?' The blood thudded to her feet. 'Stephen Keele?'

'An hour ago,' the orderly said. 'You've only just missed him.'

Noah was waiting at the side of the car, head bent over his phone, smile wide enough for Marnie to see it across the car park. Texting Dan, or his mum maybe. Happy, anyway. She started towards him, marvelling at the way her pulse had settled, although her feet itched to run off the adrenalin.

Her phone rang. 'Harry, hello.' That was better, adrenalin going to the right places.

Until she heard the sombre note in his voice. 'Is Noah with you?'

'We're just leaving the hospital. Why, what's happened?'

'I need to call him.' Harry's voice tightened. 'But I don't want to do that if he's on his own.'

Marnie stopped, her eyes on Noah's smile, the relaxed slope of his shoulders. 'Is it bad news?'

She was twenty feet away, keeping her voice low, but Noah glanced up and raised a hand in greeting, his grin broadening.

'Harry?' She held the phone close to her ear. 'Is it bad news?'

'The worst.'

She heard the pain in his voice. Felt it spreading to her cheek as if the phone was leaking distress. 'Tell me.'

Noah was coming towards her now, his grin so bright it bounced.

'It's Sol,' Harry said. 'They found him in the exercise yard. Stabbed. The prison's in lockdown, they called me because it was one of Trident's convictions. The man who stabbed Sol, he's someone I arrested last year.'

'Which hospital have they taken him to?' Marnie put up a hand to try and hold off Noah's approach, wanting all the facts before he reached her side. 'I'll drive.'

'Marnie, it's not looking good.' Harry gathered his breath. 'They're saying he won't make it.'

'No, that's—' A mistake, like the one she'd nearly made ten minutes ago, standing by Stephen's stripped bed. 'He's young, and he's strong.'

Noah had pocketed the phone. Three strides and he'd be at her side. The sun had come out, drilling through the clouds in a dozen places, setting a cage of yellow light around him.

'Marnie?' Harry said. 'I'm so sorry. I wish I was wrong.'

Noah stopped two feet away with the sun grazing his skin, making it shine.

'He's not going to make it,' Harry said. 'I'm so sorry, but Sol's— Gone.'

50

From: C87908 Edward Elms, HMP Cloverton
To: Anita Elisabeth Lamb, Harpenden, Herts

Dear Anita (if I may),

The year's turning, does it feel that way to you? In the exercise yard this morning the air smelt on the cusp, green. The leaves on the few trees we have here are bursting to bud, frantic to escape and catch the sun. There's been a fair amount of rain just lately, ripening the soil. I love the smell of the earth after rain, don't you? The way the spade fits so neatly into soil when it's ready to be turned. Digging is so much easier at this time of year.

Mum had a favourite tree, perhaps you do too? A lilac, surprisingly hardy. It collects the rain in all its furls and petals, dripping long after the rest of the garden's dry, the sound of it like little acts of kindness. Mum believed in kindness, 'A little goes a long way, Teddy,' and it did. All the way to the garden of remembrance. 'One last kindness, for me,' but it

356

didn't stop me feeling that I ought to be punished. You feel these things so keenly at the time, fear they will prey on your mind, but you have only to remember how hard it was at the end, like tilling a frozen field, to know you did the only thing possible. The only human thing.

Mothers and their sons, it's such a strange bond, isn't it? Unbreakable. You do what you have to do. I was the same. We chose fire, for our loved ones. There's a fierceness to it, and such softness to the ash afterwards. I took Mum to the hills, the place we once saw a new lamb. You took Charlie to the beach, I believe. It's the need to know they're honoured, isn't it? And our need to know it's over. It's a kindness, to them and to us. Let me do a kindness for you, please, Anita. Let me give you the gift of peace, an end to all this. If you'll allow it, I should like to wrap your pain in my words and bury it deep under the lilac where the soil is ripe and blue with rain. Your boy is free now, Charlie. I want you to be free too. I want you to be able to slip out into the sunshine, and know that it is over.

I've thought so much about you and your boy. That last day, at the beach. The shore's grit between your toes, the water making mirrors of all the little pebbles, half-buried by fingers and feet. The sun's shadow is on the beach, or else it's the remains of a camp fire, an ashy black circle on the shale. You went down to the water's edge, I expect, holding the flask firmly in both hands.

Everyone was there with someone else, only the lonely come to the beach by themselves. Children chucking laughter around like a ball, slapping the water with the open palms of their hands, making it jump. You'd come here with Charlie thirty odd years ago, when he hiccupped inside you. You wore a swimsuit to show him off.

'When's he due?' you were asked. 'Or is it a she?'

'A boy,' you said, although you didn't know for sure, not then. No black and white evidence to hold in your hand, just the blood-red rush of him, the hiccup and kick inside. 'He's a boy.'

Water curled its hand at your toes. You let it come, wetting your feet, and walked a little way from the bathers and picnickers, for decency's sake. The lid of the flask unscrewed without a sound. At the hospital they'd handed you an urn, but you didn't want to bring an urn to the beach. So you decanted, a spoonful at a time, his soft ashes into the flask. Standing with wet feet at the shore, you put the lid under your chin so you could hold the flask with both hands, one last time.

'Deep breath! Breathe, breathe! Keep breathing!'

Both arms in front of you, waiting for the wind to change direction, your eyes wide open so you could catch Charlie slipping out into the sunshine in a dazzle of golden brown, dancing and dancing to join the other children.

Acknowledgements

A book is made of many things. Sleepless nights and early days, wall-staring, and long walks by water. Patience and panic, aching wrists and quite often chaos. Coffee and cake, apples and cheese, blood, sweat and gin. And gratitude, a book is made of gratitude.

I owe thanks to my editor, Imogen Taylor, and the crew at Headline. To my agent, Jane Gregory, and her team. To the Killer Women, and the Sawday's suspects. To Anna Britten, Becky Brunning, Jane Casey, Rowan Coleman, Lydia Downey, Mick Herron, Alison Graham, Rebecca Kwo, John Lyttle, Anne-Elisabeth Moutet, Susan Pola, Alyson Shipley, Elaine and Patrick Slanksy, Jane Riekemann, and Daphne Wright.

To Joseph Coen who won the Get in Character auction in support of the CLIC Sargent charity, I hope you approve of your role in the story.

I'm grateful too for the kindness of strangers, Kerry Halferty Hardy, Carin Knoop, Donna Scherer, and Li Whybrow. To those who battled behind the scenes on my behalf, most especially Conrad.

Always, to my family. My mother, sister and brothers, their partners and offspring, and to my miraculous Victor. What a year in which to write a book.